# THE BORODINS
## BOOK IV
# HOPE and GLORY

## LESLIE ARLEN

A JOVE BOOK

HOPE AND GLORY

A Jove book / published by arrangement with
the author

PRINTING HISTORY
Jove edition / May 1982

ISBN: 0-515-06041-0

Jove books are published by Jove Publications, Inc.,
200 Madison Avenue, New York, N.Y. 10016.
The words "A JOVE BOOK" and the "J" with sunburst are
trademarks belonging to Jove Publications, Inc.

PRINTED IN THE UNITED STATES OF AMERICA

# AS THE SWASTIKAS UNFURLED OVER EUROPE, THEIR FIERCEST STRUGGLE BEGAN...

**MICHAEL NEJ.** The most important man in Russia—after Stalin. It was his mission to hold back the German onslaught with words, not tanks.

**GEORGE HAYMAN.** The American newspaper magnate whose bravery sent him into the cannon's mouth.

**PRINCE PETER BORODIN.** He viewed the Nazis as his only chance to break the grip of Stalin on his beloved homeland.

**RUTH BORODIN.** Peter's dark-eyed young daughter. Did her disappearance have to do with her Jewish blood?

**ANNA RAGOSINA.** Hauntingly beautiful, utterly deadly, she was brought back from the hell of a labor camp—to serve the secret police once more.

**TATIANA NEJ.** Her glamorous life on stage was ended, but the dream of happiness had never been nearer.

---

# HOPE AND GLORY

*By* Leslie Arlen
*from Jove*

## THE BORODINS

# HOPE AND GLORY

# Chapter 1

THE COURTYARD WAS CHILL. THE SNOW HAD CEASED AND largely melted, but the spring air retained its nip and made men shiver. Even the green-greatcoated firing squad, *shlems* settled firmly on their heads with flaps pulled down to protect their ears, gave an occasional shudder as they slapped their rifle barrels and shifted from one booted foot to the next. But perhaps they trembled because of what they had to do.

Surreptitiously, they watched the archway that led into the main part of Lubianka. This was their home. As members of the NKVD they had to regard this grim building in the heart of Moscow as the sole reason for their existence. The very square on which the building with its secret prison stood was named after Felix Dzerzhinsky, who had been the first commander of the Cheka, as the security force had been known then. Now their commander was Nikolai Yezhov, a man whose infamy had spread far and wide as, for the last four years, he had carried out the dread bidding of his master, Commissar Stalin. But this execution squad knew better than to fear Comrade Yezhov, who, after all, did no more than he was told. It was the man who did the telling whom *they* feared, Stalin's

1

true executioner, the deputy commissar for internal security, Ivan Nej.

And there he was, emerging from the archway, at the head of another squad of NKVD men, marching crisply forward. Commissar Nej was a little man, with hunched shoulders and a quick stride that made no effort to keep pace with the rhythmical tread of the men behind him. He wore horn-rimmed spectacles and a thin mustache, which left the protruding features of his face—the thrusting chin and the long nose that matched the enormous peak of his khaki cap—strangely exposed, making him resemble the man in the moon. His revolver was far too large for the thigh against which it slapped. But there was no one here today tempted to smile at that. For now he stopped and turned to watch the guard squad marching the prisoners they surrounded to the stakes at the far end of the courtyard. And once again a ripple of concern went through the waiting marksmen. For four years now they had slaughtered group after group of men, accused by Commissar Stalin of deviation and plotting against the regime. But they had been little men. Last year some generals had been marched into this courtyard, among them the great Tukhachevsky himself, the man who had led the Red armies to the Vistula eighteen years earlier, in 1920. That had been a day. But generals come and go. It is the nature of their employment. Today the group of men included Comrade Bukharin, Comrade Zinoviev, and Comrade Kamenev. These were not little men. They were not even generals. They were the men who had shared Lenin's Swiss exile with him, had returned to Russia with him in the great days of 1917, and with him—and Comrade Stalin, Comrade Trotsky, and the Nej brothers—had destroyed the Provisional Government, eliminated the last traces of tsardom, and created the Soviet state. They were the fathers of the nation. And today they were to die, shivering since they had been stripped to their shirts, in a bloodstained courtyard.

For what crime? Could a man like Comrade Bukharin really be a deviationist? An enemy agent provocateur? A Trotskyite? Or was it just that Comrade Stalin was bent on removing the very last trace of criticism or opposition from within the Politburo? But there was no man present here today who dared think thoughts like that.

Except perhaps Comrade Nej, who already knew the answer. But even Comrade Nej was in a hurry to get it over with. When Comrade Bukharin, his wrists secured behind his back to the post against which he had been placed, shook his head to decline the blindfold, and instead opened his mouth to speak, Comrade Nej said quietly, "There will be no talking, comrade, or I will have you gagged. Comrade commandant, do your duty."

The bolts clicked, the rifles exploded; the heads of the once-famous, once-powerful, drooped above their drooping bodies.

And Commissar Nej smiled.

George Hayman brought the Rolls-Royce to a stop in a flurry of scraping brakes and flying gravel. For all his sixty-one years, his wealth, and his power, he still preferred to drive his car himself, and still drove like a young man, constantly attempting to break his own best time for the journey from Manhattan, across the Queensboro Bridge and thence to Northern Boulevard, through Manhasset and Roslyn, and out to his home here at Cold Spring Harbor. Indeed, only the heavy gray streaks in his brown hair gave any indication of his age; he wore his glasses only for reading. Tall and powerfully built, his paunch concealed beneath the well-cut suit, he moved briskly; his long, somewhat solemn features could still break into a boyish and utterly delighted grin when he was pleased, as now. For as he handed the keys to Rowntree the chauffeur to garage the car, he looked up the steps of his house to the front door, and to his wife, waiting to greet him.

Her presence surprised him. Since he had agreed to let her launch her own magazine, under the general financial umbrella of Hayman Newspapers, Inc., Ilona Hayman had occupied her days with meticulous energy. To preserve her independence she had removed herself and her editorial staff from the stylish Hayman Building to rented offices in much less salubrious surroundings on Forty-second Street. From there, often working a nine-to-seven day, she had steadily built up the circulation of *You* to a very respectable quarter of a million copies a month. The readers were drawn from widely different sections of the community, as the lavishly illustrated articles ranged from reviews of current popular musicals to serious political studies of the increasingly gloomy European scene.

Her independence was not a quality George resented. Ilona

was too vital a personality to remain a housewife, now that her children were grown up. Nor did his domestic arrangements suffer in any way, as Mrs. Stephens was an excellent house-keeper. Besides, it was a pleasure to watch Ilona blossoming into a businesswoman.

But then, it was a pleasure to see her at any time. She was one of those rare women who enhance any setting, any occasion. Nearly nine years younger than her husband, she kept her figure under even better control than he did. To match him she had allowed gray streaks to appear in her magnificent golden hair, but these could almost be mistaken for intentional high-lights, since she still wore her hair long; it was the one certain link with the past, with the power and splendor she had known as Ilona Borodina, sister of the premier prince in all Russia—the hair and the features, flawlessly carved, suggesting marble in repose, but now breaking into a smile as her husband took her in his arms, while Harrison the butler carefully averted his eyes.

"I'm so glad you're home early," she said. "The girls are here. And you'll never guess what came today. A letter from—"

"Peter," he said. "That's why I'm home early."

"Peter?" Ilona was astonished. "I was going to say Tattie. That's why *I'm* home early."

He squeezed her against him. "A family gathering by mail. I wonder if they have the same news."

He left his arm round her waist as they walked through the entry hall and into the huge living room, which filled the width of the house until it ended in the French windows leading down to the croquet lawn with its borders of flowerbeds. This lawn, and the maze beyond, which concealed the stables and out-buildings, and the orchard further on, had all been designed by Ilona, and was her special world. It too helped her to reach back through the mists of time to her family home of Starogan, as it had been before the tide of Lenin's revolution had reduced it to rubble. And yet, long before that catastrophe, she had fled Starogan's peace and beauty, to follow the fortunes of her American husband. Theirs had been a stormy romance, which had brought her disgrace, a disastrous first marriage, an ille-gitimate first child, and, ultimately, exile from her motherland.

And a good deal of trauma since then as well. And yet, sure at last of his love, she counted it all worthwhile. So she said, and so he believed.

Then what memories, what considerations, he wondered, were evoked by letters from her brother and her sister, still caught up in the turmoil that was Stalinist Russia?

But first, the girls, for in the happiness of their children was a great deal of their own happiness founded.

"Daddy." Felicity kissed him on the cheek and hugged him against her. She was his youngest, twenty-five years old and a Borodin woman to her lacquered toenails. Unlike her mother, she wore her hair short, but had at the least resisted the current mania for permanent waving, so that it formed a straight golden shawl about her ears. Her height she had inherited from both of her parents, but the Borodin features were almost untempered by any Hayman influence, and she had the bright blue eyes of her mother. Yet she possessed her father's temperament, reflective rather than ebullient, although this afternoon she was sparkling, in keeping with the huge sapphire she wore on her left ring finger. If she had left it late to become engaged, she had chosen well and was the only one of the children who had done so with Ilona's complete approval. David Cassidy was the son of a wealthy man, was a charming boy in his own right, and was a lieutenant in the navy. Filly would be happy.

Beth, now getting up from the sofa to present her cheek for a kiss, was difficult to categorize. A Hayman by marriage— to George junior, Filly's brother—she was small and dark and intense, as unlike a Borodin as it was possible to imagine. Then, too, she was an artist, and in her Bohemian inclination, which she had refused to change even after six years of marriage, she was again mentally on the opposite side of the moon from either Hayman or Borodin thinking. Yet she made young George happy, and in doing that had earned Ilona's respect if not her affection. And besides, Ilona had Diana. The little girl had been in the garden, but now came bounding through the French windows to be picked up and hugged by her grandfather. A first grandchild is always a precious bond, and Diana Hayman, even at five, was already bridging the gap, at least physically, for although she had inherited her mother's midnight hair and brown eyes, her features were almost pure Borodin, a combination that suggested true beauty when she grew up.

"Yours first," Ilona said, pouring tea and sitting beside her husband, while Diana bounced on his lap.

"Oh, nothing very different than before," George said. "It's just that after damn near ten years, to get a letter . . . and you'll never guess where it's written from!"

"Don't tell me he's back in America!"

George shook his head. "Berlin."

*"Berlin?"*

"He's living there. In fact, he claims to be writing me at the request of the German government."

"Peter? Peter Borodin, my brother, in Berlin? And working for the Germans?" Ilona was incredulous. Whatever else he had been, or had become in his determined opposition to Bolshevism, the Prince of Starogan had at least never been a Fascist.

"Well, I wouldn't go so far as to say he's working for the Germans. I don't think Peter has ever worked for anything except his own crazy ideals. He just happens to believe, it seems, that Nazi Germany is the only hope of bringing down Stalin. He spends a lot of the letter quoting from *Mein Kampf*, about how Germany must expand to the East, and also pointing out Hitler's aversion to Communism."

"He's mad," Ilona declared. "He is absolutely and completely mad. This anti-Communist thing has burned a hole in his brain. When I think of the amount of time, and money, and sheer misery he has caused for the sake of fighting Bolshevism in Russia . . ."

"Well, at least John is out of his clutches now," George said.

"I wasn't thinking of Johnnie, so much. What about poor Judith?" She flushed. Judith Stein was again counted as a friend. Perhaps she had never ceased to be a friend. Yet Ilona could never hope to forget that she had been George's mistress. "Her brother was beaten to death by the Nazis, and Peter claims to have always loved her. How *can* he?"

The younger women looked from one speaker to the other in concerned interest. They were Haymans, and therefore bound up in this family history, even if the feuds and traumas of the past were not likely to affect their own lives. Or that of little Diana, George thought thankfully.

"Well, I guess he considers Judith as best forgotten, since she went off with Boris Petrov. The fact is though, my darling, that Peter has some cogent points to raise, as usual."

"Such as?"

"Well, what has been going on inside Russia these last four years. Since Kirov's murder, as he puts it. In that time nearly every prominent man in the country who has ever opposed Stalin has been liquidated, and God knows how many thousands of others. How Michael Nej has survived I have no idea."

"He survives because he supports Stalin," Ilona said.

"He has opposed him from time to time. Anyway, Peter raises two points which, believe it or not, he wants me to take up with the administration. He doesn't seem to realize that I'm not quite such a friend of Roosevelt's as I was of Hoover's."

Ilona frowned at him. "What points?"

"The first is that Stalin's wholesale elimination of opponents may well mean that he is considering launching a Bolshevik offensive against Europe. And the second is, that since the purges have involved most of the military top brass, the Russian army is probably more disorganized at this moment than it has ever been; therefore this might be the time to launch a preventive war, and eliminate Bolshevism forever."

"My God," Ilona said. "He *is* mad. Really and truly mad. And he seriously expects Roosevelt to consider that proposal?"

George shook his head. "No. He thinks Germany and Italy can do the job, with some help maybe from Hungary and Finland. What he wants is the assurance of U.S. neutrality in the event of such a war."

Ilona sighed. "Do you suppose Hitler put him up to it?"

"I would say so. With Peter doing the letter-writing, the whole caper can be disavowed by the German government whenever it feels the urge."

"Peter—Hitler's stooge. Of all the *disgusting* things," Ilona said. "What are you going to do?"

"Not a thing. I don't happen to agree with him. I think Stalin is just turning into a paranoiac. I think he was turning that way a long time ago, but I think what finally tipped the scales was Nadezhda Alliluyeva's death."

"A maniac in charge of Germany, a maniac in charge of Russia—what a world," Felicity remarked.

"Well, I don't agree with either of you," Ilona said. "I don't think Joseph Vissarionovich is crazy. I don't know what he's doing, but he's working to a plan."

"You mean you go along with bumping off several thousand people?" Beth asked.

"Of course I don't. I think his methods are abhorrent. But they are *not* paranoiac. I got a letter from Tattie this morning, remember?"

"You were going to tell me what was in it," George said.

"It blows your theory and Peter's sky high. Tattie is going on another tour."

It was George's turn to be surprised. "Where?"

"Well, Germany. It is part of a great Russian mission, diplomatic as well as cultural, and it is to be headed by Michael Nej and Tattie, as commissar for culture. Now does that sound like the action of a paranoiac government?"

George was pulling his nose, thoughtfully.

"Of course Tattie is wild with joy. It means she'll be able to see Clive Bullen again. I gather she's already written to him. And she'll have Svetlana with her. And Natasha Brusilova. Natasha is her principal dancer now." She gazed at her husband. The only blight in their happiness was the hopeless love of Ilona's son John for the beautiful Russian ballerina—love which she obviously reciprocated, but which had seemed doomed, since John was persona non grata inside Russia for having acted as his Uncle Peter's agent in anti-Soviet activities. But if Natasha was being allowed out, for a season . . .

"I don't suppose—" Ilona began.

"I was going to send John to Holland this summer, anyway. There's to be a huge chess tournament there. It's almost equivalent to the world championship. Alekhine, Capablanca, the whole lot. Even that Russian fellow Botvinnik will be there."

"Oh, George," Ilona said. "It would be wonderful for him. If you don't think . . ."

"That he'd be wasting his time?" George shrugged. "I suspect he is. But it's only right he should be able to see his father again. I'll organize it." He gave her a squeeze and got up. "How about us?"

"Us?" Her chin lifted.

"Well . . . Europe in the summer, and Tattie, and Michael . . ."

"Oh, it would be marvelous. But . . . the paper . . ."

He knew which one she meant, but decided to let her say

it. "Actually, my love, it's something I've had in mind for some time, letting George junior sit in my chair for a month or so. Just to see how it fits." He smiled at Beth.

"Oh, *would* you?" Beth cried, unable to believe her ears. They had married while young George was still at college, and even though he had automatically gone to work for his father's principal newspaper the moment he graduated, neither of them had ever been sure whether he would be considered for the succession.

"Just to see, mind you," George said, smiling.

"I was thinking of *You*," Ilona said. "I've a series of articles planned with this Disney man—the cartoonist, you know. He's making a full-length film, all in animation."

"Sounds a bit ambitious, to me," Felicity remarked.

"Sounds damn nonsense, to me," George said. "I've heard about it. Surely Helen can handle it. That'd be better. A film about Snow White has got to be a flop, even if it had Judy Garland in it. Anyway, my love, the break will do you good."

"You really *want* to go back, don't you, George?"

"Sure I do. I have to confess that I'm interested. If Stalin is sending a diplomatic and cultural mission to Berlin, I agree it doesn't sound like paranoia. It sounds like something a hell of a lot more serious."

Joseph Vissarionovich Stalin stood at the window of the Kremlin and looked down at the Moscow River, flowing by on its way to join the Volga. It was his favorite view, his favorite posture, hands clasped behind his back, expression shrouded in the huge mustache that entirely concealed his mouth. When he stood like this, others in the room had to wait, for his thoughts, for his decisions. And if none of the three men who sat in the chairs before the huge desk were quite sure how he, and not one of them, had arrived at this position of ultimate inheritor of Lenin's stature and prerogatives within the Party, none of them was prepared to question that authority now that it had arrived.

Not even Michael Nej, who as the senior Party member in the room occupied the center of the three chairs. Considerably larger than his brother, who sat beside him, or than Vyacheslav Molotov, who occupied the other chair, Michael Nej had curiously rounded features that gave an overall impression of softness, and shrewd brown eyes that gave him a not altogether false suggestion of intellectualism. For if he lacked the education of most of the other Party leaders, he had done his best to remedy this by reading everything he could lay hands on in his youth. And if the world at large supposed that he had never risen as far as he should have because of his peasant background, he knew that it was his own lack of personal ambition that had kept him always one step from the top. And then there was the matter of Stalin's distrust. Yet he, of all those who might have been expected to fall in the recent purges, remained the man on whom the Party secretary relied whenever any peculiarly difficult task arose.

At last Stalin turned. "So you understand, Michael Nikolaievich, exactly what I have in mind."

"I do, Joseph Vissarionovich," Michael agreed. "That is not to say I necessarily like what I must do."

"Nor can I see the slightest possibility of the mission's being successful," Molotov said.

Stalin slowly walked behind the desk and sat down. "And you, Ivan Nikolaievich?"

"I am sure you know best, Joseph Vissarionovich," Ivan Nej said. "I merely wonder whether the size of the mission is not too great. This cultural section is to my mind unessential."

Stalin smiled. "Why do you not just divorce your wife, Ivan Nikolaievich?"

Ivan flushed. "It has nothing to do with Tatiana Dimitrievna."

"Self-honesty is a man's most important asset," Stalin remarked mildly. "You remain consumed with jealousy at the thought of Tatiana meeting that Bullen man again, as she will certainly do. You would save yourself a great deal of misery were you to divorce her."

"Tatiana Dimitrievna is my wife," Ivan said. "I will never divorce her."

Stalin shrugged. "Then you must bear with what is necessary for the state. As I have said before, she has her faults. Within the Union she is perhaps not an ideal commissar for culture. She has too many ideas of her own, her morals are bad, and she refuses to follow the Party line in too many things. But abroad she is possibly the best-known Russian of us all, and the best-liked. It is not merely her dancing that has made her famous and popular. And important. It is the fact that she is a Borodin of Starogan, the sister of a prince, no less, the sister-in-law of an American millionaire, who still prefers to live here in Russia, to work for us and with us, that makes her invaluable. And the Germans, Ivan Nikolaievich, adore culture. More, they adore Tatiana Dimitrievna. You will not forget that her last tour there was an outstanding success. She will bewitch these Nazis. She will make Michael Nikolaievich's task that much easier. Eh, Michael?" He smiled genially. "You have no doubts about including Tatiana and her girls in your party?"

"None at all," Michael said. "I have doubts about reaching an accommodation with Nazi Germany, a beast that is dedicated to our destruction. I have doubts whether it is necessary."

Stalin sighed. "I have explained that, Michael Nikolaievich. There can be no question that Europe is moving towards war. The democracies have allowed Germany to become far too powerful, compared to their own strengths. And Germany is greedy. Germany has always been greedy, but Hitler is greedier than most. He wants all of Czechoslovakia. Do not mistake that. The Sudetenland business is just a snare. Now, will the democracies fight? That is the question we must ask ourselves."

"Of course they will fight," Molotov said. "They are committed to fighting. France is, anyway, and Britain will support France."

"May I point out, Joseph Vissarionovich, that we are also committed to supporting France?" Michael asked gently.

Stalin's smile was equally gentle. "If they fight. And if they do, comrades, it will give us all a heaven-sent opportunity for getting rid of Nazism once and for all. But if they do *not?* There is the question."

"Is there a question?" Molotov said.

"I think there is," Stalin said. "I have a notion that the democracies, having read *Mein Kampf,* which Herr Hitler has been good enough to write for us all to study, are of the opinion that in the course of time Germany and Russia must go to war, and that it will be to their advantage to let that happen *before* they try to put an end to the Wehrmacht. Now I am sure you all agree with me that the reverse situation would be better for us. In any event, it will do no harm to keep the Germans guessing, and to make the democracies more interested in being nice to us. We are in this business for the good of Russia,

Michael Nikolaievich, not to pull others' chestnuts out of the fire for them. When we go to war with Germany, it will be at a moment of our own choosing. There is your task." He smiled at Ivan. "And if Tatiana Dimitrievna can be of assistance to you, then we shall all be grateful to her, shall we not, Ivan Nikolaievich?"

A roll of drums echoed through the Tiergarten Railway Station in Berlin, followed immediately by a clash of cymbals and then the full volume of the orchestra, heralding the approach of the train. Orders were snapped, and the black-clad soldiers on the platform came to attention, rifles at present, faces looking rigidly ahead. The reception committee, also mostly in uniform but containing a scattering of civilians, moved toward the edge of the platform.

The Moscow express rolled to a stop, the doors were opened, the red carpet was laid. Michael Nej stood on the step and waved. In strong contrast to the black uniforms all around, the black and red flags draped from the roof, the aura of militarism surrounding everything to do with this new Reich, Michael wore a pale gray suit with a matching hat, which he now raised as he shook hands. But already attention was wavering to the woman stepping onto the platform behind him.

Tatiana Nej was more than a younger edition of her sister. Perhaps she lacked Ilona's elegance, but she possessed instead, even at forty-five, a bubbling enthusiasm that brought the Borodin features to life and seemed to surround her with an enormous halo of light even on a dull afternoon. Besides, there were certainly men present here today who could remember her last visit to Germany, thirteen years ago, when she had taken the capital by storm, as she had taken all Europe by storm, with the originality as well as the eroticism of her dancing.

"I saw you, Frau Nej—why, it seems like yesterday." Joachim von Ribbentrop seized her hand to kiss it with all the effusion of a champagne salesman completing a large order.

"Herr Ribbentrop is foreign minister of the Reich," Michael explained, carefully omitting the aristocratic *von*.

"You were magnificent, Frau Nej. Magnificent. But you are no less magnificent today." Ribbentrop was under orders to be pleasant to the Russians, no matter what.

"Why thank you, comrade," Tattie said graciously. "It does seem only yesterday that I was here. But your city has changed. So many uniforms . . ." She smiled at him. "Are you going to fight somebody?"

At last Ribbentrop's smile died, and Michael hastily began introducing him to the various attachés who were descending from the train. Tattie was taken in charge by Frau von Ribbentrop, while behind her, the members of her dance troupe also began to accumulate on the platform.

"My daughter, Svetlana," Tattie said.

Svetlana Nej gave a brief curtsey, while Frau von Ribbentrop smiled at her. Svetlana, being Ivan Nej's daughter, had inherited her father's size with her mother's coloring and looks, and thus possessed an altogether more petite version of the famous Borodin beauty, her five feet three inches hardly bringing her to her mother's shoulder.

"And my principal dancer, Natasha Brusilova," Tattie said.

Another curtsey. In strong contrast to the brilliant blond beauty of the Borodins, Natasha Brusilova hardly looked Russian at all, with her delicate features and slender body, her red-brown hair, her solemn eyes.

"I am enchanted," said Frau von Ribbentrop, looking at the other thirty-odd young women who were still disembarking from the train. "Enchanted. I can hardly wait to see you perform."

Michael reclaimed his sister-in-law and niece, and escorted them through the saluting soldiers to the waiting cars.

"So many soldiers," Tattie said again.

"Well," Michael muttered, "it is a military state."

"And all so handsome," Svetlana whispered with a giggle.

"They give me the shivers," Natasha confessed, and squeezed Tattie's arm. "Comrade Nej, do you suppose . . ."

"We shall find out," Tattie said, pausing to smile at the crowd waiting outside the station. "Michael will find out for us."

"Find out what?" Michael asked, completing his wave, and about to be drawn away by Ribbentrop to enter the first of the official cars.

"Whether Clive and Johnnie are here yet," Tatiana hissed.

Michael smiled at her, indulgently. "John arrives tomorrow. From Holland."

Tattie glanced at Natasha, laughed at the sudden pinkening of her cheeks. "Remember now," she said. "You are here to dance. Not to get pregnant."

"Oh, Comrade Nej..." Natasha turned away in embarrassment.

"And Clive?" Tattie asked.

"Why, as I understand it, Mr. Bullen is here now," Michael said. "He is waiting for you at the hotel."

Suddenly she was a girl again, and as nervous as when she had first come here, thirteen years before. Berlin in 1925 had probably been the most important event of her entire life, because it had justified her life. It had justified all her girlhood quarrels with her mother, when she had wanted to do nothing but dance——and dance after her own fashion, following her own instincts, rather than any time-tested and time-wearied formula. It had justified her quarrel with her brother Peter, when in the first flush of succeeding to the princedom of Starogan he had discovered that he had also inherited the problems of coping with his two sisters, one a princess who wished only to elope with an American newspaper correspondent, and the other a princess who had consorted with people like the sex maniac Rasputin. Ilona had eventually slipped through his fingers; her love and George Hayman's determination had proved too much for even a Prince of Starogan. But Tattie had been younger, and more restrainable, able to be virtually imprisoned down on Starogan for seven years, to wait for a suitable husband to be found for her, to get over her mad impulses. That Berlin triumph had justified all the anger, and indeed the hatred, she had felt for her brother and the entire rest of her family who had so willingly supported him.

But most of all it had justified her decision to survive the revolution, and even prosper from it. She did not suppose many people understood that, even now. The mob Ivan Nej had led against his master's house had been intent only on destruction. In that single catastrophic afternoon the Borodins had been torn to shreds—in the case of beauties like her cousin Xenia, quite literally. Only Ilona, safe in her American nationality, and Peter, still with his regiment, had survived the holocaust. And little Tattie. She had been spared little. Like Xenia she had been thrown across her own bed and raped. But where the mob had then dragged Xenia downstairs to be butchered, Ivan Nej, once the Starogan bootblack, had instead claimed the woman he desired, perhaps even loved, and in his love she had seen her chance for survival.

Survival had meant marriage, because he had wanted it. Marriage to a bootblack, who had murdered her mother and her aunt and her cousins. Marriage to a Red revolutionary who was to become the most feared and hated man in all Russia. How shocked they had all been—Peter, Ilona, George, even Michael. They had not been able to understand that her only alternative—fleeing with Peter, the man who had locked her up for seven years, who would never let her do anything she wished, be anything she wished save a Princess of Starogan— was impossible. She might hate Ivan Nej; she might hate having to surrender her body to him every night, but he had let her dance. And through him she had gained access to Lenin himself, and he had *wanted* her to dance.

Berlin, 1925, had justified all that.

And it had given her Clive Bullen. The Englishman had watched that first, overwhelming performance, when the audience had gone mad with delight, and he had watched almost every other performance on that entire tour. And in London they had consummated their passion, had looked forward to so much more, before their affair had been brought to a sudden stop by Peter's absurd attempt to kidnap her and take her to America and, as he would put it, to freedom. Freedom to be a nothing, instead of the most famous woman in Russia. He had not been able to understand that, either. Not even Ilona had really been able to understand that. But Clive Bullen had. For all his love, he had understood that she needed something more than a simple human relationship, that her boast of being Tatiana Nej, the golden goddess from the steppe, as the newspapers called her, was to her a plain statement of the truth.

And their love had stood the test of time. Armed with it— and with the honors that had been heaped upon her after the tour—she had been able to leave Ivan, to live her own life, to concentrate upon her dancing academy and on the girls she trained there, and on Clive. Their meetings over the past few years had been infrequent, and once, in 1932, even disastrous, when Ivan had had him arrested on a trumped-up charge of sabotage in the hydroelectric plant Clive had been building on the Volga. But Michael had been able to sort that one out, and it was Michael who was once again taking her to meet him.

Dear Michael. She glanced at him, sitting beside her in the car, and found that he was watching her. She gave a guilty smile. They were the oldest friends in all the world. Since Michael was Ivan's elder brother, he had been there, her father's servant, ever since she could remember. He had been Ilona's friend more than hers, since he and Ilona were closer in age, but to little Tattie he had always been Michael Niko-laievich, grave and thoughtful, willing to understand. A man whose love for Ilona, whose extraordinary affair with her, had carried him into some strange paths, from participation in the assassination of Prime Minister Stolypin in 1911, through Prince Roditchev's torture chambers, to exile with Lenin in Switzerland, and eventually, because of that friendship, to hav-ing a share in the ruling of all Russia. To the world at large Michael Nej was no different than his brother. Both had blood-stained hands; had not Michael Nej signed the order that led to the execution of the tsar and all his family?

Only she knew that he was as different from Ivan as a man could possibly be. She and Ilona. Only she knew that he re-gretted having to work with a man like his brother at all, that he regretted so many of the decisions of the past four years, that he hated the trauma that had swept across Russia, and perhaps himself for sharing in it. Perhaps he even hated Stalin. But, as Stalin well knew, he was so fervent a patriot, so utterly dedicated to the continuance of Lenin's dream, that he remained the most important man in the Party, after only Stalin himself.

And only she knew that he was a man who could smile, and who could escort his sister-in-law to an adulterous meeting with a British capitalist. Perhaps he did not approve, but he would do it, because she was Tattie, because it was what she wanted, and because, like everyone else in Russia, he adored her.

She blew him a kiss, and he winked in reply. But now the car was stopping, and the doors were being opened by anxious flunkies. It was time for Clive.

She always worried that he might have changed. Presumably he would, eventually; she reminded herself that he was ten years older than she, and thus fifty-five.

But not yet—and not, perhaps, ever, at least for her. There was gray in his black hair, which he kept so smoothly brushed and which she delighted to rumple. There was a slight paunch, but this only enabled her to feel him the more. Yet the essentials, the clipped features, the sudden quiet smile, the intensity of his gaze, and the utter gentleness with which he held her in his arms were still there, and would always be there, as was the tremendous latent strength, which she had discovered so early in their relationship but which she valued less than his gentleness. She had not known a great deal of gentleness. It occurred to her that she had known no gentleness at all before this man. The Borodins were not gentle people, for all the closeness of their family circle. And revolutions, by their very nature, are not gentle things and do not throw up gentle people. Ivan had only wanted to inflict hurt.

Presumably there were other gentle men in the world. She had no doubt at all that George was a gentle man, and she had a suspicion that Michael might also turn out to be gentle, in bed. But Clive was the first gentle man *she* had known—the only one. Now that was an amusing thought. Tatiana Nej, world-famous as much for her blatant immorality as for her beauty as for her talent, had only *known* two men in her entire life.

But she had all she wanted, here in her arms.

He kissed her nose. "I can hardly believe it is really happening, that you are really here." Gently he stroked damp golden hair from her forehead to join the tumbled mass on the pillow above her head. "That we are here. Tattie . . ."

She placed her forefinger across his mouth, but he shook his head.

"I must speak, my love. You can't stay any longer in Russia. You cannot."

"My work is not yet finished, Clive. *I* am not yet finished, as a dancer, as a creator of dancers. It is my life. You know that, my own sweet love."

"But it is not necessary for you to stay in Russia," he said. "Even you must see that Stalin is turning into a monster. Can you possibly justify the things he has done these last few years?"

"Some people were opposing his plans for Russia."

"So he had them taken out and shot? Thousands and thousands of them? Can you possibly condone that, Tattie?"

She shrugged. "I don't know the truth of the matter."

"You mean you don't want to know. And now, sending a mission here to Germany . . ."

"You are here in Germany."

"That doesn't mean I have to like the Nazis."

"Well, I don't think I like the Nazis either, although I don't know a lot about them. And as Svetlana says, they *are* a handsome bunch. All those young men in uniform. Anyway, your government is also negotiating with them. All the newspapers are full of the negotiations over Czechoslovakia."

He sighed. "It's a tangled world. I don't think our government truly represents the feelings of the British people any more."

She smiled. "That is a confession of the failure of democracy. In Soviet Russia it is our business to represent the feelings of Joseph Vissarionovich, not the other way around." She laughed at his frown. "That upsets you."

"It concerns me. Tattie, don't you realize that you exist only because your friend Joseph wishes you to exist?"

"Well," she said, "we *are* friends. We have been friends for years. Oh, I know he does some terrible things, but it is his business to rule Russia, and mine to bring out Russian culture. Soviet culture. Revolutionary culture. Not to interfere in his business."

"But he interferes in yours."

"That is because he is first secretary of the Party."

"He is a dictator. Can't you understand that? And in his own way he is every bit as bad as Hitler."

She refused to get upset. "He is the ruler of Russia. The tsars were all dictators. There have always been dictators in Russia. And the tsars shot people and hanged them and sent them to Siberia, just as Joseph does. Of course it would be lovely if it weren't necessary, and we must all look forward to a world when it *won't* be necessary. But since it is necessary, now, it must be done. And Joseph is the only man who can do it, and hold the country together at the same time."

"And employ people like Ivan."

She made a moue. "Again, there is nobody else who will do it." She raised herself on her elbow, her heavy breasts against his arm. "Why should we quarrel? After six years, we are together in bed, and you wish to quarrel."

"Not quarrel, my darling. But I am afraid for you."

"Then don't be. Listen. I am training Svetlana to take my place. She will never be a great dancer. But she has a keen mind, and she has been with me from the beginning. She knows the school and my methods inside out. But she is only eighteen years old. She must be given a year or two yet. When she is twenty-one, I can make her my assistant. And when she is a little older than that, certainly when she is twenty-five, I will be able to leave her in charge of the academy. Then, if you wish it, Clive, I will leave Russia and come to you. If you wish it."

"If I wish it?" he asked. "Oh, my darling, darling . . ." His arms went round her, and she lay on his stomach, shaking her hair into his face. "If I wish it. But . . . seven years! I'll be sixty-one!"

"I'll be fifty-one," she said, and kissed him on the mouth. "Then you won't want me any more."

"Want you," he said, "want you." The desire welled up from his groin, and she matched it with her own. The bed became a kaleidoscope of racing passion, of movement, and of surging feeling. Like dancing, she thought, always like dancing, while lying down. The sweetest dance in all the world.

His eyes drooped, his body relaxed. She slipped from his chest to lie beside him again, but still on her stomach, her chin embedded in his armpit, her eyes only inches from his face. "But I cannot leave my school, Clive. Not until Svetlana is ready. It is *my* school. Lenin gave it to me himself. It is all I have ever lived for, the only reason for my existence. Those girls, those musicians, rely on me. I am everything to them, and they are everything to me. Say that you understand, my darling. Say it."

His eyes opened. "I understand, my darling, that you are the most splendid creature who ever walked this earth."

She blew him a kiss. "I am a Slav goddess. The critics say so, and the critics are always right, are they not?" She pushed herself up and reached for her robe. "Now come and watch us rehearse. I want to dance." She gave a pirouette across the center of the floor, hair and robe flying. "I want to dance!"

Applause welled out of the orchestra, rose toward the roof of the auditorium, drew the dress circle and the boxes into its growing paean. People stood to clap and to cheer, to yell themselves hoarse with delighted enthusiasm.

It was an evening of black, and red and gold, Michael Nej thought. A permanent glorious sunset, shot through with the most dramatic colors in the spectrum. And now that the lights were on, the curtseying young women on the stage itself were only a minor part of the splendor with which he was surrounded. Everywhere there were uniforms, blacks and midnight blues, decorated in reds and golds. Everywhere there were clean-shaven, handsome, dedicated features. He realized that almost for the first time in his life, at such a function, he was spending his time in watching the men rather than the women. It was an eerie feeling, a suggestion of almost menacing homosexuality. This was a male world into which he had wandered, in a way in which Europe had not been exclusively masculine since before the days of the Crusades, and like that feudal society, it was based on ruthless strength, and was dedicated to only one purpose, the assertion of that strength.

What did the democracies have to set against this juggernaut they hoped to contain? Frock-coated old men with rolled umbrellas? A pious memory of past triumphs, plucked from the very jaws of defeat? It was a prospect no less disturbing to him than to Stalin, even though Michael might feel entitled to suggest that Russia was in the same position as the democracies; a paranoiac suspicion of even his oldest associates had overtaken Stalin after the death of his wife Nadezhda Alliluyeva had been rapidly followed by the assassination of Serge Kirov. Undoubtedly there had been a group plotting against the continual accumulation of power into the hands of the Party secretary and his immediate supporters. Undoubtedly many senior members of the Party had remembered Leon Trotsky's warning, given way back in 1924 after Lenin's death, that his own demotion and disgrace was but the beginning, that they were yielding everything they and the revolution stood for into the power of one man. And undoubtedly the pernicious tsarist, anti-Soviet sedition expounded by men like Peter Borodin and disseminated by his agents throughout the country, had penetrated even the ranks of the Red army. Michael had been shocked and distressed by the ruthless brutality with which Stalin had ordered his secret policemen, Lavrenti Beria and Ivan Nej, to arrest their victims and torture, cajole, or blackmail them into confessions, and then to execute them with savage efficiency; but he had not been present in the cells beneath the Lubianka, so there was no way of telling which of the confessions were genuine and which had been induced entirely by pain and terror. The thought of so many of his old comrades, men like Nikolai Bukharin and Lev Kamenev, being delivered into the hands of Ivan's terror squads was quite sickening, but, as he had asked himself so many times, what was the alternative? However bloodstained Stalin's road, however much Michael might be aware that his master at times reacted with the angry venom of a madman, Stalin remained the only possible ruler of this turbulent accumulation of peoples and religions and national states and even of races that made up the Soviet Union. He had to be supported because there was simply no alternative, just as his policies had to be supported because he remained the greatest pragmatist of all time, a man whose sole driving force was the greatness of Russia.

And since that is my only driving force as well, Michael thought, I am here, in the center of this sinister gathering, to buy time for the Red army to be reorganized, for our industries to prepare themselves for the struggle foretold in *Mein Kampf* and undoubtedly merely waiting to develop—struggle that Russia *must* win, or disappear forever from the face of the map, a German colony, as devastated as it had been when overridden by the Mongols who were his own ancestors.

But do *they* know that? he wondered, glancing at Ribbentrop's shining face beside him as the foreign minister continued to applaud the stage. If they do, what can I hope to achieve?

"They are magnificent," Ribbentrop said. "I have never seen anything like it, Herr Nej. Frau Nej and her girls make me think of valkyries, riding across our sky. It must be the dream of every man with red blood in his veins to have such a bevy of beautiful women to bear him to his last resting place."

"Oh, quite," Michael said, wondering if Ribbentrop had been about to say "Aryan blood" instead of "red." "Would you like to come backstage and meet some of them?"

Ribbentrop smiled his cold smile. "Perhaps later. There is the reception, you know. The Führer will be there. We must not be late. Besides, I have a message for you."

"For me?" Michael asked.

"Yes, it seems there is a young man, an American, asking

for you. His name is John Hayman. A newspaper reporter. Do you wish to see him?"

"John," Michael said.

Ribbentrop raised his eyebrows. "Do you know this person?"

Michael slapped him on the shoulder, for the first time genuinely smiling. "Know him, Herr Ribbentrop? He is my son."

Unlike every other man in the auditorium, John Hayman wore neither uniform nor a black tie. In his sports jacket and gray flannels he was surrounded by ushers as if he had the plague, and only they could prevent him from communicating his dread disease to the audience at large. They regarded the Russian commissar with studied disapproval as he hurried forward, arms outstretched.

He stopped suddenly, within three feet of his son. It was still a new experience, to possess a son at all. He could remember the rapture with which he learned of her pregnancy from Ilona, in that dreamy summer of 1907 down in old Starogan, before his world had fallen apart. He had imagined then, for a single crazy moment, that in her angry despairing at having been forcibly separated from George, the man she loved, and married to Prince Roditchev, a man she hated, she might actually run away with him—her brother's former valet, in whose arms she had found a substitute passion. They might be together, with their son.

Her decision, so logical and indeed inevitable for her, that she should pretend the child was her husband Roditchev's, had left him angry with her for the first time in his life. Yet such had been his love that he had surrendered completely. After Ilona fled Russia, he had seen his son only once in fourteen years, during the revolution. The boy had been brought up to believe that he was the last Prince Roditchev, even though his mother had had him adopt the name of his stepfather. That belief, which carried with it a built-in hatred for everything Bolshevik, had led him into the orbit of his Uncle Peter, whose entire life was dedicated to the overthrow of Bolshevism. And as a Borodin spy he had reentered Russia, inevitably to be arrested by the secret police and handed over to the tender mercies of Ivan and his infamous assistant, Anna Ragosina.

Michael had rescued him, and had done so *as* a father. Their week together then had been too brief for true understanding. And besides, how could a young man of twenty-five grasp the fact that within an instant he was no longer the son of a prince but the son of a Bolshevik commissar? And his tsarist activities had meant that although he could be saved by Michael from a Siberian labor camp, he had nevertheless been deported from Russia, never to return.

But now, at thirty-one, he was a man, broad-shouldered, with the thoughtful dark eyes of his real father and the splendidly contoured features of his mother.

And as a man, had he yet come to terms with himself, and his background?

"Ivan," Michael said in Russian, and then flushed. "I should remember to say, John."

"Ivan to you, surely, Father," John Hayman said, also speaking Russian, and a moment later was in his arms.

There was so much to say, so much to ask, which could never be asked. Only commonplaces, however important *they* might also be.

"Your mother is well?"

"Great. She's coming over, you know, with George. Well, they wouldn't miss a chance for a get-together with Aunt Tattie."

"How splendid," Michael said, holding him at arm's length, the better to look at him. "And you . . . still chess?"

John Hayman's mouth twisted. "As a correspondent, yes. I am covering the AVRO tournament, but George told me to take a week off, so I could see you. And them, of course. They'll be here in a couple of days. They're in Southampton now."

Michael smiled at him. "And Natasha Brusilova?"

John blushed. "Is she well?"

"Indeed she is, and dancing better than ever. You must come backstage with me to see her. And your aunt."

John Hayman looked down at himself. "I'm not really dressed for it. But the train only just got in. I went to the hotel, but I guess I couldn't wait long enough to change."

Michael clapped him on the shoulder and led him through the scandalized ushers and the guests now starting to leave the auditorium, towards the backstage area. "You are well enough dressed for Natasha Brusilova, I suspect. And besides, if you do not see her now you will have to wait until tomorrow. We are all going to a reception at the chancellery." He winked. "To meet the Führer."

"Oh," John said. "I had hoped..."

"There is always tomorrow, Ivan Mikhailovich. And the day after. And even the day after that."

"And after that? Father, is there any chance..."

"Now that is something you will have to discuss with Tatiana Dimitrievna. And with Natasha Feodorovna, to be sure." Michael opened the door for his son. "But since they are here, why do you not do so?"

"Johnnie!" Tatiana Nej cried, throwing her arms wide. "Johnnie Hayman!"

He hesitated in the doorway of the dressing room. Well, many a man had hesitated in the doorway of Aunt Tattie's dressing room. She had, as usual, been enjoying plaudits both on the stage and off it, and had not yet changed. Since she had, in this evening's dance, been the queen of the water spirits, she wore a blue costume, containing a good deal of feathers round her head, and descending from her hips, but in between, her silver-lamé leotard clung to her body like a second skin, and darkened with sweat, seemed almost to have become a second skin in places; it was against those large breasts with the pointed nipples that he was about to be hugged.

But meeting Aunt Tattie was embarrassing in other ways— a reminder of too many things past, of that insane attempt of Uncle Peter's to kidnap her on her first tour, and force her to defect to the West, a scheme in which Peter had expected the loyal support of his hero-worshipping nephew. Then he had made the choice which had kept them friends. But when, following his reconciliation with Uncle Peter and his quarrel with his mother and stepfather, he had returned to Russia as a spy, once again Tattie had had to involve herself—and not only on his behalf, for she had discovered he was secretly meeting one of her most promising dancers.

But Tatiana Dimitrievna, whose heart was as generous as her figure or her smile, willingly forgave, because he was Ilona's son, and because she loved him.

"Johnnie," she said again. "How good you look."

He was in her arms, being smothered against her powerful beauty, being kissed, and looking past her at Clive Bullen, apologetically.

"John." Clive shook hands. "You're looking well. How's the tournament going?"

"It's between Paul Keres and Reuben Fine," John said.

"Not Michael Botvinnik?" Tattie demanded. Botvinnik was the only Soviet player taking part.

"He's doing well, but not well enough," John said. "You don't want to talk about chess, though."

"You mean *you* don't," Tattie said, and went to the door. "Natasha Feodorovna," she shouted. "Come in here."

"I don't wish to disturb her," John said.

"Nonsense," Tattie declared. "She is finished for the evening. And she wants to see you. She keeps all of your letters, you know."

"Tatiana Dimitrievna," Natasha protested from the doorway.

"Well, I am sure it is something Johnnie would like to know," Tattie pointed out.

John was tongue-tied. Natasha Brusilova had been twenty-one when he first met and loved her, six years before. She was then a shy and uncertain girl, suffering all the psychological damage of having watched her parents being shot during the massacre of the kulaks ordered by Stalin in 1929, and then all the ecstasy of having been selected by the great Tatiana Nej as a future lead dancer. But now, at twenty-seven, she *was* the company's principal dancer, second only to Tattie herself, with all the sophistication that success could give her. And there was more. The slender, hesitant girl had given way to the woman. Natasha Feodorovna was still slender to be sure, as befitted a professional dancer—Tattie being the exception— but she carried her height with the grace of a gazelle, left her face exposed and austerely handsome within its cloud of auburn hair worn shorter than the other dancers', and looked at John with an assurance that reduced him to jelly. When they had first met, he had thought himself to be the son of a prince, and thus at least an exiled prince in his own right, and she had supposed the same. Instead he had turned out to be the son of a commissar. Well, he tried to remind himself, in Russia that probably meant a great deal, and Natasha Feodorovna lived in

Russia. But he knew that it meant nothing at all outside of Russia, and more, he knew that he was one of life's entire irrelevancies, a chess player who would never be a master and therefore must content himself with reporting what the masters did, a newspaperman who worked for his stepfather and had therefore never *proved* any ability in his life, a man who would always be half-way up the professional tree where she had already reached the top of hers.

And he loved her. Yet, he had never done more than hold her hand and kiss her with a youthful innocence. Six years ago. When she had thought him a prince.

"I think I will use your room this evening, Natasha Feodorovna," Tattie decided. "Come along, Olga Mikhailovna. Come along, Clive."

She bustled Clive and her maid to the door, while Natasha suddenly woke up to what was happening.

"Oh, but you cannot, Tatiana Dimitrievna," she protested. "I mean—"

"Silly girl," Tattie said, and closed the door.

"Your aunt is very generous," Natasha said. "She supposes there is a great deal we must say to each other."

"Isn't there?" John asked.

Natasha crossed the room and sat down in the one easy chair. "I do not know."

"Natasha." He knelt beside her. "I have written you every week. Every week for six years."

"And I have enjoyed receiving your letters."

"And kept them."

A faint flush. "As Tatiana Dimitrievna has said, I have kept them."

"Then . . ." He bit his lip. "There is nobody else?"

"How could there be anybody else?"

"Well . . . six years. And you are so beautiful, so lovely in every way. And so famous, now."

"A principal dancer has no time for romance," Natasha said, watching him carefully.

"Thank God for that," John agreed. "And now we are here, out of Russia, together . . ."

Natasha gave a faint sigh. "I am here to dance, Johnnie."

"Of course you are. But it is to be a long tour, I am told. You will have lots of days off."

"If Tatiana Dimitrievna permits it."

"Of course she'll permit it. I'll ask her. She would really like you and me, well . . ."

"Tatiana Dimitrievna is very fond of you," Natasha agreed gravely. "She often speaks of you as her favorite nephew."

"Well, so that's not a problem. Natasha, there'll be time. We have so much to talk about. So many plans to make. So many—"

Natasha stood up. "I will look forward to that, Johnnie. But now I must hurry and dress. We are due at the chancellery. There is to be a reception there, given by the Führer himself."

"I know." John also got up. "I wish I were coming with you."

"I wish you were too," she said.

"Natasha." He seized her hand, kissed it. "May I see you tomorrow?"

"I do not know. I do not know our schedule. You will have to telephone."

"Then I will do that. Natasha—" He resisted the faint tug she had given to free her hand. "Six years."

She hesitated, then allowed him to draw her into his arms. Her kiss was as chaste as he had remembered it, just the slightest parting of the lips, the softest touch of her tongue against his before she pulled her head away, suddenly, as if she had been surprised by her own temerity. And he would not force her. It was not possible for him ever to force Natasha.

"I must hurry," she said again. "Telephone me at the hotel tomorrow, Johnnie."

He allowed her to slip through his fingers.

Michael was disappointed. Here was a short man, with lank black hair and strangely uninteresting features, except for the bright little mustache. A man one would easily lose in a crowd, he thought, except that he was chancellor of the Reich. But a strange chancellor, as well, he decided, obviously ill at ease in his black dinner suit, and even more ill at ease to be in the presence of so many tall and beautiful young women.

"I am told they dance well, Herr Nej," he said. "Ribbentrop tells me they dance well."

"Indeed they do, your excellency," Michael agreed. "But will you not come to a performance?"

Hitler looked positively startled. "A performance? Why, I might, Herr Nej. But these are pressing times. Pressing times. The theater is a luxury I can seldom afford. There is work to be done, eh? Work with you, Herr Nej."

Michael had the strangest feeling that he had nearly added "even". He inclined his head.

"I am here to work, certainly, your excellency."

"Yes. Well, you must talk with Ribbentrop, and then, no doubt, you and I will have a talk. Yes, indeed. You've met the Reichsmarschall?"

"It is my pleasure, Herr Göring," Michael said, carefully refraining from using any title.

The big man was once a dashing air ace in the World War, Michael had been told, but now he was grotesquely overweight, with a bulbous face into which his eyes all but disappeared. Göring frowned at him, and then forced a polite smile. "All these lovely little girls, Herr Nej," he said. "To be surrounded by them, all the time . . . why, you are a fortunate man. You must bring them out to my country estate, for a private performance, eh? Ha ha."

"For that you will have to ask Madam Nej herself, Herr Göring. And here she is. Your excellency, may I present Tatiana Nej, our commissar for culture, and the greatest dancer in the world."

Hitler looked still more uncomfortable as he was confronted with a woman both taller than himself, and glowing with blond beauty. Tattie wore a white georgette evening dress with wine-colored trimmings at shoulder, thigh, and hem, a velvet sash, and soft gloves that concealed her elbows. Her décolletage, for Tattie, was remarkably modest, but it was impossible, ever, to be unaware of her physical attributes.

"It is my pleasure, your excellency," she said, giving a brief curtsey. Unlike Michael, she had not troubled to learn German very thoroughly.

"Is she not a perfect representative of Aryan beauty, my Führer?" Ribbentrop whispered.

"Why, yes, yes," Hitler said, for a moment animated. "Indeed she is. Do you not think so, Hermann?"

Göring was lingering over her hand. "You *will* come to see me, Madam Nej? And you will bring all of your lovely young ladies?"

For a terrible moment Michael thought that Tattie was going to stick out her tongue at him. "We are here to dance, Herr Reichsmarschall," she pointed out.

"I adore dancing," Göring assured her. "Now, will you not introduce me to some of your girls?"

Tattie glanced at Hitler, and received a benevolent nod. "Oh, please go ahead, Frau Nej. I cannot stay long. Affairs of state, you understand. Affairs of state."

"Well, then, your excellency, let me see. There is my daughter, over there."

"I could have told that at a glance," Göring said enthusiastically. "Such beauty could belong to no one else. May we begin with her?"

Tattie was frowning. "I do not know who that is she is talking to."

Svetlana was deep in conversation with an extraordinarily handsome young man, wearing the deep blue and black dress uniform of the SS. Their heads were close together, and his yellow hair was even paler than hers.

"Why, isn't that young Hassell?" Göring said.

Hitler looked in the required direction. "So it is," he said. "Paul von Hassell, Frau Nej. He is one of our best and brightest young men. As he has shown by his choice of your daughter as a conversational partner, eh? Ha ha. Ribbentrop, I must go. Herr Nej, I welcome you to the Reich. Use your time profitably." He gave a wintry smile. "And our time, to be sure. Frau Nej, this has been one of the most memorable evenings of my life."

His associates came to attention, and conversation came to an end as, at a signal from Ribbentrop, the band struck up the national anthem. Hitler left the room, hands clasped behind his back, smiling to left and right, several of his aides scurrying behind.

"And now," Göring said, tucking Tattie's hand under his arm. "The formalities are over. Now we can enjoy ourselves. Now you can introduce me to every one of your lovely little girls. Beginning with your daughter, of course. Hassell will have to take his chances with me, eh?" His bellow of laughter rose above the hum of conversation, and heads turned.

Tattie raised her eyebrows at Michael, who gave a faint shrug. "Well, then, Herr Reichsmarschall—" she began.

But Ribbentrop interrupted. "Before you hurry off, Frau Nej, we have a surprise for you. A great surprise." He winked. "A special guest, who will be equally surprised to see you."

He turned to one of the side doors of the huge room, through which two men were entering. One was short and grotesquely ugly, limping towards them on a club foot, his face twisted into a smile.

"I would have you meet Herr Goebbels," Ribbentrop said. "Our Gauleiter for Berlin, and, more important, *our* minister for culture."

But Tattie was not interested in Goebbels. She was staring at the other man as if she had seen a ghost. For he was taller even than she, and possessed her blond hair and coloring, as well as her perfectly carved features, in his case softened by a little mustache.

"But the other gentleman I am sure you already know," Ribbentrop chuckled. "Frau Nej—your brother, Prince Peter Borodin of Starogan."

# Chapter 2

"MADAM NEJ," GOEBBELS SAID, TAKING BOTH TATTIE'S HANDS and drawing her towards him. "How beautiful you are. Your photographs do not do you justice."

For one of the very few times in her life, Tattie was aware of being embarrassed by a man. His eyes were never still; his gaze moved from her face to her neck and then to her décolletage, seemed able to penetrate the material to uncover the delights that lay beneath.

Besides, she wasn't interested in him. She allowed him a perfunctory kiss, had to jerk her hand to get it away.

"Peter?" She could not believe her eyes.

"I understand it is some time since you have had the opportunity of seeing your brother," Ribbentrop said, with a malicious smile.

"It is thirteen years," Tattie said. "But Peter... You are here in Berlin?"

Peter kissed her hand. "Is it not the new capital of Europe, Tatiana Dimitrievna? You are looking well."

"Thank you. And you. I wrote to you, when Rachel died, but you never replied."

"It was a trying time for me," he said, and looked at Michael Nej, patiently waiting.

"You remember Michael," Tattie said.

"Indeed I do," Peter said coldly. "What is he, your watch-dog?"

Michael held out his hand to his old master. He wondered at the lack of sensation, the absence of any feeling of alarm. He had not laid eyes on Peter Borodin since 1907, when he had resigned his position as valet. Peter had been furious, had warned him that he would end up badly, and had no doubt felt justified in his prediction when Michael had been condemned to death for the murder of Stolypin. But since then a great deal had happened. The Prince of Starogan was now the fugitive, and his erstwhile valet was second only to the ruler of his country. That was sufficient cause for dislike, he supposed, but there was even more. In the interim he had known and loved Prince Peter's own mistress, Judith Stein. There could be no forgiveness there, nor would he wish any. But Michael himself found it difficult to hate.

Now he smiled. "I doubt that Tatiana Dimitrievna would take kindly to a watchdog," he said.

"Tatiana Dimitrievna," Peter said thoughtfully, as if slowly digesting the fact that a servant could so refer to a princess, in her presence. "What of the other watchdog? The murderous one? But of course, I forgot. You are no less successful a murderer than your brother."

Ribbentrop cleared his throat uneasily, and Goebbels signaled for some drinks to be brought over.

"If you are going to fight," Tattie said, "I am going to knock your heads together. I had to do that the last time we met, you know, Herr Ribbentrop," she explained. "He tried to kidnap me. My own brother."

"Have some champagne," Goebbels suggested. "I am sure he did it for your own good, Frau Nej."

"Everything Peter does is for somebody's good," Tattie pointed out. "The trouble is, he never thinks to ask them first."

"I see you have not changed at all, Tattie," Peter said, taking a glass. "Well, as you are here, we must have a meal together. I am sure Ruth would like to meet . . . Svetlana, is it?"

"Oh, I'd love to meet Ruth. I never have, you know," she explained to the indifferent Germans. "My own niece, and I have never met her. But do you mean Ruth is in Germany with you?"

"Of course," Peter said. "We are living here now. These gentlemen have been good enough to give me a home."

"A home?" Tattie demanded. "Here in Germany? With the Na—"

It was Michael's turn to look alarmed. "I imagine you must be very happy here, Herr Borodin," he hastily interrupted. "After all, historically, Germans and Russians have always been very close." He smiled. "Half of our tsarinas, in the old days, were German princesses."

"Quite," Peter said, still speaking coldly. "And I have no doubt at all that Germany and Russia will continue to have close links in the future."

"Yes," Ribbentrop said, uncomfortably.

"Oh, yes," Tattie said. "That's why we're here. Well, really, I'm just the gilt on the gingerbread. That's what Joseph Vissarionovich says. But Michael is here to discuss trade, and the future, and even a political agreement. Aren't you, Michael?"

Michael stared at Ribbentrop, and Ribbentrop returned the stare. Goebbels hastily downed another glass of champagne.

Then the men all looked at Peter.

"A political agreement?" Peter demanded quietly. "Between Germany and the Soviets?"

"A discussion on the future of Europe," Goebbels suggested euphemistically.

"A political agreement?" Peter asked again, his voice rising. "Between Nazi Germany and the Bolsheviks? The people you—we—are sworn to destroy?"

"I do beg you to remember, Prince Peter, that this is a social gathering," Ribbentrop said. "Really, sir—"

"You would sign an agreement with . . . with *that?*" Peter shouted, pointing at Michael.

Heads turned, and all conversation ceased. But Goebbels was equal to the crisis. He gave a quick signal to the band, which had hitherto been playing light, quiet dance music to permit the talk to flow freely, but now burst into a Wagnerian overture, drowning out every other sound.

"I do apologize," Ribbentrop bellowed, trying to make himself heard above the din. "Prince Peter does not understand at all."

"Understand?" Peter bawled. "I understand only too well. You, sir, have misled me, and tried to make a fool of me. Well, sir, I'll not have it. I'll—"

"You'll excuse us, Herr Nej," Goebbels said, seizing Peter's arm. "It has been a lovely reception. Frau Nej, meeting you has been the greatest occasion of my life. I look forward to renewing our acquaintance, at the earliest possible moment."

"I am not leaving," Peter declared. "I am not going anywhere. Why should I? I came here—"

He discovered that his other arm had also been seized, and this time by a brawny man in uniform.

"It is time we left," Goebbels explained. "There is work to be done."

"Well," Tattie said, as her brother was escorted through the door. "He doesn't change. I don't suppose he ever will. All he ever wants to do is fight. Do *you* really want to fight, Herr Ribbentrop?"


"You really must try to control your temper, Prince Borodin," Goebbels said, hustling Peter Borodin into an antechamber.

"Control my temper?" Peter shouted, able to make himself heard now that they were away from the blaring music. "Control my temper? That man is a red-handed murderer. Worse, he is a seducer of my sister. And he signed the tsar's death warrant. And I find him here, being entertained by you, having discussions with you—"

"Surely, Prince Peter, a diplomat is forced to hold discussions with many people he might not wish to entertain in his own home." Ribbentrop had left the reception to join them.

"Herr von Ribbentrop," Peter said. "I came to Germany for one reason, and one reason only, as you well know. I am engaged in a fight against Bolshevism—Bolshevism in all its forms, wherever it rears its ugly head. Of all the nations in Europe, all the nations in the world, it seemed that only Nazi Germany, the Germany of the Führer, was prepared to oppose Bolshevism by all the means at its disposal, by force of arms, if necessary. Thus I came here in good faith, and offered your government my services. Services, I may add, Herr von Ribbentrop, of which you have been pleased to avail yourself. I am speaking of my network of agents within Russia, of the men and women who, like me, have dedicated their lives to the downfall of Stalin and all his crew. Do you expect me to condone the entertainment of one of the most infamous of that crew here in Berlin? Treating Michael Nej as a diplomat, by God! The man is a valet! The son of a serf! His brother used to polish my boots. *He* used to polish my boots. And you treat him as a *diplomat?*"

"The Third Reich does not require its guests to *condone* its actions," Ribbentrop said, his voice a blast from the Arctic.

"Times may change, Prince Peter," Goebbels said soothingly. "But an enemy remains always, an enemy."

"I'm afraid I do not understand you," Peter said.

"As I am sure Herr von Ribbentrop means to explain to you," Goebbels said, glancing at his colleague, "there can be no question but that the life of the German nation, of the Third Reich, demands a war with Russia, a victorious war, and in the not so distant future. Our Führer has explained this, and it is the will of the Nazi Party, the will of the nation. Living room, breathing space, that is what the German nation requires, and where can such living space be obtained, except at the expense of the East?" He gave another glance at Ribbentrop, who was watching him a trifle anxiously. "The East, where the Bolsheviks have alienated so many of their subject peoples, peoples who would far rather be ruled by Germany than by 'red-handed revolutionaries,' as you so aptly describe them."

"I understand that," Peter said, impatiently. "When the war is won Germany will have the Ukraine. I have raised no objection to that."

"Quite so," Goebbels agreed. "But make no mistake, Prince Peter, a war with Russia will be no light affair. Think of those who have tried to conquer that vast land. Napoleon. Charles the Twelfth. They both failed, and each was the greatest soldier of his generation."

"They fought a united country," Peter pointed out, "rallying to the call of God and tsar. And they fought against a well-trained, disciplined army. These are the points I have been making for the past six months. Russia is more disunited now than it has been since the days of the Mongols. And the army is mere rabble. I'd be the first to admit that the Bolsheviks discovered some excellent generals—"

"Indeed they did," Ribbentrop said. "Didn't they defeat you in 1920?"

"We lost because of lack of supplies," Peter retorted. "Supplies, which, if granted us by the then allied governments, would have stopped this Bolshevik catastrophe from overtaking the world at all. But that is by the by. Those generals have now been liquidated by Stalin. The army is in a state of total disarray. You will never have a better opportunity then now, gentlemen."

"At least one of those generals is still alive and is attending our reception," Ribbentrop remarked.

"Michael Nej? Bah. He is a peasant and the son of a peasant."

"Did he not command the armies that opposed your own?"

"He had supplies," Peter shouted. "He had tanks, when we had none. He had—"

"This is irrelevant," Goebbels broke in. "If you will excuse me, Prince Peter. You are probably right, and at this moment Russia is at her most vulnerable. But we too are vulnerable. We cannot fight Russia until our frontiers have been rectified, until there is no risk of encirclement by the democracies. Great Britain and France will not stand by and watch us go to war with Russia."

"Nonsense," Peter said. "They will never fight for the Bolsheviks. They hate them as much as we do, only they lack the courage to say so."

"The democracies will always fight where they see the chance of a profit," Goebbels said. "They are getting very excited now because of this Sudetenland business. It is necessary for us to sort out that problem before we can think of attacking Russia. And do not forget that if they decide to fight for Czechoslovakia, Russia is obliged by treaty to help them. Now we know, thanks to your agents, Prince Peter, that Russia is in no condition to fight anyone, and would very much like to avoid that obligation. Does it not make sense to you for us, as a purely temporary measure, to increase that reluctance? To suggest to the Bolsheviks that, despite what is written in *Mein Kampf,* we are prepared to live and let live, to divide Europe into spheres of influence, within the boundaries of which we may exist to each other's mutual advantage?"

"It is hypocrisy," Peter grumbled.

"It is necessity," Goebbels insisted. "There is nothing for you to fear. We will have Russia, eventually. You will have Michael Nej. I give you my word. You may have him, and his brother, to hang with your own hands."

Peter stared at him. "Do you take me for an executioner? I am the Prince of Starogan. My interest is to see justice done. Nothing more and nothing less than that."

"Of course, of course," Goebbels said. "And it shall be done. Have I not given you my word? But you will agree that murderers should be hanged. Just let us give them enough rope to make sure that such an end is attained. Trust us, Prince Peter. We shall not let you down."

Peter hesitated, looking from one man to the other. "You cannot expect me to sit down to dinner with the man. He was my valet."

"Of course," Goebbels repeated. "Tonight was a mistake. It was carelessness on my part. Now I think you should go home. There are papers for you to look at tomorrow. Let me escort you to your car. I am sure Herr von Ribbentrop will excuse you."

"Of course," Ribbentrop said, taking his cue from the minister of propaganda.

Peter nodded and went down the stairs, Goebbels at his elbow. Ribbentrop lit a cigar and stared moodily out the window until he heard the limping tread return.

"I am amazed that you can put up with him," he said. "The man's hatred of the Bolsheviks is quite pathological. I do not see how anyone who has so little control of himself can possibly be of any use to us."

"He knows his job," Goebbels said. "His network of agents inside Russia is invaluable to us, and you know that. What is more, they are people activated by an *ideal*, just as he is. They do not ask for pay. And they cheerfully die for him. We would have to look far and wide to find anyone as useful to us. And I have not mentioned the propaganda value of having him here in Germany, openly working for us."

"Bah," Ribbentrop said. "I doubt he is half as valuable as you think. And what of the future? Don't you suppose we are going to have trouble with him? He 'understands' that 'we can have the Ukraine', indeed. What a farce! Doesn't he 'understand' that we want all of European Russia? Let him have Siberia and the steppe, if he wants to set up a kingdom, another tsar."

"He does *not* understand that, Joachim, and I would be grateful if you would not enlighten him on that subject. When our war with Russia is won, why, Prince Borodin will have outlived his own usefulness." He clapped Ribbentrop on the shoulder. "He could well wind up hanging on the same gallows as the Nej brothers. Wouldn't that be fine sport?"

"That I would like to see," Ribbentrop agreed. "With that blond bitch of a sister hanging right beside them."

"Now that would be a waste," Goebbels said. "Madam Nej is one of the truly beautiful women in the world today." He sighed. "Although, I have heard that her American sister is even more beautiful. Ah, well, I must see what can be done with this one." He winked. "And for heaven's sake don't let Borodin get under your skin, Joachim. He is a tool. Nothing more than that. A tool."

"The reviews all seem to be good." Clive Bullen sat on the terrace of the hotel bedroom, in his dressing gown, and folded the last newspaper.

Tattie poured coffee. "Don't sound so surprised."

"Well, as I remember, one or two were a little bit shocked the last time you were here."

She placed his cup before him, held his head to tilt it back and kiss him on the mouth. "That was 1925. This is 1938. Times have changed. Attitudes have changed. People have become more civilized."

"Would you really say that about these people?"

She sat down. "They are revolutionaries. Like us in Russia. It takes time to smooth the rough edges. Anyway, they seem to like my dancing."

"Or they are so determined to be polite to the Russian mission that they have ordered all their newspapers not to dislike it."

"Wretched man." But she smiled as she said it. "I would not care if they hated it. I am here, and you are here. For a whole month. I can hardly believe it. And I am going to enjoy every minute of it."

"Before we are separated for... what did you say, six years?"

She made a moue. "Not so long as that. But six years, from now, we shall never be separated again. I have promised you. There will be other cultural missions before then. Joseph Vissarionovich is determined to remain at peace with everyone in Europe. There will be other missions."

He gazed at her; it was not something he could ever tire of doing, gazing at Tatiana Nej. But he did worry about her almost dangerous insouciance, her remarkable confidence that whatever she decided, would happen, because it always had in the past.

"You like Joseph Stalin, don't you?" he said. "You trust him."

"Well..." Tattie considered while drinking coffee. "I do like him, because he likes me. I like everyone who likes me. As for trusting him, why of course I trust him. I work for him."

"Not quite the same thing."

She leaned across the table to place her finger on his lips. "No politics. I do not travel two thousand miles to see you, and then talk politics. Here are the girls. Svetlana, my own sweet love." She left the table to embrace her daughter. "Natasha." A kiss for Natasha Brusilova. "Now, come and sit down and tell me all about last night." She escorted them to the table; they also wore dressing gowns and looked a trifle bleary-eyed. "And kiss Clive," Tattie commanded.

Natasha Brusilova flushed as she presented her cheek, but if Svetlana was embarrassed to be eating breakfast with her mother's lover she did not show it.

"It was a wonderful party," she said, sitting down and buttering toast. "They were all so kind. After we left the reception we went on to some kind of nightclub, down in a cellar, where they sang and danced and there was a floor show up on the stage—"

"A disgusting affair," Natasha said. "All suggestion and innuendo and obscene posturing."

"Oh, it was fun," Svetlana protested. "And everyone was so charming, so attentive..."

"Anyone in particular?" Tattie inquired.

"Well..." It was Svetlana's turn to flush. "I met the loveliest young man, Mama."

"His name is Paul von Hassell, he is a lieutenant in the Waffen SS, and I can tell you that he is highly regarded by Hitler himself."

"There's joy," Clive remarked, quietly, and Tattie kicked him under the table.

"How did you know?" Svetlana cried.

"It is my business to know. Did he bring you home again?"

"Oh, yes, Mama."

"And?"

Svetlana stared at her for a moment, then gave a peal of laughter. "Oh, nothing like that. He kissed my hand. But Mama, he wants to take me to dinner tonight."

"I really don't think it would be a good idea to get *too* close to these Nazis," Clive suggested.

"Clive is quite right," Tattie said. "Not *too* close. But the boy is Hitler's protégé, and we are here to make a friend of Hitler. I think you could let him take you to supper, after the performance. Don't you agree, Natasha Feodorovna?"

"I have no idea," Natasha said, shrugging.

"Why?" Tattie asked. "Did you not meet a handsome German?"

Another shrug. "I suppose I did. Several."

"But your mind was filled with Johnnie. Is he coming here for lunch?"

Natasha nodded, and flushed all over again. "Tatiana Dimitrievna, I would like to have a word with you in private, if that is possible."

"Of course it is possible, especially if it is about Johnnie. After breakfast. Clive always smokes a cigar after breakfast, and I cannot stand the smell. After breakfast." She watched the door open. "Well, Olga Mikhailovna?"

The dresser curtsied. "There is a young woman here to see you, Comrade Nej."

"A young woman? Has she a name?"

"She probably wants to join your outfit," Clive suggested.

"Her name is Ruth Borodina, Comrade Nej."

"Ruth!" Tattie cried, leaving the table in a long bound. "My niece." She paused in the center of the room to look over her shoulder. "Your cousin, Svetlana. She is Peter's child, by Rachel Stein. Oh, I'm so glad she's come."

"Let's hope she's not like her father," Svetlana muttered

under her breath. But Tattie had already pulled the door wide,
had seized the girl outside, and was dragging her into the suite.

"Ruth!" she said. "Ruth Borodina. Stand there and let me
look at you."

The girl obeyed, casting a curious glance at the table and
its occupants. She was very slender, although not lacking in
either hip or bosom, and dark like her mother, her hair thick
and black and drooping past her shoulders. Her features were
large and well-shaped, and dominated by enormous black eyes.

"Why, do you know," Tattie declared, "you're the spitting
image of your Aunt Judith, when I first met her. How old are
you, Ruth?"

"I am seventeen, Madam Nej." Ruth Borodina's Russian
was perfect, although she had left the country as a baby.

"Seventeen. Why, I think Judith was just about that age,
too. Oh, to be seventeen again. And what is this Madam Nej
stuff? I am your Aunt Tattie." She threw her arm round the
girl's shoulders, hugged her, and then half-carried her toward
the table.

"I . . . I have come to apologize," Ruth explained. "For
Father, last night. I am afraid he must have been very rude."

"Your father is a very rude man," Tattie pointed out. "It is
not something to concern yourself about."

"But he was rude to Commissar Nej, as well," Ruth said.
"I would like to apologize to you, sir, also."

Tattie gave a peal of laughter. "This isn't Commissar Nej,
Ruth. This is my friend, Mr. Bullen."

"Oh." Faint color crept into the pale cheeks. "I am sorry,
sir." She hesitated, glancing from his dressing gown to the
rumpled bed that could be seen through the open door.

"Clive is my friend, Ruth," Tattie said again. "And this is
your cousin Svetlana."

Svetlana hurried round the table for a kiss.

"And my principal dancer, Natasha Brusilova."

"Oh," Ruth nearly curtsied. "I have read of you, Madam
Brusilova. I so admire your dancing. I . . . I wish I could be a
dancer too."

"Then you *shall* be a dancer," Tattie said, sitting down.
"Now do have some coffee."

Ruth cautiously lowered herself into a chair. "Father would
never permit it."

"He does not like coffee?" Svetlana inquired roguishiy.

Ruth flushed. "I mean, he would never allow me to dance in public. He says that I—"

"That you are the future Princess of Starogan," Tattie said. "I can just hear him saying it. Fathers are such nuisances. Although," she said thoughtfully, "mine wasn't a nuisance. Peter takes after my mother. Now *she* was a nuisance. But I want you to tell me all about yourself, Ruth, about why you are now living in Germany, about where you go to school . . ."

"I have a governess," Ruth explained.

"Oh, la la. I used to have a governess too. A French thing. I can't even remember her name. Well, then, tell me about . . . oh, really, Olga Mikhailovna. What is it now?"

"A message, Comrade Nej," Olga explained. "From a Dr. Goebbels."

"*A* Dr. Goebbels. I have heard that name."

"You met him last night," Natasha said. "A little man, with a lame leg."

"He is minister for propaganda," Ruth said reverently.

"That creepy little man? My God, I never met anyone so unlikable. What does he want, Olga?"

"He invites you to lunch with him, comrade."

Tattie looked at Clive, who shrugged.

"I suppose it is part of the reason for your being here," he said. "After all, if he *is* minister for propaganda—"

"And you'll have fun," Svetlana said, and gave a shriek of laughter. "I was hearing about him last night. They say he is the most lecherous man in all Germany. They say he can have the pants off any girl who is alone with him in five minutes."

"Svetlana!" Natasha protested.

"He can, can he?" Tattie said.

"Herr Goebbels is a great man," Ruth said. "Father says so."

"I'm sure he does," Tattie said. "Well, you may refuse the luncheon engagement, Olga."

"Refuse Dr. Goebbels?" Ruth was horrified.

"I am here to dance," Tattie said, "not to be pawed by club-footed little Nazis. Besides—" She smiled at them. "—Ilona and George are coming in today. We shall all lunch together."

\* \* \*

"It's so amazing, being able to meet like this, every so often," Ilona said to Michael. She sat on his right, obliquely opposite Tattie, who sat on George's right at the other end of the table. Clive Bullen was on Ilona's right, with Svetlana between himself and George; Natasha was on Michael's left, with John on her left, next to his aunt. "Suddenly it seems only yesterday since we all sat down to lunch."

"It was six years ago," Michael said. "And it was dinner. And Judith and Boris Petrov were with us."

"I'd forgotten," Ilona confessed. "We never hear from them. How are they?"

"I think they are very happy. They haven't married, you know. I do not think Judith could ever bring herself to marry a Bolshevik, even one like Boris, who doesn't really approve of us anymore. But they are living together quite contentedly in Paris, from all accounts, where she can be very busy helping Jewish émigrés. It is what she always wanted to do."

"There was so much that Judith always wanted to do," Ilona said thoughtfully. They had first met in the Kitai-Gorod, on that never-to-be-forgotten night in December 1905, when the Moscow revolution had started. She had been the Princess Roditchev, wife of the military governor of the city, the man who, eventually, would use his cannon on women and children to crush the revolt into nothing. And Judith Stein had been the young Jewish revolutionary, only a girl, who had dreamed of overthrowing tsardom and replacing it with a model socialist republic. They had shared the misery of those days, before flying apart, Ilona to resume her life of gracious aristocracy during the day, the horror of the nights in Roditchev's bed, and Judith to progress through all the subterranean layers of terrorism and anarchy until she had reached Siberia, her back still wealed from Roditchev's whip. As had been her own, Ilona thought wryly.

But in time they had both escaped from their respective prisons, and sought the sunshine. She had succeeded, thanks to the powerful love of George Hayman. Judith was still searching. And yet, incredibly, they had spent their lives loving the same men, if in entirely different ways. Judith had been her brother Peter's mistress. Ilona had loved Michael Nej out of angry despair at what she was forced to suffer as Roditchev's wife, Judith had loved him as part of a bargain of survival.

And she loved George as his wife, while Judith had had to rest
content with the shadowy substance of being his mistress.

They had shared so much that they would either have to
love each other no matter what, or hate each other, no matter
what.

Michael gently wrapped her fingers around her champagne
glass. "Memories should be confined to happy events."

She started, drank, and flushed. "How did you know I was
remembering?"

"It seemed likely."

She smiled. "Perhaps I was remembering that when we last
ate together, Catherine and Nona were also with us. But they
too are absent today."

"Well," Michael said, "Nona has to go to school, you know,
and Catherine . . . well, she does not like travel, and she is not
really cut out for diplomatic receptions." They gazed at each
other, each aware that Michael's marriage to Catherine Lissit-
sina had been decided on suddenly, after he had met Ilona
again. It was a subject he was anxious to abandon. "Anyway,
you were thinking of Judith."

"How did you know? We're going to Paris next week, when
we leave Berlin. George intends to take in all the capitals of
Europe on this tour. He says it will be the last we shall ever
make. So we shall certainly call upon the Petrovs, I suppose.
Shall I give her your love?"

"Please do," Michael said. "Why does George say this will
be your last tour of Europe?"

Ilona shrugged. "I suppose because he believes Europe as
we know it will no longer be here, in a few years time. Do
you agree?"

"It is my business to attempt to make sure that it is here."
But his eyes had shuttered in that way she remembered so well.
He was not prepared to discuss politics. "Let us talk of happier
things. John is looking well."

Ilona glanced at their son, deep in conversation with Natasha
Brusilova. "Why, yes, I suppose he is."

"But you worry about him?"

"Well . . . he isn't *doing* anything, is he? I mean, you can't
call reporting chess tournaments doing something."

"If it makes him happy—"

"You can be happy lying on a beach throwing stones into

the water. But there comes a time when you have to leave the beach."

"There speaks the wife of one of America's wealthiest publishers," Michael said, gently smiling. "If someone is not making a million dollars a day he is wasting his life."

"And you don't agree that he should be doing something more?"

"Not everyone can be a human dynamo," Michael pointed out. "It takes all kinds to make up the world. Someone has to report chess tournaments, for the benefit of the millions of people who love chess, wish to play like the masters, and cannot afford to attend every congress. John is making people happy. He is also making himself happy. I do not think that can be so bad."

"Comrade Philosopher Nej," Ilona said. "But I don't think he *is* happy, except maybe when playing chess." She glanced at Natasha, but could say no more without risking the girl's overhearing her.

Michael nodded. "That too will work itself out, I am sure. Tell me, did you know that Peter is living in Berlin?"

Ilona nodded.

"Have you seen him?"

"I believe we are having lunch with him tomorrow."

"He has changed."

Ilona smiled. "What you mean is, he hasn't changed a bit. And he never will. You just haven't seen him for a long time. But he *is* my brother, Michael. I can't ignore him. Anyway, I worry about Ruth, being dragged about from country to country, having no proper schooling . . ." She sighed. "Not that I'll be able to influence things in any way. My God, what a gloomy lot we are! We're here, alive and well and drinking champagne. We should be celebrating. Let's drink a toast, Michael. Please let's drink a toast."

"Of course." Michael banged on the table and stood up. "A toast. We have all survived a great deal, to meet here like this. May we have many more such meetings. To the Borodins, to the Haymans, and to the Nejs. To us. Let us drink to us."

Ilona rang the doorbell of the apartment, took out her handkerchief, and wiped a bead of perspiration from her upper lip. She knew so little of this girl. Only that her life had been an utterly tragic one. Born to Peter Borodin and Rachel Stein, Judith's sister, in the closing days of the revolution, when the White Russian armies had been shattered by the growing Red strength of Trotsky and Michael Nej, Ruth Borodina had been an exile from the moment she had first drawn breath. In New York, during the twenties, for all of Peter's pretense and bombast, she and her parents had been but poor relations of the Haymans, and following her mother's tragically early death she had been dragged behind her father, first to England and now here to Germany. At least for a while she had had the company, and the protection, of her aunt Judith. But since Judith's quarrel with Peter, she had been all alone, keeping house for her father, and surely even more alone here in Berlin, in 1938, when she could hardly be unaware of her Jewish background, no matter how she was protected by her Borodin name.

The door opened, and Ruth peered at her. She wore an apron over an inexpensive day gown, and her hair was tied up in a bandanna. She had on no makeup, save for the color that now flared into her cheeks.

"Mrs. Hayman? How . . . how nice to see you."

"Aunt Ilona," Ilona said. "May I come in?"

"Of course." The chain was taken from the latch. "Father makes me keep the chain on," she explained. "He says you can't trust anyone, nowadays."

"And he's quite right, I'm sure," Ilona agreed, replacing it behind her. The apartment was surprisingly large. They stood in a small hall, off which opened some five doors, the one to the living room standing open to allow them into a light and airy room. But the furniture was cheap and shabby, and the carpet had seen far better days. "Is your father home?"

"Oh, I'm terribly sorry, but he's out."

"Good." Ilona said. She drew off her gloves and sat down on the settee by the window.

"But . . ." Ruth frowned. "He's lunching with you."

"I know, but not until later. It is you I came to see," Ilona said. "Do you remember me at all?"

"Well . . ." Ruth hesitated.

"I can see you don't, really. Well, you were only seven when you left New York."

"I . . . I called on Aunt Tatiana—Madam Nej—yesterday,"
Ruth said.

"She told me. She was delighted to see you. Ruth—" Now
Ilona hesitated. "May I ask how old you are?"

"I'm seventeen." Ruth sat on a straight chair, perched on
the very edge, hands clasped in her lap.

"Then why aren't you at school?"

"Well, Father doesn't send me to school. It's so very expensive. And I know everything I need to."

"But . . . you're not going to spend the rest of your life keeping house for Peter. I will most certainly have to have a talk
with him."

"No." Ruth said, with surprising firmness.

Ilona raised her eyebrows.

"I mean . . ." Ruth flushed. "Not if you wish to speak about
me. I . . . I am perfectly happy."

"Are you?" Ilona asked. "Do you know what happiness is?"

"Does anyone?"

"Well . . . there have to be better things to do with your life
than hiding away in this apartment all day, cleaning and cooking. Do you go to any parties?"

"Father doesn't approve of parties."

"I see. So how are you ever going to meet any nice boys?"

"Why should I wish to do that?"

"Don't you want to get married?"

"Here? In Germany?" Ruth gave a little shiver. "When we
move on, perhaps. Father says we are sure to move on, soon.
Perhaps back to Russia."

"Oh, my God," Ilona said. "Even he must know that is just
a pipe dream." She got up and held out her hands. "Ruth, my
darling, I *am* going to speak with him. The way he treats you
is cruel. I'm going to ask him to let you come to America.
Just a visit. But we'll make it a long one. Ruth . . . there's so
*much* to life. Believe me."

"No." Ruth said. "Please don't do that, Aunt Ilona."

"But . . ."

"Please," Ruth cried. "Don't you understand? I'm all Father
has. Oh, I know he lives in the past, dreams of Starogan and
the old days. It's all the pleasure he has. But he has to *live* in
the present, here and now. And he needs me. I . . . I can make

him smile. Sometimes. Sometimes he calls me his little Rachel. He did love my mother, Aunt Ilona."

Ilona remembered the embarrassing quarrels, Rachel's constant humiliations, and decided against arguing.

"So I can't leave him," Ruth explained. "Not now."

Ilona sighed. Then she held the girl's hands and drew her against her for a kiss. "He doesn't deserve you," she said.

"He's got me," Ruth insisted. "Nobody can change that."

"Yes," Ilona said, and kissed her again. "Just remember, my dear, sweet girl, that you owe yourself a duty as well. Do please remember that. And if you ever need anything, at all, remember that George and I are there, just waiting to hear from you."

"I like your mother," Natasha Brusilova confided to John. "I liked her when we first met, six years ago. I thought then that you are a lucky man." She smiled shyly. "And that she is a lucky woman."

They had lunched together at the hotel, and the dancers were supposed to be resting before the evening performance. But it was just as pleasant to rest by the hotel swimming pool, enjoying the hot sunshine, and here they could talk. John was not really sure Natasha wanted to be alone with him, but it was time to take the bull by the horns. Soon she would be on her way back to Russia.

"You've no comment to make about my father," he said.

"He is a commissar," she pointed out.

"Which could mean, and therefore is a loathsome creature—or, therefore there *can* be no comment."

"The latter, I think," she said, still smiling.

"Natasha—" He hesitated, giving her the opportunity to interrupt and attempt to change the subject. But she waited, patiently, turning his resolution to water, glad to be momentarily distracted by the splash of someone entering the pool from the high board. It was not merely being in her presence again after so long. It was, perhaps, seeing her for the first time in a bathing suit, being able to appreciate the length and beauty of her legs, and the true slenderness of her body, inadequately concealed by the white one-piece, the splendor of her complexion, so pale, and yet lightly dusted with freckles.

Although he had loved before, he suddenly now desired as well. As if every man in Berlin were not at this moment desiring the principal dancer of the Nej troupe, he thought; her photograph had been in every newspaper this morning.

"You know how sorry I am," he said, "about everything that happened. About my part in it."

"Of course I do. And you had no part in it, except as an innocent bystander."

"You don't suppose so? Your parents were murdered by my uncle. My God, how can I ever forget that? How can you?"

"You did not know he was your uncle," she said gently.

"Does that excuse it, or him? And then, pretending to be a prince—"

She shook her head. "You thought you *were* a prince. Believe me, Johnnie, I know what you must have gone through."

"Yeah." He brooded at the pool. The high diver, clearly one of Hitler's bright young men, was now free-styling up and down at fantastic speed. "Tell me something?"

"If I can."

"Would you have met me that night if you had known that I was not a prince? If you had known I was the son of Michael Nej?"

She gazed at him for several seconds. "If I had known you were the son of Michael Nej, I do not think I would have come," she said at last.

"Well, then—"

"But if I had merely known you were not a prince, I think I might have."

"Natasha..." He seized her hand, and then his shoulders slumped. "But now you do know."

"No man can be responsible for his own father, John. And I happen to like and admire Commissar Nej. I cannot like Commissar Ivan Nej, but I do not suppose many people in Russia do like him. And certainly you cannot be responsible for your uncle."

He looked down at the hand which lay in his. He could not bring himself to meet her eyes. "Natasha, will you marry me?"

The hand jerked free. "Marry you?"

He raised his head. "You must have known that was what I would ask you. I asked you six years ago."

"Yes," she said. "But not quite like that."

"I had to leave Russia, and they would not let you come with me."

"You never asked me to."

"I would have. But my father told me it would not be possible, in the circumstances. I was being deported as a spy, and there had been a lot of publicity. He told me to wait. Well, I have waited."

"For six years? To marry me?" She was obviously genuinely surprised.

"I have written you every week."

"I know."

"And you have kept the letters."

"I like receiving letters from you. They tell me of a world entirely different from my own."

"In my letters I told you that I loved you."

"One puts things like that in one's letters," Natasha pointed out.

"But you never put anything like that in your replies," John said sadly. "Because you do not love me, not enough to marry me. Because my name is really Nej."

"No," she said. "Really and truly, no."

"Well, then?"

Natasha gazed at him, for another long period. Then she sucked her upper lip beneath her teeth and slowly released it again.

"Don't you even love me a little?" he said.

"I think I could love you a great deal."

"Well, then—"

"But I do not know about love! How can I? Listen," she said, as he was about to speak, and this time *she* took *his* hand. "As you say, my parents were murdered when I was seventeen. Just after I had first met you, remember? How could I know about love, then? How could I know about anything? I think I wanted to die, too. I think I would have died, but for Tatiana Dimitrievna. Indeed, I *know* I would have died. I would have been executed by the OGPU, had Tatiana Dimitrievna not interfered."

John sighed. "Ivan Nej may be my uncle, but she happens to be my aunt, you know. We're not all bad."

"I didn't mean that, Johnnie. What I mean is, Tatiana Dimitrievna protected me, and took me into the academy, and looked after me. I am eternally grateful to her. But I was only one of several hundred girls, and she had a daughter of her own. She could not teach me how to love again. All she could do was teach me how to dance. How to forget everything but dancing. Dancing became my entire life, because it was the only way I could forget my misery."

"And then I came along and taught you to be miserable all over again."

"You gave me a glimpse of a happiness which I had never supposed could be mine. But how long did we have together, then? Only a week, before you were arrested. Then they took me to Lubianka as well."

"I remember," John said, grimly.

"I don't know why," Natasha said. "That is, I know now. It was to frighten you. I didn't know then. I was too terrified. I thought they would interrogate me, accuse me of being a spy. When they merely marched me along that corridor and then took me home again, I didn't know what to do, or say. I just lay and shivered. And even when you were released, I was still shivering. I wanted only to dance."

"And now you are one of the great dancers of the world," he said.

She shook her head. "I am one of the great dancers in Russia. The world will only recognize me as a result of tours like this one. But there will be others like this one. Tatiana Dimitrievna has promised me."

John frowned at her for several seconds. "And you want to dance."

"It is my life, John. It is the only substance I possess."

"You don't suppose marriage, children, might put a little substance in as a replacement?"

"Johnnie," she begged, "I hardly know you."

"After three hundred letters?"

"Do you really know an author because you have read a few of his books?"

"But . . ." He decided to take refuge in facts. "You can't be a dancer all your life."

"I know that. I have only a few years left, at the top. Only a few."

"Only a few," he muttered.

"But Johnnie..." Her fingers were tight on his. "I would like us to go on being friends, until then, at least. I would like you to go on writing to me. I would like—" She hesitated, once again biting her lip, staring at him, while a rosy flush filled her cheeks.

"To ask you again, in a few years' time," he finished.

He thought she was going to shake her head. Then she sighed, and said, "I would be most grateful, if you still felt that way about me, in a few years' time."

Tatiana Nej sipped cold hock and regarded her nephew with a speculative expression. "Tell me again," she said. "Repeat exactly what she said."

"Oh, really, Aunt Tattie," John protested. "She said no. All of that sweet talk really boiled down to that one word, no. She wants to dance."

"Well of course she wants to dance," Tattie said. "She is a great dancer, and everyone should do what they can do really well. But that does not mean she should devote her entire life to it."

"So I just wait about for another three or four years," John said bitterly.

"Clive has been waiting for thirteen years," Tattie pointed out. "And he is prepared to wait another six as well. He loves me. Do you love her?"

"Of course I love her, Aunt Tattie, but be fair, you and Clive...well...it's more like long separations than actually *waiting,* isn't it?"

Tattie held out her glass for him to fill. "Now tell me exactly what she said, all over again."

John sighed, and obeyed. Tatiana Nej was really a very difficult woman to argue with.

"Yes," Tattie said. "I thought that was what she said. You great silly oaf, what have you been doing these last six years? Oh, don't tell me, playing chess. If there is a quicker way to addle the brain I don't know of it. Don't you understand what she was trying to say? She was saying, 'I can't marry you for a few years, but there is no need for us to *wait* that long.'"

John splashed wine over the table as he poured and raised his head at the same time. "Aunt *Tattie.*"

"God give me patience!" Tattie said. "You're not a boy any

longer, Johnnie, you're a man. Haven't you ever been with a girl?"

"Well, of course. But not... well, not girls like Natasha."

"What's so different about Natasha? She has two legs, hasn't she? And she has a bosom. And I can assure you she has a vagina."

"Aunt Tattie, *please!*" John protested.

"Oh, you Americans really annoy me. Those things are there. They are what you will use when making love to the girl, and yet you are afraid to hear them spoken. It is all so childish. All right, I will be polite. Natasha is as every other woman of twenty-seven, except that she is lovelier than most. She is dying to have a man, but she has kept herself for you, for six years. And now she offers herself to you—and you do nothing about it."

"But... she's Natasha Brusilova. *The* Natasha Brusilova."

"God give me patience. Aren't I *the* Tatiana Nej? That doesn't discourage Clive, believe me. If anything, it excites him."

John chewed his lip.

"So my recommendation to you, John Hayman, is to invite her out to dinner, and then take her back to your hotel room, and take her to bed. But don't get her pregnant. She has too much to do."

"I couldn't do that," John said. "I mean, I couldn't... well, I just couldn't. Anyway, I'm leaving the day after tomorrow."

"There's tonight, and tomorrow night."

John shook his head. "No, really, Aunt Tattie, I don't think—" He looked up in relief as the door of the suite burst open to admit Svetlana. She wore a pale green trouser suit, to which a few leaves were clinging, and there was a leaf in her hair. Her face was flushed and excited, and the entire room seemed to fill with her racing pulse.

But she stopped when she saw her cousin. "Oh," she said. "Oh, I'm sorry. I didn't mean to butt in."

"You aren't butting in," Tattie said. "Pour Svetlana a glass of wine, Johnnie. And maybe you will tell us which haystack you have been rolling in."

"Oh." Svetlana ran to the mirror and hastily pulled a leaf from her hair. "Oh, dear."

"There is one stuck to your bottom as well," Tattie said.

"But at least that makes me optimistic that you didn't actually take off your pants."

"Mama!" Svetlana turned, cheeks scorching. She gave John a nervous glance as he held out the glass, and her blush deepened.

"Maybe I should go," John said. "It's been great talking with you, Aunt Tattie, and I'm very grateful for your advice. Really I am."

"But you won't take it," Tattie said regretfully.

"Well, I'll think about it."

"For another six years," Tattie said. "Come and give me a kiss." She squeezed his hand, then watched the door close. "And now, miss," she said.

"Is he going to marry Natasha, Mama? Is he?"

"I very much doubt it, the way things are shaping up," Tattie said. "Unless I do something about it. And whom do you suppose you are going to marry?"

"Oh, Mama." Svetlana knelt beside her chair. "He really is the most wonderful man in the world. We went walking in the park, and we went to the zoo, and we had a cream tea..."

"And you are dancing tonight?" Tattie cried.

"Only a very little cream tea. And we talked. And talked. And talked."

"Lying on the grass," Tattie said.

"Well, it was so warm and pleasant. Nothing *happened,* Mama. Truly. Paul is such a gentleman."

"Paul being this Herr von Hassell?" Tattie suggested.

"Of course. But you know, Mama, if he hadn't been a gentleman, oh, I don't think I'd have refused him. I do love him so."

"For heaven's sake, you've only known him a few days," Tattie shouted.

"Aren't you always telling me how you fell in love with Clive Bullen at first sight?"

Tattie sighed, and then in a sudden explosion of energy hurled her glass against the wall, where it shattered.

"Mama!" Svetlana protested, scrambling to her feet.

"My favorite nephew," Tattie declared to the room at large, "won't do anything about the girl I want him to marry, while my daughter takes up with a Nazi. A *Nazi!*"

"You can't hold that against him, Mama. I mean, he's not really a Nazi. He's a Nazi because everyone else in Germany is a Nazi."

"Oh, yes?" Tattie demanded. "He's in the SS. That's as Nazi as anyone can get."

"The Waffen SS," Svetlana explained. "That's the fighting regiment. It's the elite. Paul only wants to belong to the best."

Tattie looked down at her daughter. "And you love him. Does he love you?"

"Oh, yes, Mama. I'm sure he does."

"Well, well," Tattie said, and ruffled Svetlana's hair. "Then who am I to object? But your father will never give you permission."

"Then we'll wait until I'm twenty-one," Svetlana said. "It's only two years."

"Only two years," Tattie said. And shrugged. "Only two years. You have time, my poppet. You have time."

Judith Stein had aged in a manner which for Ilona, only a year her elder, was inconceivable. There were heavy gray streaks in her black hair, deep lines in her face, and if her figure remained slender it seemed the thinness of worry and *concern,* rather than the trimness of health and exercise.

Yet Judith's big, handsome features remained calmly relaxed, and if she was slow to smile as she opened the door of the flat, that was surely because of the difficulty of facing the woman whom, as George's mistress, she had once betrayed. The fact that she and Ilona had been old friends made the difficulty still greater.

But that was in the past. "Judith," Ilona said, and hugged her close. "You did expect us?"

"Of course." Judith presented her cheek to George. "I just did not know when." She stepped away from them. "Boris," she called, "George and Ilona are here."

Boris Petrov was inclined to bustle. He was both younger and shorter than Judith, and he had allowed himself to put on weight. Still, with his firm features and strong jaw, he was not an unattractive man. And he was undoubtedly the reason for whatever happiness Judith had succeeded in finding, even if to Ilona it was the strangest of paths for her to have trod—

from being a socialist revolutionary, to fleeing the horrors of Bolshevik extremism—including her parents' execution—to discovering happiness in the end with a Bolshevik commissar.

But then Boris was not really a Bolshevik. He was a diplomat, and his years in Washington and Paris had made him less of a Russian than a man of the world, who kissed Ilona on both cheeks, gave George's hand a hearty squeeze, and immediately poured them large glasses of Calvados, which made even Paris suddenly seem that much brighter.

"You know there are problems here," he said to George when they had taken seats. "Serious problems."

"I've seen some," George agreed. "But I thought maybe they were the sort of problem you'd enjoy. Isn't the main one that the Communists all but control this government?"

"It is part of the problem, to be sure."

"And it is encouraged by you, surely."

Boris smiled. They had been friends for too long for him ever to take offense. "Up to a point. But when it comes to opposing Hitler and the Nazis, why, a country should have a strong government, a government prepared to make whatever decisions are necessary, however unpleasant." He shrugged. "Insofar as we can, we have been telling these French Communists this, but they are difficult people to convince. They do not like change, eh?"

"They make me sick," Judith said, "when they say that they will not fight for their country. How can people be like that?"

"We met Ruth last week," Ilona said brightly, hoping to change the subject. "What a pretty girl she has become! She looks very like you, Judith. I mean, when you were a girl, of course."

"You met her in Berlin?" Judith said.

"Why, yes."

"I do not know how she can live there. Her Uncle Joseph was beaten to death by those thugs, and yet she can *live* there."

George watched Boris's hand creep over hers, give it a squeeze at the mention of her brother's death.

"Well, I suppose it's because Peter is living there," Ilona said. She gave an embarrassed shrug as she looked at Boris. "Chasing his mad schemes."

"I doubt they are mad, when he is involving the German government in them," Boris said. "George, you have been to

London, and Berlin, and Rome, and now you are in Paris. Tell me who you saw and what you think of the situation."

George sighed. "I saw Halifax and Beaverbrook in London, and I have a feeling the British don't really know what is happening, can't believe it yet. They keep hoping that if they stall, it'll all go away."

"You saw Churchill as well," Ilona reminded.

"Oh, sure. He knows what's happening. But he's almost a retired elder statesman. Most people view him as a prophet of doom. And here in Paris I've seen Reynaud. He's relying on the British to sort it out for him."

"And will it go away, George?" Ilona asked.

"No," George said. "I had a chat with Ribbentrop in Berlin, and a brief audience with the Führer himself. They were very accommodating. They want a good press in America, and they're not exactly getting one. But there's no escaping the fact that they regard central and eastern Europe as their own back-yard, from which they'll take whatever they want."

"And they don't consider they're sticking out their necks?"

"They don't," George said, "and I'm inclined to agree with them. I had a chat with Ciano when I was in Rome. Now you can take it from me, Boris, Ciano loathes the Nazis. He doesn't trust them and he's afraid of them. Well, aren't we all? But you can also take it from me that, personal feelings or not, Italy has made its choice. The Italians think the Nazis are going to run Europe for the next couple of generations, and they intend to be on the German side for those generations. And you know what? I get the feeling you people in the Kremlin are adopting the same point of view."

Boris sighed. "The Nej mission. Yes, it is incomprehensible to me."

"It is madness," Judith declared. "Stalin has finally lost his mind. There can be no other explanation. For God's sake, Nazism is opposed to everything Communism stands for. It is dedicated to its destruction. How *can* he?"

"Maybe he feels there is nothing else he *can* do," George said. "After what's been happening inside Russia these past four years, he's in no shape to take on Germany on his own."

"That is true enough," Boris admitted. "But he will support the French, and even the British, if it comes to a fight. If, just for example, the Germans do not drop their demands on Czechoslovakia, well, we may see a repetition of the sides at the beginning of the Great War. That will settle Mr. Hitler."

"And suppose the British and the French choose not to fight for Czechoslovakia?"

Boris frowned at him. "They are obliged to, George. They have given guarantees."

"Well, I wouldn't put too much faith in any guarantees given by the present bunch in Westminster. Not from what I saw and heard."

"I can't believe it," Judith said. "I just can't believe it. Everybody is going to sit around and let them do what they like. They are *evil*. It's not just what I saw when I lived there, those bands of horrible young men wandering around beating up anyone they didn't like the looks of. It's not just the way Joseph died. It's what I see and hear from the people who come here. The people I help. That's all I do. I find them places to stay while they're in Paris, and I find them passage on ships, to America or to Palestine or to South America or to somewhere, anywhere, where the Nazis can't get at them. And the stories they tell... George, why don't you let the American people know what the Nazis are really like? Tell them about the concentration camps, just for a start."

"I intend to," George said. "But you can't really hate a people for shutting up political opponents." He turned to Boris. "It's an old-fashioned pastime."

"Shutting them up?" Judith shouted. "Do you have any *idea?*"

"I have, as a matter of fact," George said. "I was taken to one of those camps. Okay, so it's entirely against the grain to think of people being shut up at all, merely for holding a different point of view from that of the government, or merely for being part of a minority race. And I'll admit that it's humiliating to have to wear that ridiculous pajama uniform. But there's no evidence that they're ill-treated. None that I saw, anyway."

"None that you were allowed to see," Judith said.

"I'm not in the propaganda business, Judith. My business is to report the truth, as far as I can."

"I'm amazed they let you into one of those camps at all," Boris remarked.

"I asked, and they didn't object. And I have to say that the people I met seemed perfectly content. They are being allowed to continue their trades, to live their own social lives within the camps. Okay, as I said, I abhor the idea of *anyone* being deprived of their liberty. I intend to stress that point, in the paper. But it does all depend on your point of view. As Goebbels said, Germany is still in the midst of a social and cultural revolution. When it is over—and he estimates that will be soon—the camps can be closed, and these people let out."

"And you believed him," Judith said bitterly.

"I saw no reason not to."

"And you don't realize that you were shown a *specific* camp, especially prepared for your visit? They'll show anyone a camp, if they're given sufficient notice. That gives them time to hide the ones who've been flogged or starved half to death."

"Judith, there is no evidence that such things actually happen. I'm prepared to help your people all I can. I'll condemn the Nazi government in the strongest possible terms. But you can't ask me to tell lies about them. Have any of these people you help actually been inside a concentration camp?"

"Well, of course they haven't, or they wouldn't be here, would they?"

"So everything is hearsay, rumor."

"Oh, for God's sake, so we all just sit back and wait for the Nazis to take over Europe," Judith said. "What a mess! What an absolutely awful mess." She gazed at Boris. "What are we to do? What can we do?"

"Have supper," he said. "And then sit on the terrace, with a bottle of wine. It is Paris, in the summertime. And the Nazis are far, far away. There's the whole Rhine between us and them."

"I'll say amen to that," George agreed. "And let's hope it stays there."

# Chapter 3

JOSEPH VISSARIONOVICH STALIN GOT UP FROM HIS DESK AND walked around it, arms held wide. "You have done well," he said. "Well." He took Tatiana Nej into his arms, held her close, and kissed her on each cheek in turn. "As I knew you would. You took Germany by storm. You are a treasure. Has she not been a treasure, Ivan Nikolaievich?"

Ivan Nej glanced at his brother, Michael, seated in the other chair before the desk. "Yes, Joseph Vissarionovich," he mumbled. "She has been a treasure."

"Then get up and kiss her," Stalin commanded. "I hate to see people being foolish. So you and Tatiana Dimitrievna no longer find it possible to live together. You are still man and wife. Kiss your wife, Ivan Nikolaievich."

He released Tattie and stepped back. Ivan got up in turn, regarding her with hatred. In conquering Tattie, on that unforgettable spring day in 1918, he had imagined he was achieving his every dream, the dreams of a bootblack sick with longing for his master's daughter.

And yet he himself had been conquered. He had not known it then. Caught up in the tumult of the revolution and of his

61

emerging role in it, he had encouraged Tattie to drink away her hours in the Red army camp. Never once did he suspect the bog in which he had caught his feet.

For in time the vodka had worn off, and Tattie had understood that she had accomplished her first objective: survival. Then she had started to think again, and Tatiana Dimitrievna, for all her life dismissed by her parents, and her brother and sister, as a weak-minded halfwit, because of her obsession with dancing, possessed the shrewdest brain and most single-minded will he had ever encountered. Ivan Nej might have raped her and appropriated her as his wife, but she was alive and beautiful and talented, and there was a whole new world to conquer. Certainly she had conquered Lenin, just as she had conquered Stalin, whatever specious reasons the Party secretary might give for humoring her moods and her ambitions. And as she had conquered, so had she grown and grown, until she had become too great for his arms to hold, until it had been her desires which had mattered and not his—until, eventually, she had been able to escape him altogether, after humiliating him in public.

So only hate was left. Hate and a looming determination that one day he would have her back, and even more, have her in his cells in Lubianka, listen to her screams.

One day. But clearly not today. He held out his arms, and she mechanically stepped forward for a kiss on the cheek. He might have been a small nephew, wasting her time.

"And now, Joseph Vissarionovich," she said. "I think I am entitled to some reward."

"Indeed you are," Stalin agreed. "And I have already decided what it shall be. Do you know Minsk?"

"Of course I know Minsk," Tattie said. "I have performed there."

"Certainly," Stalin said. "But I doubt you know the country south of Minsk."

"South of Minsk there is the marsh," Tattie pointed out.

"Oh, indeed. But the Pripet Marshes are well south. I am talking about the country around Slutsk. It is lovely there— hot in the summers, and yet good farming land. There is an enormous farm not far from Slutsk, which belonged to a nobleman in the bad old days when such things were possible. I am giving it to you."

"A farm?" Tattie asked. "What am I to do with a farm?"

"Oh, the kholkoz will do the farming. But the buildings—and there is an enormous number of them, including a real old-fashioned manor house—are all still intact. It struck me that *there* would be the place for you to train your girls, far away from the hubbub of Moscow. Why, you know the academy is now surrounded by apartment houses and roads, and there is the noise of traffic all the time. Down in Slutsk you will be at peace, the way you should be. Does that not sound delightful?"

"Well . . . I suppose it does," Tattie said.

"Good. Then I will make the necessary arrangements for your school to be transferred there."

"Yes," Tattie said absently. "It is quite overwhelming, Joseph Vissarionovich. I had not expected anything like that."

"But I am grateful for the part you played in making Michael Nikolaievich's mission a success," Stalin said. "Russia is grateful."

"Yes," Tattie said again. "I was going to ask for something else, though."

"Well, why not ask?" Stalin said jovially. "Nothing ventured, nothing gained, eh? The farm is yours in any event."

"Well," Tattie said. "I was thinking that under the circumstances, it would be nice to have the order barring John Hayman from Russia rescinded. After all," she hurried on, as Stalin raised his eyebrows, "it is in our interest to be friendly with the Americans, and John is Michael Nikolaievich's son. I can promise you he is entirely finished with my brother. He only worked for him because he did not know who he was."

"And of course he is in love with your principal dancer," Stalin said.

"Well," Tattie said, "I do not know if that will come to anything. But it would be good propaganda."

"I think you are quite right," Stalin agreed. "Yes, I think that may be possible, in the course of time. I think that may be quite possible."

"And in that case," Tattie said, "it would be unfair to maintain the deportation order against any of the Britishers who were involved in that business."

"Now wait a minute," Ivan said.

"I think she is quite right," Stalin said.

Ivan made a strangled noise.

"Yes," Stalin said. "I think you may safely leave that with me, Tatiana Dimitrievna. Yes, indeed." He took her hands, drew her close for another kiss. "I am pleased with you. Pleased. Give my warmest congratulations to your girls."

"I thank you, Joseph Vissarionovich," Tattie said. "Oh, I thank you." She hurried from the room.

"Joseph Vissarionovich—" Ivan said.

Stalin shook his head. "She *has* done well, and I believe in rewarding success. As you have done well, Michael Nikolaievich." He sat down at his desk and turned his attention to Michael Nej, who had not yet spoken. "So, you think the prospects for a nonaggression pact are good?"

"There is a great deal yet to be done, Joseph Vissarionovich," Michael said. "But the Germans are certainly interested."

"Yes," Stalin said. "Well, we shall have to wait and see how this Czech business turns out. If it leads to war, we will have to reconsider our situation. But if the democracies accept it, as I believe they will, then we may take things further. But what of this Peter Borodin? Is he not influencing the Germans against us?"

Michael shrugged. "Not very successfully, on the evidence I saw. They seemed to find him to be something of an embarrassment."

"That is good," Stalin said. "Yes, very good. I am very pleased with the way things have turned out, Michael Nikolaievich. Now come; will you not confess that the mission was a good idea?"

"They are detestable people," Michael said. "Utterly detestable. They lack all stature, all dignity. The thought of dealing with them makes my skin crawl."

"They are the present rulers of Germany," Stalin pointed out. "We must hope that they are not the permanent rulers of Germany. Now take a holiday, Michael. Take Catherine and your daughter and go down to the Crimea. You have done well."

Michael got up, glanced at his brother, left the office. Stalin waited for the door to close, then leaned back in his seat.

"He *has* done well. I feel much happier than before about the situation. But certain aspects remain troublesome."

"All this rewarding of Tatiana Dimitrievna," Ivan mumbled.

"It is quite unnecessary. Do you know that she is actually suggesting that Svetlana Ivanovna marry a Nazi? The silly girl has fallen madly in love with some blond beast. Well, I have absolutely forbidden it."

"That is your right, as a father," Stalin said, somewhat wearily.

"But of course the girl is nineteen," Ivan grumbled. "Soon she will be able to ignore me. It is all Tattie's doing, turning my own children against me. And now, a farm of her own! It is absurd, Joseph Vissarionovich. And it is not socialism."

"I am sure you are right, Ivan Nikolaievich. But still, the farm serves a purpose, and a reward keeps her happy."

"A purpose?"

"I think it is time that Tatiana Dimitrievna was less in the public eye. Slutsk is a long way from Moscow and Leningrad. I think it is the ideal place for her to train her girls."

Ivan's eyes gleamed. "You mean, at last..."

"I mean that I am coming to the conclusion that she may have completed her useful life as commissar for culture. She and I have never seen eye to eye on what is truly revolutionary culture and what is not. I had occasion to speak to her about this back in 1932. And then, because of all the circumstances, she was willing to listen. Shostakovich, for example, was writing the most deviationist rubbish I have ever heard. Well, she sorted that one out. We had a public recantation from him, and now he is keeping strictly to the Party line. But now Tattie herself is slipping back into her old ways. I have been looking at the musical scores, and in fact the very themes of the dances she has been performing, and I can discern several anti-Communist ideas."

"She is certainly guilty of deviation," Ivan said eagerly. "And I have always believed she is secretly a Trotskyite. While, as a Borodina... you must know she met her brother while in Berlin."

"I wished to discuss that with you," Stalin said.

"Just give the word, Joseph Vissarionovich. I will arrest her in a moment."

Stalin regarded him with a benevolently tired expression. "And haul her down to your cells and reduce her to a gibbering wreck?"

"Well..."

"I doubt you would succeed, with Tatiana Dimitrievna. And then what, supposing you did? Put her against a wall and shoot her full of holes?"

Ivan was frowning, uncertainly. "If she is proved to be a Trotskyite, or a tsarist agent—"

"You are starting to sound like Yezhov. Which is something else I wished to discuss with you. I think we have eliminated enough Trotskyites and tsarist agents. I think, in view of stormclouds gathering around us, that we should devote our efforts to unifying the nation and preparing it for the trials that lie ahead."

"Yes," Ivan said sadly. "It will take time. And in the cases of known criminals—"

"It can be accomplished more quickly than you think," Stalin asserted. "The country, even the world, needs just one example, a definite indication that the Soviet government is calling a halt to the state trials, is preparing to move forward and upward."

Ivan merely looked puzzled. And worried.

"I think," Stalin went on, speaking more quietly, "that Comrade Yezhov has also served his purpose. I think that it is time to prove that he has exceeded his authority, and that a great many of his arrests and his executions were in fact carried out to conceal the evidence of his *own* deviation, his *own* Trotskyite leanings. I would like you to do that for me, Ivan Nikolaievich."

At last Ivan smiled, but still uncertainly. "A great number of those orders were signed by me, Joseph Vissarionovich."

"Then concentrate on the ones that are not."

Ivan nodded slowly. "Yezhov," he said. "I have never liked the man."

"Neither have I," Stalin agreed. "His name has become synonymous, the world over, with assassination and judicial murder. He is giving the entire Party a bad name. We must be seen to be capable of putting our own house in order."

"Yes," Ivan said. "Yes." He got up. "It shall be done immediately. And then . . ."

"And then," Stalin said, "Comrade Beria can take over the NKVD."

Ivan sat down again, slowly.

Stalin smiled at him, "Still searching for the outward signs of power, Ivan Nikolaievich? Have I not told you they are unnecessary?"

"But, Joseph Vissarionovich, if I can never be head of the NKVD, what can I be?"

"What you are. My *éminence grise,* they call you. There is no more powerful position than that, Ivan. No, no. You will stand at Lavrenti Pavlovich's shoulder, as you have stood at Yezhov's shoulder, and you will make sure that he obeys my orders. And should he ever fail to do so, why, you and I can then decide what is best. You follow me?"

"Yes," Ivan said miserably, his shoulders hunched.

"Good. Now, the moment you have settled the Yezhov matter, I have a task for you. A task I know you will appreciate."

Ivan raised his head.

"These people you are training," Stalin said. "They are good?"

"Oh, yes." Some enthusiasm returned to Ivan's voice. Then he frowned at his master. "I did not know—"

"That I knew of them? Why did you not tell me of them?"

"Well—"

"I do not approve of secret armies, unless they are my own."

"But of course they belong to you, Joseph Vissarionovich," Ivan protested. "As I do. And it was you who gave me the idea. You remember the girl Ragosina?"

"Indeed I do. You sent her to a labor camp for five years, for exceeding her authority."

"On your instructions, Joseph Vissarionovich."

"Ah, yes," Stalin said. "Well, the way the Americans and the British were acting over that stupid sabotage affair back in 1932, it was necessary to make an example of someone. Where is she now? She must have finished her sentence."

"I have no idea," Ivan said. "But it was because of Anna Ragosina that I conceived my idea. I trained her to be my absolute slave, and to be absolutely deadly. She killed without compunction, without hesitation, once I told her to. She could destroy a man or a woman in minutes, and still leave them able to stand up in court and confess their crimes."

"It seems to me that you miss this girl, Ivan Nikolaievich."

"Well..." Ivan flushed. "But anyway, when she was sent away, I began to think. I realized that my mistake was in having just one Ragosina. I decided then to create a whole squad of them, a dozen young men and women who would carry out my absolute bidding, and each of whom would be as skilled and as cold-blooded as Anna Ragosina."

"*Your* bidding, Ivan Nikolaievich?" Stalin's voice was soft.

"As I carry out yours, Joseph Vissarionovich."

Stalin regarded him for several moments. Finally he nodded. "I never doubted it. And are they ready now?"

"Well. It is still early in their training. I have to confess that none of them is a Ragosina. That girl was amazing. But they will continue in their training. I promise you that."

"Then I wish you to find Anna Ragosina and take her back into your company."

"Find Anna Ragosina?"

"I have an urgent commission for you, Ivan Nikolaievich. A commission that can be carried out only by a highly skilled squad such as you describe. It is a commission that must not fail."

"Well, then, under my command—"

Stalin shook his head. "No, no. On this mission, *should* anything go wrong, we must be able to disclaim any involvement. That would not be practicable were you to take command. Besides, Ivan Nikolaievich, I would not like to lose you."

Ivan's frown was back, contorting his entire face. "This 'mission,' as you call it, sounds very dangerous."

"It is. But also very important." Stalin leaned forward. "Listen to me. You will agree that, however much we may dislike it, some sort of accommodation with Nazi Germany is absolutely necessary for us until the Red army has been reorganized, until our industries are capable of sustaining the burden of a great war."

"Well, of course, Joseph Vissarionovich. I have never argued against this."

"Quite. And thanks to your brother's efforts, such an accommodation now seems possible. But it will never be possible, in my opinion, so long as Nazi minds are being poisoned against us by tsarist claptrap."

Ivan stared at him for several seconds. Then he said, slowly, "Peter Borodin."

Stalin leaned back.

"Peter Borodin," Ivan said again, also leaning back. "How I have longed to hear you say those words, Joseph Vissarionovich. But we will not need a squad. A single dedicated assassin..."

Stalin shook his head. "I wish Borodin to be brought here, alive, to Russia." He smiled. "Would you not like to have him here? Alive?"

"My God, if it could be done! If—"

"It shall be done. Your people will do it, Ivan Nikolaievich. Anna Ragosina will do it. Restore her to her rank, restore her to everything she ever had, everything she ever wanted. Make her a colonel in the NKVD, and tell her that if she carries out this mission, she will know our gratitude forever."

Ivan bit his lip. "After five years in a labor camp?"

"She will have been hardened even more."

"She will have learned how to hate."

"Hate us, you mean? She will also have learned how to succeed. And she can only succeed by regaining her power. Handle it any way you like, Ivan Nikolaievich. As you know, I wish to learn none of the details. I only want to have Peter Borodin here in Russia. I want him telling such a tale as we can appreciate, in a court here in Moscow, by next summer. That is your charge, Ivan Nikolaievich. Fetch me Peter Borodin."

Ivan Nej stood on the mezzanine that surrounded the gymnasium and looked down into the room below, at the people beneath him. Twelve of them were instructors, brawny men in undershirts and sweat-stained trousers. The other twelve were six young men and six young women. They were naked, and they stood against the wall, hands clasped behind their heads, while the instructors hurled soccer balls at them with all their strength. Each blow left a splotch of red blood gathering beneath the white skin, hardly having the time to fade again before it was regathered. Each time the ball slammed into face or genital it brought a sharp intake of breath. Yet not one of the twelve bodies moved, and not one of the twelve pairs of eyes closed. To fail was incomprehensible, because there could be no failure. No one in this room could ever be allowed to return to a normal life outside, to tell anyone what they had experienced here, what they had been trained to do.

His people. The very feeling gave him a warm glow as he watched them. He had picked them individually, from orphanages, as he had taken Anna Ragosina. He wanted people with no relatives, no ties. And he had wanted youth and beauty. They were the most attractive young people he had been able to find. And they knew that, having agreed to work for him, with all the rewards that that would eventually entail, they were also entirely dependent on him. They were puppets dancing to his strings, fulfilling his requirements, pandering to his needs, whether physical or emotional, as Anna Ragosina had done, a decade before. And learning to kill, under any and all circumstances, as Anna had done. He knew their curriculum by heart. They would already have jogged, round and round the gymnasium. They would already have done fifty pushups each, and chinned themselves twenty-five times. And now, when their bodies had been sufficiently battered by the flying balls, they would be taken straight into the indoor pistol range and made to hit their targets, while hands were still slippery with sweat, hearts were still pounding, groins were still aching, and cheeks were stinging. They would, in time, be the deadliest people on earth.

In time. For as yet, not one of them was the equal of Anna Ragosina. Anna Ragosina. To see her again would make nonsense of these children. What would she be like, after five years in a labor camp? She had certainly had no doubts about her fate. It was the only time she had ever begged for anything in her life. And he had sent her just the same. Anna Ragosina.

If she was still alive.

The door behind him opened, and he turned. One of his secretaries stood there, a thin, bespectacled woman with a harassed expression. She looked past him at the naked bodies.

"Yes?" he asked.

"There is someone requesting an interview, comrade commissar."

Ivan frowned at her. "An interview? I do not grant interviews."

"This is your son, comrade commissar. Comrade Nej."

"My son? Gregory Ivanovich is here? In Lubianka?"

"Yes, comrade commissar."

Ivan brushed her aside and hurried along the corridor. Her heels clattered behind him. "What is he doing here?" he asked over his shoulder.

"He wishes to see you, comrade commissar."

Ivan reached his office, pulled open the door, and gazed at the young man. Normally he saw him only once a week, when they formally took tea together. Svetlana he saw even less often, since she was always performing or practicing at the academy. He had not really thought much about them. They were children, like any other children. He had had children by Zoe Geller, years ago at Starogan. And he had disliked them just as much as he had disliked their mother. One of them was still alive, quite a well-known chess-player. But he had nothing in common with any of them. They all took after their mothers.

Gregory, for instance, had the rather sharp features of his father, and the dark hair, but he was already, at eighteen, a true Borodin in size, towering above Ivan as the boy shifted uneasily from foot to foot.

"Gregory Ivanovich." Ivan shook hands. "Why have you come here?" He permitted himself a smile. "People do not usually come to Lubianka voluntarily. I do not encourage it." He pointed to a chair. "Sit down."

Gregory Nej slowly lowered himself into the straight chair. "Mother tells me she is leaving Moscow. For Byelorussia."

Ivan nodded. "Comrade Stalin has made her a present of a farm down there. It is a big place, I understand. He feels that the academy is no longer suitable now that Moscow has grown around it."

"She wishes me to go with her," Gregory said.

"Well, I imagine she would."

"I am not a dancer, Father."

"Yes. Well, we shall have to discuss your career. First of all, you must complete school and get into the university. Then we shall see what is best for you."

"I would like to work for you, Father."

Ivan leaned back in his chair. "For me?"

"Yes."

"Your mother would never permit it."

"She cannot stop me," Gregory said. "I am eighteen. And I am volunteering."

Ivan frowned at him. "May I ask why?"

"Well—" Gregory flushed, and bit his lip. "I do not wish to leave Moscow. And I do not any longer wish to live entirely surrounded by women and musicians. I have no interest in music. I wish to do something for Russia. And I thought—"

"That working for me you would have an easy time of it."

"I do not wish an easy time of it," Gregory said. "But I do wish to work for you."

Ivan considered him, allowed himself a quick mental image of Gregory, naked, standing against the wall downstairs while someone hurled a soccer ball at his private parts. It was a strangely fascinating image; he hardly knew the boy. But this was no orphan, without ties or relations. He was the son of the commissar for culture, the nephew of the deputy Party leader. To accept him would be to break every rule by which he had sought to mold his squad.

On the other hand, if he too could be made into a slave, a willing instrument, what a way to strike back at Tattie!

But there could be no running home to Mother.

"To work for me is very hard," he said. "Very, very hard. And once you agree to work for me, you can never change your mind."

"I understand that," Gregory said. "I do not wish it to be easy."

"You will have to do hard things, for the good of the state," Ivan warned. "There can be no hesitation, no pity, no attempts to understand motivations. Only the requirements of the state are to be considered and obeyed. Do you understand that?"

"Yes," Gregory said.

Ivan regarded him for several seconds.

"Very well," he said at last. "I wish you to go home and think about it for one more night. Do not mention it to your mother. But if you come back here tomorrow, then I will take you."

"Thank you, Father." Gregory stood up, appeared about to hold out his hand, then changed his mind and left the office.

"It is hard," the secretary said, "to use your own son."

"Yes," Ivan agreed. "Tell me. Is there news of the Ragosina woman?"

"Oh, yes, comrade commissar. She has been found."

Ivan's heart leapt. "Where?" He sat up.

"She is living in Tomsk. But she has been told to report here. She will be here in a week."

"What has she been doing in Tomsk?"

"She has been working in a factory, comrade commissar."

"Married?"

"No, comrade commissar."

"And she will be here in a week. I thank you, Vera Igorovna. You have done well."

He leaned back again. His heart was pounding. His entire body was swollen with anticipation. After six years. The most miserable six years of his life. His attempt in 1932 to arrest Ilona Hayman, to destroy Clive Bullen, had turned out to be a disaster. He himself had escaped disgrace only by sacrificing Anna Ragosina, and ever since then he had been left with a total sense of failure, a sense of having accomplished nothing with his life. Thus he had been able to throw himself still more savagely into the liquidation of every Trotskyite named by Stalin, but without ever feeling the slightest pleasure, even the slightest interest in what he was doing.

But suddenly . . . permission to deal with Peter Borodin, after so long. His own son, coming to work for him. And Anna Ragosina coming back. After six years.

"Yes, indeed, Vera Igorovna," he said, getting up. "You have done well. Fetch your coat, and I will take you out to lunch."

The secretary stared at him with her mouth open.

The train began to slow, and Anna Ragosina sat up. Her bottom ached, and her back ached; she had traveled all the way from Tomsk in a hard-class carriage, sitting and sleeping on wooden boards, surrounded by odoriferous bodies and swirling cigarette smoke, huddled in a corner, so terrified of recognition that she would not even exchange a word with her fellow passengers. The aches in her body, which were there even when she was not sitting on hard boards, were a constant reminder of what she had suffered, of the kicks as well as the lashes, of the scratching, pummeling, *angry* beatings she had received from her fellow prisoners, once they had discovered who she was. To send Anna Ragosina to a labor camp was to condemn her to death.

As perhaps had been intended. She knew too many of the secrets Ivan Nej protected for his master. Only by surrounding her with people who would believe nothing she might say, who would accept no conversation with her at all, could Stalin and Nej feel safe. But she had survived. Since she had already existed for years on hatred, having to exist for another five years had not been so very difficult. She had not tried to fight back. She had had more sense. As each blow thudded into her body she had merely curled herself into a tighter ball, endeavored to protect her breasts and her groin and her kidneys, allowed her mind to tighten with hate.

The only time she had responded had been when they destroyed her hair. It wasn't the guards. She had known they would give her the obligatory cut every prisoner received, and she had prepared her mind for it. And although they had cut it short, they had left a vast fringe that fell just beneath her ears. Her hair had always been her proudest possession, that thick straight black mass she had allowed to surround her Madonna face like a shroud, parted in the center and prevented from falling across her eyes by a barette at each temple, and lying gently on her shoulders and back. To have it cut was a tragedy, but she knew it would grow quickly. But that was not the end. To be held down while the rest of her hair was torn from her head by her angry hutmates, that had been more than she could stand. Then she had supposed it might never grow back; her scalp seemed too battered to permit such a miracle.

Yet it had grown again, and by then they had tired of tormenting her. Instead they had ignored her, left her to herself. No doubt they had supposed that also a punishment, but for her it had been the greatest boon she could be granted. In the last four years in the camp she did not suppose that she had exchanged more than half a dozen words with any single person. She had, finally, been able to think.

She had kept herself sane by thinking of John Hayman. Although she had only had him in her custody for twenty-four hours—or perhaps, she sometimes thought, *because* of that— he remained the only human being, certainly the only man, in whom she had ever felt the slightest real interest. It had to do with his Borodin good looks, certainly; he was one of the handsomest men she had ever seen. But more than that, he was the first Western male she had ever come into close contact with, almost like a creature from another world, with a totally different and utterly fascinating outlook and set of values. Thinking about John Hayman had helped her to organize her hate, but now with a growing sense of futility.

She had hated ever since the day, when she was only ten years old, that the Reds had shot her parents, carted herself and her two young brothers off to the orphanage. At ten her hatred had been nothing concrete. She had not been able to formulate plans, make decisions. And then, too, she had been afraid. The orphanage had first isolated her feelings. Nearly all the girls there had lost their parents in the revolution, and most of them had been on the White side. Their mistresses, and most of all the commissar, Comrade Tereshkova, had made it perfectly plain from the start that *they* did not really understand the theory behind executing the parents and saving the children, but that since the girls had been granted, by a benevolent state, this opportunity to live and to make something of themselves, it was entirely up to them to do so. They could wind up in a railway repair gang, or as street sweepers; or they could progress toward university and a worthwhile place in the Soviet society.

Remarkably, in the entire school there had been only one suicide. Anna supposed it was because by the time any of them had reached an age, the middle teens, when suicide became a mentally acceptable form of protest and escape, they had been exposed for several years to an active program of communization, been taught time and again that their parents and relatives, if not bad people, had certainly been misguided, that Soviet society, if sometimes appearing a trifle harsh and unsympathetic to the individual, and down right brutal to the noncomformist, was doing its best to become a paradise for anyone prepared to work hard and accept that the Party knew best, and that they really could create a very good life for themselves if they would just follow those golden rules. There had not seemed much alternative, not even for Anna Ragosina. But Anna had at least found a sop for her conscience. She would survive, and even prosper, as the state required her to do. But she would still hate. She would hate the men who had killed her mother and father, the men from the Cheka. And one day, perhaps . . . one day. If it was a childish concept, this placing one's trust in a remote and certainly unattainable future, it was no less satisfying for that.

And then the miracle had happened. Ivan Nej had come to the orphanage, searching for a woman. It had been as simple as that, however he had dressed it up as a search for a personal assistant. His wife had left him, and, as Anna had very rapidly discovered, he was hopelessly inadequate anyway as a lover or even merely in the company of women. He could only hurt them, and he had wanted one of his very own, to hurt. In return he had offered her the use of the very secret police uniform on which she had centered all her hate, and offered her, too, the power to expiate that hate, on innumerable innocent and help-less victims.

He had not known of the hate, of course. Neither had Com-rade Tereshkova. But Comrade Tereshkova had known there would be disaster ahead. She had warned Commissar Nej that Anna Ragosina was not really the girl he was seeking; she was too moody, too introverted, too intense. Given what he would offer her, she would become a monster. She had said as much to Anna, too. But Anna had not hesitated for a moment to wear that uniform, to belong to the NKVD, as it had come to be called, actually to be a part of that state-within-a-state which really ruled Russia. What better chance would she have of destroying that body than by becoming a part of it?

A senseless dream, though, because she had, very rapidly, become the monster Comrade Tereshkova had foretold. If her hatred had to remain a blind thing, then her only pleasure had to be in instilling such blind hatred in others. Blind hatred and even blinder fear. The sight of that pale, composed face in its shroud of black hair, of those white hands with the blue veins surging only just beneath the skin, the sound of that quiet voice, had become synonymous with terror to hundreds of men and women, and even children. And to Ivan Nej she had become indispensable. Or so she had supposed. He had valued her as much for her submission in bed—that was what he yearned for in a woman—as for her vicious cruelty, her total compo-sure. But he had not valued her above his own skin. In the pursuit of his crazy dream, he had arrested George Hayman's wife on a trumped-up charge, his mind a swirl of obscene desires from rape to destruction. When, as Anna could have told him would happen, the resulting explosion had very nearly rocked the Kremlin, he had sought only to save his own rep-utation and his own face. Thus, Anna Ragosina was pointed to as the one who had done the actual arresting, just as it had been Anna Ragosina who had arrested John Hayman to lure his mother into the web, and Anna Ragosina who had assaulted Boris Petrov and Judith Stein when they had sought to interfere.

No matter who had given the orders, Anna Ragosina had done the work, and therefore Anna Ragosina had to be punished.

When she was finally released from the labor camp she had wanted to do nothing more than crawl away into obscurity. Once she had dreamed of regaining contact with her brothers; indeed, she knew that one of them was now a factory inspector in Kharkov, married and a father, able to provide her with a good home. But the thought of seeing him again had been impossible, because surely he would know what she had become. Of course, she still had her beauty; despite all the scars on her body and in her mind, men were attracted to her, and she had obtained a small pleasure in allowing them to fall in love with her before crushing them with her indifference. But that had been a sterile joy. And she had foreseen nothing better.

Until now. He wanted her back. And she was coming, because of all the men in the world, she now knew she hated only Ivan Nej.

And there he was, standing on the platform to greet her.

"Anna," he said. "Anna."

She allowed him to take her hand. "Comrade commissar."

He peered at her through his glasses. "You have not changed," he said, as if to reassure himself. "Nothing will ever change you, Anna Petrovna."

"No, comrade commissar," she said. "Nothing will ever change me."

He smiled at her, then looked left and right. People were watching them. Commissar Ivan Nej was easily recognizable, and perhaps there were people recognizing the woman as well, now that they stood together.

"Come," he said, and led the way to the car. It was six years since she had traveled in a car. "There is much to be done," Ivan said. "Much." He glanced at her, in the way she remembered so well, allowing his gaze to travel from her neck to her knees, and then back again.

There would, she knew, be no more welcome than that. Just as there would be no apology for having betrayed her, six years before. Just as, in his peculiar mentality, there would be no doubt that she would be happy to return to his employment, and even to his bed. But having sent so many people to labor

camps in his time, he *was* interested in what had happened to
her. No doubt he would wish to explore, to trace each mark
on the white skin of her back and her belly, to spread her legs
to *look,* in that clinically fascinated fashion which she found
so unpleasant.

He did not speak again until they were in his apartment, and
then he asked, "What is your dearest wish, now?" It was near,
as he would ever come to making amends, she thought.

"To have a hot bath," she said.

He frowned at her.

"I have not had a hot bath in six years, comrade commissar."
She shrugged. "I have not had a bath at all in three days."

She supposed he might have noticed, might indeed have
insisted she at least shower before he began to nose his way
through her system, as he inevitably would. She had forgotten
that Ivan Nej had been born and raised on a farm, and had
never really progressed, aesthetically.

But now he smiled. "Then have your bath, Anna. But do
not be long. There is much to be done."

And much for her too, once she had the chance. Six years
ago, her mind and her body a frenzy of frustrated torment, she
had sought her own salvation, and a private revenge, in the
arms of Nikolai Nej, the chess player—a man who had hated
his father as much as she did, but who, like her, like so many
children of the revolution, had been able to map out no better
future than the Soviet way. Where was Nikolai now? Married
no doubt, and a father. But it was something to be discovered,
once she was again fully installed as Commissar Nej's personal
assistant. Once she was retrained to the edge of the razor-sharp
physical and mental awareness she had once possessed. And
once she had become accustomed to the fact that she was no
longer alone, but that there were now more than a dozen Anna
Ragosinas, men as well as women, training alongside her.

She stood surveying them, in the supremely well-equipped
gymnasium that was reserved for them alone. Here was cause
for hesitation, for a sudden reawakening of that deep-laid fear,
that resentment and mistrust and distaste for all humanity, and
for womanly feelings as well. They were all between eighteen
and twenty-three, so far as she could estimate. Not a great deal
of difference; she was only twenty-eight herself. But they were

young and fresh, and unmarked—even, she supposed, in their minds, although she did not doubt that each of the girls had been exposed to Ivan Nej's lusts. She, on the other hand, even if she had only spent twenty-eight summers on this earth, was a very old woman.

The discovery that she need not have worried was pure joy. Her muscles were as good as theirs, and if her belly was not quite so flat and her breasts not so high, she was Anna Ragosina, returned from exile to lead them. This was the greatest pleasure of all. She could not believe her ears when Ivan announced it to them; she turned to look at him with her mouth open, and then hastily closed it again. She did not want her people to suspect she had not known in advance.

Ivan was enjoying himself. "You will have heard of Anna Petrovna," he said. "Well, comrades, let me tell you this: if any one of you can even equal her you will be a remarkable person. She is your commander, as of this moment. Her word is law among you. Obey her, and prosper. Disobey her, and she will destroy you." He glanced at her, and she nodded, briefly. But her heart was sending the blood pumping through her veins. Power. It was all she had ever really wanted.

"I wish you to select three of them," Ivan said, when the recruits had been returned to their exercise. "Three of them to accompany you on a mission of great importance, great delicacy."

She gazed at him. She had been on a mission before, and found herself in Siberia.

He understood at once. He laughed, and gave her a hug. "It is for the good of the state, but you must not involve the state."

She nodded. "I understand, comrade commissar. Three, from those twelve."

"There are a few more, but they are very new. They cannot possibly be made ready in time."

"But they are under my command?"

Ivan Nej hesitated. Now why did he do that, she wondered?

"Yes," he said. "The entire squad is under your command, Anna Petrovna. Use them wisely."

More youth, and beauty. Including a tall young man with a handsome face made peculiarly intense by the depths of the black eyes, the black hair, the determination with which he approached his every task. The facial resemblance to his father was unmistakable. She glanced at Ivan.

He flushed. "Yes," he said. "My son." He looked as if he would have said more, but changed his mind, because to have said more would have been to reveal human weakness. For this son he loved, she realized, whereas Nikolai had never been anything more than an unwanted nuisance. Ivan Nej, she thought, you have delivered yourself into my hands.

But she smiled gravely. "Than I shall take care of your son, comrade commissar. I give you my word on that."

"You are very young," she said.

"I am eighteen," he answered fiercely, and flushed. But the flush was induced by more than the suggestion that he might not measure up. He *was* very young, and he was new to this world. He could not stand in the same room with a naked woman, himself naked, and not respond. And when that woman was Anna Ragosina, his entire body seemed affected.

"That is young," she said.

"I am as good as any of the others," he asserted, trying to keep looking at her eyes, which was difficult, since she had no compunction about looking at his body.

She shrugged. "Physically, Gregory Ivanovich. But physical strength, physical health, is nothing. It is the mind that matters. A cripple can kill, if he has the mind, where an Atlas will fail, if he lacks the mind."

"I understand that," he said. "That is why I am here."

She nodded. "I wish you to beat me, Gregory Ivanovich."

He frowned at her.

"I wish you to beat me unconscious," she went on. "Now. Because if you do not, I will beat you unconscious. Do you understand me?"

Still he hesitated, unsure whether this was some sort of a game.

"I will count to three," she said. "Then it must be you, or me."

He looked along the room, hopefully. But she had dismissed the others. Since he was the youngest, and the newest, it was he who required the extra lesson. Besides, it could be justified, even to his father. He came from no orphanage. He came from the Tatiana Nej Academy, the very lap of luxury. He needed all the training he could get, if he would succeed.

"Three," she said, and drove her hand, flat and with the fingers rigid, at his genitals. He gave a startled exclamation and attempted to sidestep, and her nails scoured the flesh on the inside of his thigh. The pain brought a reaction; his right hand started to swing, but only to catch her arm and force her away. Behind it his entire body was moving forward, pivoting on his left foot. Anna half turned, hurling her thigh into his groin. The gasp of pain threw him further off balance, and her hands went up, behind her own head, to grasp his hair even as she bent her back and thrust forward yet again. Gregory Nej went over her as if somersaulting, half-turning in the air to land heavily on his shoulder, legs and arms flung wide as he rolled, his head now striking the floor.

For a moment he lay there, blinking at the ceiling, then he sat up, to encounter the toes of Anna's right foot, hurtling through the air to smash into his neck. He seemed to arch away from her, then lie on his face, retching as he reached for air. Anna sat astride his back, her fingers on his neck. "Now I shall kill you," she said into his ear. It was a simple matter, really, of locking her hands beneath his helpless chin, of thrusting her knee into his neck, and of pulling upwards. And perhaps he expected her to do it. His body twitched, his toes drummed the floor for a second in despair.

Anna laughed, and got up. She went to the tap in the corner, filled the bucket, came back and emptied it over him. For a moment he hardly moved, then he rolled on his back, lay there with his head in the water, his eyes alternately opening and shutting as he struggled for breath. Anna refilled the bucket and emptied it over him again. This time he spluttered, and sat up, scraping water from his eyes, blowing his nose on his fingers.

Anna went to the table, filled a tumbler of vodka, and brought it back. She knelt beside him. "Drink."

He blinked at her.

"Have you never drunk vodka?" she asked.

He shook his head.

She smiled. "It will not harm you. It will make you feel good. I will show you." She drank herself, felt the heat coursing through her chest to meet the heat rising from her belly. "Drink."

Gregory Nej drank, and gasped.

"Some more," Anna commanded.

He drained the glass and stared at her.

"Now you understand something of what I mean," she said. "But you have a great deal to learn. I have a great deal to teach you." She stretched out her hand, stroked water away from his eye with her forefinger, and saw his gaze drifting to the sweat rolling from her own neck and down to her breasts. She allowed her hand to slide from his face to his chin, then drop to his chest and sift down through the water-matted hair to his belly, and then lower, to hold him and feel him respond. He continued to stare at her, eyes wide. "Have you never been with a girl?" she asked.

Slowly he shook his head.

Anna Ragosina laughed softly. "Then that too is a part of your education, Gregory Ivanovich." She released him and stood up, watched his head tilt as he followed her body with his gaze. "There is a mattress, over there."

"You are my father's woman," he said.

She leaned on her elbow to look down at him. "Does that matter to you?"

Whatever his reply, it was irrelevant. He could not leave her alone. His fingers traced patterns on her thighs, wanted to pass between her legs, finger her labia, move upwards to her breasts, stroke the nipples into erection, touch the firm line of her jaw. He loved, in this instant, with the tremendous fervor of a young man introduced to the delights of an older woman. An older, willing woman. An older woman determined to please, and thereby to conquer.

"I wish you to be mine," he said.

"I am yours," she said. "Whenever it is possible. But I must be your father's too. You must understand that. Your father is one of the most powerful men in the country. Without his power, I could not be here with you now."

He kissed between her breasts, holding them together with his hands to enclose his mouth and nose, sighing into her flesh. "Do you love my father?"

She drew a long breath. "I hate your father," she said.

His face moved, jerking away to allow him to look at her. Her heart gave a sudden lurch. Had she entirely misjudged him?

"But you work for him," he said. "And you sleep with him."

"Because I must. He sent me to Siberia once before. He can again, with a stroke of his pen."

He nodded thoughtfully. "My mother hates him too," he said.

"And you?"

A faint shrug. "I do not know him very well. It is difficult to hate your own father."

"You must make up your own mind, form your own opinion, when you get to know him better." She smiled. "You will get to know him much better, working here." She pushed herself up and knelt beside him. "Now we must get dressed, and then get back to work. There is much to be done."

"Your mission?"

The squad knew of that, of course, even if they did not know who or what or where.

"That, among other things."

He held her hand. "Let me be one of the squad, Anna."

She frowned at him. "You?" For a moment she was tempted. But her professional instincts and her common sense came to her rescue. "You are too young, and you are not yet sufficiently trained."

"Anna—"

She shook her head. "No. There will be other missions."

"I love you, Anna."

Anna Ragosina laughed. "On the strength of one screw? Soon perhaps you will hate me, as you will hate your father."

"No," he said. "I will never hate you, Anna."

She leaned forward and kissed him on the mouth. "You should try to find a girl more your own age, Gregory Ivanovich." She stood up, allowing him to gaze up the length of her body once more. "Now I must go."

"To be with my father."

Anna smiled at him contentedly. "I have no other choice. At the moment."

Anna did not like Berlin. She had only been there once before, in 1932, and then too she had been engaged upon an abduction, of Peter Borodin's sister, Ilona Hayman. How strange that her entire life should be spent in combatting one family.

And that last episode had turned out disastrously for Anna. The kidnapping itself had been the simplest thing in the world, because it had not occurred to Ilona Hayman that she was *being* kidnapped. She was in a great hurry to get to Moscow, to be with her son, and here was a polite young woman offering her a plane ride that would shorten the train journey by days. And all the while she had been heading straight to Ivan Nej's cells.

This one was not going to be so easy. Peter Borodin would not be fooled by pleasantries. And as Ivan Nej had repeated so often, the Soviet government could not be involved. Thus they had obtained an aircraft from one of their Swedish agents, and had flown into Berlin from Malmö, pretending to be a party of young Swedish aristocrats out for a weekend joyride to the new Reich. No matter that only Jonsson the pilot spoke Swedish; they were all fluent in German.

Now, sitting at the dinner table in their hotel, looking out onto the Unter den Linden, she checked through her handbag while the others watched her anxiously. They were the beginners, she the expert. She had told them what they must do; she had even told them what would happen. Yet they waited, desperately, for her command, or her reassurance that everything would be as she had planned it.

And what did she feel about it all? Remarkably, she felt almost nothing. She had never in her life laid eyes on the Prince of Starogan, and she understood only a little of the personal animosity felt by Ivan Nej towards the entire family. She could reason that as both Ilona and Tatiana were beautiful women, Prince Peter would be a handsome man, but he also happened to be fifty-six years old, twice her own age, and she had no taste for older men. Ivan Nej had seen to that. Ivan, and the labor camp, where women had become old at thirty, had formed within her a hatred of age, a terror of that inescapable fate overtaking her own body, her own mind. Old people had consciences, and complexes, and they feared the future, because annihilation was rushing upon them.

And did she not fear the future, fear the shades that would surely cluster around her deathbed, eager to get their hands on her? Not yet, because she was young. Those shades were a long way in the future. She did not even fear the immediate future. By all accounts the Gestapo were just as bad as the NKVD. She found this difficult to believe. Certainly they were not people to be afraid of. No German concentration camp could be quite such a hell as a Siberian labor camp. And besides, if she were arrested here, she had no doubt that Ivan would soon get her back out. Ivan valued her. And like his son, he worshipped at the shrine that was her body.

There was no reason for her to fear anything anymore. She had experienced it all, and she was still Anna Ragosina.

She closed her handbag with a snap and stood up. The three men stood with her, uncertain in their smart suits, their neatly brushed hair, trying to take their cues from her sophisticated assurance, the way she wore her frock, dangled her bag, smoked her cigarette.

Jonsson held her coat for her, but she left it draped around her shoulders. The night was chill, but summer was not far away now. The summer of 1939. She would be twenty-nine.

As she walked up the street, the others drifted away. They knew where they were going, but each had his own task, and it was essential for them to arrive separately. Anna walked along the pavement, looking at the shop windows, glancing at passersby, exchanging greetings. Here was an ebullient people, amazed at their own success, unable to restrain their somewhat boisterous humor, just a little afraid of what their remarkable leader might choose to do next, where his insatiable ambition, having successfully swallowed both Austria and Czechoslovakia with nothing more than a verbal protest from the democracies, might lead him, but slowly realizing that whatever he decided, however frightening it might appear at first glance, he would do it and he would succeed in it, and the might and power and reputation of Germany would grow a little more.

A people to be destroyed before they became *too* powerful. Anna knew all about that plan. Tonight's work was just a part of it.

She went up the steps to the apartment building, took the elevator, and emerged on the fourth floor. She stood smoking a cigarette until she heard the sound of feet on the stairs. Then she rang the bell, watched the door being opened by a slight, dark girl who peered past the chain.

"Fräulein Borodin?" Anna asked in German. From the corner of her eye she watched Gutchkin take up his position at the end of the corridor. Jonsson would not be far behind him; Plekhov would already be waiting with the car.

"Yes," Ruth Borodin said.

"I am Fräulein Schmidt, of the *Frankfurter Zeitung* newspaper. I telephoned about an interview with your father."

Ruth frowned at her. "An interview? My father did not mention it."

"Yes," Anna said. "If you would tell him I am here . . ."

"But I cannot," Ruth said. "My father is away."

Anna frowned at her, little alarm bells starting to jangle in her mind. "Away? I did not know of this. He was here yesterday."

Ruth smiled. "He did not know of it himself. But he left this morning. It is for a meeting with the Führer, down in Berchtesgaden."

Of all the atrocious luck, Anna thought. Definitely, she was starting to hate Berlin. It was an unlucky city. But she continued to smile. "Then obviously it was so important he forgot to inform me," she said. "When do you suppose he will be returning?"

"Not for several days," Ruth said.

Anna bit her lip. That was that. A quick telephone call to Frankfurt would establish that they had sent no one to interview the Prince of Starogan. She had failed. It was the first time in her career that she had failed to carry out Ivan Nej's wishes, and it was her first assignment since returning from Siberia. She felt as if she had been kicked in the stomach.

"I am very sorry," Ruth said.

Anna Ragosina gazed at her. This was the prince's only daughter. The very last true Borodin of Starogan, even if she did not look in the least like the blond beauties the Borodins had always been. But she was the very last Borodin of Starogan.

"So am I," she said. "Do you suppose it would be possible to make a telephone call? I sent my car away, you see, as I thought I would be here for some time. It will not be returning for me for an hour if I do not call it."

"Oh, of course," Ruth said. "It was thoughtless of me to keep you standing in the hall. Do come in, Fräulein Schmidt." She stepped back, and Anna stepped inside. Ruth Borodin carefully closed the door and replaced the chain. "One cannot be too careful," she said. "Even in Berlin."

"I know," Anna said sympathetically. "The entire world is in a mess, is it not?"

"The telephone is just here," Ruth said, leading her down a narrow corridor between two bedrooms. She stopped in front of the polished table, and indicated the instrument. Her back was to Anna, and Anna had already taken the small bag of sand from her handbag. Now she flicked it against the girl's neck.

# Chapter 4

JOSEPH STALIN STOOD AT HIS WINDOW AND LOOKED DOWN AT the Moscow River. His shoulders were hunched—a bad sign. Ivan Nej cleaned his glasses with his handkerchief, replaced them on his nose slowly. He could only wait.

"Tell me about Yezhov." Stalin said.

"He was arrested on a charge of exceeding his authority," Ivan said. "He was shot yesterday morning."

"Did he protest?"

"He asked for an interview with you, Joseph Vissarionovich. But I refused to permit it."

"That was well done. You will make the news of his execution public."

"As you wish, comrade."

"It will be good for our reputation." At last Stalin turned. "But in this other matter you have failed me, Ivan Nikolaievich."

Ivan licked his lips. "The woman Ragosina is not what she was, Joseph Vissarionovich," he said. "I cannot help but wonder if it was not a mistake to bring her back at all. Five years in a labor camp..."

"Yes," Stalin said, and sat down.

Ivan waited more hopefully. Bringing her back had not been his idea.

"What have you done with her?" Stalin asked.

"As yet, nothing. I waited to hear your opinion first. But she will be punished. Oh, she will be punished. I promise you that."

"I was not talking about Ragosina," Stalin said. "I think you would be making a mistake to be too harsh with her. Perhaps she needs closer supervision, more detailed direction. But from what you have told me, she carried out the operation itself flawlessly, except that her victim was the wrong person. No, no. Do not be too harsh with her. I was talking about Borodin's daughter."

"Well, Joseph Vissarionovich, since she is here—"

"The Germans are still talking with us. Beria tells me they are now thinking in terms of Poland. That, and Czechoslovakia, will bring the Wehrmacht to the very borders of Russia. And as I prophesied last year, the democracies are sitting back and doing nothing. This guarantee England has given Poland, just like the one they have given Rumania, is clearly nonsense. They are not going to fight, Ivan Nikolaievich. Therefore it is more necessary than ever for us to reach an accommodation with Hitler. I am instructing Molotov and Michael Nikolaievich to step up their discussions with Ribbentrop. I wish nothing, nothing at all, to interfere with that process."

"We could try again," Ivan said hopefully.

Stalin sighed. "You are missing my point, Ivan Nikolaievich. Try again? Is it not true that since the disappearance of his daughter Peter Borodin does not leave his flat without being accompanied by armed guards, that they sleep there with him? On the other hand, whatever he may be saying in private, no one has yet accused us of having a hand in the girl's disappearance. This suggests that Hitler and Ribbentrop are more interested in talking with us than in accusing us of kidnapping. I would like things to remain that way. You will not touch Peter Borodin."

"Yes, Joseph Vissarionovich." It was Ivan's turn to sigh.

"On the other hand," Stalin said, "we cannot risk this girl ever being able to identify her kidnappers, to say a word even to another prisoner that might one day be used as part of an accusation against us. You follow me?"

Ivan cleaned his glasses again. "She may well prove useful, one day."

"I doubt that, Ivan Nikolaievich. I do not really see how that could ever be possible. I think that, since she has mysteriously disappeared, she must stay gone. That is an urgent matter, Ivan Nikolaievich."

Ivan waited, but when he saw his master was clearly finished, he got up and saluted. "As you say, Joseph Vissarionovich. She will remain gone." He went outside and down to his car, his brain seething.

The car stopped in the courtyard of Lubianka, and he went downstairs immediately, into the observation room, and looked through the concealed window into the cell beneath him. The girl sat against the wall, in a corner, head cocked as she tried to listen. She had been stripped and searched, but not otherwise harmed. On the other hand, she was blindfolded and her wrists were handcuffed behind her back, so that she could not see and could scarcely move. But she would of course have been able to listen.

She was certainly a danger.

The door behind him opened. He turned his head and saw Anna Ragosina.

"What do you wish done with her?" she asked.

She still thinks she has succeeded, Ivan thought bitterly. She does not understand the dilemma she has placed me in.

"Does she understand what has happened to her?" he asked.

Anna shook her head. "I injected her, and kept her sedated and blindfolded until we got here. There was no difficulty."

"But she will have heard Russian spoken here," Ivan said.

Anna gave another brief, almost impatient shake of the head. "I have allowed no one near her, since her arrival here. I have fed her myself, and I have addressed her in German."

Ivan stood up. "You have failed me, Anna Petrovna."

Her head came up as her brows drew together.

"I sent you for Peter Borodin," Ivan said, his voice grating. "Not for his daughter."

"I did the best I could, comrade commissar," Anna said quietly. "Prince Peter was not there. He had left unexpectedly.

I had reconnoitered the situation carefully. His departure was just bad luck."

"Do you suppose I am interested in luck?" Ivan demanded. "Luck is the excuse of failures. You have failed." His hand slashed out and whipped across her face. She had seen the blow coming, and instinctively started to raise her own hands in defense, but then changed her mind, allowing his hand to bite into her skin, bringing a fleck of blood from her cut lip. Her head swung, before straightening again. The look in her eyes was pure venom, because she knew, as he knew, that if she wished to she could probably break his aging body in two with the use of her special skills. If she dared. But she would never dare. He was Commissar Nej, and she was his creature.

Now she licked her lips. "The girl is not entirely useless, comrade commissar," she said softly. "Was her mother not a Jewess?"

Ivan glanced at her.

"I do not think the Nazis know that, comrade commissar," Anna said. "I do not think Prince Peter Borodin has told them."

"How can that affect him?" Ivan asked. *"He* is not a Jew."

"He loves his daughter," Anna said. "Were she to be returned to Germany, denounced as a Jew . . . were we to *threaten* that . . ."

Ivan returned to his chair, sat down, and again looked through the window at the girl. Her head had slumped. Perhaps she was asleep.

"I can arrange it, comrade commissar," Anna said.

"You will take her to cell forty-seven," Ivan said.

Anna frowned at him. "Cell forty-seven? But that is . . ."

"Yes," Ivan said. "It is where we put Comrade Glinka to starve to death. I do not wish this girl to be starved, Anna Petrovna. I wish her to be fed and treated well, and I do not wish her to see anyone in this prison except yourself, and I do not wish anyone in this prison to see her, except yourself. Do you understand me? As of this moment, she is your sole charge, your sole responsibility."

"I am your assistant," Anna said. "I am the commander of the squad."

"Not anymore," Ivan told her. "You have failed me. You are not yet ready, apparently, for such responsibilities. You will devote yourself to this girl. Since she has seen your face before, it can do no harm. But you will give her only German books to read, and you will speak to her only in German. You will not inflict any physical punishment on her, Anna Petrovna. I will wish to see her, from time to time, to make sure of that."

"You are insulting me," Anna said. "I am no jailer."

"I am punishing you," Ivan said, "for your failure. If you do not wish a more severe punishment, if you do not wish to find yourself in a cell beside hers, you will obey me."

Anna opened her mouth, closed it again. "And my suggestion?"

"It may be possible to implement it, one day. But not now. Until that day, she is in your care. See to it."

Once again he thought she would speak, and wondered what it was she really wished to say. Then she turned and left the room.

Anna placed the bundle on the table. The cell had been newly furnished, and contained a cot as well as the table and chairs, a washstand with basin and ewer and slop bucket. It was almost comfortable, for a cell. But it had no windows, and not even the heating could entirely dispel the chill of being several feet underground. Down here it was not even possible to hear the other prisoners screaming.

The girl watched her with deep black eyes, the blanket held to her throat. She was braced for physical assault.

"Here are some clothes," Anna said. "There is no need to spend all your time in bed. It would be good for you to dress, from time to time, and to walk about the cell. Get some exercise. Would you like me to show you?"

The girl stared at her.

Anna took off her jacket and trousers, sat down to remove her boots. Then she got up and jogged on the spot for several minutes, until sweat stood out on her flesh and her breathing had quickened. Next she got on the floor and did fifty pushups, before turning on her back with her legs in the air, raising the lower half of her body without using her hands for support, and pedaling an imaginary bicycle with tremendous energy. When she stood up again she was panting. She opened the parcel, took out the towel, and delicately dried herself, watching the girl.

"If you do that twice a day, you will remain healthy. It does not do to be ill, down here. And then, there are books for you to read. I have brought Goethe and Schiller, and there are German editions of Shakespeare and Tolstoy, too. There is no need for you to be bored."

"Who are you?" asked Ruth Borodina.

Anna shrugged. "I am your jailer," she said. "And, if you behave yourself, I will be your friend."

"Am I still in Germany?" Ruth asked.

"Where else do you think you could be?" Anna asked.

"I don't know," Ruth said thoughtfully. "I remember you standing beside me, then everything is vague. But I am sure I remember traveling, from time to time."

Anna smiled at her. "You are certainly no longer in Berlin."

"But you are not German," Ruth said. "I know you are not German. And you are not a Nazi."

Anna raised her eyebrows. "You are very sure."

"The Nazis burned all books by Goethe and Schiller, six years ago," Ruth said.

Anna bit her lip. So much needed to be known, for her to function properly. But she smiled again. "Then, as you say, I am not a Nazi." She crossed the room, sat on the bed beside the girl.

"Then who are you?" Ruth begged. "Why have you brought me here? Why did you hit me? Do you hate my father? Are you a Communist?"

"I am your jailer," Anna said again, and reached out to smooth hair from the girl's face. Power. She was suddenly realizing that she had lost none of her power. It had become concentrated, that was all. Now it was focused entirely on this girl. But it was none the less enjoyable for that. Ivan had said Ruth Borodina must not be harmed, physically. But a bruise here and there, if she felt like it, if it became necessary, could hardly be called harming. And she *was* a Borodin. She would be John Hayman's cousin. This girl might even help to allay that memory.

Ruth moved her head back.

"You are going to see nobody else, for a very long time," Anna said. "Perhaps for the rest of your life. If you are not my friend, you will have no friends at all. And if you become my enemy, you will have a very miserable time of it." She picked up Ruth's hand and gave it a gentle tug, but Ruth refused to move.

"You have knocked me unconscious, injected me with drugs, kidnapped me, and locked me in this prison. Doesn't that make you my enemy?" she asked.

"I obey orders," Anna said. "I do exactly what I am told, because I wish to survive. If you wish to survive, you will do exactly what you are told by me. Now put down that blanket, and come here. I wish to touch you."

Ruth Borodina pushed herself further up the bed until she reached the wall, the blanket clutched to her throat. "If you touch me—" she whispered.

Anna stood up. "What will you do, Princess Borodina?" she asked. "Will you scream? No one will hear you. And no one would care if they could. Will you resist me? I could kill you with three blows of my hand. What will you do?"

"You are *Russian,*" Ruth whispered. "I should have known. You are Russian."

Anna frowned at her. "What nonsense!"

"You addressed me in the Russian way," Ruth said. "I know you are Russian." She looked around her. "Am I in Moscow?"

"I would not think things like that, if I were you," Anna said. "It could cause you a great deal of grief." She looked at her wristwatch and hastily began to dress. "I must go now. I suggest you wash yourself, and then eat something. There is vodka in this parcel. Drink some vodka, and then lie down with a good book. I will come back in due course. But think of what I have said." She closed the cell door behind her, leaned against it for a moment. What a silly mistake! But she had made two silly mistakes already this morning. If Ivan were to find out...

On the other hand, why should he ever find out? He could not let the girl see him, however much he enjoyed watching her through the observation window. The girl was hers. All hers. She felt a peculiar sense of elation. For five years she had belonged to other women, to be treated as they pleased, to be raped or loved or beaten, as the mood took them. This girl was hers, in that same sense. Complete possession.

But never wholly satisfying. Never to be compared with the real thing. Ruth Borodina could never be anything more than a placebo. She hurried up the stairs, along the corridor. She was no longer allowed within the training gymnasium, but she knew the hour the sessions ended. And there they were, emerging from the doorway, laughing and talking to each other, aware that they were an elite, an army within an army, perhaps relieved to be rid of their unsmiling leader. All except one, surely. She stood in the corridor as they passed her, glanced at her. Some averted their eyes, one or two muttered, "Good afternoon, Anna Petrovna."

Gregory Nej was last. He must have deliberately allowed himself to be last, so that they could have a word, arrange a meeting.

"Good afternoon, Gregory Ivanovich," she said softly as he reached her.

He gazed at her for a moment, then averted his eyes. "Good afternoon, Comrade Ragosina," he said, and hurried on behind his friends.

Anna stared after him for several seconds, until she felt her fingernails biting into the palms of her hands. But she would not cry. Not for a Nej. Slowly she unclenched her hands, then she went back down the stairs, into the depths of Lubianka, down to cell number forty-seven.


"The president is waiting for you, Mr. Hayman," the aide said, hurrying in front of George Hayman down the polished floor. George decided against being inquisitive. He could wait. It was the first time he had been inside the White House for seven years, since the Hoover administration had come to an end. He did not know Roosevelt at all well, although they had come into contact often enough when the president had been governor of New York. He had always respected the man, had occasionally reflected, a trifle ruefully, that he voted Republican, in the first place because his father had always voted Republican, and in the second because as proprietor of America's largest international newspaper chain he had to be a conservative businessman. Nor did he approve of featherbedding, in any direction, from individuals to businesses. But he would cheerfully admit that a great deal of Roosevelt's New Deal made sound common sense.

The door opened, and he was in the Oval Office. He knew each of the other three men in the room, nodded to Secretary of State Cordell Hull and Under Secretary Sumner Welles, reached across the desk to shake the president's hand, and felt a certain sense of shock. George was five years the president's elder, but Roosevelt looked much more than his fifty-seven years. Obviously the aftermath of his illness, which left him unable to rise to meet his guest, contributed to his tiredness, but his face was also drawn and anxious, and his lips turned down.

The voice was as brisk and as clipped as ever, however. "Good of you to come, Hayman. Sit down. I'd like you to read this."

George took the paper labeled Top Secret Memorandum, glanced at it, and frowned.

"That's not for publication, George," Hull said.

"Not yet," Roosevelt said. "But it's going to be common knowledge, soon enough."

George replaced the memorandum on the desk.

"No comment?" Roosevelt asked.

"I'm not surprised," George said.

Roosevelt nodded. "When you came back from Europe last year, and I asked you to stop by for a chat, you told me then that the Nazis were negotiating with the Soviets, and I was sure you had to be wrong. Okay. Now they've got a trade pact and a nonaggression pact about to be signed, if that report is accurate. You believe it is?"

"I do."

"So tell me what you think it means."

George pulled his nose. "It means that within a month Germany will invade Poland."

"The Russians will never stand for that," Hull said.

"It'd bring Nazi Germany to the frontiers of Russia," Welles pointed out.

Roosevelt gazed at George.

He shrugged. "You asked for my opinion. Hasn't Hitler made it plain that he's going to have Danzig and the corridor? Doesn't that mean an invasion of Poland, or, supposing the Poles refuse to fight, an occupation of their country, just as in Czechoslovakia and Austria? Stalin must have allowed for that when he agreed to this pact."

"Will the Poles fight?" Roosevelt asked.

"My guess is they will," George said. "The Poles have been

fighting *some*body, including each other, ever since they became a nation. They don't bother too much about the odds."

"And Great Britain and France have guaranteed to support them," Hull said.

"So we'll have a replay of the World War," Roosevelt said. "Is that how you see it, Hayman?"

"That's how I've seen it since Hitler came to power."

Roosevelt nodded. "And the Russians?"

"Will sit this one out, in my opinion. At least for a while."

"And what do you think this country should do?" Roosevelt asked.

George sighed. "The only hope there is of preventing another World War is for this administration to declare publicly and loudly that if Great Britain and France become involved in a defensive war with Nazi Germany, the United States will support the democracies, with force of arms if need be."

"That's hardly Republican philosophy," Hull remarked.

"It happens to be my philosophy, and has been for a long time."

"It'd be a blank check," Welles said. "An absurdity."

"It's impossible, anyway," Roosevelt said quietly. "I have no constitutional powers to make such a statement, and you know I'd never swing Congress."

"You'd never swing the country," Hull said.

"Well, then, we can all sit back and watch the fireworks, until they start hurting us as well," George said. "They will, you know, just like the last time."

"Isn't there a strong chance, even a likelihood, that the British and the French will sidestep again, as they did over the Czechs?" Welles asked.

"I imagine there is," George agreed. "Then Germany will absorb as much of Poland as is practical, and wonder where to go next. Rumania, I imagine. Do you really want to sit back, Mr. President, and see the swastika fly over all of Europe?"

"No," Roosevelt said. "But we must be sure that's what Hitler intends. I'm sending Sumner here over on a mission, early next year. He'll go to Berlin and Rome and London and Paris, and talk things out with the people there. When he comes back we'll have a clearer picture of what's going on."

"By the time he comes back," George said, "we are going to be in the middle of a war."

"We must hope not," Roosevelt said, and held out his hand. "It was good of you to come, Hayman. You've no objection to giving Sumner a private briefing on the people he's likely to meet?"

George shook hands. "It'll be a pleasure. Give me a call."

The plane was waiting to whisk him back to New York, but he did not feel like returning to the office, and drove to Cold Spring Harbor instead. He was aware of a feeling of utter sadness combined almost with relief. For so long there had been such confusion, such uncertainty. There was no uncertainty any longer. Hitler had got what he wanted, a guarantee that there need be no war on two fronts, the nightmare that had haunted the German General Staff for seventy years, and which had certainly brought about the German defeat in 1918. They must, he thought, be dancing in Berlin tonight.

And what were they doing in Moscow? Undoubtedly this represented a triumph for Michael Nej, however willingly he might allow Molotov to take the credit. His mission was not something that Michael had believed in, in George's opinion, but it had been something he had been told to do by Stalin, and he had done it, as ever, faithfully and well. As Michael had confessed, the Russians were buying time. But it was equally possible they were buying more than that, a division of Eastern Europe into German and Russian spheres of influence, which would allow the spread of Soviet doctrine and Soviet methods just as Trotsky had dreamed in 1918, and just as Lenin had realized was impossible.

In which case the future looked bleak.

"George." Ilona met him in the front hall and kissed him. "Mrs. Killett said you were at the White House."

He winked. "They've found a use for me again."

"Any news of Ruth? Oh, please say there's news of Ruth."

"I'm afraid there isn't. But Michael has pulled it off. The Russians and the Germans, according to a secret report from Berlin, are about to sign a nonaggression pact to support the trade pact of last month."

"I can't believe it," she said. "It's just incredible."

"It's going to happen. And that means there's going to be a war. I told Roosevelt and Hull that, but they still hope for a miracle, apparently. What your brother is saying, I simply can't imagine."

"Peter..." She held George's hand as they walked towards the living room. "I sometimes think I should go to him, you know. It's been five months now, and not a word about Ruth. He must be desperate. George, haven't you heard from Michael?"

"Now you know I have, my darling. He's just as mystified by the whole thing as I am. Okay, so one would immediately think of Ivan and his nasty little tricks, but Michael has his ear fairly close to the ground in Moscow and there has not been a whisper of any Russian involvement. Anyway, you know, it just doesn't make sense. Peter is apparently still quite popular with the Nazis, even if they don't seem very eager to take his advice, and the Russians know this. Would they have risked botching up the negotiations with Berlin by staging a kidnapping?"

"Well, if they don't have her, who does? I mean, taking her out of her own apartment... George, I'm getting a terrible feeling that she may have been the victim of some kind of sex crime, and is buried in a ditch somewhere."

"I doubt that. To my mind there are only two possibilities. One is okay, one is pretty grim."

Her fingers were tight on his as they reached the closed living-room door. They paused there. "Tell me."

"Well, it happened while Peter was away. So at least one possibility is that Ruth eloped with somebody. Somebody she knew her dad wouldn't approve of. She must know Peter as well as you do. You tried to elope from his custody, once, remember?"

She sighed. "That was a long time ago. I can't see Ruth doing that. She's very dutiful, and she loves her father. And she was fairly well aware of his opinions, as I remember. What is the other possibility?"

"That someone in Germany may have remembered, or found out, that her mother was Jewish."

She stared at him. "Oh, my God!"

"Because, you see, while the Nazis might not want to antagonize the Prince of Starogan, who is, after all, of tremendous propaganda value to them, they might also have decided that they could not have a half-Jewess parading with him at official functions."

"Oh, George . . ."

"My love, it's only a possibility. Nothing more. And the more I think about it, the less likely it seems. The Germans have denied any knowledge of her whereabouts. Their police have been going wild trying to find her."

"Well, they'd pretend that, wouldn't they?"

"They wouldn't rest with a blanket denial. Knowing those fellows, I'll bet they'd have someone all ready to accuse of the crime, even to arrest, if need be. And there is still another possibility, you know—that Peter found out some such plan was in the wind and shipped her out."

"Where?"

"Well . . . why not Paris? Judith. She'd be safe there. And the fact that Judith also seems to be worrying like mad may be just a cover-up."

"My God, I wish I knew. Every time you think life is settling down fairly smoothly, something else happens. George, Johnnie is here." She opened the living-room door.

George went in and kissed Felicity on the cheek. "Hi. Any news of young Cassidy?"

She shrugged. "Oh, he's prowling up and down the Pacific. He called me from Pearl, last week. He's having fun."

"Too much fun to get married?"

"Oh, *Dad*. You know he doesn't want to get married until he's a full lieutenant. We want to be self-supporting. He'll be through in three months."

"I'll believe that when I see it." George looked at his stepson. "Aren't you supposed to be in Chicago?"

John Hayman stood up. "Caught red-handed. But the tournament doesn't start until tomorrow. I'm going down tonight. I wanted to see Mother first, and you, of course. George—"

"Tattie wants him to visit them in Russia," Ilona said.

"What? Aren't you still banned?"

"It's been rescinded," John said, his voice becoming excited. "She's managed to have the ban revoked. I can enter Russia to cover the main chess tournament there. There's an all-Russian championship early next year."

"I don't think he should go," Ilona said. "It's not safe. It has to be some kind of a trick, on Ivan's part, to get hold of him again."

"Now, Mother," John said patiently, "you know that isn't so. The order is signed by Stalin himself. It can't be a trick. And . . . well . . ."

"You want to see Natasha Brusilova again. Didn't you ask her to marry you, and didn't she refuse you?" Ilona persisted.

John flushed. "Not altogether. I would like to see Natasha again, very much. May I cover the championship, George?"

"You realize Europe is probably going to be at war by next year?" George asked.

"Not Russia. Aunt Tattie agrees with you about there being a war, but she says Russia is determined to keep out of it, just as we are. And besides," he added with a smile, "if things are happening over there, well, maybe I could do a bit more than just cover chess. You'd have a reporter inside Russia itself. That should have to be worth something."

George looked at Ilona, who shrugged helplessly. "Yes," he said. "It sounds an exciting project." He clapped his stepson on the shoulder. "Do you know, if I didn't think it would cramp your style, I'd come with you."

Ilona Hayman sat at her desk and brooded on the table of contents of her magazine. Helen Meynon, her editor, hovered rather anxiously at her elbow. Being editor of *You* was the peak of her career, so far, but she wished that the proprietor would allow her more independence. And today, she felt sure catastrophe was hovering above her head.

Her instincts were correct.

"It's not right," Ilona said.

"Well, Mrs. Hayman, Artie Shaw is very popular just now, whatever his . . . well . . ." She was remembering that the proprietor also had a few conjugal indiscretions in her background.

"I am not the least bit interested in Mr. Shaw's problems with women," Ilona said. "I merely think it is absurd to make him the lead story under the present circumstances."

Helen Meynon frowned. "What circumstances, Mrs. Hayman? It's a little early to start running profiles of the possible presidential candidates. Besides, you yourself said you didn't want a specifically political slant. The arts, you said, and fashion, and even sports, must all have their fair share of lead stories."

"I am talking about the war," Ilona said, icily.

"What—Oh, that war."

*The* war," Ilona said.

"Well, to be frank, Mrs. Hayman, I don't think people over here are really interested in what's happening in Europe. It isn't as if we were involved, or anything like that. And in fact, nothing *is* happening. I was talking to John Brien the other day, and he says the whole thing will be over in another couple of weeks."

"He thinks so, does he?"

"I think most of the foreign correspondents feel that way, Mrs. Hayman. Poland is over and done with, and Hitler has been very careful not to fire a shot more than he has to against France. Chamberlain did what he had to do. It's almost certain he'll call the whole thing off. I mean, what can Britain and France do about the situation now?"

"Well, I don't think he's going to call it off," Ilona said. "I think it's just beginning. I want a lead story on the British at war. How they see the situation. The ordinary housewife, the children. I want to be able to tell Americans how they feel over there. Oh, I know we can't change this month's edition. Run this absurd article on Artie Shaw, if you must. But next month I want that London story. Get whoever we have over there, or the *American People* has over there. Send someone, if you have to. But have it ready for next month."

"Mrs. Hayman, if Chamberlain does make peace, we are going to be left with egg all over our face."

Ilona leaned back in her chair, and smiled for the first time that morning. "Would you like to take a bet on it, Helen?"

The applause was tremendous, swelling out of the auditorium, cascading over the stage as the lights went up and the dancers could at last see their audience. Natasha Brusilova blinked into the sea of faces, her eyes filling with tears as they always did after a performance. Only slowly was she able to identify them, the huge moustache of Stalin, the glittering décolletage of Tatiana Nej, now rising to make her way backstage, the quieter features of Catherine Nej, the gentle smile of Michael Nej, and then the moustache of Ivan Nej, the policeman. Hastily she looked away, smiled at the rest of the auditorium, curtsied again, and had a bouquet of flowers thrust into her arms by one of the chorus. Then the curtain dropped for the last time, and she could hurry off the stage to join the rest of the cast outside, who were already gathered around Tattie, to be told how well they had done.

"That was splendid," Tattie said. "A fitting finale. I am very pleased with you. And with you most of all, Natasha. You were quite delightful." She kissed her protégée on each cheek. "One day you will be as good as I am—perhaps. Now come, I have something for you." She led Natasha into the dressing room and gave her an envelope. "A letter from Johnnie."

Natasha sat down and slit the paper, her mind going strangely dead, as it always did when she received a letter from John Hayman, or even heard his name.

She raised her head. "He is coming to visit. Next spring."

"I know," Tattie said. "He wrote me as well. The letters arrived yesterday."

"Yesterday? But..."

Tattie smiled at her. "I was not going to give you yours until after the final performance. It would have distracted you. But now you can think about it. It's you he is coming to see, you know."

"Me?"

"Of course he is. He is going to ask you to marry him, as usual. And are you going to say yes, this time?"

Natasha carefully read the rest of the letter. All commonplaces. But it bubbled with his excitement at being able to see her again.

"Because I think you should make a decision about that," Tattie said.

Natasha raised her head, and Tattie sat beside her. "You are going to be thirty years old next year. If you ever intend to marry and have children, you don't want to leave it much after that."

"But...my career?"

"You have had a great career, already," Tattie said. "Now you must decide if marriage would be still greater than continuing your career. And if so, whether John Hayman really is the man you want to marry. It will mean leaving Russia."

Natasha gazed at her. Leaving Russia. Did Tattie really suppose she wanted to stay here, if she had somewhere better to go? Here, where her mother and father had been murdered by the state?

She had not been on her father's farm when the Cheka men led by Ivan Nej, with Anna Ragosina at his side, had destroyed it, and shot her Mama and Papa for the great crime of being kulaks, farmers who had done better than the rest. The news had reached her second hand, when she was inside the safety of the Tatiana Nej Academy in Moscow. She had felt at once sick and vengeful, but could not even imagine what it would have felt like to be there when the Cheka came. She had only known that she hated the very name of Ivan Nej, of the secret police, of the entire Soviet government, with an intensity she could hardly express even to herself.

These were not feelings she had dared communicate to either Tattie or Svetlana, her only two real friends in all the world. Tattie probably loathed her husband as much as anyone did, but it was for entirely personal reasons—which was strange, because by all accounts her own mother and family had been murdered in exactly the same way as the Brusilovs, and by the same man. But Tattie was unique, a law unto herself. And Svetlana could hardly be expected to hate her own father, especially since she had never been allowed to witness any of his handiwork.

But at the same time, as a girl Natasha had never really considered escaping Russia. She was Russian. The rest of the world promised her nothing but the misery of being a refugee. And before she had been able to grow sufficiently to consider the possibility that being a penniless refugee somewhere else might just be preferable to living in a society of murderers, she had been caught up in the glamour of the dance, in the real possibility that she could be a lead, and soon, that she was, indeed, going to be famous. She supposed that in many ways she was a coward. The truth was that, as a star, life for her in Russia was very good. It gave her some pride to feel that she had risen to the top even through this society that had destroyed her family. And what promises could John Hayman make her? However much she might hate Bolshevism, she could not help but believe some of the things that were said about American capitalism, about the thousands starving to death, according to *Pravda,* and about the ruthless way in which the rich exploited the poor.

Besides, it had never seemed an urgent decision. Therefore, was it urgent now? It gave her great pleasure to be loved by someone so remote, and so very, very nice.

"You cannot expect him to wait forever," Tattie said softly.

He had already waited ten years. But ten years ago they had both been children. She had, certainly. Now...

"He is rich," Tattie said. "Very rich. And remember, Ilona is his mother, Natasha, far more than Michael is his father."

"Should I marry a man because he is rich, Tatiana Dimitrievna?"

"I'm trying to remove your fears, child," Tattie said. "His stepfather is also very powerful. You need not suppose that you will be going to some hovel. And they are happier in America than we can ever be here."

Natasha stared at her. That was tantamount to treason.

Tattie smiled. "It is true, you know. Here we are all children, ruled by a stern stepfather, Joseph Vissarionovich, and his mob. In America, people are adults. As adults they are responsible for their own actions, and they make mistakes. Sometimes they elect the wrong people to office, and sometimes they pass the wrong laws. But those are *their* mistakes. They have the right to correct them, and then to make others. This is their system. Here, we just endure Joseph's mistakes. So do not fear America."

"Why did you never go there yourself?" Natasha asked.

"I will leave Russia," Tattie said, "when I am ready."

"But you will come back here."

"Perhaps."

"But why?"

"I am Tatiana Nej," Tattie pointed out.

There was no answer to that. And besides, it was irrelevant. John was coming back to Russia. He was coming to see her. And as Tattie had said, he would again ask her to marry him. Tattie was suggesting she say yes, now. Was she therefore hinting that Natasha Brusilova could never be as great as Tatiana Nej? That she had reached the height of her career, and should retire while she was at her peak?

And then leave Russia? Because, without her fame, it might be remembered that she was the daughter of a kulak?

"But of course," Tattie said gently, "it must all depend upon whether or not you love Johnnie."

They played at croquet. Aunt Tattie had become positively bucolic in her new surroundings, wore an enormous floppy hat and a sheer muslin gown, and encouraged her girls to do the same. She sometimes seemed determined to recreate a Chekhovian life here in Byelorussia. She was happy as ever, but now in a passive fashion. Perhaps, John Hayman supposed, it was because she was approaching fifty. Or because, as she had told him with mock self-pity, her friend Stalin had reshuffled the Politburo and replaced her as commissar for culture. "Rather a relief, really," she had confessed. "I hated their stuffy old meetings."

But most likely it was because, during this visit of his, Clive Bullen was not also in residence. It was not likely she was going to see much of Clive over the next few years, since, like everyone else in England, apparently, he had been inducted into the army for the fight against Germany, despite his age. Presumably this also was some cause for personal concern. And yet she was filled as ever with enthusiasm, even for knocking wooden balls about with wooden mallets. She marshaled Svetlana, who was her partner, with a series of staccato commands, seemed about to break her mallet between her hands at each missed shot, and finished by kicking down the finishing post when Natasha Brusilova sank her last ball against it to win the game for herself and John.

"We must play again," she decided. "Tomorrow we will play again. This afternoon I will show you the farm."

John looked at Natasha, and raised his eyebrows. Aunt Tattie persisted in regarding the farm as her own, although it was in fact only part of a vast kholkoz with which she had nothing to do.

"But you would rather walk with Natasha," Tattie said regretfully. "Ah, well, my love . . ." She rumpled Svetlana's hair. "Paul will soon be here."

"You don't approve of Captain von Hassell," Natasha suggested. Lunch was over, and the huge house slept, except for them, sitting next to each other on the side veranda.

"I hardly know the fellow," John confessed. "I only met him once, two years ago. I suppose it just seems odd, with all of Europe at war, for him to be able to take time off, and come to holiday here in Russia."

"Bah," she said. "Everyone knows the war is over. It does not really matter whether or not the British make peace now, does it? Germany has all of Western Europe, which is what they wanted in the first place. Did *you* notice anything like a war?"

"Well, I came across on a Swedish ship, direct from New York to Stockholm and then Leningrad, so I couldn't have seen anything. But I didn't know you were interested in politics."

"Everyone has to be interested in politics," she pointed out. "Besides, the whole thing is interfering with our dancing. We were to go on another tour this summer, but it has been put off. Tatiana Dimitrievna says it may be possible next year."

*"We* aren't at war," John said gently.

She smiled. "I am glad you are not at war, Johnnie. So glad. So glad that you could come here."

It was the first actual welcome she had uttered since his arrival the previous night. Partly, he supposed, it was because of his own shyness. But she must have been shy as well, after another two years had passed. He had almost dreaded seeing her.

And Natasha was more beautiful than ever, more desirable, and more distantly unapproachable. He had no means of knowing whether or not Aunt Tattie's suggestion, in Berlin, had been founded on anything more than her own overdeveloped libido. But he had come here determined to find out. He would never have a better opportunity. She was relaxing down here outside Slutsk between performances, doing nothing more than practice for half the day, along with the other girls. The rest of the time she could enjoy herself. And he would never, he was sure, find more congenial surroundings for himself. The place was actually reminiscent of Starogan itself, lacking the intense summer heat, but hot enough certainly, with the same great fields of wheat surrounding the village, the same farmyard smells, and farmyard sounds, the same lazy river drifting by a mile away, liable to dissolve into mud in the summer just to encourage the mosquitoes, and with an added attraction in the

form of an enormous brooding forest beyond the water, a place
longing to be explored, but which Aunt Tattie claimed was
inpenetrable because of its bogs and its undergrowth.

Even the house was on a grand scale, although different
architecturally from Starogan; huge stone chimneys suggested
that the winters here were colder than they had ever been in
the basin of the Don. But the house had the same silent hall-
ways, the same verandas and porches where the afternoon
breeze could be enjoyed as now, and even the same retinue of
servants, all "comrades" to be sure, but all happy enough to
serve the legendary Tatiana Nej and her famous girls.

And the same orchard, which he remembered so well from
Starogan; the trees were heavy with leaves and with apples.
A place of quiet contentment.

"Would you like to take a walk?" he asked diffidently.

She stretched, at ease in the porch swing. "I would rather
stay here."

"Oh." He chewed his lip.

Natasha laughed. "We will not be interrupted, if that's
what's bothering you. I overheard Tatiana Dimitrievna giving
instructions after lunch that no one was to come on this veranda."

"Oh," he said again, still uncertain.

Natasha sighed, but she continued to smile. "Tatiana Dimitrievna has spent a great deal of time lecturing me, during the
last couple of years. She points out that next year I shall be
thirty."

Johnnie held her hand. "Natasha..."

"And still a virgin," she said thoughtfully, glanced at him,
and laughed at his flush. "It is I who should be blushing. Do
you still love me, Johnnie?"

"Love you? Oh, my darling..." He held her close to kiss
her mouth and her eyes and her hair, allowed his hand just to
touch the curve of her breast, and felt the emotion ripple through
her body. "I love you."

"I thought you did," she agreed, "since you kept on writing,
all this time. Do you know that I have five hundred letters from
you, all bound up in blue ribbon?"

He could never be sure whether or not she was gently poking
fun at him. And he had never received a plainer invitation than
just now.

"Natasha . . ." Once again he held her close, could look over her shoulder at the row of buttons that crept up her spine. Was he a coward, then? There was nothing to be cowardly about. She was not going to say no to his invitation.

"So I think," she said into his ear, "that if you still wish to, I would like to marry you."

His head jerked away from hers, the better to look at her.

"But you have changed your mind," she said, with mock sadness.

"Oh, Natasha . . ." Once again he held her close, but this time thoughts of sexual encounter were forgotten. There was something so magnificently pure about her, so tremendously, healthily feminine, that he wanted to do nothing more than hold her in his arms. That she would be sexually delicious he did not doubt, but it could not be a transient delight, a matter of moments. It had to be something permanent. To *know* Natasha Brusilova, and then to have to leave her again, even for a second, was unthinkable. Besides, if they were to be married—

"Then I say yes," she said, and kissed him on the nose. "Next summer."

"Next *summer?*" he cried.

"Well," she explained, "I do not suppose you wish to come and live in Russia."

"I couldn't even if I did want to."

"Of course not. Then, you see, I have to apply for permission to emigrate to the United States."

"And that's tough?"

"For most people it takes years. Oh, we shall get the permission. Tatiana Dimitrievna has assured me of this. But it will take time. Several months, even for Tatiana Dimitrievna. And then, there is this last tour I wish to make. As soon as Tatiana thinks things in Europe are sufficiently settled. A last tour, Johnnie. You would not begrudge me that?"

"Of course not," he said. "It's just that next summer seems so far away." He sighed. "I can't stay here with you, you know. There'd be nothing for me to do, even if your government let me stay."

"I wouldn't want you to," she said. "I have to work. I have to practice, and then I have to dance. We have a very full calendar of engagements, even if we cannot make our tour.

But it is only twelve months away, my darling Johnnie. Only twelve months."

She had never called him "my darling" before. She had never actually allowed herself to indulge in any endearments. All the years of uncertainty and even unhappiness were suddenly rolled away. It was only in the company of this girl that he had ever found true happiness. Unlike him, she was one of life's successes, a born dancer, a girl who, however tragic her girlhood, was destined for nothing but triumph. How could a mere chess-playing reporter, however well-born his mother, however high his connections, both in Russia and in the United States, aspire to so much beauty and talent?

But now . . .

She had been watching his changing expressions, his eyes, almost with anxiety. Now she smiled, and kissed him again. "Only a year, Johnnie," she whispered, and held him close. "Only a year."

He wondered if she had been disappointed. If so, she had not shown it. Besides even more than before, the idea had been unthinkable. She was his, promised to him. All that slender, hard-muscled, superbly fit flesh was going to be his, together with that gentle, half-mocking smile and that determined mind. Things to be held, carefully and gently, and irrevocably. Not things to be borrowed for a hasty half-hour, even if they were promised to him.

She was giving him her career, too. There was the greatest responsibility of all. To be sure, he understood that a principal dancer, unless she happened to be a Tatiana Nej, could begin to see the writing on the wall at the age of thirty. He felt no responsibility for taking her away from the glitter and the romance of thrilling thousands of people in the capitals of Europe. But he felt an immense responsibility for making sure that her future life did not suffer in the comparison with her exciting youth. And thus he felt almost anxious to be away from her again, to arrange it all.

"Are you sure, Johnnie?" Ilona asked, frowning at him. "Are you very, very sure?"

"I seem to have loved her all my life, Mother. It's been ten years." He shrugged. "I guess I had come to suppose it would never happen. Oh, yes, Mother, I'm sure."

"And you can't knock the family, Ilona," George said with a smile. "The Brusilovs were big farmers in their time. They even come from the right part of the country."

"I suppose it's because it's all so sudden," Ilona complained.

"Sudden?" George and John asked together.

"And it's not for another year," George said. "Time to change your mind, John."

"Or for her to change hers. George, I . . ." He chewed his lip.

George nodded. "You're marrying an internationally famous dancer."

"You mean you understand that?"

"Don't forget, thirty years ago I set my sights on marrying a princess. But this means you're going to have to give up chasing around the world, and settle down. How about the sports desk?"

John stared at him. "The sports desk?"

"Well, old Hapgood is due to retire next year. I did have you in mind all the time, although I never thought you'd be willing to take the job. But now, why, I guess you are."

"Sports editor of the *American People*," John muttered.

"Why, George," Ilona said, "that would be marvelous." She blew him a kiss. "You're being very kind."

"But . . . do you think I could do it?" John asked.

"Of course you can. You'll move in as assistant editor right away, begin to get the feel of the thing." He smiled. "Don't worry, you'll have time off next summer."

"Next summer," Ilona echoed. "I don't want any more elopements like George junior's."

"Ah," John said. "Aunt Tattie has some ideas about that."

Ilona frowned at him. "You're not getting married in Russia, are you, John? Say that you're not. It would only be a civil ceremony over there."

"You can have a church wedding in Russia if you wish it," John explained. "It just doesn't happen to be legal. But you see, Aunt Tattie knows that there is no way, with things as they are at the moment, that she and her girls can come over here. And she so wants to have the wedding as well. After all, Natasha is virtually her daughter."

"So you'll have two weddings," George said.

"That's exactly it. I'll join Natasha in Moscow next summer, and we'll go to Slutsk. All the girls will be down there training, and we'll have a house wedding, and then Natasha and I will come home again—"

"How do you plan to get there?" Ilona asked.

"Well, I thought I'd use a different route. Boat to Lisbon and train all across Europe. It certainly ought to be interesting."

"I hate the thought of those Atlantic crossings," Ilona said. "I really do."

"Now, love, no one is going to sink an American ship," George reminded her. "And I agree with John. A first-hand look at Nazi Europe should be very interesting."

"It's a long trip," Ilona said. "You and that girl. You won't have been properly married."

Husband and son gazed at her with their mouths open.

"Well," she said, flushing, "things were different before the war."

"Which war?" John inquired. "Anyway, Mother, we will have been properly married, at least in our eyes. But we can be married in a civil ceremony as well, if you'd prefer it. And then, when we get over there, we can be married all over again. Think of it, a September wedding in New York."

"That will be wonderful," Ilona said, growing enthusiastic at last as she began to consider the possibilities. "Felicity can be bridesmaid, and little Diana can be a flower girl . . . It'd be so nice if you'd have David Cassidy as your best man, Johnnie."

"I don't see why not."

"Oh, lovely," Ilona said. "The lists. We must start making up the lists right away. It'll be the wedding of the year! Oh, George . . ."

He put his arm round her shoulders, offered her his handkerchief to wipe away the tears. John was her first-born, and he had been a love child at that. He was everything to her, as George well understood—a constant reminder of the glory that had been Russia, of the excitement that Ilona Borodina had engendered and experienced, and loved, thirty years before.

"I tell you what," he said. "I know who'd damn well better make the effort to get over here for the wedding. Michael Nej. He's never visited America before."

Ilona sat at her desk, glasses perched on the end of her nose as she surveyed the typewritten sheets of paper in front of her.

Helen Meynon chain-smoked. A year ago she had been prepared to resign, and had not done so. But the fact that her
employer seemed to have some gift of foreseeing the future
didn't make her any easier to work with.

"Is this true?" Ilona asked at last.

"He's a good man."

"And he has been to these places, seen these things? I find
it hard to believe."

Helen Meynon waited.

Ilona got up, walked to the map that adorned one of her
walls, and gazed at Europe. "France," she said. "Austria, Belgium, Holland, Norway, Poland, Hungary—they all belong
to Germany now, virtually. How am I to believe a story like
this, that all over those countries people are being tortured and
murdered, whole villages taken hostage and then shot, and no
one is doing anything about it?"

"There's nothing they *can* do about it," Helen pointed out.

"But, Helen, people have been ruled by brute force before,
and have done something about it. Almost an entire continent . . . It just doesn't make sense."

"It soon will *be* an entire continent," Helen said. "There's
a rumor that Hitler is about to conclude some sort of a pact
with the Yugoslavs, so that he can send an army through there
to help Mussolini against the Greeks and the British. Bulgaria's
on his side too. And Rumania, I think."

"On his side," Ilona said. "Not having their people butchered. We'll wait on this one, Helen."

"But—?"

"My husband once told me that his job was to report the
news, not make it. That applies to us just as much. Besides,
I can tell from our mail, lately, that people are desperate for
some cheerful stories. It's time for something light. Marriage.
We'll run a feature on famous international marriages. You
know John is marrying the Russian ballerina, Natasha Brusilova?"

"I had heard."

"Well, you see, if we run a series, we'll be able to top it
with one of our very own. That will be splendid. We'll put a
little sanity back into people's lives. There's nothing like a
good wedding. And John's is going to be the best. He's having
two, you know. One in Russia, and one in New York. You

have no idea the organization that's going into it. I mean, think of it. Communist Russia, allowing one of its principal dancers to marry an American. My sister is responsible, of course. But it's still quite a feat."

It occurred to Helen Meynon that Mrs. Hayman was nervous. It was the first time she had ever noticed such a weakness. She stubbed out her eleventh cigarette, got up, and collected the article. "And this? It could just all be true, you know."

"If it is true," Ilona said, "then of course we'll run it. Later on this year. George and I are going to Russia for the first wedding, you know. We'll be visiting Nazi-occupied Europe as well. By the time we come back, I'll be able to tell you whether this story is true or not. We can only pray it isn't."

The train roared across the Polish plain, already sweltering in the early summer heat. But then, all Europe was sweltering, and not just from the heat, John guessed.

For the past few years he had endeavored to stay out of politics. When, in his youthful enthusiasm, and his youthful confusion as well, he had gone to work for his Uncle Peter, he had not really considered the implications of what he was doing, the possible physical results. He was Prince Sergei Roditchev's son, he had thought, and it was his duty to help his uncle in every possible way for the overthrow of Bolshevism, the restoration of the Russian aristocracy to its proper place in the scheme of things. The sudden realization that he had been fighting against his own kind, against his own real father, had left him floundering. Brought up a capitalist by George, and besides, having seen how the Bolsheviks managed their state from inside a cell in Lubianka, he knew he could never possibly sympathize, much less admire them. But he could no longer fight against them, either. Better to stay entirely divorced from the reality of life, reflect that when the Russian people got tired of their red-handed overlords they would throw them aside as they had thrown aside the tsar and *his* red-handed executioners.

From that determination had come a divorce from all things political, all things even remotely real, as George would no doubt have it. There was no reality about chess, where an entire life situation was created with every game, and then scrapped for the next encounter. Besides, chess players on the whole preferred not to have politics. It was too international a game. If, during the past two or three years, it had been impossible to ignore the militarism of Germany and Italy, the German and Italian chess players themselves had deprecated this intrusion into their private worlds; the end of each big international tournament, and even more, the close of each biennial Chess Olympiad, had always been an occasion for looking forward to the next time rather than worrying what might happen in between.

Well, he supposed, now they were all being overtaken by events. Europe in 1941 lay under a heavy hand. Even Spain, so far uninvolved in the conflict, was a police state as it sought to recover from its civil war. France had been a pitiful experience for someone who could remember playing chess in Paris in 1938. He had had an overnight stop, but had remained in his hotel, although his mother had reminded him to be sure to call on Judith Stein. Judith, secure in her position as mistress of a Russian diplomat, must be untroubled by the Nazis, despite her background. But she could not be less than miserable at what was going on around her.

And after Paris, there was the somewhat hysterical happiness and confidence of Germany itself, as if they could not really believe that all this was happening, that their Führer had indeed conquered all Europe, was now opposed only by a handful of intransigent islanders, that the only actual fighting going on, apart from at sea, was in the unwanted sandy wastes of North Africa, and the police actions in the Balkans. After Germany came Eastern Europe. And reality. Poland remained shattered physically, and from what he could see of the people, shattered mentally as well. Since the Germans had now occupied Yugoslavia and Greece, as well as Romania, he presumed those countries were in a similar state. It was impossible not to feel a glow of relief and even self-satisfaction at belonging to the most powerful nation on earth, able by its very strength to remain remote from the miseries of other, smaller nations. And to be traveling to another nation similarly endowed.

Somber thoughts for a bridegroom on his way to his wedding. In another couple of hours the train would be at Brest-Litovsk, to which the Russian frontier had spread since 1939, and he would be within two hundred miles of Tattie's academy.

It was far more profitable for him to continue his analysis of the games played the year before in the match between the Dutch ex-champion of the world, Max Euwe, and the young Estonian genius, Paul Keres, who many said would be the next champion. Who, he realized with a start of surprise, was now by force a Russian citizen, since the Bolsheviks had taken over the Baltic republics too.

The door of the compartment opened. John raised his head, and as always when he saw one of those black uniforms, felt his heartbeat quicken. It was not merely association of ideas, remembering how everyone else automatically seemed to bow to these superb young men; it was that the uniform itself seemed to carry an omnipotent violence, reducing in a single glance his shabby sports jacket to irrelevance.

But this black-clad young officer was smiling, and John suddenly remembered that he need never fear *this* man.

He stood up. "Paul," he said. "Paul von Hassell." He shook hands. "You're not going to Slutsk?"

"Briefly," Paul said. "Look." He sat beside John and flipped open the lid of a little blue box to reveal a diamond sparkling against a red velvet cushion. "Do you think she will like it?"

"She'll love it," John said. "Does she know it's coming?"

"Ah." Paul von Hassell leaned back, took off his cap and flicked it onto the other seat, where the death's-head above the brim seemed to wink at them. "She knows it is coming one day. So I thought, why not now? If there's to be one wedding in the family, then why not two?"

"What about old Ivan?"

"The Terrible?" Paul smiled. "Oh, yes. But Svetlana is going to be twenty-one in three months. Don't forget that. And Madam Nej is certainly on our side. We shall be related, John. What do you think of that?"

It was hardly something he had considered before. But Paul was one of the most charming fellows he had ever met, even if he was a Nazi. Last summer, when he had been in Slutsk, they had gone hunting together, played chess together, taken walks together with the women they loved. Paul, of course, had overflowed with the confidence John entirely lacked, and he guessed their methods of courting had been slightly different. But there could be no doubting Svetlana's happiness.

Yet strangely, he thought, today the German was less confident than usual. Or perhaps the mass hysteria that had seized his nation was affecting even him. He seemed excessively, rather than normally, bright and cheerful. Now he threw himself back on the cushions to smile at his friend. "Tell me all the arrangements," he said.

"The wedding itself is scheduled for July 15," John said. "My mother and stepfather are arriving on the tenth. This is the Russian wedding, you see. We'll have another one in New York in September."

"Why do you bother with the Russian one at all?" Paul asked him. "Why do you not just collect Natasha and take her back to the United States with you?"

"I don't think that would go down very well with Aunt Tattie, frankly. She wants all the girls in the school to have a share in it too."

"Then why are you waiting until the middle of July? It is only the beginning of June. Six whole weeks? Why not have your Russian wedding right away? Then you can be back in America by the end of this month."

"Impossible," John said. "For one thing, Mother and George can't get over here for another month, and for another, Natasha doesn't finish her final season until the end of next week. I'm actually on my way to Moscow to pick her up, then we'll go down to Slutsk together."

"Ah, yes," Paul said. "I see. Circumstances dictate our lives, do they not? Still," he reflected, "you are an American, and Natasha Brusilova becomes an American the moment she marries you."

"That's the general idea," John agreed, wondering what point Paul was trying to make.

"That is good. And when Svetlana marries me, she will become a German citizen." He smiled, almost guiltily. "It is a pity that we cannot discover some such citizenship for Madam Nej. Still, you know, John, we Germans will never destroy real talent, especially in the arts. You may rely on that fact."

Svetlana Nej peered at the box. "It's beautiful," she said. "Quite beautiful. I've never seen anything so beautiful."

"Then why don't you try it on?" Paul asked.

She raised her head and gazed at him. He was asking her to marry him. The strange thing was, she had known from the beginning that he would ask her to marry him some day, and had looked forward to it with every intention of saying yes, but without allowing herself to consider the implications of that one little word.

He was a dream, which she sometimes thought she might have had all her life. Russia was so drab. And if life for Tatiana Nej's daughter was less drab than for the majority, her privileges only seemed to accent the drabness with which she was surrounded. Besides, her mother was a romantic, and when Svetlana heard tales of life on old Starogan, or of social events in St. Petersburg when the tsar had ruled, it was like listening to a magnificent fairy tale—except that she knew the fairy tale had actually happened.

She had been prepared to resign herself to the fact that she had been born at the wrong time. Even her faint hope that through her dancing she might achieve a fame, and a way of life, like with her mother's had eneded with the growing awareness that she would never be a great dancer. She would have to be content with dreams.

But that had been before Berlin. Berlin was another world, of brilliant uniforms and handsome young men. It was a reincarnation of the St. Petersburg of her imagination, and if the Führer made a somewhat insignificant tsar, there could be no gainsaying the splendor with which he was surrounded, all of which had reached a focal point in this man who wanted to marry her.

But she hardly knew him. She only knew that he would be gentle, and kind, and amusing. And that he was a Nazi, which was generally regarded as a very bad thing. But *he* could never be involved in anything bad, or even unpleasant.

And he would take her away from Russia. She would actually live in Berlin, amidst all that glitter and excitement. In a country at war. But a war that existed in name only, existed only because the British refused to make peace and end it all. Therefore a state of war that could be enjoyed, for its excitement.

She realized that she was about to begin a life as dramatic as her mother had had.

Slowly she took the ring from the box, slipped it onto her finger, and raised her head for his kiss.

*   *   *

"He's an odd guy," John confessed. "Don't get me wrong, I like him enormously. But he almost seemed to be trying to reassure me about being an American."

"Yes," Tattie agreed, "he *was* very odd this time. Do you know that he asked Svetlana to elope with him?"

"He couldn't have!" Natasha said. Like John and Tattie, and indeed, Svetlana herself, she sat at the huge dining table in the manor house and opened letter after letter, replies to the wedding invitations, stacking the acceptances on one side and the refusals on the other. But there were very few refusals. Almost the entire country seemed to be coming to Slutsk for the wedding.

"Mama," Svetlana protested, blushing to the roots of her golden hair, "you promised."

"Well, family doesn't count," Tattie said.

"But you didn't agree," John said.

"Well . . . I asked Mama, and she said no."

"Eloping," Tattie snorted. "I'll have no daughter of mine eloping. Who ever heard of such nonsense? Svetlana is going to have a bigger wedding even than yours, Natasha Feodorovna."

"But what made him want to elope?" Natasha inquired.

"Well," Svetlana said. "I won't be twenty-one until September, you see, and since Father won't give me permission to marry Paul, we would have to wait until then."

"But it's almost the end of June now," Natasha pointed out. "Only another three months."

"Yes, but as Paul explains, Germany is at war, and he might get sent anywhere . . ."

"There's scarcely any actual fighting," Tattie said.

"There's North Africa," Svetlana said. "He could be sent to North Africa."

"Nonsense. Only Panzers are sent to North Africa, and Paul is an infantryman. I cannot understand this impatience."

"Anyway, you're still friends," John said. "I see you're wearing his ring."

"Well, of course, I am," Svetlana said. "We *are* going to get married, as soon as possible. He didn't get angry. He was just very sad. And then he became very strange. He told me that he thought the air down here in Slutsk was bad for me, and that I should get away back up north to Moscow, and stay there until we were married. And when I told him I would probably stay, and go up to Moscow after the summer, he said that it was the summer he was worrying about."

"He actually suggested we bring the entire marriage forward," Tattie said, "and have it this month instead of next. As if such a thing were possible."

"That's odd," John said. "He made virtually the same suggestion to me about my own wedding. Apart from also suggesting that I persuade you to elope as well, Natasha."

"He seems to have eloping on the brain," Tattie commented.

"And you never asked me." Natasha smiled.

"Well . . . I didn't think Aunt Tattie would really approve."

"I would have been furious," Tattie declared. "Absolutely furious. There, is that the last of the notes?"

"That's it." John leaned back and yawned, and sipped his after-dinner brandy. How quiet it was on the farm! There was hardly a sound, not even a breath of air to disturb the evening.

"But nothing from Gregory," Tattie said.

"He's probably not going to bother to reply," Svetlana said. "Or he's too busy. What does he *do*, Mama, that he can't come down here?"

"Didn't you know?" Tattie asked. "He is working for his father."

"In the NKVD?" Natasha was incredulous.

"Oh, well, I don't think he is actually a policeman yet. He's too young. Ivan tells me he's given him some sort of a desk job. But that's no reason not to reply to a wedding invitation. I will telephone him tomorrow." She glanced at John. "A boy must stretch his wings. You know that."

"I do indeed," John agreed.

"And besides," she said, as if to herself. "I suppose it is good for him to be with his father, from time to time." Once again she regarded John speculatively. "Yours is coming down here in a couple of weeks, the day before Ilona and George arrive. Isn't that going to be fun? You really should spend more time with him, you know."

"Yes, I look forward to it," John said, and got up. "Coming for a walk, Natasha?"

"I think that's a delightful idea." She joined him at the door.

"Good night, Tatiana Dimitrievna, Svetlana Ivanovna."

Tattie sighed noisily. "Oh, to be young again, walking in the moonlight..."

"Isn't Mr. Bullen coming for the wedding, Mama?" Svetlana asked innocently.

"How can he?" Tattie demanded. "Even if he could get leave, which he can't, it wouldn't be possible with this stupid war going on. Why don't the British make peace? Johnnie? Why don't the British make peace?"

"I don't know, Aunt Tattie. I'm not Churchill."

"The man is a warmonger," Tattie grumbled. "He always has been, ever since the Great War. And do you know something else? He has never liked the Russians. Michael has told me so."

"Well," John said, winking, "maybe now that the Germans have even got down as far as Crete, they'll *have* to invade England, because there'll be nowhere else for them to go."

"Never," Svetlana cried, jumping up. "Oh, they couldn't! If they did, Paul would have to get mixed up in it."

"It was only a joke," John reassured her. "I bet you the British are suing for peace right this moment. You wait and see." He closed the door behind Natasha and himself, and took her hand as they walked down the steps. "You know what? I think she wishes she *had* gone off with Paul."

"Tatiana Dimitrievna would never have forgiven her," Natasha said. The grass of the lawn felt soft underfoot, and above them the moon was beginning to loom beyond the cowsheds. "And I don't think she really wants to leave this place. I know I don't. I think it is the most heavenly spot on earth, even lovelier than Papa's farm, I suppose because it's so green."

"Yes. It reminds me of Starogan," John confessed, and squeezed the fingers that lay in his. "But you're not really sorry to be leaving, are you?"

She smiled. "Of course I am nervous. I am going to a great, strange land, about which I know nothing..."

"You'll love America," he promised. "And America will love you."

"You talk as if I were going on tour." She reached the garden bench and sat down. "I am never going on tour again."

He sat at her feet and leaned back against her knees. "Does that bother you?"

She ran her fingers through his hair. "Not as much as I thought it was going to. I felt quite a sense of relief when I finished my final performance last week. But that was partly because I knew you were waiting in the wings."

He turned on his knees. "Really, Natasha? Really and truly?"

She kissed his nose. "I *am* going to marry you, silly."

"Yes," he said. "I still can't believe it. I still can't believe that I am here, with you, that in three weeks we are going to be married."

"And that then you will give me lots of babies."

"Oh, Natasha, I wasn't thinking of that."

She sighed very softly. "Are *you* happy?"

"Yes," he said. "I am wildly, deliriously happy."

"Then," she said, kissing him again, "the babies will come of their own accord. And now I think we should go to bed. It is very late. I heard midnight strike in the village when we were doing the last of the letters."

"Natasha..." He caught her hand as they both stood up. "Are you... well... do you wish that we..." He paused again.

She smiled at him. "Do I wish that I was no longer a virgin?" She shook her head. "Not now. Now I am glad that we waited. That I have waited. But you will have to be gentle with me," she said seriously. "A thirty-year-old virgin will be... what do you say in America?"

"Repressed? You aren't repressed. You're Tattie's protégée. She doesn't have any inhibitions at all."

"To be like your Aunt Tattie must be the dream of every woman," Natasha said. "I do not think that many attain that dream. But with you, I will not be repressed. Don't tell me you are regretting it now? Can't you wait another three weeks?"

"I can wait forever," he said. "Sometimes I think I have waited forever. Natasha, I do love you so. It's just that I can't believe that someone like you, so... well, so everything, could possibly wish to love someone like me."

"What is the matter with you?"

"Well, I've no talent for anything, and I've no conversation, and I'm not sexy..."

"You have talent. Are you not sports editor of the *American People* newspaper?"

"Nepotism."

She shook her head. "I do not think your Mr. Hayman indulges in nepotism. Anyway, I would love you if you were the hunchback of Notre Dame."

"Tell me why."

"Why? Because you're so gentle. Because you are so kind. Because you are so thoughtful. Because I do not think you would ever hurt anybody in your entire life."

"Natasha..."

"Bed," she said firmly.

But not to sleep. For the first time he actually believed it was going to happen. He had lived with a dream for too long. But now at last it was all to be his. His in a way he had not believed last year, when he had put the ring on her finger; had not even believed during all the preparations, with all the letters going to and fro; had been quite unable to believe when he had got to Moscow, had seen her last performance, had watched the near-adulation with which she had been bid farewell by the theater audience, the flowers and the champagne, the kisses and the cheers. She was giving them all up, to marry a sports editor.

But she loved him. At last he could believe that. She loved him.

He stood at the window, watched the great swath of moonlight cutting across the yard, listened to the faint soughing of the dawn breeze beginning to rise, the drone of the distant aircraft, slowly and steadily growing louder.

Aircraft? At four o'clock in the morning? A great number of aircraft. He peered out his window, but could see nothing. And then he heard a series of sharp punctuations, crisp bangs, also coming closer, like the planes.

John Hayman stood absolutely still, unable to believe his ears, unable to believe what his ears were telling him, that a vast fleet of airplanes was flying over Russia, and dropping bombs on it.

A woman screamed.

# Chapter 5

THE SCREAM WOKE TATTIE. SHE SLEPT HEAVILY, AS A RULE, AND had not been disturbed by the distant droning or the steadily approaching explosions. But the suggestion that one of her girls might be in danger had her sitting up and getting out of bed in the same motion, gathering her dressing gown from its chair as she ran for the door, and then on to the gallery that surrounded the great hall.

Every other bedroom door was opening as well, and the hall quickly filled with excited girls and young women, all in their nightgowns and robes, among whom John Hayman, the only man allowed to sleep in the manor house, looked startling.

"Be quiet," Tattie bawled, clapping her hands. "Johnnie, what is happening? Who screamed?"

"I did, Tatiana Dimitrievna," one of the younger girls gasped. "I heard the sound of the bombs. There they go again! Oh, Tatiana Dimitrievna, I'm so frightened."

As if given a signal, the girls clustered round their idol, begging her to help them.

"Be quiet," Tattie shouted again. "Natasha Feodorovna, are you there?"

"I am here, Tatiana Dimitrievna." Natasha looked as calm as ever.

"Take these girls downstairs and give them some cocoa. You too, Svetlana. Take them downstairs. Johnnie, what is happening?"

John stood beside his aunt. "I'm very much afraid you—we—are being attacked, Aunt Tattie," he said in a low voice.

"Attacked?" she demanded. "How can we be attacked? Who would attack us?"

"It can only be the Germans."

"The Germans? Nonsense! We have a pact with them. Oh, I will have to telephone." She stormed into her office, picked up the receiver, drummed the lever, and again, glared at him in impotent fury.

"Aunt Tattie," John said urgently, leaning over the desk. "I think we should leave."

"Leave? Leave Slutsk? Whatever for?"

"We're barely a hundred miles from the border."

"You suppose Russia is going to be invaded? Don't be absurd!" Once again she banged on the lever, without result. "They are all asleep. At a time like this, they are all asleep. Oh, I will have their hides for this!"

"At least have the girls get dressed, Aunt Tattie," John begged. "And pack up your things. Then if necessary we can get into Slutsk in a hurry and catch the train."

"And go where?"

"Anywhere," John shouted. "Otherwise they'll be caught up in the fighting. They'll be killed."

"My girls? Killed? What nonsense!" she said again. She got up from the desk, paused to glare a last time at the telephone, and cocked her head. "Listen."

Even the sound of the planes was suddenly obscured by the rumble of wheels and the barking of orders. A moment later Svetlana burst into the office, face flushed, pigtail flying. "There are soldiers in the yard, Mama! They are coming into the house."

"Soldiers? In my house?" Tattie marched to the door, threw it wide, stood at the top of the steps to look down at the green-uniformed men beneath her, tramping on her parquet floors, bringing in machine guns and boxes of ammunition, pushing tables to left and right. "You there," she shouted. "What are you doing?"

The men paused, gazed up the stairs at the women they had never seen except on the stage or on posters. A captain came into the room, glanced at the door to the pantries, where the girls were gathering, then up the stairs, and saluted. "Comrade Nej. I am sorry. I have been ordered to take over this house and prepare it as a strongpoint."

"A strongpoint? What is happening?"

"It is the Germans, Comrade Nej. They have broken the truce and are invading. They are bombing our airfields and our military installations. They have crossed the frontier and are advancing very fast. Now we must make haste. Gather all the mattresses," he commanded. "Place them over the windows. The beds, too. Hurry."

Tattie thrust both hands into her magnificent hair as if she would pull it out by the roots, then withdrew them again and went down the stairs. "And what is to happen to my girls?" she inquired, her voice deceptively soft.

The captain turned back to her with a tired expression. "I do not know, Comrade Nej. I have no orders concerning them."

"But they can't stay here," John said. "Can you not lend us your trucks to take us into the town, to catch the train?"

The captain stared at him.

"Yes," Tattie said. "That would be best."

"There is no train," the captain said. "It has been canceled."

"Well, then, lend us your trucks to go to somewhere where there *is* a train."

The captain shook his head. "I am destroying my trucks, Comrade Nej."

Tattie looked through the open front door as, from the yard, there came a whoosh of flame, and the first truck exploded. The others immediately began blazing. Several of the girls screamed.

"Destroying your trucks?" Tattie shouted. "In the name of Lenin, why?"

"Orders, Comrade Nej."

"You have been ordered to barricade the house and then destroy your transport?" John asked.

"It is all here," the captain said, patting his breast pocket.

"Let me see that," Tattie snapped, ripping open his pocket and seizing the paper before he could stop her.

"Comrade Nej," he protested.

Tattie scanned the typewritten lines. "It says, in the event that withdrawal proves to be impossible, all transport is to be destroyed. Withdrawal is not impossible, comrade."

"But I have been ordered to hold this place to the last man," the captain explained. "Thus withdrawal is impossible. Thus I must destroy my trucks."

Tattie gazed at John, while handing back the paper without a word.

"Then what is Comrade Nej to do with her girls, comrade?" John asked. "And with herself? You cannot expect them to walk away from here."

"I suggest you get yourselves dressed, Comrade Nej." He looked around him at the nightgown-clad girls, who were obviously distracting his soldiers. "You and your young ladies, and await the outcome of the battle. It will not take long. We will throw these Germans back without difficulty. And I have been promised support. There are tanks and artillery on their way to assist me. It will all be over by breakfast. And if there should be any fighting around here, you can always hide in the cellar."

"Ugh, it's so damp down here." Tattie led the way down the stone stairs, peering into the ill-lit gloom.

For twelve hours they had waited, and listened, and watched, and exchanged fear-induced rumors. They had looked at the sky, and the German planes flying across it in immense flocks, apparently unmolested by any Russian. And they had listened to the rumble of gunfire coming closer. The Germans had not been defeated by breakfast, and the captain had had to revise his estimate to suppertime. But now, as the afternoon began to draw in, and the sound of artillery had come even closer, he had recommended the cellar.

"And there are rats, Mama," Svetlana said, holding the skirt of her dress clear of the floor. "Nina Alexandrovna saw one the other day. Didn't you, Nina Alexandrovna?"

"A big one," Nina agreed.

"And what were you doing down here, Nina Alexandrovna?" Natasha inquired.

, "Well..." Nina began.

"Oh, be quiet," Tattie said, taking her place in the middle of the floor, looking around her at the empty bottle racks; all the fine wines had been removed years ago. "Now, then, we may be down here for a little while. You've brought the bread and the meat, Olga Mikhailovna? Good. Well, you can start making sandwiches for supper. Put the vodka over there with the water. Now, we have some playing cards, and Natasha Feodorovna has brought some books... Oh, I wish those men would stop stamping about our heads like that." She sighed. "Anyway, as I was saying—My God, what's that?"

The lights went out.

"They've cut the lights," John said, unnecessarily.

"They must have shut down the station in Slutsk," Svetlana suggested.

"We can't just stand here in the dark," Tattie boomed. "My God, I can't see my hand before my face. Who is that sobbing?"

"Lena Vassilievna," a voice sniffed from the darkness.

"Well, stop it. Where are the flashlights?"

"I have one." John switched his on and shone it round the frightened faces.

"Only one?" Tattie inquired.

"I brought one, Tatiana Dimitrievna," said Olga Mikhailovna, the head dresser.

"Good," Tattie said. "Now, Johnnie, I should have thought about the lights before. There are candles in the upstairs storeroom. Go up and get them. And bring matches as well."

"Right away, Aunt Tattie."

"I will come with you," Natasha volunteered.

"And hurry," Tattie commanded.

John waited for Natasha at the stairs. They went up together and cautiously pushed open the door to the kitchen. This was built away from the main building to lessen the risk of fire, but was connected to the downstairs hall by a corridor. The lights were out here as well, but that didn't matter since it was still broad daylight. There were several soldiers in the kitchen, waiting by the windows with their rifles already resting on the sills, as they had waited all day. They had broken most of the glass sashes. They had even become quite used to being surrounded by pretty girls, although they still turned their heads to look at Natasha Brusilova.

"What a mess," Natasha said, as broken glass crackled beneath her shoes. "It's going to cost a fortune to put all of this right." She was keeping the conversation matter-of-fact, as she had done all day. The bitter disappointment which she must be feeling that such a catastrophe should have happened immediately before her wedding had not been allowed to show; she had submerged her feelings in being busy, in helping Tattie and encouraging the girls.

Or perhaps, John thought, like him—like them all, he suspected—she was merely numbed by the unbelievable immensity of what was happening.

"I don't really think they'll bother," he said. "It'll mean a new house for Aunt Tattie." He opened the door into the hall for her. Here again soldiers were waiting, and more at the top of the stairs. He led her past the sitting room. It was incredible to think that only days ago he had sat in there with Paul von Hassell, playing chess, and now Paul was out there... He slapped his hands together. "Von Hassell knew this was going to happen."

"What?"

They climbed the next flight of stairs, and John opened the door to the storeroom; the three soldiers inside looked round at them. "We've come for some candles," he explained, pointing at the cupboard in the corner.

They shrugged, and resumed looking at Natasha.

"He knew," John said, opening the cupboard door. "Remember what he said? Trying to get us to move the wedding date forward, or at least to go to Moscow. Trying to get Svetlana to elope with him."

"Give me some of those," Natasha said, holding out her arms. "If he did know, I shall never speak to him again. I shall never speak to any German again."

John placed a row of candles across her arms, and she held them against her chest.

"Don't forget the matches," she said.

He felt deeper into the cupboard. "What an incredible mess," he said, suddenly unable to suppress the thoughts that were tumbling through his mind. "Mother and George are on their way here..." He stopped, looking over his shoulder.

"Well," she said. "Maybe we won't be able to have a big

wedding, here in Russia, but we are certainly going to get married. Aren't we?"

"You can bet your life on that. In fact—" He emerged from the cupboard holding a large box of matches. "—I won't be too sorry to skip the fuss. We can just go to the magistrate and—"

The morning exploded into sound, a series of tremendous roaring wails ending with a crash that shook the entire house and made it seem to rock on its foundations. Plaster came down from the roof and scattered across them, and John discovered he was lying beside Natasha, his arm over her head.

The men at the window started firing their rifles, adding to the din, while from below them the rest of the company also opened fire with rifles and machine guns. The room filled with acrid smell and smoke.

"My God." Natasha sat up. "What was that?"

"Tanks," one of the soldiers said, still firing at an unseen enemy.

"Let's get downstairs," John said. "Don't stand up." He seized Natasha's wrist as she would have risen, pulled her back to her knees. "Put the candles in your pockets."

They were broken anyway. He crammed some into his pocket, beside the matches, and patted her on the thigh. "Stay down." Amazingly, he was not afraid. But then, he did not remember being really afraid when he had been arrested by the secret police in 1932. Then, as now, he had been too concerned with Natasha.

The continuous roaring was suddenly overlaid by an even greater explosion. John was picked up by a blast of hot air and thrown forward. He cannoned into Natasha and she fell as well, rolling through the door to come to a rest against the banisters over the stairwell, which promptly cracked away from her. She gave a despairing scream and John grabbed her ankle just in time to stop her from falling the ten feet to the next floor. With a tremendous effort he rose to his knees, and tugged her back up until she could get her hands onto the stumps of the banisters, and push herself back beside him.

"What on earth . . ."

They looked together at the room they had just left. The entire outer wall had been blown away, and two of the three soldiers had disappeared; no doubt they had fallen out into the yard. The other man lay on his back, staring sightlessly at the ceiling. His face had disintegrated into bloody pulp and blood cascaded from his chest.

"Oh, my God." Natasha slipped so far back into the forgotten ethics of her childhood that she crossed herself.

John continued to stare out at the afternoon, at the huge lumbering tanks that were cutting swaths through the wheatfields, so confident of their opponents' helplessness that the hatches were open and he could see the helmeted heads of the commanders looking out. Behind them there was a swarm of gray-clad infantry, advancing in extended order and every so often raising their rifles and shooting. He could see the flashes without at the moment feeling afraid of them, but a moment later there was a whine and a crash, and a bullet slashed into the remains of the inner wall, bringing down more plaster.

"Come on," he shouted, although Natasha was only inches away. His ears were singing with noise. He grabbed her arm, forgetting the candles which were falling out of their pockets and rolling all over the floor, slid towards the stairs, and saw that they too had collapsed.

"We're trapped," Natasha screamed, and he smelled burning wood.

"Wait." He eased himself over the edge, hung by his hands for a moment, and dropped. "Come on. I'll catch you."

She hesitated, but another wailing crash and a fresh fall of lath and plaster spurred her on. She turned on her stomach and lowered her legs over the edge. He caught her calves.

"Let go," he shouted.

She came down in a rush, sliding down his body to reach the floor, turned, panting, and kissed him on the mouth. "We're going to die," she said. "I know it."

"Like hell we are." He held her hand and ran for the next staircase, which was still intact. "We'll fetch Aunt Tattie and the girls and get the hell out of here." Bending double, they ran down the stairs, reached the hall, looked around them at the destruction, the dead soldiers, and were seized with a sudden thought that they were the only survivors. They ran for the kitchen door, were halted by a shot whining above their heads. They stopped instinctively, dropped to their knees, and gazed at the gray-clad men coming through the door.

* * *

"Madam Nej." Colonel von Spicheren, a tall, spare man with a hatchet face and a monocle, spoke perfect Russian. "This is a great honor. I saw you dance in Berlin in 1938. I only wish the occasion of our meeting could have been more pleasant."

Tattie glared at him, and then turned to look at the house, which was now blazing fiercely. The heat spread across the courtyard and scorched their arms and faces. The girls huddled together in horrified amazement; if there had been one thing they had always been certain of, it was that under Tatiana Nej's protection they were safe from everything ugly in the world.

"You have destroyed my house," Tattie said. "That house was given to me by Comrade Stalin himself."

"I am sorry, Madam Nej," the colonel said. "The fortunes of war. But I assure you that one of the farm cottages will be placed at your disposal, and that of your young ladies." He beamed at them. He was pleased. It was the first evening of the invasion, and he had achieved far more than his original objectives.

"A *cottage?*" Tattie said. "And what is to become of us? What shall we do for food? Where are all our servants? The workers from the kolkhoz?"

"Ah," the colonel said. "That I cannot say. I think they have all run off, either into the woods or into Slutsk. They will be rounded up and returned, I promise you. But for tonight I should be delighted if you and your young ladies would honor my officers and myself with your company at dinner. And once the front is advanced, as we intend it will be tomorrow, our administrative forces will move into this area, and you will be properly looked after."

"By tomorrow morning," Svetlana said fiercely, "our soldiers will have killed you all."

The colonel bowed. "In that case, fräulein, you have nothing to worry about. But dare I say that Captain von Hassell asked me especially to look out for you, Fräulein Nej?"

She glared at him, a smaller Tattie.

"Can we not be sent to the Russian lines?" Natasha asked. "We are not soldiers."

"That is something to be discussed with our administrative forces when they arrive," the colonel said. "To be frank with you, Fräulein Brusilova, there *is* no Russian line at this moment. Your people are in full retreat, or are confined to isolated pockets that we intend to surround and liquidate. You will be better off here, I promise you. The young man, of course, will have to join a labor battalion."

"I'm an American citizen," John protested.

The colonel raised his eyebrows. "You have a passport?"

"Of course." John pulled his wallet out of his jacket pocket.

"In that case, Mr. Hayman," the colonel said, "you do not belong here at all. It will be my pleasure to provide you with transport back to an intact railhead, from where you may travel to Berlin, and thence to the United States."

Natasha drew in her breath sharply.

"Of course you must go, Johnnie," Tattie decided. "Ilona will be very worried about you."

John chewed his lip. After all the years of waiting, to be separated from Natasha again, just as they were about to be married . . .

He shook his head. "I would rather stay with my aunt and my fiancée, if you don't mind, colonel."

Colonel von Spicheren shrugged. "I don't mind in the least. But I must tell you that it will not be possible to treat you any differently from the rest, if you do stay."

"Are we, then, to be ill-treated, colonel?" Tattie inquired.

"Of course not, Madam Nej. But naturally there will be some restrictions, and from time to time there may be food shortages. We are in the midst of a great war, which may not end until late in this year . . ."

"Late this year?" Svetlana asked. "It will end long before then, when you have been defeated."

The colonel looked rather tired. "No doubt, Fräulein Nej, but as I say, there may be hard times before then. However, Mr. Hayman, if that is your decision . . ."

"It is my decision."

"Very good. Then you may share the school's billet. And I repeat my invitation to dinner, Madam Nej."

"Oh, we shall accept," Tattie said. "But I must tell you that we shall have to come as we are." Once again she brooded on the burning building. "Over there are all of our clothes, not to mention my piano, and the score of my next production. All gone up in flames."

"Again, my apologies, believe me. But I shall assign a squad of my men to help you make yourselves as comfortable as possible in your temporary quarters."

"We would like some cloth," Tattie said.

"Of course. There will be dry-goods stores in Slutsk."

"You will have to fetch it," Tattie pointed out. "We have no transport."

The colonel sighed, then bowed. "It shall be done, first thing tomorrow. Have you any money?"

"Of course I have no money," Tattie said. "That's all burned up as well. Tell them to give me credit. They know who I am. It will all be repaid. Oh, I am so *angry*." She stamped her foot, then raised it to look at it; mud had seeped over the shoe to discolor the white flesh inside. "Oh... balls to you all," she shouted, and marched towards the cottages. "Come along. There's work to be done. Come along."

John and Natasha brought up the rear. "I'm so glad you decided to stay, Johnnie," she said. "So very glad."


"I suppose," Tattie said, "as soldiers go, he is not so bad."

It was four o'clock in the morning, and they stood outside the cottage to watch the Germans assembling in the yard, preparatory to departing. Having burned all night, the main part of the manor house was now a heap of ashes, and the heat had died. Yet the morning remained close and still, except for the tremendous, all-pervading *sound*, the rumble of hundreds of vehicles warming up their engines for the day's push, the rustle of thousands of men packing their arms and equipment onto their backs. The sound seemed to stretch forever, certainly beyond Slutsk, as far back perhaps as the Polish border, indicative of the immense German force concentrated in this area.

Also indicative of their success was that there was no noise of firing anywhere to the east. The Russians were in full retreat.

The girls had not been to bed. They were all still too excited, and none of them really wanted to bed down in a farm cottage; those surrounding the manor house had stood empty for years, had been used only as storerooms. Besides, the dinner to which Colonel von Spicheren had treated them had not ended until after midnight, and it had been during the dinner that the wireless operator had come in with fresh orders, which required the infantry and the tanks to move out again at dawn. Really, Natasha thought, it was quite exhilarating. She was sorry about the killing earlier, and the burning of the manor house, but in view of her feelings about the Bolshevik state and all it stood for she could not help but feel that everything that had happened, if it led to the downfall of Stalin and his friends like Ivan Nej, was in a good cause. The German soldiers were the nicest young men imaginable, almost apologetic at what they had to do. She hoped not many of them would be killed, that they would win their war as quickly as possible, and make Russia once again a good place to live in.

And far more important than that, what had happened was helping to clarify her feelings about John. She had agreed to marry him, had even taken the lead, but she still wasn't always sure she loved him. And up to this moment she had doubted that he truly loved her, because he had never attempted to make love to her, whereas most of the men to whom she was introduced immediately tried to proposition her, or at least get their arms around her waist. But suddenly even those doubts had disappeared. He had chosen to stay with her, for however long the war took. There was true love. And in his coolness under fire yesterday, he had revealed a side of his character she had doubted was there, a very reassuring side.

If she didn't love him now, she had no doubts at all that she was going to love him, and very shortly.

Now his arm *was* about her waist, and she could rest her head on his shoulder. Yet he still never attempted to touch her breast or her thigh. He was the most perfect gentleman she had ever known. And he would be similarly perfect after they were married, which was a reassuring thought—even if, then, they would both wish more, and they would both have more.

More motor cars roared into the yard, to send more mud splashing. And Colonel von Spicheren was marching towards them, with another officer at his side.

"Madam Nej," the colonel said. "I must take my leave. But the administrative forces have arrived, and I am placing you in the hands of Colonel von Harringen. Madam, I salute you. I hope to see you and your girls on the stage again in the near future."

He saluted, touching the brim of his cap rather than throwing his hand out in front of himself, made a remark to his replacement in German which Natasha, who possessed only a few words of the language, did not understand, and strode toward his command vehicle. The noise became tremendous, as every truck and every tank roared into life. With a tremendous clanking and banging and rumbling the column moved off. For several minutes it was quite impossible to hear anything above the din, then it slowly began to fade, and the girls watched a new series of trucks rumbling into the yard, and a new set of men disembarking. But these were different men. Instead of olive green they wore black, as did Colonel von Harringen. And on his cap there was the emblem of the death's-head.

Natasha suddenly felt John's fingers biting into her arm.

Harringen was staring at Tattie. "Did the colonel address you as Madam Nej?" he asked, his face stiff. It was a large, moonlike face, rising out of his uniform like a pink melon.

"I am Tatiana Nej, yes," Tattie said.

"The dancer?"

"I dance," Tattie said stiffly. "These girls are the members of my troupe. The Colonel placed us in your care."

Harringen was still staring at her. "You are married to a man called Ivan Nej."

Tattie made a face, and nodded. "Yes," she said.

"A commissar."

"Oh, indeed, Colonel von Harringen. He is a commissar."

Harringen turned to his aide. "This woman will be shot," he said. "Sentence is to be carried out immediately."

For a moment Natasha's brain seemed to have gone numb, as indeed had everyone else's, apparently, even Tattie's. They just stared at the colonel, while the noise of the advancing army faded into the morning, and was replaced by the noise of the SS men parking their vehicles and unloading their gear, and the sun, huge and round and red, peeped above the trees of the orchard and brought faces into sudden focus, created a world of light and shadow.

The aide had snapped an order, and two of his men had advanced to seize Tattie's arms.

"Now wait just a moment," John shouted, coming to life.

Colonel von Harringen regarded him coldly. "You must be the American, Hayman," he said.

"That's right," John said. "And Madam Nej is my aunt."

"You are to be deported," Harringen said. "This is a military area, and neutral civilians are not permitted here."

"If you lay a finger on my aunt—"

"As the American is clearly a Communist sympathizer," Harringen told his aide, "he is to be placed under arrest until transport can be arranged for his return to Berlin. See to it."

They were entirely surrounded by black-uniformed soldiers now, and two were seizing John's arms, while he hesitated, unsure of what to do.

"You are mad," Tattie declared. "Stark, staring mad. I am Tatiana Nej. How dare you bring your Nazi methods into my school? I suggest you get through to your superiors and find out from *them* what you have done."

She did not seem the least afraid, obviously because, Natasha thought, being Tatiana Dimitrievna, she refused to believe anything so bizarrely horrible could happen. And she seemed to have won at least the opening skirmish. Having stared at her for several seconds, and been stared at in return, Harringen snapped his fingers.

"Place this woman in solitary confinement," he said. "And get me headquarters on the telephone."

The aide saluted, and Tattie's arms were seized.

"Let go of my mother," Svetlana shouted, pummeling the colonel on the sleeve. He turned violently, and for a terrible moment Natasha thought he would strike her. Then he controlled himself.

"Ah, you will be Fräulein Nej," he said. "Yes?"

"Aren't you going to shoot me too?" Svetlana cried. "Ivan Nej is my father."

Harringen nodded. "Yes," he observed. "But it seems you are to be granted a reprieve, fräulein. On the other hand, you had better be locked up too. See to it, Dieter."

The aide saluted, two more guards were summoned. John made an abortive attempt to free himself, and was thumped in the ribs and forced towards the house, Svetlana behind him. Natasha suddenly realized that she was exposed, standing just in front of the girls, the morning breeze whipping the skirts of her dress about her ankles. She looked over her shoulder; the girls had huddled together, pressing their shoulders against each other, as if by presenting a united front they could avoid catastrophe.

"You are Natasha Brusilova," Harringen said.

Natasha's head jerked back to face him. Amazingly, he was smiling at her.

"I saw you dance in Berlin, fräulein," he said. "You were magnificent."

Natasha opened her mouth, closed it again, and then pulled herself together. If he was an admirer of hers... "You cannot really mean to harm Madam Nej," she said. "She is far more famous than I."

"She is the wife of a commissar, and was once a commissar herself. My orders are to destroy everyone connected with the Soviet regime. I am sorry, but there it is."

"And not Svetlana?" she demanded, her courage growing. He seemed to be quite a reasonable man, only hidebound by his orders.

"Fräulein Nej is engaged to a German officer, who has obtained a special dispensation for her."

"Then what about me? I am connected with the regime."

"Nonsense," Harringen said. "You are a dancer. A great and famous dancer. No one is going to shoot you, Fräulein Brusilova. Of course you are also a Russian, and therefore an enemy of the Reich. But you have with you thirty delightfully attractive girls. I place them in your charge, Fräulein Brusilova. I hold you responsible for their behavior, their obedience."

Natasha glared at him. "In doing what?"

The colonel gave another wintry smile. "In doing what every woman does best, fräulein. I am instructed to set up a military brothel for this district. You and your girls will staff it. Pick out half a dozen—including yourself, of course—to be reserved for officers, and make sure no enlisted man ever gets at them. Your quarters will be assigned to you shortly. Dieter here will see to it."

The words were only slowly sinking into Natasha's brain, they were so hideously incomprehensible.

"A—" She could not frame the word. "Are you crazy?" she shouted. "Do you think those are common girls? They are the best in Russia. They are all great dancers, they are all going to be famous dancers. And you suggest—"

The colonel's gloved hand slashed across her face, sent her reeling into the arms of his lieutenant, blood dribbling down her chin. Her mind went blank for a moment, and she could hardly breathe. She had never been hit like that in her life. Not even Ivan Nej's men, not even Anna Ragosina, had ever hit her, when they had arrested her on suspicion of complicity in the 1932 plot.

"You will address me properly, at all times, fräulein," the Colonel said. Then his tone softened. "You will soon learn. Now tell me this, have you any Jews in your school?"

Dieter had released her, and she found herself kneeling. Slowly she pushed herself to her feet. She opened her mouth, but it was filled with blood, which she had to spit out before she could even inhale properly.

The colonel turned away from her, faced the girls. "Come now," he said. "Are any of you Jews? Did you hear what I said to Fräulein Brusilova just now? You are going to be military whores. You will enjoy that, eh?"

The girls stared at him, huddling even closer together. Someone—probably Lena Vassilievna, Natasha supposed—began to cry.

"But Russian Jews cannot service German soldiers. Come now, girls, step out."

There was another brief hesitation, and then Hannah Jabsky stepped out, holding her hands in front of her as a sort of shield.

"You are a Jew?" Harringen asked.

Her head bobbed up and down.

"But you are not the only one, eh? There are others. Point them out to me. You do not really wish to be a whore, do you? Not a good Jewish girl."

Hannah bit her lip, and then turned to point at two others. They came through the group slowly, holding hands. Like everyone in the troupe they were slender and athletic and pretty. The colonel smiled at them, and Natasha felt her heart constrict. If they were not good enough to be whores, what *could* they be good enough for?

"No others?" Harringen asked.

Hannah shook her head. The two other girls continued to hold hands.

"Very good," Harringen said, in German. "Put them in with

the other Jews and commissars we have arrested, and have the shooting done immediately."

The lieutenant saluted, and the girls stared at him in total mystification as he signaled some more of his men.

Natasha's brain seemed to burst. She gave a long wailing cry and threw herself forward, striking at the colonel with her nails. She thought she had managed to reach his cheeks, but it was only the collar of his jacket as he swayed away from her and caught her hands, while Dieter grasped her waist, allowing his hands to go round in front and squeeze her stomach so that she lost her breath.

Once again she fell to her knees, the morning swinging in front of her, while the three girls were hustled across the courtyard. Hannah suddenly woke up.

"Help us," she said thinly. "Natasha Feodorovna, help us."

The girls seemed to tremble, in unison. But it was only in order to huddle more closely together.

"Help us," Hannah shouted again, her voice fading. Then they were out of the yard and being marched onto the road, to the other Jews and commissars who had already been arrested. Natasha hadn't realized that the SS had been so busy.

Voices were speaking German around her, and now she was dragged to her feet by two soldiers. Each gripped one of her arms, and like John she was being forced towards one of the farmhouses. She twisted her head from side to side, but only caught a brief glimpse of the girls. What was going to happen to her? Undoubtedly she was going to be punished for attacking the colonel. Perhaps she was going to be shot as well. Perhaps...

She came up against a command car, her stomach pressed against its hood, her ankles tripping on its fender. She lost her balance and fell as the men were actually pulling her forward; their grips shifted from her arms to her wrists. Her face banged into the already sun-hot metal, and she jerked it up again, to stare at the colonel. He stood between the two soldiers, who had gone round the other side of the car, still holding her wrists, so that she was flattened across the hood, with her legs hanging down the other side.

"I told you that you are responsible for those girls," the colonel said, once again speaking Russian. "Your own behavior will guide them in theirs. Your own misbehavior will encourage them to misbehave. Therefore we must set an example. Do you understand me, fräulein?"

She stared at him, listened to Lena Vassilievna weeping. So the girls had been brought forward to watch. And now she felt hands on her back and waist, listened to the ripping of material, suddenly felt the morning sun on her back and legs. For a moment she was paralyzed with horror. She was naked before half the German army, and before her own girls. She, Natasha Feodorovna Brusilova, who had waltzed on the arm of Joachim von Ribbentrop himself. She, regarded as one of the finest dancers in Europe, perhaps in the world. She ... she attempted to kick, to hurt whoever it was was standing behind her, and instead had her ankles seized, pulled apart, held close to the ground so that she was anchored there, while at the same moment the men holding her wrists pulled tighter so that she was pressed against the car hood, her skin seeming to stretch. She stared at the colonel's face, half-smiling now, and her head jerked in sheer surprised agony as a thin line of pain suddenly stung her buttocks, for a moment doing no more than that, and then suddenly spread upwards into her belly and groin and downwards into her thighs in the same moment.

Her mouth flopped open even as she told herself that she must not scream. No matter what happened she must not scream; it was simply a matter of willpower. But the next blow caught her before she was ready.

Natasha felt her face being washed, soft hands holding her against a softer bosom. She opened her eyes and gazed at Olga Mikhailovna, who was mopping her face. She opened her mouth, was struck by the soreness of her throat. She had been screaming. She had screamed her lungs dry.

She touched her lips with her tongue, and someone held a glass of water to her mouth. They were all in here, all the girls, in what appeared to be a kitchen. All except for Hannah and the other two Jewish girls, and Svetlana, and John ... and Tattie. Her heart lurched and she attempted to turn, and uncovered the pain.

It had been there all the time, she supposed, but dully, at the back of her not altogether conscious mind. Now it leapt at her, like a series of tacks being driven into her buttocks, dribbling agony down her legs and into her groin. She moaned, and turned away, onto her face, tried to scream as hands touched her cuts, found she could not make a sound, realized they were attempting to help her by rubbing butter into the wounds.

"She cannot speak," Olga said. "My God, she cannot speak."

Natasha inhaled, slowly. Every movement of every part of her body caused a fresh surge of misery. "I can speak," she whispered. "Where . . . where are we?"

"They have put us in this kitchen," Olga explained. "It didn't burn with the rest of the house, remember? They say we can cook for them until our quarters are ready, until we have to . . . to . . ." She sighed.

"I have never been with a man," Lena Vassilievna wailed. "Never. I shall go mad. Natasha Feodorovna, what is to become of me?"

"As you say, you will probably go mad," Natasha said, and with a tremendous effort pushed herself to her knees, to look at them. They looked back. "We must not be afraid," she said fiercely, trying to concentrate, to stop her face from twisting in agony. "So what is to happen to us? We are not going to be shot. We are only going to be made to lie on our backs. We must . . ." She frowned at the expression on Olga Mikhailovna's face and turned her head. Two Germans sat in chairs against the wall by the door, their rifles across their knees. They were smiling at her; apparently they understood Russian.

"You must learn to behave, fräulein," one said. "Otherwise you will be flogged again. After you have been flogged twice, the officers won't want you anymore, and you will have to lie with us, eh? We would like that, Natasha Brusilova. But you would not."

Natasha chewed her lip, because she knew that if she were ever hit across the buttocks with a whip again she *would* go mad. The very thought of it made her want to start screaming once more.

To her horror she discovered that her hands were trembling, and realized that her lips were also trembling. No doubt her entire face was trembling.

The guards had noticed too. Now they were smiling even more broadly as they looked at her. But there was more to their smiles than contempt. They had a great deal to look at. For the first time she realized that she was naked.

Olga Mikhailovna realized it too, and took off her own skirt to wrap around her friend. Natasha shook her head, because Olga's slip really concealed very little, but Olga smiled gently. "I am old and fat," she said. "They will get no pleasure out of looking at me. But Natasha Feodorovna, what are we to do?"

Natasha pulled the skirt close around her shoulders, and felt almost human, even though her legs remained exposed. Then she tried to stand, and the rivers of pain began all over again. She gritted her teeth and forced herself, turning away from the grinning soldiers. If only she could drive away the fear, the horror, the disgust at what was happening! She thought that if she could empty her mind of those emotions, she would come to a very important realization. But for that she needed to be alone, not surrounded by the girls, anxiously watching her, each one at least as terrified and as shocked as she, each one secretly hoping and praying that the great Natasha Brusilova, who had led them through so many dances with such supreme confidence, would be able to extricate them from this catastrophe, tell them what to do, *lead* them.

The kitchen door opened, and half a dozen men wearing fatigue clothes came in and dumped sacks on the ground. They were accompanied by a sergeant, who stood in the middle of the room with his hands on his hips.

"Get to work," he shouted in Russian. "Up off your asses. You're here to work. There are potatoes in those sacks. Cook them. Make potato soup." He waved his arm, and another squad came in, bearing a dozen chickens, their necks already wrung. "And chickens," he said. "Pluck them and cook them. Get on with it."

The girls looked at each other. None of them had actually cooked in her life. And the sight of the dead chickens was already bringing Lena out in a fresh burst of weeping.

"A good meal," the sergeant said, "or I will take the hide of a couple more of you, personally." He stamped from the room, and the door closed.

Natasha suddenly realized that she was hungry. And she wanted to do something, anything, to stop herself thinking.

"Well, come along," she said. "Let's get to work."

\* \* \*

They listened to the ripple of gunfire, looked at each other, and then glanced at the German guards, who merely grinned. They did not speak. They knew that the sound meant that Hannah Jabsky and her friends—their friends—as well as many other men and women, were dead.

And Tatiana Dimitrievna? Was she also tumbling into that pit, her magnificent body riddled with bullet holes? They could not believe that. Tatiana Dimitrievna had been there since any of them could remember. Tatiana Dimitrievna could not die.

They cooked, apparently, only for the officers, who ate in the largest of the farm buildings. The men cooked for themselves, using their own pots and primus stoves in the fields outside the farm yard. The girls also had to serve the meal. Natasha knew she was being a coward, but she could not force herself to serve. She could not face Colonel von Harringen or the man Dieter, who had whipped her. And she knew they would not be content just to be served.

"They kept putting their hands on us," Nina Alexandrovna said. "Oh, it was terrible! They put them under our skirts. And Colonel von Harringen said I was to tell you to put me in the selected six. What did he mean by that, Natasha Feodorovna?"

Nina was excited. She was a pretty little thing, a fluffy blonde with large breasts who would never progress beyond the chorus line, not because she couldn't dance, but because it was inconceivable to have anyone with a figure quite that voluptuous leaping about the center of the stage, unless her name happened to be Tatiana Nej.

Natasha hugged her. The pain was starting to dwindle, and she could think again. "He was paying you a compliment, Nina Alexandrovna," she explained.

They spent the afternoon washing dishes, and then had to settle down to prepare dinner. They listened to distant bangs and crashes, and supposed more people were being shot. But somehow it no longer mattered a great deal. And then, in the early evening, they heard a scream from close at hand, a shout of utter despair, and they recognized the voice.

"That's Svetlana," Olga muttered. "What can they be doing to her?"

There were no more screams.

"Nothing," Natasha said grimly. "They must have told her that Tatiana Dimitrievna is dead."

Now several of the girls were following Lena's example and crying. They were exhausted, and they were frightened, and there was no one to help them. Tatiana Dimitrievna was dead, and Natasha Feodorovna was showing no sign of leadership.

But what can I do? she thought. What *can* I do? Except submit, like the rest of them, and suffer. I will not even be allowed to say good-bye to Johnnie. And having left, will he ever wish to come back to an army whore? Even supposing I survive?

She held a kitchen knife in her hand, and wished to use it, to drive it deep into her own belly, to laugh at them as she died, because she would have escaped them. But she could not desert her girls. And besides, she was too tired, and her bottom hurt. She couldn't think straight. Time enough to consider suicide when she could think again.

They cooked dinner, and served it, and washed up. No one had said anything about where they were to sleep, so apparently it was to be on the kitchen floor. There were no blankets to soften the stone, but at least it was a warm June night, and the guards had been removed from inside the kitchen; the girls were regarded as cowed enough to be left unwatched. "We will just have to lie down as best we can," Natasha told them, and attempted to smile. "At least we are sleeping alone, for the last time, eh?" The officers, and the men on sentry duty outside, had been loud in their ribaldry, reminding them that by tomorrow a house would have been made ready for them in Slutsk, and they could then start on their duties.

Slowly the girls lay down. Natasha decided she would sleep on the outside, nearest the door, but she soon discovered that while it was impossible to lie on her back, it was also next to impossible to be comfortable on her front on the cold stone. She was wondering if she would sleep at all, when the door opened. She sat up immediately, wincing, peering into the darkness, and a flashlight beam played over her face.

"Fräulein Brusilova," said Lieutenant Dieter. "Get up."

She pushed herself up and gave an anxious glance at the girls. None of them would be sleeping yet.

"Come out here," Dieter said.

Natasha stepped out of the kitchen into the burned-out passageway. The collapsed roof had been cleared away, and only the stars shone above her head. When the lieutenant pointed, she stepped away from the building out into the yard. The supper fires still smoldered, but the men had gone, having pitched their tents in the destroyed wheatfields.

"In there," Dieter said, pointing at the cottage being used as an officer's mess.

"Why?" she asked.

He smiled at her; she could see his teeth flash in the darkness. "I wish to talk with you."

She hesitated, then walked in front of him into the darkened doorway.

"Quiet now," he said. "The colonel is sleeping upstairs." He opened a door, shone the beam of the flashlight into a small room. She thought it might be an office, because there was a desk, pushed back against the wall, but no other furniture. A sleeping bag was spread on the floor. "It's a hard floor," he said. "But then . . ." He smiled again. "I shall be lying on you."

She turned sharply, and the flashlight again played on her face.

"If you resist me," he said, "I will flog you again. I will take the skin from your pretty little ass, Natasha. I shall enjoy doing that, just as I enjoyed beating you this morning. Besides, why should you resist me? You will be doing this fifty times a day from tomorrow. I am just going to break you in."

The flashlight held her face, hid his. Blind panic caught at her mind. She wanted only to escape, to be away, to be anywhere but here. And she was going to beg. She knew it, however much she might hate herself.

"I am a virgin," she said.

For a moment the flashlight faltered; he was surprised. "You are Natasha Feodorovna, the famous dancer," he said.

"I am a virgin," she repeated.

"How old are you?"

"I am thirty years old."

"You are thirty years old, you are a famous dancer, you are betrothed, and you are still a virgin?"

She nodded, getting her breathing under control.

He closed the door, gave a brief laugh. "Then I am a lucky fellow. But you need not worry. Since you are a dancer, your hymen will hardly still be intact. I know about these things."

She stared at him, her eyes slowly becoming accustomed to the gloom. For a moment she had thought she might escape.

"Besides," he said, "you must not cry out. It would disturb your boyfriend."

Natasha caught her breath, looked from left to right.

Dieter smiled, and began to unbutton his jacket. "He is not here. But he is right next door, in the coal shed. So you will wish to keep quiet. And I will make a bargain with you. Keep quiet, and please me, and I will allow you to say good-bye to him tomorrow morning, before he leaves. I will even allow you to say good-bye to Frau Nej."

"Madam Nej is still alive?"

"For the moment. But she will be taken to Germany tomorrow. Orders from Dr. Goebbels himself. It seems she insulted the good doctor, when she was in Berlin in 1938. The doctor never forgets. He wished to watch her execution. He is going to hang her, I believe." His jacket was off, and he was carefully laying it across the desk, placing his belt on top of it. His pistol holster shone in the brief gleam of the flashlight, and beside it, an ornately decorated dirk in a sheath which he also wore on his belt. He turned, the flashlight flicking up again to shine on her. "Take off that absurd skirt. I wish to look at you. Again."

It was the word *again* that cleared her mind. Before, there had been only fear, and pain. The knowledge that Tattie still lived, if only for a few more hours, that John was only a thin wall away from her, had added to her confusion. But the word *again* brought back all the horror of the morning. This man had torn the clothes from her body, exposed her to the gaze of the girls and the assembled German soldiers, and had then laid his whip across her back, no doubt smiling as he had done so. Suddenly the understanding she had been seeking all day was vouchsafed to her. Her body ached, but she had become used to that now. Her mind was clear. And she could hate. That was what she had sought, throughout every unending hour. She had always imagined she hated Ivan Nej and Anna Ragosina and all the secret police. Now she knew that she had never even understood the meaning of the word. To hate, one must be prepared to kill, to destroy; otherwise the emotion was nothing more than dislike.

But one must kill successfully, when the moment was ripe. When it could be done to a purpose, and when it could be done without detection. Slowly she released Olga's skirt, shrugged it from her shoulders. She should have lost her virginity years ago. She should have surrendered it to John Hayman, way back in 1932, when they had sat together on a park bench, two innocents who knew nothing more than to hold hands. She supposed they had always remained innocents, despite the years that passed. And now they would never know intimacy with each other, because he would go back to America and she would remain in Russia, perhaps a whore, perhaps a murderer, and . . . she did not know what else.

But she would not simply submit. This man could save his life now only by escorting her back to the kitchen, to her waiting girls. And he was not going to do that. The beam of the flashlight played slowly up and then down her body, hovered at small breast and tight belly, at pubic hair and at the curve of well-muscled thigh.

"I think you are quite delightful," Dieter said. "I too saw you dance in Berlin, three years ago. I thought you were delightful then. I never supposed that I would one day possess you."

You will never possess me, she thought. But she did not speak. If it was going to happen, then it must happen quickly. She could do nothing until he was sated, and relaxed. She knelt on the sleeping bag, and then sat. The beam of the flashlight followed her down.

"Spread your legs," he said.

She stretched her legs, and waited. He removed the rest of his clothing and she realized with something of a shock that it was the first time in her life she had seen a man naked, except for that very brief glimpse of Johnnie himself, when she had been taken down to Lubianka, and hurried past the door of the cell where he was awaiting interrogation. Dieter, with a narcissistic sense of his own beauty, allowed the flashlight to pass down his body before he switched it off, plunging the little room into darkness.

Then she could only wait, and feel. His hands slid over her breasts as his mouth sought hers. She allowed him that, was surprised when he wished to part her lips and take her tongue as well. Surely he could not desire so much. But now his hand was sifting through the hair on her mount, his fingers probing. He would demand even more than she had expected. She attempted to close her legs, received a pat on the inside of her thighs and spread them again. He could not be angered, or he might not relax sufficiently, afterwards.

The preliminaries were over. His body was on top of hers, and she could feel him resting on her thigh. A moment later there came a stab of pain, and at the same time a tremendous filling of her groin. And yet it was surprisingly easy. He worked himself up and down, his body thumping into hers several times while he sought her mouth with his and then left it again, to gasp into her ear. And then to lie still, breathing hard, and a moment later to roll off her and lie on his back beside her.

"That was good," he said. "You are good, Natasha Feodorovna. As good as I had ever hoped. I will come to you again."

She raised herself on her elbow in genuine surprise. She had done absolutely nothing.

His eyes were shut, and he was breathing slowly and evenly. Perhaps he was even asleep. Slowly she pushed herself up and knelt.

"Do not go," he said. "Lie here with me."

There was semen trickling down the inside of her thigh. "I am going to wipe myself," she said. "I will come back in a moment." Her hands slipped gently across the top of the desk, found his coat and the belt, and the dirk in its holster. Very carefully she withdrew it. It seemed to make a terrible scraping sound, but the man lying against her knee did not move.

She turned, still on her knees, threw her leg over his to straddle him, and looked down on him. His eyes opened, just visible in the darkness, and she saw his teeth again as he smiled.

"That is good," he said. "That is good. Lie on me, Natasha Feodorovna."

Natasha drove the dirk through his throat.

Natasha slipped the bolt on the coal shed, opened the door, and shone the flashlight into the interior. John sat up, blinking.

There was coal on his hands and his face, coal on his trousers and shirt.

"Who is it?" he asked.

She turned the flashlight on herself, and only then remembered that she was naked. It no longer seemed important.

"Natasha?" He started to move towards her, and then checked. "Natasha? What have they done to you?"

"I have come to say good-bye," she said.

"Good-bye? But—" He reached for her hand, and she allowed him to take it. She switched off the flashlight. "I don't understand. Natasha. I heard you screaming, I heard the whip, I couldn't see. Oh, my darling . . ."

"Good-bye," she said, and stepped back to close the door.

He blocked it with his shoulder. "Tell me what you are doing."

She shrugged. "I have just killed a German officer. They will certainly shoot me, or hang me, as they mean to hang Tatiana Dimitrievna. I think I am going to kill as many Germans as I can before then."

He drew her close, and she allowed him to feel the knife. "My God," he said, as he also felt the blood on her hand.

"So now I will lock you in again," she said, "and then you will have had nothing to do with it."

"Nothing to do with it?" Carefully he took the knife from her hand. She did not really want to hold it, anymore. "Would it not make more sense to try to escape?"

"Where?" she asked. "Where can I escape?"

"The forest is not far from here. We could get there. We could hide there, until the Russian counterattack. There *is* going to be a Russian counterattack, I am sure of that."

"We?" she asked, turning up her face.

"Did you suppose I would go away, and leave you here?"

Relief started all the way in the pit of her stomach. Sudden joy cascaded through her system. Then she remembered.

"I have just been raped," she said. "That is why I killed him."

His arms held her close.

"Johnnie," she said, "I have just been raped."

"And so you killed him," he said. "I expected nothing less of you, Natasha Feodorovna."

She moved her head back, to look at him in the gloom. She wanted to scream her joy. And then she wanted to weep.

"How can we run away," she said, "without the girls?"

"We'll take them with us."

How enormous was his confidence.

And how inadequate.

"Without Tatiana Dimitrievna?"

"We'll take her as well. Her more than anyone, since she is condemned to death."

Her shoulders sagged. "We do not even know where she is."

"Svetlana knows. She was taken to see her today, as soon as the confirmation of the sentence came through."

She stared at him. "And where is Svetlana?"

"Right next door. There is an outside lavatory there."

She shook her head. "It cannot be so simple."

"It is, Natasha. It can be. If you will it."

He was magnificent. He was everything she had ever dreamed he should be, or could be. She stepped backwards, into the moonlight of the yard, turned to the toilet door, and heard feet behind her. She turned again, and saw the sentry slowly advancing, his automatic rifle thrust in front of him.

"Halt there," he said in German. "Identify yourself."

Natasha sucked air into her lungs, and glanced into the shadows beside her. It was all simple, he had said. If you will it. But she had already killed—she knew she could do that—and he never had, and it was he who held the dirk.

Slowly she formed the words. "Natasha Brusilova," she said.

"The dancer?" The sentry came closer, peering at her naked body, unable to believe his fortune.

"Yes," she said. "Yes . . ."

He was close enough to touch. John stepped out of the shadows, and drove the knife into the soldier's body at the same time as he threw his hand across the man's mouth.

Natasha caught the rifle before it could hit the ground. Suddenly she knew it was going to be all right. They would escape. And she would be married. To a man she could trust completely.

# Chapter 6

JUDITH STEIN WAS AWAKE. SHE HAD BEEN DREAMING OF WALK-
ing down a boulevard before the war, with the chatter of conversation overlaid by the roar of traffic. That had to be before
the war. In the last two years Paris had become a silent city.

It was just past dawn, but still only four-thirty in the morning, and the bedroom was hot, despite the windows left open
all night. The sheet was a storm-swept sea from the folds of
which their legs emerged and then disappeared again like half-
tide rocks. Boris's head was tucked into her shoulder, as he
liked to sleep, and he breathed slowly and evenly.

It was no more than the dawn of another day, in which Boris
would take himself to the embassy, and she would go shop-
ping—a necessary daily occupation, for there was little to be
had, and so she would join the patient, but sullen lines waiting
for bread, or drink a cup of coffee in one of the pavement cafés
and watch the tragically despondent Parisian world go by. She
spent her time in a strange limbo, because everyone knew that
she was Jewish, not least the German soldiers who might share
the café with her. But by virtue of her Russian lover, with his

diplomatic immunity, she was untouchable. It was probably, she reflected, the safest situation she had ever been in during her entire life, except for those few marvelous years when she had sheltered within the protection of George Hayman.

And one day, she supposed, even Paris would regain its gaiety, when the black tide of Nazidom had receded, and she would again hear the hubbub of conversation, and the growl of traffic.

She frowned at the ceiling. It was the growl of traffic that had awakened her. And even the chatter of conversation. Or if not conversation, of shrill comment and barked orders.

She nudged Boris in the ribs. "Boris. Wake up. Something is happening."

"Hm?" He opened his eyes.

"Listen." She sat up, the sheet falling to her waist. "There are troop movements."

"I must see." He scrambled out of bed, reached for his robe, and turned as the doorbell rang. He opened the bedroom door and hurried toward the front of the apartment. Judith also got out of bed, instinctively reached for the dress and underclothes she had carelessly draped across a chair last night. Her heart was sagging into her stomach. She knew what was going to happen next, because it had happened before, because for Judith Stein, it would continue happening, until the day she died.

The group of men filed into the large room and took up their positions in a line along the wall, facing the huge desk with the high windows behind it. Clive Bullen was the last to enter.

He wore a uniform, as did the others, whatever their ages. Most of them he knew by sight, from prewar trade missions, as they knew him, therefore there could be no doubt in any of their minds why they were here, or what they were going to be asked to do. But he would have been here anyway, volunteering. The war had suddenly become a terribly personal matter.

The man seated behind the desk got up, his aides stepping aside to allow him to come into the center of the room. Alone of them all, he wore civilian clothes, somewhat untidily. A gold watchchain drooped from his waistcoat, and his massive head and shoulders seemed to droop, too, from their own sheer weight. An unlit cigar hung from his fingers, was occasionally transferred to his lips as he paused for effect, or was used as a wand, to punctuate his statements.

"You will know," he said, "that yesterday morning the Nazis invaded Russia. I am informed that it is a country you all know well. You will know, therefore, that it is in the grip of one of the most brutish regimes which has ever stalked this earth, a regime which is dedicated to the eradication of all individuality, all personal freedom, in favor of a monolithic system of state control, and a regime which has murdered millions of its own citizens in pursuit of this aim. It is a regime I have opposed from the moment it took office in 1917.

"But gentlemen, I will tell you this, wicked as is the Soviet system, it is a degree better than Nazism. It is now twenty-one months since we took up the burden of resisting Hitler and his minions. In that time we have seen every one of our allies, France and Poland, Belgium and Holland, Norway and Denmark, Yugoslavia and Greece, crushed beneath the heels of the Nazi jackboot. He will never defeat England. But for us to defeat him, unaided—" He paused, and glanced at a large signed photograph of Franklin Roosevelt that hung on the wall, "—remains a long, a daunting task. But now we possess an ally. These are not people to be trusted, and they are not people with whom we would normally wish to associate. But they are people who will defend themselves, and they are strong, and undoubtedly valiant. It therefore follows that we shall fight shoulder to shoulder with them until the Nazi filth is crushed into the ground, and driven from the minds of men. But we must know what is happening there, what they require in the ways of arms and equipment, how determined they are to carry on this fight to its proper conclusion. This is your task. By your knowledge of the people and the language, and by your personal acquaintance with their leaders, you men will be the link between His Majesty's government and that of Joseph Stalin. I know it will be an onerous and at times dangerous task, and I know too that you will be greeted with suspicion and that you will be treated with mistrust. But you will bear with these things, because your country asks it of you. Thank you, gentlemen. Major Bullen."

The others filed from the room. Clive stood at attention until they had left.

"You have a personal interest in Russia, I am told, Major Bullen," Churchill said.

"I have, sir."

"Have you news of her?"

"No, sir. Save that her home lies directly in the path of the invading armies."

"Poor woman," Churchill said. "Poor woman. Your passage has priority. Your ship sails from Bristol in three days' time. I hope you find your Madam Nej. But remember, you have other tasks. God speed you, Major Bullen."

The office was silent. This was not unusual, for those who habitually gathered here. But today was not like any other. Normally, when these men met, it was in an attempt to foresee the future, to control it to their own advantage. This morning the future had overtaken them and their country. Theirs was an angry silence.

The telephone rang. Stalin picked it up and listened. The other person spoke for several minutes. Then Stalin replaced the receiver.

"Grodno has fallen," he said. "And so has Lvov. The Germans have crossed the old frontier and are driving for Minsk."

"Minsk?" asked Michael Nej. "But—"

"Tattie is down there," Ivan Nej said, "with the academy. Is there news of the academy, Joseph Vissarionovich?"

"How can there be news of individuals?" Stalin demanded. "Nobody knows what is happening, except that the Germans are advancing everywhere."

"Individuals do not count, at moments like this," Molotov declared. "And especially individuals like Tatiana Dimitrievna. It is as much her fault as anyone's that this is happening. Her fault and yours, Michael Nikolaievich."

Michael raised his eyebrows.

"You assured us that the Germans wanted peace," Molotov insisted, his harsh voice even more grating than usual. "You said their one desire was to avoid having to consider two fronts when it came to war. Well, you were wrong, comrade commissar."

"I also stated from the beginning, and before you all," Michael pointed out, "that any pact with Germany could never be anything more than a delaying tactic. Germany is our natural enemy, because they have selected us as theirs. We always knew that they would have to be destroyed. Well, they also always knew that, about us. And they have struck first."

"Without warning," Beria said, polishing his rimless spectacles. "Without the slightest indication. This is barbarism."

"Nazi Germany is a barbaric country," Michael said.

"Your intelligence has been at fault, Lavrenti Pavlovich," Ivan said to Beria. "Now, if I were operating the espionage section—"

"You are quarreling like children," Stalin said. The room fell silent again. "The important point is that both Grodno and Lvov have fallen, and on the same day. That is a front of several hundred miles, and my information is that the Germans are advancing all the way from the Baltic to the Rumanian border. That must be the biggest attack in history. We are drowning in a sea of Germans, and you are arguing about whose fault it was, who may or may not have perished. There will be time enough to count the dead, time enough to decide whose responsibility this debacle is, when we have thrown back the Germans. And at the moment we do not seem to be able to do anything about it. Our air force has been destroyed. Our army commanders appear to be suffering from paralysis. Our country is being gobbled. Comrades, we are fighting for our lives, *our* lives, here in this room. I want to hear no more arguments. I want only action."

"I would like permission to go to the Byelorussian front, Joseph Vissarionovich," Michael said.

"To find Tatiana Dimitrievna?"

"And her school. My son is there also."

"Of course. The American. Well, he will have to survive as best he can, Michael Nikolaievich. I cannot waste men, and brains, in fruitless searches for someone who may already be dead. The Germans must be halted, comrades. Now, I know that historically our best defense against an invasion has been our country itself. Militarily, there always comes a time when the aggressor outruns his lines of communications, and that is the moment for the defender to strike. I accept both of those tenets. I also have the most complete faith in the future. I have already had assurance of support from Great Britain—"

"Britain?" Molotov snorted. "Churchill? He hates us. He has always hated us."

"Not as much, apparently, as he hates the Nazis," Stalin said.

"Anyway, what help can the British give to us?" Ivan asked.

"A great deal, in supplies, and also, perhaps, by attacking the Germans in Europe. But that is not all. I have been promised help by the Americans as well. The end of the tunnel is bright, comrades. But it will still be a long tunnel, and it is no use being sure of survival at the end if we drown in the middle. A line must be drawn beyond which we will not permit the Germans to advance, even if it means dying ourselves, gun in hand."

"They will never get past the Urals," Beria said.

The other four heads in the room turned to stare at him.

"They are not going to get past Moscow," Stalin said. "Nor are they going to get the Crimea. Nor are they going to take Leningrad. That is my decision, and it must be our will. But that will still mean sacrificing a great deal of our country, and nearly all of our heavy industry. Lavrenti Pavlovich, I put you in charge of dismantling all of our industrial plants and shipping them to beyond the Urals, and re-erecting them there. It must be done quickly, both to keep the Germans from capturing them or destroying them, and because we cannot afford a break in production. If the German advance is not stopped soon— and there is no sign that it will be—then I wish this task accomplished within two weeks."

It was Beria's turn to stare. "Two weeks? Two weeks to dismantle several hundred plants, transport them, and rebuild them?"

"And get them into production again," Stalin reminded him.

"That is quite impossible."

"I do not wish to hear that word again, Lavrenti Pavlovich. I want it done. You have carte blanche to requisition men— providing they are not of military age—and women, and even children, if you find it necessary. But get the job done."

Beria pulled his ear, but did not reply.

"Now you, Vyacheslav Mikhailovich," Stalin said to Molotov, "your task is to insure that the Japanese do not invade Siberia in support of their German friends. We certainly cannot afford a war on two fronts, even if Hitler imagines *he* can. Offer whatever you have to, but guarantee me peace in the east."

Molotov nodded.

"You have selected certain points on the map beyond which we will not permit the Germans to go," Michael Nej said. "Is that not a dream, Joseph Vissarionovich? If we cannot stop the Germans now, while our armies are still intact, why can we hope to stop them later on?"

"For three reasons," Stalin said. "First, because Leningrad and Moscow and the Crimea are all at the limit of the possible German lines of communication. By the time they reach them, they will be ripe for a counterstroke. Second, because our armies are *not* in full war readiness, at this moment. We must pull them back to regroup them, we must train new armies, and we must bring men from the east, as soon as Vyacheslav Mikhailovich tells us we can. And third, because it must be our *will*. It must be above all the will of our commanders. I will take command here in Moscow."

"You?" they asked together. Stalin had never before commanded in war.

He smiled. "I will keep Timoshenko as my army commander," he said. "Khrushchev can go to the south, with Budenny. A mixture of experience and talent, eh?"

"And Leningrad?" Beria asked. "Leningrad is the most vulnerable of all. If the Finns were to come in on the German side—"

"The Finns *are* in on the German side," Stalin said quietly. "That was part of the report I have just received."

"Then Leningrad is finished," Molotov said.

"Not so. We can hold the Finns," Stalin said. "A good commander can hold the Finns, while preparing the city to hold the Germans as well, if need be. Michael Nikolaievich, I am sending you to Leningrad."

Michael raised his head.

"You have fought a war before, Michael Nikolaievich. You have held on, without proper supplies, with too few men, against an overwhelming enemy. I wish you to do so again. I will give you Voroshilov as your army commander."

Michael looked as if he would like to speak, then changed his mind and merely nodded.

"And I promise you," Stalin said, "that the moment any news is received concerning your son, or Tatiana Dimitrievna, I will let you know. Thank you, comrades. You all have tasks ahead of you. I wish you to get to them immediately."

"You have given no task to me, Joseph Vissarionovich," Ivan said.

Stalin nodded. "Stay, and talk."

The other three gave Ivan a glance as they filed out. Like everyone else in Russia, they both hated and feared his intimacy with the Party secretary.

"I told you this would happen," Ivan said. "I told you from the beginning that it was madness to attempt to deal with Hitler."

"Yes," Stalin said. "And it would seem that you are right."

"Had I been commissar for the NKVD," Ivan said, "I would have found out. I would have brought you dates, times, places . . . this catastrophe would never have happened."

"No doubt," Stalin agreed. "However, that is looking over your shoulder. In time of war the one mistake no man can make is to look over his shoulder. The Germans have seen fit to wage war on us. Well, we will wage war on them. These people of yours, they have been waiting for too long to occupy themselves. Trotsky was nothing more than a rehearsal, in my opinion. And it was successful."

"We lost the operative," Ivan said.

"That must be expected. By the very nature of their operations, they are a suicide squad. Well, now I wish you to put them to work."

Ivan shook his head. "It will be impossible to get them into Germany," he said, "much less to enable them to reach people as securely guarded as Hitler and Göring."

"I am not thinking of assassination, anymore," Stalin said. "We will not win this war by murdering a few people. We will win it by destroying the German armies, by whatever means we have. Now, as far as I can gather, our soldiers are simply melting away whenever the Germans attack. A few are killed, a great number surrender, but an equally great number are reported as missing. What do you think has happened to them?"

"Well—" Ivan began, cautiously.

"They have deserted," Stalin said. "I am also hearing reports that in places like the Ukraine and Byelorussia the people are welcoming the Germans as friends."

"You are thinking of Tatiana Dimitrievna?"

"It would not surprise me. She is far too cosmopolitan. But

I am thinking of everyone—the ordinary people. The Ukrainians have always been an unpatriotic bunch, and the White Russians are not much better. That is why the Germans are advancing so easily, Ivan Nikolaievich. Our soldiers are deserting, and our civilians are fraternizing. This must be stopped. Your people are trained to fight, and kill, and be loyal. You will send them behind the German lines, in groups of two and three. They will have orders to take command of any soldiers who may be hiding there, and of any civilians they require, and to wage war on the Germans—sabotage, murder, anything they can think of."

"The Germans will surely retaliate on the civil population."

Stalin smiled. "Then the civilians will *have* to fight."

"It will be very dangerous," Ivan said. "The Germans will destroy them."

"They will have died like soldiers, which they should have done in the first place."

"But my squad—"

"You can train another squad, Ivan Nikolaievich. In fact, I would like you to commence doing that immediately. But you must not make the mistake of becoming too attached to your people. They are there to be used, and now their country needs them. Do not fail me in this, Ivan Nikolaievich. Send your people to work."

"There is a telegram," Catherine Nej said. She stood by the table and watched her husband, as their daughter Nona, sixteen years old and possessing her mother's broad Tartar features and crisp black hair, waited on the other side. Like everyone else in Russia, they were stunned by the events of the past two days, and they knew that Michael had come straight from the Kremlin.

Michael took the envelope mechanically. His brain was consumed with what lay ahead, with what he must do. And with John's possible fate. "We are to go to Leningrad," he said, "today. So pack your things. You too, Nona. We will put you back in school in Leningrad."

"Leningrad?" Catherine echoed.

He nodded, sat down, slit the envelope with his thumb. "I am to take command of the defenses there. The Finns have come in against us, you know."

"The Finns?" Catherine cried.

"Yes. And Joseph Vissarionovich has some doubts that we will be able to stop the German advance before they have penetrated even deeper into Russia. He wished Leningrad to be made as strong as possible. That is my task."

"But . . . we will not have to fight! Surely the Germans will never reach Leningrad. It is hundreds of miles from the border."

Michael squeezed her hand. "It is not hundreds of miles from the Latvian border, Catherine Petrovna. And the Latvians are Fascists, like the Germans. Nor is it hundreds of miles from the Finnish border. We may well have to fight. But we have fought before."

"When we were young," Catherine said. She gazed at Nona, whose cheeks were flushed with excitement.

"So now we shall fight when we are old," Michael said. "It is not so very different, except that we shall know more and thus make fewer mistakes. This cable is from England. It must be Clive Bullen, inquiring after Tattie. God knows what I am going to tell him."

He scanned the sheet of paper:

DEEPLY SHOCKED BY NEWS AND CONCERNED AT GERMAN CLAIMS STOP HAS MINSK FALLEN STOP PLEASE CONFIRM SAFETY OF TATIANA NATASHA AND JOHN STOP PRESUME BORIS AND JUDITH RETURNED TO RUSSIA STOP PLEASE INFORM ANY USEFUL TASK STOP GEORGE.

"George," he said. "Of course. He and Ilona are on their way to the wedding."

"Where are they?" Catherine asked.

"London." He suddenly snapped his fingers. "Judith! My God, I had forgotten about Judith."

"Boris is a member of the Paris embassy," Catherine said. "Not even the Germans would disregard that. They will be sent home."

"You think so?" Michael drummed his fingers on the table. "George will be able to help. He is a neutral. Yes . . ." He pulled a notebook towards him and began to compose a message: "Minsk under attack. No news on academy. Any information would be gratefully received. Nothing on Petrovs yet but will inform as soon as possible."

"George Hayman will find them," Catherine said. "If anyone can find them, and see that they are safe, George will do it."

Michael glanced at her. He had often wondered just how intimate his wife had been, before their marriage, with George Hayman. Catherine had been his official escort in Russia on the Haymans' first visit following the revolution. Perhaps, like so many women, she had fallen in love with him. George Hayman had that effect upon women. Women who mattered. Women who were capable of summing up a man and knowing which was the best.

But envy of George was a waste of time. Besides, however often he had needed George's help in the past, he needed it more than ever now.

"Yes," he said. "If anyone can find them and bring them out, George will do it." He got up. "Now we must get packed. We leave on tonight's train for Leningrad."

"And you?"

"I am going down to the office to send this telegram, and then I must find out what has happened to the Petrovs."


"My God." Ilona stood at the window of their hotel room, stared at the trees waving gently in the park on this hot, dry day. It had been the best June in years, said the weather experts.

And the most terrible June that had ever been.

George looked from one to the other of the telegrams on the table. His brain seemed to have gone blank. This was to have been a happy time. A family reunion, in Russia. Shades of Starogan, but this time with Michael and himself playing the parts of the elders.

And now . . . he simply had to concentrate. And however traumatic Michael's telegram, the other must be dealt with first. It read:

PRESIDENT HAS DECIDED TO OFFER KREMLIN ALL POSSIBLE MATERIAL SUPPORT INCLUDING EXTENSION OF LEND LEASE STOP IMPERATIVE REQUIREMENTS ESTABLISHED EARLIEST POSSIBLE MOMENT STOP IN VIEW YOUR KNOWLEDGE AND UNDERSTANDING RUSSIAN LEADERS AND AVAILABILITY IN EUROPE REQUESTS YOU UNDERTAKE PRELIMINARY NEGOTIATIONS PENDING ARRIVAL MILITARY

MISSION STOP PLEASE CABLE ACCEPTANCE AND COM-
MENCE IMMEDIATELY WELLES.

There could of course be no question of refusing. But the
quickest way to get to Russia, for a neutral, was certainly to
travel across Europe, and if he was going to do that . . .

"Paul," he said.

Ilona turned her head.

"Young Paul von Hassell. Isn't he virtually engaged to Svetlana? He must know what has happened to them. In fact, he
has probably taken care of the whole thing already."

"Do you think so, George? Do you really think so?" She
came back to sit beside him.

"Of course he has. But I think I'd better stop by and see
him for myself. John is in no danger, of course, but presumably
Tattie and her girls are technically enemies. I wouldn't want
to think of them being sent to a camp or something like that.
I think the sooner I get to Berlin the better."

"I'll pack now," Ilona said.

"Now, sweetheart—"

"I'm coming with you," Ilona said. "Do you really expect
me to sit here in London?"

"No, I don't," George said. "But there are Felicity and
George junior to think about. And yourself. Europe is a pretty
miserable place at the moment. And with this German invasion
of Russia, who can tell where the next eruption might come?
Anyway, I have to go on to Moscow. I may well have to pass
through some militarily affected areas—"

"And if you're going to be killed, you'd rather do it on your
own."

"Now, darling, it just won't be very pleasant. Believe me,
I have no intention of getting shot."

"But you have every intention of acting the war correspondent again. It's in your blood. But at your age, George, really!"

"I'm as fit as I ever was. And this is quite a scoop.
Ilona—" The telephone jangled. He picked up the receiver.

"I have a call for you, Mr. Hayman," said the hotel operator,
"from a Colonel Bullen. Will you take it?"

"Of course. Clive? Where are you?"

"I'm in Bristol," Clive said. "I've been trying to get through
to you all day. Have you heard the news?"

"Of course I've heard the news."

"I mean about Tattie."

"I know she's missing."

"She's a German prisoner," Clive said. "It came over the radio just now, that in the battles before Minsk the famous dancer Tatiana Nej and her entire troupe fell into German hands."

"Thank God for that," George said.

"Thank God? Tattie, a German prisoner?"

"At least we know she's alive. John is with them, you know."

"My God, yes. The wedding! I'd forgotten. George——"

"I'm on my way to Germany now," George said. "I don't know what I can do, but if it's humanly possible I'll get to see her. I give you my word. I'll see them and I'll make sure they're all right."

"Yes," Clive said. "If only there was some way... well... why should they want to keep a troupe of dancers? Is there a chance they could be exchanged?"

"I'll see what can be done," George said. "But you do understand that this isn't the sort of war you and I knew. This just isn't two armies fighting and being nice to the civilians and gallant to the ladies."

"I know that," Clive said. "But still, Tattie—she's as popular in Germany as she is in Russia."

"You're right about that. Leave it with me, Clive. I'll get back to you the moment I find out anything. Where can I contact you?"

"I'll be in Russia," Clive said.

"Russia?"

"Well, now they're in it with us, we're going to give them all the help we can. I've been given a place on the mission we're sending. We leave tomorrow. So I'll be there if you can get her out."

"Yes," George said thoughtfully. "How the devil are you planning to get to Russia with all Europe controlled by the Axis?"

"By the North Pole, I understand, or something like that. Don't worry about me, old man. I'll be there. Just get hold of Tattie."

"If I can," George said. His head turned as there was a

knock on the door. "My busy day. Have a safe trip." He hung up.

Ilona had already answered the door, was holding the telegram in both hands. "Another one from Michael."

"Maybe they've come through the lines." George almost snatched it from her, ripped it open:

PETROV DEPORTED FRANCE WITH REST OF EMBASSY
STOP JUDITH ARRESTED GESTAPO STOP SHE NEEDS HELP
GEORGE STOP MICHAEL.


John Hayman looked down at the man he had just killed, a barely discernible lump in the gloom of the doorway. Then he looked down at his hand. He still held the knife, but the knife no longer gleamed, and his hand was discolored and sticky. And it smelled, an odor he had never known before.

But then, he had never killed a man before. He felt sick.

"Johnnie? Johnnie, are you all right?"

Natasha might have been a stranger. But she was Natasha, and she held the automatic rifle the guard had been carrying.

"We must hurry," she said. "Did you say Svetlana was next door?"

He tried to speak, found that his mouth was full of saliva. So he nodded, and pointed.

Natasha hurried across and bent to examine the bolt. "It's padlocked," she said. "Give me the knife."

"It's—" He wiped his hand across his lips, nearly retched. "It's bloody."

"German blood," she said, and took it from his fingers to work on the lock. From inside the toilet they heard movement.

"Who's there?" Svetlana whispered.

"Me," Natasha said. "And Johnnie. Hush."

"But—"

"Sssh," Natasha said again, and the padlock flew open. She pulled the door wide. "Come on."

"But . . . where are you going?"

"Away from here." Natasha took her hand and drew her into the moonlight.

"Away? But—" Svetlana stared at the dead German, and then at Natasha's naked body.

"It was necessary," Natasha said fiercely. "Johnnie killed him. Now we must escape."

"There's nowhere we can go," Svetlana said. "Besides—"

"Besides, you are in no danger," Natasha said. "Well, we are. Your mother is going to be sent to Germany tomorrow to be hanged. Can't you understand that? Hannah and Rivka have already been shot. And the rest of us are going to be made into whores. Can't you understand that? I . . ." They could hear the air being sucked into her lungs. "I have already been made into a whore."

Svetlana continued to stare.

"So we are going, and you must come with us," Natasha said. "And you must tell us where your mother is."

"She . . ." Svetlana pointed at the house they had just left. "She's in there."

"With the German officers?"

Svetlana nodded, her head bobbing up and down.

Natasha frowned. "Then we will have to kill them all," she said.

"Now hold on a moment," John said.

"They are our enemies," Natasha insisted. "Yours as much as mine, Johnnie. You have killed one of them."

He glanced at Svetlana.

"Did you, John?" she asked. "Did you really kill one of them?"

"I had no choice."

"And instead of just standing here, we should be killing more Germans," Natasha said. Suddenly she was a stranger to both of them. This was Natasha Brusilova, the great dancer, who had always commanded the stage, now commanding a greater stage. "Where exactly is your mother?"

"Upstairs. The back bedroom. That's where I saw her."

"She'll still be there. Now listen to me, Svetlana," Natasha said. "Go to the kitchen of the house, and tell the girls to wake up. Tell them to be quiet, but to be ready to leave the moment we call for them. Can you do that?"

Svetlana hesitated, and then nodded.

"Well, then, stay in the kitchen until we come for you. Now, Johnnie, you and I must rescue Tatiana Dimitrievna."

"In a house filled with German officers?" he said. How

simple it had all seemed, a few minutes ago. Like a boy's adventure story. But that had been before he had blood on his hand.

Natasha knelt beside the dead sentry. "One of them is already dead," she said.

"You . . . you killed him?"

"He raped me," she said, pulling at the sentry's equipment. "He took the only truly private thing I was going to give to you, Johnnie, and stole it from me. I had no compunction about killing him, as you had none about killing this sentry."

"I feel ill, if you must know," John said.

"Understandable," Natasha said. "But in war it is a feeling that must be overcome." She stood up, the four grenades in her hand, and the cartridge belt.

"How did you know where to find them?"

"I have seen photographs of German soldiers," she said. "Do you know how to use the grenades?"

"You pull out the pin, count to four, and throw the bomb at your target," he said. "Sounds simple, doesn't it?"

"If you have the nerve," she said, and held out the knife.

He shook his head. "I won't use that again. I can't. Give me the rifle. I was in the team at college."

She hugged it against her, as if afraid to let it go. "I know where there is a pistol," she said. "Come on."

She led him across the yard, gently opened the door of the house, and stepped into the hall. He stood at her elbow, and she closed the door again.

"Shouldn't we leave it open?"

"There may be another sentry," she said, and opened the door to the office on the left. John waited in the doorway, blinking into the darkness. Natasha went into the room, bumped against a chair and knocked it over. He held his breath, but there was no alarm, and he realized that he was in the presence of a dead man, naked on the floor, his blood a coagulated pool around him. The man who had raped Natasha. Killed by the woman *he* was going to marry.

Natasha turned and pressed the Luger into his hand. "Do not be afraid to use it," she said. "There will be several bullets in there."

"This is madness," he said. "There are too many of them."

"And apart from you, they have only girls to deal with,"

she said. "So they will expect nothing. Johnnie..." She held both his hands, brought him against her. "Johnnie, we must succeed, or we must die. There can be no alternative. You must forget about nice things like surrender and shaking hands and seeing what happens next. You have killed a German. I have killed a German. They will torture us to death if they catch us, just as they will torture Tatiana Dimitrievna if we do not rescue her, just as they will, slowly, kill all our girls, if only with disease. Johnnie, you must not fail."

He sighed, and nodded. "I guess you think I'm not up to much."

She squeezed his hand. "I think you are up to a great deal. I think you are magnificent. It is just a matter of composing your mind, to *do* something. Something dreadful. Something you have never considered doing before. But something that *must* be done. Must, Johnnie, *must*."

"Yeah. I won't let you down, Natasha. I promise you."

They stepped into the hallway, and heard the sound of booted feet on the cobbles outside.

"Christ almighty," Johnnie muttered. "Another sentry."

"I thought there must be more than one," Natasha said.

"He'll find that dead man, and give the alarm."

"So we must deal with him first." She hesitated, and then gave John the automatic rifle and the cartridge belt and grenades. "I will do it. Give me the knife."

"Natasha..."

"Get Tatiana," she said fiercely. "And kill if you have to. And join me here. Give me the pistol, too. Now go."

He hesitated, looked back at her, and cautiously opened the door. The moonlight streamed into the hall and made seeing easier. The German's feet stopped thumping the cobbles, and he asked, "Who is that?"

"A lonely woman," Natasha said, and stepped outside.

John ran up the last few steps, looked around the landing, listened to snoring coming from beyond the first of the doors, saw the rear door, and tested the lock.

"Who is there?" Tattie whispered.

"John," he said. "Wait a moment." He would have to smash the lock with his gun butt. That would make too much noise.

From the yard there came a scream. For a moment he froze, supposing it Natasha, then he realized that it had been the

German. But everyone would have heard it. There was no more time to lose.

"Stand away," he shouted, reversed the rifle, and fired into the lock. It burst open, and Tattie ran out, hair flying.

"Johnnie," she shouted. "Oh, Johnnie."

She was in his arms; behind him a bedroom door opened.

"What is that noise?" asked a voice in German.

John fired over Tattie's shoulder at the door, and the man gave a startled grunt and fell backwards. To his right he heard someone shouting. "Down the stairs," he snapped. He could see Natasha standing in the doorway. She waved her arm and then left, running towards the kitchen and the girls. Tattie was halfway down the stairs when the second door began to open. John fired from the hip, and heard more shouts from within. But the door remained open. He brought up the first grenade, pulled the pin with his teeth, and counted. It was the longest four seconds he had ever known. A man reappeared in the door, wearing only underwear, but armed with a Luger. John threw the grenade at him, hard, a baseball pitcher's throw. The man ducked, but the grenade hit him on the shoulder and spun him round, back into the room. Someone screamed "grenade," and then there was a sheet of red and a rumbling roar. John went blind for a moment, lost his footing, and tumbled down the stairs. Tattie was waiting for him and pulled him to his feet.

"That was magnificent," she panted. "Look!" Her voice had raised. A man had come out of the other bedroom and was looking down at them, holding a pistol. There was a flash and something hit the wall behind him with a tremendous thump. But he was already firing back, searing the top of the stairs with bullets. The man came down the stairs, rolling and bumping, the Luger falling from his hand to the floor beside him. Tattie picked it up.

"I've always wanted one of these," she said.

"Come *on*," Johnnie begged, opened the door, and ran into the moonlight. Instantly a shot from an upstairs window reminded him of how exposed he was, and he ducked back into the shadows, against the wall, Tattie beside him. They watched the kitchen doors open and the girls come streaming out into the moonlight.

"Take cover," he yelled.

Natasha hesitated, looking across the courtyard, and then several shots rang out from above. One of the girls gave a shriek and half-turned before collapsing on the ground, a shapeless mass of white material.

"Oh, God," Tattie said.

The rest had ducked back inside. But they could not get out while the yard was commanded by the men upstairs, and soon the alarm would spread.

"Stay here until you hear the bang," John said. "Then get them out."

"Where can we go?" Tattie said. "The German army is all around us."

"Over the river," he said.

"That swamp?"

"They won't find us in there. And beyond the river is the forest. That's best. Take them there."

From above his head there was more shooting, and now he heard the distant sound of whistles being blown.

"And you?" she asked.

"I'll be behind you. Now hurry."

He went back inside, stepped over the dead body, smelled the acrid tang of burning wood—from the bombed bedroom, no doubt. He fed a fresh clip of bullets into his magazine, ran up the stairs, faced a man coming down, shot him through the chest. Behind him were others; they had left only one officer to command the courtyard. But Lugers were no match for the automatic rifle. He ran towards them, the gun bucking in his hands and becoming red-hot, sweat trickling down his chest. At the doorway he fired again, and the man at the window fell back with a scream. John ran to the window himself, looked down into the courtyard. "Now," he shouted. "Now."

There was the roar of an engine, and a truck crashed into the arched gateway to the courtyard. Men spilled out, half-dressed, but carrying rifles. John had already drawn the pin from the second grenade, and now threw it onto the hood of the truck. A sheet of flame shot upwards, and the archway began to crumble. He watched Natasha and the girls fleeing towards the rear of the courtyard, joined by Tattie. John left the window to gain the back of the house, and faced an unarmed man, clearly one of the officers' servants, standing looking in bewilderment at the carnage about him.

"Don't shoot," he shrieked. "Don't shoot. I'm unarmed."

He was German. And he was in the way. John shot him through the head.

Heart pounding so that it seemed it would smash its way out through his chest, breath coming in great pants, John threw himself from the back door of the house, ran past the pigsties, and saw the open ground beyond. Behind him whistles blew and trucks roared, men shouted, and one or two even fired their rifles. But they assumed that it had to be a counterattack by organized Russian forces, and they were for the moment more concerned with defense than with looking for the girls from the academy. To his enormous relief, the moon slipped behind a cloudbank, and the night was suddenly intensely dark.

His eyes were soon accustomed to the gloom, and he could see the girls in front of him, straggling across the meadow, shrinking away from the cattle who looked at them in patient bewilderment. He forced his feet forward, refusing to think of what he had just done, of anything he had done this night. He was a sports editor, not a soldier. As a youth, he had always enjoyed weapons, had been proud of his ability as a marksman at college, had even briefly thought of a military career, because as the son of a prince, that was his birthright; but as a man, the son of a Russian commissar, he had sought only to remove himself as far away as possible from all conflict except those of little pieces of wood.

And now he had just killed several men, at least two of them in cold blood.

The girls in front of him had halted as they came to the first of the soft ground.

"Ugh," Nina Alexandrovna said. "It's wet and soggy."

"I'm sinking," someone wailed. "Oh, I'm sinking."

"Hush," Natasha commanded. "Be quiet. Johnnie? Johnnie, are you there?"

He panted up to them, felt the mud tugging at his ankles.

"Listen," Tattie said.

Behind them the firing was dying down.

"Yes," John said. "They're realizing they aren't being attacked, after all. Now they'll start to think, and in a little while they'll be looking for us."

"It's going to be dawn in two hours," Natasha said.

"And we'll be here, stuck in the mud," Lena Vassilievna wailed. "They'll shoot us all. I know they will."

"Yes, they will," Natasha said. "They'll shoot us all. So if you don't want to die you'll follow me. We're going to cross the river."

"The river? I can't swim."

"Nor I," said another of the girls.

"Those who can will tow you over. You have no *choice*. Don't you realize that? It's the river or a German bullet. Come on!"

"Natasha Feodorovna is quite right," Tattie said, taking charge. "We have no choice. So you will follow us. I can swim. Those girls who cannot must stay close to me."

"I can swim also," Natasha said.

"And I," Olga Mikhailovna said.

"And I."

"And I."

"There," Tattie said. "There is no need to be afraid. Johnnie?"

"Oh, I can swim," he said. "But I'll bring up the rear."

"Make sure to stay close," Tattie said. Her confidence was as magnificently reassuring as ever, and he knew that she could not yet really have attuned her mind to the fact that she was not, after all, going to be put against a wall and shot. Or perhaps, being Tattie, she had always known the Germans wouldn't make it. Now he walked behind the girls, listening to their stifled shrieks and whimpers as their bare feet sank through the mud to touch submerged wood and stones, watching them huddle ever closer. But soon they were in water to their waists, and pushing themselves out of the mud to float, with more moans and wails. He slung his rifle and swam after them, staying close to two girls who were clinging to each other, gasping and panting.

From behind him he heard the sound of whistles; the shooting had entirely stopped.

And then there came the barking of dogs.

The splashes from in front of him grew louder. The girls had heard the sound too. "Don't stop," he gasped, spitting water. "They can't smell you once you're across here."

Someone shouted: "Help me." The voice wailed through the darkness. John left the two last girls and struck out in the direction of the cry. Dimly in the darkness he saw a hand waving, drove himself forward through the water and reached the girl. He couldn't tell who she was because black hair was all over her face, but he got her under the armpits and pulled her head back to the surface. She turned and struck at him, her arms and legs rigid, stuck away from her as she choked and spluttered, and he realized that she had cramps.

"Easy," he said. "Easy. I'll tow you." He turned her on her back, still holding her beneath the arms, and kicked with his feet, but immediately she gave another roll and a shriek, and her head dipped beneath the surface as she was inhaling. Desperately he jerked her up again; her legs were still rigid, and her arms pounded him with such force that he sank.

When he regained the surface she was several feet away, drifting. He had to force himself through the water again to reach her, and then a moment later his feet hit the bottom, and there were women around him, led by Natasha, dragging him and the girl into the shallows.

"Johnnie." Natasha held his arm as he knelt and retched, trying to drive the water from his lungs. "Are you all right, Johnnie?"

"I'm fine," he gasped. "What about her?"

Four of her friends were carrying her up the bank, laying her on the grass. He crawled towards them as they crouched about her. "She's not breathing."

"Let me get to her," Tattie said, and knelt astride of the silent body, skirts pulled to her thighs as she worked the girl's arms, slapped her chest, pummeled her stomach. And sighed. "My poor girls," she said. "My poor girls."

"Better to drown than to live as a German slave," Natasha said. "We can do nothing for her now, Tatiana Dimitrievna. It is the living we must think of. We must get on. Listen."

Behind them the whistles were coming closer, as were the barking dogs, and now too they could hear the rumble of a truck engine, and a moment later a searchlight cut through the darkness—several hundred yards away, since the current had swept them downstream, but still scorching the riverbank and turning it brightly visible, and moving in their direction.

"Hurry," John said, getting up and pulling Aunt Tattie to her feet as well.

"Where can we go?" asked Nina Alexandrovna. "Where can we go, that they won't find us?"

John looked at Natasha.

"The forest," she said. "They won't find us in the forest."

They reached the first of the trees just as fingers of light began to stream above the eastern horizon. By then the girls were in the last stages of exhaustion; their feet, toughened by dancing, had served them well, but their clothes were shredded by the tangled bushes through which they had pushed their way, their bellies rumbled, and their throats were parched. But for the moment they were safe. John, bringing up the rear to help stragglers along, pick them up where they had fallen, sometimes having to kick and slap them to get them to move at all, had looked back to see the searchlight come to a sudden stop and point at a crazy angle; clearly the truck had approached too close to the water's edge and had sunk in the mud. The sound of the dogs had also dwindled; undoubtedly they would eventually cross the river and pick up the scent, but it was proving a difficult task for men not prepared actually to swim; the nearest bridge was several miles away.

If only he could decide what came next. Now they lay panting under the trees, and ahead of them lay nothing but a forest and swamp in which even a sizable army would get lost. It was unlikely the Germans would pursue them in here. But how would they live? These girls were not pioneers, they were not even peasants. And they were not, regrettably, he thought for the first time, members of the Komsomol. Tattie had decided that her girls were superior to that sort of thing, and they had not even been taught the rudiments of camping. Their world was that of the stage, of greasepaint and cheering audiences . . . and of absolute luxury in which their every physical need was cared for. And his own world had scarcely been one of hardship. He didn't know if he could do what had to be done.

But then, a few hours earlier, he had not known he could kill. And neither had Natasha.

He pushed himself to his feet. "We must keep moving."

They stared at him. Even Aunt Tattie merely blinked. Never had he seen her so disheveled, not even when he and Uncle

Peter had so foolishly tried to kidnap her, back in 1925. Now the magnificent golden hair was matted, the beautiful face was streaked with mud and sweat.

Natasha was the first to get up. She looked little different from Tattie, except that there was mud even in her auburn hair, and she was naked. All at once he realized that during this remarkable night, he had hardly noticed the disturbing fact of her nakedness. He took off his sodden jacket and wrapped it round her shoulders. She seemed almost unaware of what he was doing.

"Johnnie is right," she said. "The dogs will soon be after us again."

"And they will catch us," Nina Alexandrovna said. "They will tear us to pieces."

"They'll not find us in here," John said. "Not if we go deeper in."

"But we'll starve," Lena Vassilievna moaned. "I'm so hungry. Oh, I'm so hungry. My stomach hurts, I'm so hungry."

"I thought it was your feet hurting," Natasha said unkindly.

"My feet hurt too," Lena said. "But not so badly as my stomach."

"That's because you've stopped moving," Natasha pointed out. "If you get up, your feet will start hurting again, and you won't have time to think about your stomach. Come along. Let's—" She stopped speaking, and they all held their breaths and turned their heads, alarmed by the click that seemed to echo through the morning.

John also turned, keeping his hands away from the rifle slung on his shoulder. He gazed at the Russian soldier covering them with his weapon, then at the other three men, one wearing the stripes of a sergeant, who also stood on a slight rise, looking down at them.

"Who are you?" asked the sergeant.

"We are from the academy," Natasha said. "We have escaped the Germans. Who are you?"

"We are from the Ninth Army," the sergeant said. "What is left of it."

"Then we will join you," Natasha said. "We will return to our lines with you."

"Our lines?" sneered the sergeant. "There are no lines, comrade. The Russian armies no longer exist. The Germans have bypassed this forest, because it means nothing to them. They are driving for Moscow. There is nothing we can do, now. And we have not the food to share with civilian refugees. You must find your own way."

"If you abandon us, we will starve," Natasha said.

"That happens, in a war," the sergeant said, and turned away.

Natasha glanced at John, who stared at the sergeant in indecision. To kill Germans was one thing. To fight Russian soldiers for some scraps of bread was another, even if they dared risk the noise.

"Wait," Tattie said, getting up. The men frowned at her. John supposed not one of them had ever seen quite so commanding a figure of a woman, even in her current state of dishevelment.

"I am Tatiana Nej," Tattie said. "You will take your orders from me, comrade sergeant."

"Comrade Nej?" The sergeant peered at her. But he would certainly have seen her photograph.

"Comrade Nej." Tattie added, for good measure, "My husband is Commissar Ivan Nej, deputy commissar for internal security, and my brother-in-law is Commissar Michael Nej, deputy chairman of the Communist Party. You will take your orders from me, comrade sergeant."

The sergeant hesitated, glancing from left to right. "We have no food," he mumbled. "We can only hope to survive by ourselves."

"Nonsense," Tattie said. "You will find it easier to survive, with pretty girls to keep you company. We will come with you, comrades. Together we will form our own army, here in the forest."

# Chapter 7

"WE CANNOT STAY HERE," THE SERGEANT POINTED OUT. "IT'S too close to the river, and the Germans will certainly come after you."

"Look at my girls," Tattie said. They were scattered everywhere, lying on the muddy earth, too exhausted to care about their appearance, even if it was by now broad daylight. "They need food and water."

"There is none here, comrade commissar," the sergeant said. "Further into the forest..." He shrugged. "There is a little food. And a clear stream."

"Then we must go there," Tattie decided. "How far is it?"

Another shrug, as he looked over the girls. "Five miles."

"Five *miles?*" Tattie demanded.

"Five miles?" Lena Vassilievna burst into tears.

"It is a big forest," the sergeant pointed out, unnecessarily.

"And we must go into it, to be safe," Natasha said, getting up. The sergeant and his men stared at her naked legs. She did not seem to notice. "Well," she said. "Come along."

They tramped through the forest, led by the sergeant, with Tattie just behind him. After them the girls straggled, gasping and moaning as they tripped over fallen branches and exposed roots, stepped into soft earth or upon sharp twigs. The three soldiers walked with them, eager to assist, arms around waists, fingers sliding over buttocks and even breasts. It occurred to John, bringing up the rear beside Natasha, that the fate of these girls was inevitable, whether it came in the person of Germans or of their own countrymen.

"I think we may have a problem," he said. He was desperate to converse with her, regain something of their earlier mental intimacy, because he suspected that all other intimacy had slipped away, with the dead German officer on the office floor, the two dead sentries. It was going to be very difficult to regain.

"I am considering that," Natasha said. "It is all a matter of how long we must spend in this forest. How soon the Russian armies come back to us. I should like your opinion on that."

"I don't know that I'm qualified to give an opinion," he said. "But I don't think they're going to recover for a week or two."

"Then the situation will have to be regularized," she said. "We cannot have any promiscuity. Each man will have to choose one girl, and sleep with her alone."

Her voice was entirely matter-of-fact. But then, he was realizing that her reaction to the entire catastrophe had been entirely matter-of-fact. She had been as afraid as he was, in the manor house, when the tank shells had been bursting all around them. She had been as bewildered as any of them when the SS troops first arrived. But somewhere between her flogging and her rape she had changed. Many a woman would have collapsed completely at so much pain, so much humiliation. But Natasha Brusilova had reacted with anger, and with char-acter. This Natasha was not the girl with whom he had fallen in love. But perhaps this Natasha was a far greater prize, if *he* possessed the character to grasp her. He desperately wanted to say something to let her know that his feeling for her had not changed, but he could think of nothing that would not sound either banal or critical.

So he said the most obvious thing he could think of. "There are only four men," he said. "And twenty-five girls."

"Yes," she agreed, her face suddenly hard, and he guessed she was thinking of the two they had left behind, the crumpled white mass in the courtyard and the sudden white mass on the riverbank.

And perhaps also of the three Jewish girls.

"There will be other men," she said, "who have fled to the forest."

And she was right. After an endless two or three hours, they were led to a clearing in the depths of the forest. Here they were surrounded by some fifty soldiers, leaning against tree trunks, kneeling and sitting, watching the girls with hungry eyes.

"I must have a word with Tatiana, Dimitrievna." Natasha hurried forward. John was glad of the opportunity to sit down himself, to watch the girls quickening their movements as they saw the stream tumbling through the trees. He rested his rifle across his knees and returned the gazes of the men who gathered round him. Their clothes were as mud-stained and disheveled as his own, and not all of them still carried their weapons. They asked no questions. To do that would be to give him the right to ask them where *they* had come from.

Soon they wandered off to watch the girls, who were paddling their tired feet, gathering water in their cupped hands to soothe their equally tortured throats, modesty forgotten as they washed mud and sweat from their hair and their legs.

And soon each was to be allotted to a man, John reflected. For Natasha had been talking to Tattie, and Tattie was summoning the sergeant and the other senior soldiers, who were listening with great interest to what she had to say. In about five minutes, he supposed, there would be an old-fashioned slave market—except that he had an idea that after all that had happened, the girls would not be the least reluctant to be mated, not even Lena Vassilievna.

Then what of John Hayman? He leaned back, looked up through the trees at the sun, just high enough to send its beams slanting through the leaves, creating sudden patches of light and dramatic pockets of gloom. The sky above the trees was almost cloudless, but not empty. A single-engine reconnaissance plane circled up there, only just over the treetops, seeking the whereabouts of the impudent young women who had challenged the might of the Reich. It was difficult to suppose the pilot would not be able to locate them, difficult to believe a

German force would not be here within hours, impossible to convince himself that he could be alive by this time tomorrow. The whole thing was incredible, like a nightmare that refused to end with his own awakening. He was an American, a citizen of a country that had declined to have anything to do with the brutal passions surging across the European scene. He had come here merely to secure his bride. And now he had killed, again and again, and his bride...

He watched her walking toward him, carrying a canteen of water and half a loaf of bread, throwing her long, superbly muscled legs in front of each other, her now-dry auburn hair rippling in the morning breeze, his jacket loose on her shoulders and, as it possessed only two buttons, constantly threatening to flap open and once again expose her beauty. His woman, perhaps. If he dared. But no longer his bride.

She knelt beside him, gave him the bread. "Tatiana Dimitrievna has persuaded them to share their rations. But tomorrow they will have to go looking for food. We all will, I suppose. But it is so good, to be able to think of tomorrow."

He broke the bread in half, gave her a portion, chewed his own, slowly and carefully; only the sight of the food had reminded him of how hungry he was.

"Or don't you want to think of tomorrow, Ivan Mikhailovich?" she asked quietly.

"I want to think of today," he said. "Tomorrow may never come."

She gazed at him for several seconds, while she swallowed the last of her bread. Then she got up. "Yes," she said, and walked away from him into the woods.

He watched her go, uncertain as to her intention, unwilling to intrude on her privacy, if that was what she wanted. But then she stopped, and looked over her shoulder, and in an instant he was on his feet and following her, casting a quick glance over *his* shoulder to see how many more were watching, and then realizing that it did not matter, that nothing mattered anymore, save the essential fact of Natasha and himself, for this moment, and for however many more moments they were to be allowed to share.

Once again she knelt, in the shelter of some bushes, took off his jacket, allowed it to settle on the ground behind her.

He knelt beside her, and her eyes opened. "You must possess

me, Johnnie," she said, "as he possessed me. You must touch
me everywhere he touched me. You must do everything he
did, and be so much better than he was." She saw his hesitation,
and held his shoulders to bring him against her. "It will be
better," she promised. "Because I will help you. Because we
are alive. We are so much more fortunate than those who are
already dead, or those who are only waiting to die. We are
*alive*."

Ivan Nej walked slowly down the corridors of Lubianka.
He spoke to no one, greeted no one. Those of his policemen
he passed saluted and hurried on. They accepted the fact that,
like all the leaders of the Party, he was shattered by the German
invasion, by the ease with which the German armies appeared
able to scatter and destroy the Russian forces, by the sheer
immensity of the catastrophe that had overtaken his country.

And they knew nothing of the true extent of his misery.
Tattie was dead, or at best, a prisoner in the hands of the
Germans. And so was Svetlana. And now he had been ordered
to send Gregory as well to almost certain death. Because he
knew, better than anyone, far better than Stalin, that of all the
republics that made up the Soviet Union, the Ukraine and
Byelorussia were the least willing members, the most likely
to welcome the Germans as friends and deliverers, and thus
the least likely to give any aid to soldiers cut off from the army.
They were far more likely to treat them as bandits, and help
the Germans to their liquidation.

So all those superbly trained young men and women, every
one of whom he regarded as an extension of his own personality, who together would have been able to control Russia in
the course of time, for him and for whoever he decided should
be Stalin's successor—because Joseph Vissarionovich was past
sixty and showing signs of age—were to be sacrificed one by
one, among them his own son.

And he could not even concentrate on their fate. He could
only think of Tattie. There was no way of knowing for sure
what had happened to her. In the case of Tatiana Dimitrievna
almost anything was possible. She might, as Stalin had suggested, have accepted the Germans as once she had accepted
him; certainly she had never been a devoted Communist. She
might be dancing for them now, sleeping with their generals . . .

His fingers curled into fists. However much she had humiliated him, however often she might have left him with a feeling of total inadequacy when he had attempted to make love to her, and however often he had tried to eradicate her memory by using young girls who knew nothing of other men, or who, if they *had* known other men, were far too afraid of the deputy commissar for internal security ever to pretend to anything less than total ecstasy when in his bed, she remained the only woman he had ever truly wanted—wanted for a lifetime.

And Svetlana would no doubt suffer beside her mother, together with Natasha Brusilova and all the others. And John Hayman. But John Hayman, being American, would not suffer at all. John Hayman would be patted on the shoulder and told that he was consorting with bad company and then be sent home. John Hayman, like his insufferable stepfather, was one of those men who would go through his entire life merely being patted on the shoulder.

By the time he reached the lowest of the observation rooms his mood of miserable despair had changed to one of seething anger, bubbling hatred. Hatred of everything he was not, of everything he could not do. He had come down here, as he came down here most days, to look at his prisoner. That there was a prisoner in cell forty-seven was of course common knowledge throughout Lubianka. Presumably even Beria knew of it. But Beria had too healthy a respect for his second-in-command's intimacy with the Party secretary to ask questions or to interfere. If Ivan Nikolaievich saw fit to keep someone in perpetual solitary confinement for the rest of her days, then he was undoubtedly acting on Stalin's orders. What was happening to the prisoner was another taboo subject. That too would be between Ivan Nej and his master.

No doubt, Ivan thought, they would have been totally surprised by the truth. The girl beneath him sat at her table reading a book, from which she was making notes on a sheet of paper. Her black hair was neatly brushed back, and ended in a pigtail tied with a pink ribbon. Her dress was clean and recently pressed, her face and body were healthily plump. In fact she looked a lot less like her mother after two years of captivity, for she had put on weight, despite Anna Ragosina's assurance that she insisted upon regular daily exercise. Only her dead-

white complexion revealed that for nearly two years she had
not seen the sun.

The girl was a delight to watch, and he had managed, over
the past two years, to catch her in every mood, and performing
nearly every aspect of human activity. She was a living, breathing fantasy for him to enjoy. What had happened to her mind,
to her personality, over the past twenty-four months he did not
know. She was, to him, a silent fantasy. At first she had wept
and spent long hours staring at the ceiling of her cell in despair.
But for a long time now she had appeared resigned to her fate,
even contented. No doubt she talked with her jailer, complained
or begged or just passed the time of day. But he preferred not
to ask Anna Ragosina about that. He preferred his silent fantasy.

And now it no longer mattered. Ruth Borodina was as much
a part of the hatred consuming his mind as anything else.
Perhaps more so. She was Peter Borodin's daughter, and Peter
Borodin was as dangerous an enemy as Russia possessed.

The door behind him opened softly. He did not turn his
head.

"The news is very grave, comrade commissar," Anna said.
"I am sorry about the capture of Comrade Nej."

He gazed at her. She, of all the people in Russia, knew
something of the mental hell he endured. But was that not a
reason to hate her more than most? Or was it a reason to admit
her again to her former intimacy? Acting the jailer for two
years must have been just as disagreeable for Anna Ragosina
as it was for Ruth Borodina to be a prisoner.

So now he would end it all. "At least we are out in the open
at last, Anna Petrovna," he said. "Fighting Germans, as nature
always intended us to. Destroying Germans. And all who help
them. I wish that girl to be executed."

"Ruth Borodina? But—"

"Do it as slowly and painfully as you like. I will watch from
here. But it must be done today. You will take photographs
of her when you are finished, and send them to her father."

Anna Ragosina seemed to be having trouble with her breathing. "I had not supposed you would want her to be executed."

"Then you were mistaken. I wish it to be done as soon as
possible. Prepare whatever equipment you will need, then inform me. I will return here to watch." He got up.

Anna Ragosina stood at attention. "No, comrade commissar."

Ivan turned to look at her.

"I will not execute this girl, comrade commissar."

Ivan frowned at her. "You intend to disobey my order?"

"I . . ." Anna licked her lips.

Ivan pointed at her. "You have formed an attachment for her. *You* have formed an attachment for *her*. I have heard that these things can happen. Well, well. Tell me, should I not have you executed beside her?"

Anna's face was pale, save for the pink flow in her cheeks. But she had regained her composure. "It is impossible to be in charge of someone for two years and not become intimate with her, comrade commissar. But I happen to think that there is a better use for her than merely to be killed. You wish to strike at Peter Borodin. Then do as I suggested two years ago, and send the girl back, as a Jew. More, send her back as a Jew who has spent two years with us in Russia. That will destroy your enemy far more surely even than a bullet could, certainly more than the news that she is dead."

Ivan gazed at her. What she was saying was undoubtedly true, yet he hated her more than ever for saying it.

"It will destroy her as well," he said. "They will put her in a concentration camp. Two years' solitary confinement here in Moscow, and then a concentration camp? Is that not a fate worse than death?"

"It will accomplish your purpose, comrade commissar," Anna insisted.

"Yes," he said. "Yes, it will. We will do as you suggest, Anna Petrovna. We will send her back. And afterwards, I will reward you for your loyalty these past two years. I will reinstate you in the squad." He patted her on the shoulder. "We are going to need people of talent, to beat the Germans."

Anna Ragosina opened the door of cell forty-seven, and Ruth Borodina raised her head, quickly and eagerly, to smile her welcome. Her pleasure was genuine. Well, Anna thought, so is my pleasure genuine, at seeing her. Just as my sorrow is genuine, at having to say good-bye.

She had never expected such an attachment to develop, would have laid odds against it, two years ago. And yet, to possess her had been a pleasure. But the very nature of the possession had tended towards intimacy rather than satisfaction. Since she had been unable to vent her feelings by physical brutality, or even such primitive methods of subjection as starvation or inducing sleeplessness, she had been left with only mental and sexual domination as her weapons—without understanding where they were bound to lead.

She had never possessed any close friends at the orphanage. Her dormitory mates had regarded her as too self-contained, and had quickly learned to fear her vicious anger when they had attempted, with girlish innocence, to haze her. In their juvenile pranks she had found *them* puerile. When Ivan Nej had marched her into his bedroom for the first time and commanded her to undress, she had had no idea what he would wish of her, what he would make her do or feel. She had not enjoyed what had happened—it was impossible to enjoy sex with Ivan Nej—but she had gained a rare insight into the power a woman might achieve over a man who wanted her very badly. That had certainly been a pleasure, and it was one she had been able to indulge to her heart's content as chief interrogator of OGPU, glorying in allowing her male victims a suggestion of interest on her part before reducing them to screaming misery with her whips and her pepper. Only with John Hayman had the interest ever been real, and since he had been whisked away from her grasp before she had been able even to touch him properly, she did not know if destroying him would have been a pleasure or a tragedy, or even if she would have been able to do it at all.

And if, for ten years, having John Hayman at her mercy had been almost her only daydream, it had no part in the reality of her existence. As for women, she had always viewed them as nuisances, and after her experiences in the labor camp, when she had been the victim, she had been filled with distaste for her entire sex. The pleasure in molesting Ruth Borodina could only come from witnessing the utter consternation of the girl at what was happening to her.

But there had *been* no pleasure in that. Ruth had certainly resisted, to the best of her ability but uselessly against a woman who was older and stronger and more experienced and also a mistress of unarmed combat. And *Anna,* to her total dismay, had found herself quite unable to force the issue, had been reduced to schoolgirl attitudes such as sulking, refusing to speak, even weeping. For a while she had been bewildered by her emotions, but she had had enough practice analyzing her victims' emotions to be able to view herself with similar detachment. The understanding at which she arrived had been quite shattering: She realized that she was just as much a victim as this girl. In all Russia, in all the world, Anna Ragosina possessed no friend at all. She had long ago lost touch with her brothers; her ability to command lovers, which had helped her ego to sustain itself in Tomsk, had been taken away when she had been recalled to Lubianka. Then she had seen the squad as her life's work and Gregory Nej as a peg on which to hang her emotions—only to have it and him ripped from her grasp, because of this girl.

Suddenly hatred had no longer been sufficient. It might have sustained her had Ruth been a hateful person. But in fact the girl possessed both charm and beauty, added to a pragmatism that she shared with her Aunt Tatiana. Once the initial shock of realizing that she was in prison, and possibly for a very long time, had worn off, she had settled down to make the best of it, and if Anna Ragosina was to be the only human contact she was allowed, then Anna Ragosina would have to be humored. There was no way for Anna to know if Ruth enjoyed physical love; she at least pretended to. She certainly enjoyed conversation and company, and was prepared to accept that a physical extension of such intimacy was necessary, as now, when she put up her mouth to be kissed, gave Anna's hand a squeeze—and immediately took her revenge, as she supposed.

"I have accumulated," she said, tapping her notes, "sufficient evidence to *prove* that your Lenin's politics bear very little relation to Marx's theories. I think I am going to combine all these notes into a book. *That* will pass the time."

Anna sat on the bed. She wondered why she had refused her master's original instructions. It had been an instinctive rejection of something too horrible to contemplate, that *she* should put an end to this vibrant personality, the first human being ever to call her *friend*. But was she not in reality being even more cruel? What would the Germans do to Ruth Borodina? They would starve her, and if she chose to resist them, as she certainly would, she would be flogged. But it was pos-

sible to survive starvation and whips. Anna had done it. Ruth
Borodina could also do it. And in Ruth's case it was even
possible to believe that they might all be wrong, and that Peter
Borodin's standing with the Nazis might be so high, that she
wouldn't suffer at all.

Certainly it was necessary to believe that.

"I have come to say good-bye," she said.

Ruth Borodina raised her head, her eyes suddenly watchful.
For all her composure and her courage, she had lived these two
years in the knowledge that her life continued at the whim of
her captors.

Anna smiled at her. "You are to be set free."

Ruth could only stare.

"You are to be returned to Germany," Anna said. "To your
father."

Ruth's stare turned into a frown, which slowly cleared. "To
Father? I don't understand."

Anna shrugged. "Circumstances change. It is no longer considered necessary to keep you here."

Ruth closed her book. "Free," she said to herself. A variety
of expressions crossed her face—incredulity, uncertainty,
slowly giving way to sheer happiness, a private happiness, a
personal contentment with the turn her life was taking. It was
as quickly replaced by doubt. "You are making fun of me,"
she said. "Cruel fun."

Anna shook her head. "No. You leave today." She hesitated.
"I shall miss you," she said.

Ruth glanced at her, then sat beside her on the bed, put her
arm around her shoulders. "As I shall miss you, Anna Petrovna.
Without you I should have gone mad." She kissed her on the
lips. It was the first time she had ever done the kissing. In her
sudden joy it was possible, Anna realized, that she would even
enjoy making love, might even take the lead there too. An
experience to which she had looked forward for two years.

But it would be meaningless. This girl was no longer interested in her. This girl had never really been interested in
her, never really been her friend. She had been interested only
in survival. She was, after all, a true Borodin.

Well, Anna thought, in a sudden resurgence of her always
latent hatred, let her try surviving the Gestapo.

She pushed her away, got up, and locked the cell door behind herself.

George Hayman glanced around the Tiergarten Station. Except for Dick Conway, who had come to the station to meet his employer, he saw nothing but uniforms. Berlin had been rather full of uniforms the last time he had been there, George recalled; now it seemed to be inundated with them.

But the atmosphere was different. In 1938 this had been an ebullient, confident nation. At the end of June 1941 the ebullience was gone; instead he saw expressions of almost self-conscious bravado. Perhaps it had to do with Germany being at last vulnerable to the RAF; the rubbled evidence that British bombers paid regular visits to Berlin was all around him. More likely, he thought, it was an inability to grasp the enormous implications of the Führer's latest thunderbolt. Every newspaper poster shrieked the amazing German victories and advances of the past week, making incredible claims—one million Russian soldiers already killed or taken prisoner; whole armies swallowed up, with their tanks and their artillery. Presumably the average German found such exaggeration equally hard to believe, and there remained always the *immensity* of Russia, and therefore of the task which had been set the Wehrmacht. If they won, all Europe was theirs, from the Channel to the Urals; but if they lost, what Pandora's box were they opening, not merely for themselves, but for the entire continent?

Bomb damage and headlines apart, though, there was precious little evidence that Berlin was the center of the greatest war in history. It was nearly dusk when he left the station, but no one was paying much attention to blackout regulations, so far as he could observe, and the restaurants along the Unter den Linden were as crowded as he had ever seen them. Perhaps there were a few less cars than usual.

"Gas is difficult to get," Conway agreed in answer to his question. "So are all imported items—coffee, for instance. But there's no food shortage, really, none of the rationing, the total mobilization of the population as there is in England. As a matter of fact, women have been left to get on with the business of being housewives. Do you still think the British are going to win this one, Mr. Hayman?"

"I sure as hell think they're not going to lose," George said, and turned to more immediate matters. "Did you get hold of the prince, and Captain von Hassell?"

"I did, sir, and they both promised to come by your hotel tonight."

But when they arrived, they found Peter Borodin was already there, stamping up and down the lobby. "You're late," he boomed, causing heads to turn.

"Blame the railways. Or the British bombs." George shook hands, let Conway take care of the business of registering him.

"You said it was important," Peter said. "Ilona isn't sick?"

"Ilona's fine," George said, and drew his brother-in-law into the bar of the Hotel Albert. He had expected some embarrassment; he had not seen Peter since Ruth's disappearance. But it was impossible to feel embarrassed about Peter, because Peter so obviously did not feel embarrassed about himself. "Whiskey?"

The bartender was already pouring, and it was Scotch.

"We do not have shortages in Nazi Germany," Peter pointed out.

"I'm glad to hear it. Peter, I want you to do something about Judith."

Peter's brows drew together. "Judith? What have I to do with Judith?"

"A great deal, I thought. For God's sake, you loved her once."

"That was a long time ago."

"And you married her sister."

"That too was a long time ago," Peter said. "Anyway, Judith made her choice when she went off with that fellow Petrov. She always was a revolutionary at heart. Well, let her build a few more barricades in Moscow, and see if it will keep out our tanks."

"Judith isn't in Moscow," George said patiently. "I think she's in Germany."

"Judith Stein, in Germany? That's impossible."

"I wish it were. She was arrested in Paris, as a Jew. I've been to her flat. It's a total shambles. I went to Gestapo headquarters there too, and they merely shrugged. They spoke of Ravensbrück Concentration Camp."

"Judith? My God."

"Exactly," George agreed. "Now, you have a lot of influence here in Berlin. You have to find out exactly where she is, and get her out of there."

Peter stared at him. "Me? Why the devil should I? If she is an enemy of the Reich—"

"For God's sake," George shouted, once again causing heads to turn. "How can she be an enemy of the Reich? By being a Jew?"

"Keep your voice down," Peter said. "There are certain things even visiting Americans do not discuss in public. In case you didn't know, when Judith lived here with her brother ten years ago, she was engaged in Communist activities. They were trying to have themselves elected to the government then, you may remember."

"And *that* is a crime? The word was 'elected.'"

"It is regarded as a crime now," Peter said. "Add to that the fact that she is the common-law wife of a Soviet diplomat— well, I'm not surprised she's been arrested. There is absolutely nothing I could do for her. There is absolutely nothing I would *want* to do for her."

"You—" For a moment George was quite speechless. He looked up, and saw Conway coming toward them, threading his way through the late-evening drinkers with Paul von Hassell at his elbow. Von Hassell looked as handsome as ever, and as flawlessly uniformed and groomed as ever, but his face was unnaturally serious.

"Mr. Hayman." He shook hands. "You are seeking information about Madam Nej, and Svetlana?"

"And John," George said. "And Natasha Brusilova. The entire school, in fact."

"Yes." Paul accepted a whiskey, and sat down. "The news is very bad."

"Well?"

"The school was overrun, as all Russian positions were overrun, by the initial onslaught of our soldiers," Paul explained. "But naturally, since they were ladies, they were treated very well. John, of course, as an American, was invited to leave, but he refused."

"He would never leave Natasha," George said, "or his aunt."

"Perhaps," Paul agreed. "But the fact is that we have received information that the night after their capture, the girls broke out."

"The girls?" Conway asked in surprise.

Paul flushed. "It appears they were led by John Hayman. I'm afraid it really is serious, Mr. Hayman. Your stepson behaved like some enemy commando. He seems to have killed or gravely wounded no fewer than twelve officers and men of the Wehrmacht."

"My God!" George said. "How absolutely—" Hastily he changed what he had been going to say. "—dreadful."

"Quite," Paul agreed. "I am afraid he is in serious trouble. Obergruppenführer Heydrich, who is in overall command of these liberated areas, is very angry indeed. Colonel von Harringen has been relieved of his command. However, there is some hope. I have obtained permission to visit the area, to make contact with them, if I can, and obtain their surrender. Obergruppenführer Heydrich has promised the utmost leniency. I leave the day after tomorrow."

"Where exactly are they now, so far as you know?" George asked.

"They have fled into the marshes. You know, those around the River Pripet. It is a huge area, virtually impenetrable to large bodies of men. It is estimated that they may have linked up with certain army fugitives from the forces we destroyed when we took Slutsk. But the new commander, Colonel von Bledow, has been instructed to leave them alone for the time being. Frankly, with our armies advancing at such a rate, there simply has not been time to deal with these isolated groups that have been left behind by the battlefront. So if I can get to Minsk in time to secure their surrender, it may yet be possible to save the situation."

"Minsk?" Peter Borodin demanded. "I am also going there, next week."

"You are going to look for Tattie?" George inquired.

"Good God, no. I didn't even know she was there. I am going to begin raising a White Russian army, to help the Wehrmacht in destroying the last vestiges of Communism."

"You're not serious!"

Peter looked down his nose at George. "I have never been more serious in my life."

"That will make you a traitor."

"Don't be childish. Don't you suppose that in the eyes of the Bolsheviks I have been a traitor since 1918?"

"I suppose you're right," George said. "But—" He glanced at Paul, and decided it was not a conversation he could continue in present company, especially in view of his coming mission. "What will happen to John?"

"Well, he will certainly have to be deported, but if I can make the point that he felt he was defending the women, well...We Germans are very understanding about attitudes like that. And as I say, I have been promised all the leniency that can be managed, by the Obergruppenführer."

"I hope to God you're right," George said.

"What are you intending to do? I'm afraid I telephoned the Obergruppenführer as soon as I knew you were arriving in Berlin, but I could not obtain permission for you to visit the area, since it is under martial law."

George nodded. "I'll leave it to you, Paul, for the time being. But I'll be around if there's any question of John's being put on trial. Right now I'm going to attempt to have a chat with Herr Goebbels—" He glanced at Peter. "—regarding a friend of mine who's also in trouble. Then I'm off to Turkey and Russia."

"Russia?"

"In time for their surrender?" Peter suggested.

George shrugged. "Could be. I was with the Russian army once before, when it surrendered, remember?" He smiled at his brother-in-law. "But we all survived. I imagine most of us will do so again. Let's have a nightcap."

The train stopped with a jolt, and Judith Stein awoke. Her dreams had been so tumultuous, so immediate, that it now seemed strange to realize that she had been asleep. But her back ached from the hard boards on which she lay, and her head ached from banging on the sides of the cattle car in which she had spent the last week. She was acutely aware that she hadn't brushed her teeth or washed her face in all that time, and that no one in the crowded car had done so either, and that not everyone had been sufficiently able to control their bowels as to be able to wait for the brief and irregular halts when they were allowed out.

At least they were only women, now. The men had been removed the day before yesterday. Or had it been the day before that? Hunger made it difficult to tell time. Indeed, she supposed that but for Michelle, still fast asleep with her head on her shoulder, she should have starved by now. How strange that her life should depend on a woman she had never seen before last Saturday.

The situation had all the ingredients of a classic, unending nightmare. The truly horrible thing was that it was a nightmare she had experienced before. This time she was surely better off. The tsar's policemen, the Okhrana, had torn the door of her bedroom from its hinges, thrown her to the floor and kicked her as they had ransacked the room, dragged her down the stairs and forced her into their truck although she would willingly have walked. The Gestapo officers had merely stared, and spoken quietly. Even when Boris had given a howl of rage and anguish at the suggestion that she would not be allowed to accompany him to Russia, they had been scrupulously polite, had restrained him rather than hit him, had indicated the door through which she should go rather than throwing her through it.

She had asked if she could be allowed to pack some clothes and cosmetics, and they had said no. The Okhrana would have hit her for being so bold. And they had placed her in a motor car, and driven her straight to the railway station and this overcrowded cattle car. It was degrading to be treated so impersonally, so like an animal, but the very impersonality, the anonymity of the crowd, was infinitely preferable to the isolated horror of her arrest by the Okhrana. *They* had taken her before Prince Roditchev himself, Ilona's husband and the tsar's chief of police. Roditchev had held her once before that, and that first time had been stopped by Peter Borodin—what a magnificently noble figure he had been then—before he could lay a finger on her. For four years Roditchev had nursed that humiliation, and when she came before him again, Prince Peter was far away.

So, nothing that had happened this last week—being treated like an animal, having to sleep on bare boards, having to smell other people's sweat and feces and urine—could possibly compare with the horror experienced by a twenty-two-year-old girl, who had never even been kissed with passion, at being stripped by laughing, jeering men, at being caned, at being spread-eagled on a table, and raped, slowly and conversationally, by that same cane. She had spent several weeks in Roditchev's cell, and he had visited her every day, to beat her or to push his cane into her, to torment her in every possible way. She had thought she would go mad, but she had not, just as she did not go mad when the judge pronounced sentence of death on her, or when Prince Peter brought news of her reprieve, or when she realized that the reprieve meant eternal exile in Siberia, or when she saw the mud-filled patch of desolation that was to be her home for the rest of her life, or when she met the criminals and prostitutes who were to be her companions.

So, was she going to go mad now that she had been arrested by the Nazis, and for no other crime than that of her birth?

She would not have supposed so. In fact she kept telling herself that it was quite impossible, that she would certainly survive this catastrophe as she had survived the first. Only this time *seemed* just as bad as the first. Perhaps, she supposed, at fifty-three one is not as resilient as at twenty-three. More important was her feeling that, having gone through such an experience once, Fate had no right to inflict it on her again. During the eight years she had lived with Boris Petrov, she had for the first time in her life known the meaning of the word security. Her pride had made her refuse to marry him, because she had not been able to convince herself that she loved him. And yet she had never worried about the impermanence of such a situation; she never analyzed it at all. Boris was younger than she, he was a Soviet diplomat, and however much she might still believe in the principles of socialism, she retained her hatred of the Soviet system, which had been responsible for the murder of her mother and father. But with all that, he was one of the kindest and gentlest men she had ever met. And he loved her—as much, she suspected, for her reputation as a revolutionary as for herself. But he certainly seemed to find her attractive, just as she found his lovemaking exciting, without ever knowing the ecstasy of George's embrace.

They were comfortable, and that was it. They had *been* comfortable, until last Saturday. The comfort and security had softened her, ruined her for coping with insane surroundings like this cattle car. She had found herself completely inarticulate, her brain numbed by the incomprehensibility of what

was happening, the shock of having her lovely flat invaded,
the fetid intimacy of her moving prison. When they had first
stopped, when the doors had been thrown open and their guards
had thrust in half a dozen loaves of bread and a few pails of
water, she had been incapable of moving, had refused to join
the struggle. Michelle had secured enough for them both, had
insisted she share, and since then had obviously decided that
this graying, middle-aged woman was her special care. She
had no idea who Michelle was, or what she had done for a
living before last Saturday—they had tacitly agreed that questions were out of place until they had some idea of what was
eventually going to happen to them—but she was plump and
obviously good-natured, unmarried, for she wore no rings at
all, and plain, possibly in her early thirties; Michelle was one
of those invaluable personalities prepared to make the best of
the worst of situations.

Judith hoped she would never change, because now the
doors were opening again, and they were being summoned out
to face the day—and their destination, she feared. In front of
them was a gate in a wire fence, and beyond the gate there
were barrackslike buildings surrounding a rough compound,
while over the gate to which they were being directed there
was a large notice with a single word on it—RAVENSBRÜCK.

Judith caught her breath. She had heard of Ravensbrück,
from the women she had helped to leave Germany, before the
war.

The girl was small, dark, and intense. In her severe uniform—white shirt, black tie and skirt, cotton stockings, and
sensible low-heeled shoes—she looked almost like a schoolgirl, but Peter Borodin suspected she was a good deal older
than that. She regarded him with suspicion, but he suspected
that was how she regarded most men.

"Obergruppenführer Heydrich will see you now, your excellency," she said.

Peter nodded and got up, leaving his hat and cane on the
seat, conscious that the other secretaries in the outer office,
men as well as women, were all surreptitiously watching him.
They all knew who he was, of course. Did they also know that
he had come to beg?

He had never begged anyone for anything, in his entire life.

No, that was a lie. He had begged once. In 1911 he had begged the tsar for the life of Judith Stein, and had been granted his request. Now he was about to do the very same thing, but this time there would be no Tsarina Alexandra standing behind a red velvet curtain, to listen, sometimes to condemn, but in the case of the young Prince of Starogan to sympathize with a boy in love, however unwisely.

In the name of God, he asked himself, why? It was possible to reason that even that first time had been a mistake. Had Judith Stein hanged in 1911, she would have always been a tragic memory, of a beautiful and passionate young girl who had got herself caught up in something she did not really understand and could not control, and who had died because of it. Certainly the woman who had returned from Siberia three years later had not been the least like the nervous, idealistic girl with whom he had fallen in love. She had not even seemed grateful to have been returned to the land of the living.

But she had not hanged, and now she was again in dire need of help. But why should he worry about her, out of all the thousands, perhaps the millions, of Jews who had been rounded up by the Gestapo as enemies of the Reich? Zionism was not a matter he had ever considered very deeply. Jews had been regarded as nuisances in tsarist Russia as well. They had so often refused to be Russians first and Jews second, had preferred to live according to their own laws and eat their own food, mingle only in their own communities, marry only their own kind. They had even, from time to time, refused to serve in the army when required to do so. There was no doubt that in a nation such as Nazi Germany entirely dedicated to war, Jews would qualify as, at best, subversives and, at worst, traitors.

He had tried to explain this point of view to George, without success. It was because of George that he was here. That was an admission he would make only to himself. But there it was. It was impossible to refuse George, not because George possessed any real power, not over him, anyway, but simply because to refuse George would be to surrender to the feeling of inferiority which the man invariably created in those around him. How Ilona managed to put up with him for thirty years and more, he had no idea.

"Prince Borodin." Richard Heydrich was the epitome of the state within a state that he had created for his master, Heinrich Himmler, who had in turn conceived it for *his* master, Adolf Hitler. Heydrich was tall, blond, and handsome. His black uniform might have come straight from his tailor. His hands were carefully manicured and his chin was shaven clean. His manners were impeccable. "This is a great pleasure, your excellency," he said. "But of course not an unexpected one. Had you not come to see me, I would have come to see you."

"Indeed?" Peter sat down and accepted a Turkish cigarette. "But of course, you would have a file on her."

"A file?" Heydrich shrugged. "I am going to start one, certainly. But I must confess I never considered it necessary before. No doubt the civil police have a file somewhere, but they will probably have closed it."

"Yes," Peter said. "Well, I suppose it must be nearly ten years since she left Germany. The fact is, Herr Obergruppenführer, that I know this is an imposition, but she *is* my sister-in-law."

Heydrich was frowning. "Excuse me, your excellency, but who is it we are discussing?"

Now Peter frowned. "Why, Judith Stein."

Heydrich leaned back in his chair. "Judith Stein?"

"Of course. She was rounded up in a Paris sweep, last week."

Heydrich nodded. "Indeed she was. She is on her way to Ravensbrück Women's Camp at this minute. Judith Stein. My God! Oh, indeed I have a file on Judith Stein, Prince Borodin. I have always had a file on Judith Stein."

"Yes," Peter said. "I know of her activities and her writings. But I was wondering if—"

"So you have come to me to ask for the release of Judith Stein," Heydrich said thoughtfully.

"Why, yes, I suppose I have. I'd be prepared to answer for her."

"And there was no other reason for your coming here?"

"I wish you'd tell me what you are talking about," Peter said, beginning to feel irritated.

Heydrich smiled at him. "Prince Borodin, I have some tremendous news for you. Your daughter has been found."

Peter sat up straight. "Ruth? You have found her body?"

"She is alive, your excellency. She has been returned to us." He paused theatrically. "By the Russians."

Peter stared at him.

"You had no idea your daughter was in Russia these past two years?"

"Ruth, in Russia? You must have the wrong girl."

Heydrich shook his head. "She is most certainly Ruth Borodin. You will wish to see her for yourself, of course. But she *is* your daughter."

Peter looked from left to right, almost as if expecting to see her sitting in a corner. "Where is she?"

"Well, she is also in Ravensbrück."

"You have sent *my* daughter to Ravensbrück Prison Camp?" Peter asked, his voice deceptively soft.

"May I ask what else I am supposed to do with her, your excellency? By her own admission she has spent two years in the hands of the NKVD. Now, what does that suggest? She is very lucky that I did not hand her over to my people downstairs."

"You are absurd," Peter said. "My daughter hates the Bolsheviks more than I do. They kidnapped her, of course. I have always said she was kidnapped."

Heydrich nodded. "I entirely agree with you, and I apologize for not believing you two years ago. Oh, undoubtedly she is quite innocent of any Russian sympathies. Do you know why I am so sure? It is because when I spoke with her, she did not even know there was a war on. Can you believe it? For two years, your excellency, she has been kept entirely incommunicado, seeing no one but a solitary jailer. Truly the Russians move in a mysterious way."

Peter got up. "I must go to her. I would like an order from you for her release, Herr Obergruppenführer. I can give you my word as a prince that she has been guilty of no crime against the Reich. My God, the poor child. Two *years*, in the hands of those monsters! I must hurry." He snapped his fingers. "The order, Herr Obergruppenführer."

Heydrich continued to lean back in his chair, and to smile. "I'm afraid that Fräulein Borodin will have to stay in Ravensbrück, your excellency."

Peter's brows drew together.

"It has been pointed out to us," Heydrich explained, "by the Russians, I am sorry to have to admit, that your daughter is half Jewish. That is of course within the prohibited degree."

"You are calling my daughter a Jew?" Peter shouted.

"Her mother was a Jew, your excellency. That is an inescapable fact. And you are an important man, Prince Borodin. Shortly you will be leaving for the eastern front, there to commence the recruiting of this anti-Bolshevik army you have promised us. Your background must be irreproachable, your family must be irreproachable, as of course it is, since you are the Prince of Starogan. But you will agree with me, surely, that we cannot carry out our very necessary policies to rid Europe of this verminous race who have poisoned the very air of this continent for two thousand years, and yet make exceptions. There will be people saying, 'But you cannot send *us* to a camp. Look at the Prince of Starogan's daughter. She is Jewish, and she is free as air.' No, no. She must stay in Ravensbrück. Do not fret. I have given orders that she is to be well treated. And Ravensbrück, I can assure you, is infinitely preferable to some other places. As long as she and you behave yourselves, she will come to no harm."

"You are threatening me," Peter said. "You are attempting to threaten me, and you are risking antagonizing me, now, at this very important moment of the war, just when your government needs my aid more than ever. Herr Obergruppenführer, you are making a grave mistake. Suppose I resign, refuse to help you?"

Heydrich shrugged. "Go ahead." Suddenly his lazy manner disappeared, and he leaned forward, his face rigid with passion, energy bursting out of every word. "But I suggest you listen to me first, your *excellency*. As of this moment you are virtually of *no* use to us at all. Your espionage network is finished. You are being sent to the east to rally a Ukrainian army on our side, if you can. Well, sir, I have to tell you that a large number of my colleagues, and my superiors, doubt that you can, or that any force you *do* raise will be worth a damn. So, sir, your importance is nil, from this moment forth. It is up to you to *prove* what you can provide. And it will have to be something very good if you intend to avoid a concentration camp yourself, much less ever be in a position to tell me what I can and what I cannot do." He relaxed, leaned back, and once again smiled at the shocked face in front of him. "But I have said that you may visit her, and I am a man of my word. You may visit Judith Stein as well." His smile became a grin. "You should be pleased that I have put them both in the same camp, Prince Borodin. They will be company for one another."

"Come on, come on." The woman was tall, heavily built, and yellow-haired. She wore a green uniform with a soft peaked cap, and knee boots, and presented an appearance that might have seemed ridiculous to an impartial observer. But the women trailing through the gate were not in a position to be impartial. They were suddenly aware that the woman also carried a short whip, with which she was flicking her skirt. "Come on," she bawled. "Halt there. Halt, you vermin. Halt."

The procession halted before the first building in the compound, not exactly a barracks, Judith decided, because it lacked a roof. But she was determined not to be inquisitive. She had learned that lesson thirty years before, on her way to Siberia. For someone in her position, what would happen would happen. It did not pay to anticipate, but rather to live every moment *as* it happened, waiting patiently for the bad moments to end, enjoying the good moments to the utmost.

So, for the moment, there was no cause for complaint. It was a blessed relief to be out of the cattle car and in the fresh air, and it was a glorious summer's day, warm and sensuous. If she felt dirty and hungry, well, presumably they would soon be fed again, and it might even be possible to have a wash. She studied the guard. The woman had an attractive face; at least it should have been attractive, in the regularity of the features, the pale blue eyes, the mass of waving blond hair. Why, Judith thought, she might almost have been a Borodin; and certainly she had a Borodin-like figure. But there was no nobility in her expression, not even any humanity, as she regarded the women standing before her. There was no particular animosity, either. Basically, Judith supposed, she was as uninterested in them as had been the guards on the train.

But now she was speaking again, her words for a moment incomprehensible. "All right," she was saying, "strip. Come along now, everything off."

They stared at her, and then at the guards, who leaned out of their watchtowers to look at them. But surely . . . They were in the open air, on a bright summer's morning... The woman just wasn't making any sense.

"Are you deaf?" she shouted even more imperiously, her whip flicking her boots now. "I said strip. We're going to wash the muck off you." She seized the nearest woman by the front of her blouse, shook her to and fro. "Take it off."

The woman looked from left to right, and then slowly began to undress. Her fingers released buttons with a faintly desperate air, slid her crumpled skirt past her thighs with a suggestion of disbelief. Judith felt an acute sense of embarrassment. She realized that because of the singularly private life she had lived for so very long she could not remember when last she had seen a woman undress. Probably not since she had nursed the tsarevnas, just before their arrest in 1917. And they had been such healthy, happy young animals, even in captivity, there had been nothing *intimate* about such moments. But for an overweight middle-aged woman to be suddenly naked in the middle of a dusty compound surrounded by watching men, in the bright sunshine... and the woman was no longer alone. They were all taking off their clothes, as rapidly as possible, obeying the most primitive of herd instincts.

Judith was suddenly isolated, and immediately afraid. Her intuition warned her that her one serious mistake would be to stand out from the crowd, to be an individual. Up to now not one of the guards, and certainly not the blonde, had even appeared to notice her, despite her height and, she would have confessed privately, her still considerable attractiveness. She was just one of the crowd, and it was terribly important that she remain that. Desperately she tore at her clothes, felt the hot sunshine on her shoulders and then her back as she instinctively turned away from the light, still waiting for laughter or comment, as she would have received from Roditchev's policemen. But if there *was* laughter or comment it was not aimed at her. There were too many naked breasts and bottoms suddenly on display for anyone, even a woman as statuesque as Judith Stein, to be quickly noticed.

And now they were moving forward, bare feet padding over the dry earth; apparently they were required to abandon their clothes. Michelle was in front now. Judith kept her eyes fixed on the plump shoulders before her. By staring between Michelle's shoulder blades she could limit thought, prevent that normal human urge to know the worst that might happen, from taking control of her brain and thereby inducing hysteria. She could only remind herself that nothing that could happen to her could possibly be as bad as to be in the hands of Sergei Roditchev's policemen.

The sun faded in the same instant as the jet of water hit her face, so hard it almost knocked her over. But the water itself was warm, and deliciously relaxing, and as they were now concealed between stone walls, out of which the shower heads protruded, she could turn and allow it to play over her back as well, to soak the hills and valleys of her body, to drive out the sweat and the smell, even to open her mouth to catch and drink some of the water and relieve her parched throat. She did not suppose that the water was safely drinkable, but she suspected that an upset stomach was going to be the very least of her problems.

When she emerged from the showers she felt almost human, was quite disturbed to discover that once again they were required to stand in line, in the sunshine, watched by the guards, while more uniformed women patrolled up and down. This line was moving very slowly, so that one of the women sank to her knees, only to be forced to her feet again by a bellow from one of the guards.

But humanity and fellowship had been restored. Michelle looked over her shoulder to smile, her initial embarrassment dissipated. Yet anxiety remained, and even grew as they approached the next doorway and heard someone weeping. Once again Michelle turned her head, and this time the smile was gone. Then she was gone too, and Judith faced the door, and listened to a rapid and continuous clicking sound, followed by a low buzz. Suddenly she realized what it was, and instinctively put up her hand to hold her thick, gray-streaked black hair almost protectively, for the door was opening and she was being thrust inside, her feet wading through an enormous mass of hair, brown, black, gray, and yellow, and she saw to her distress that the barbers were men, who grinned at her and commented upon her figure, and held her breasts to pull her into the required position, and assaulted her head with their scissors and then their electric clippers, before turning their attention to her pubes. In a few minutes they had effectively stripped her of her individuality in a way neither the cattle car

nor public nakedness had been able to accomplish, and the fact
that the other women were similarly grotesque was this time
no comfort at all.

The others seemed to share her shame. They didn't look at
each other now, or at the guards, or even at the sky. They
studied the ground between their feet, waited to be ordered into
yet another room, where they were examined by two male
doctors and a dentist. This was the most distasteful and humiliating experience yet, Judith thought, just as it was poten-
tially the most threatening, for at the end each prisoner was
given a colored card, either black, red, or yellow, to be hung
around her neck by a string. They were being labeled.

On emerging from the examination room she found herself
in the compound proper, and in the presence of a much larger
crowd of women, all recently shaved and showered. Another
trainload of inmates must have arrived just before the one from
Paris, she thought. Again the women were divided into three
groups. Those with black cards round their necks were the old
and the obviously ill; they huddled closely together, as if aware
of the danger of their condition. Those with the red cards round
their necks were young or middle-aged, looking healthy
enough, but with no pretensions to beauty; Michelle was in this
group. Those with yellow cards were the young girls and
women who were also pretty or at least had good figures. If
it was possible to dwell on what might happen to the women
with black cards, it was impossible not to be sure of the fate
of those wearing yellow. Judith shuddered, and instinctively
stepped toward those wearing red, only to be halted by a bellow
from a guard and a push on the shoulder. She looked down at
her yellow card in consternation; another push sent her staggering into the ranks of the girls. They caught her, and prevented her from falling, and she heard an incredulous whisper;
"Aunt Judith? Aunt *Judith?*"

Her head jerked, and she stared at Ruth Borodina. She
blinked, because it was impossible to accept what she was
looking at. Ruth was dead, had been dead for two years, surely.
Everyone had accepted that. Her disappearance was just one
more tragedy in the long tragedy of the Steins, who had been
tainted with disaster ever since that afternoon she had accepted
an invitation to tea with the Princess Ilona Roditcheva, and
been sucked within the orbit of the Borodins.

But it was Ruth, and a healthy, well-fed Ruth. Incredibly, she was smiling with joy as she threw her arms round her aunt's neck. "Oh, Aunt Judith. I'm so *glad* to see you." Her head moved back, and she bit her lip at the absurdity of what she had said, and then winced and jumped away as a whip slashed across her back.

"Face front," said the woman, another big, strong woman, with outlandishly hennaed hair curling out from beneath her cap. But she was attempting to smile. "You're the lucky ones," she said. "Oh, yes. There'll be good food for you, and maybe even a drink from time to time, if you behave. So line up and march off. Line up! But not you two." She pointed at Judith and Ruth.

Oh, God, Judith thought. There must have been a mistake about her. And where five minutes ago the thought of being made a prostitute had filled her with horror, now it was actually desirable, if she could be with Ruth.

The guard was smiling even more broadly. "Judith Stein," she said. "And Ruth Borodin." She glanced from the note book in her hand to them again, as if to reassure herself that she had the right women. "Our *special* guests," she said. "The commandant wants to see you two."

Judith's stomach seemed to constrict. At the end, and as had happened to her all her life, she had been singled out, *the* prisoner rather than *a* prisoner.

And this time she had involved Ruth in her misfortune.

# Chapter 8

IVAN NEJ STOOD IN FRONT OF HIS DESK AND SURVEYED THE nineteen young people standing before him. They crowded his office, rigidly at attention, faces severely composed. His people. His creations. He gazed at them for several seconds. He had observed them under all conditions of training, under stress and during joy, when reduced near to tears by exhaustion and despair, and when consumed with the ecstasy of having succeeded.

And he had observed the female members of the squad even more closely than that.

And now he must say good-bye to them, from Anna Ragosina, who returned his gaze, her face as usual a pale mask of intensity, to his son Gregory, standing at the other end of the line, also watching his father, his face a glow of exhilarated anticipation. The poor young fool would go charging off to join his mother and his sister, either in a grave or a Nazi prison camp. Or his brothers, for that matter. There had been two of those, by Zoe Geller, his first wife. One had starved to death during the civil war. The other, Nikolai, had made a name for himself as a chess player, during the thirties. He had never sought to regain touch with his father. No doubt the poor fool blamed *him* for his mother's death; Zoe had also starved, during the terrible days following the Bolshevik takeover in 1917. Nikolai was undoubtedly now in the army. In any event, he was as lost as if he too were dead.

Gregory would wish to follow those senseless examples, and leave his father more alone than ever. That at the least could not be allowed to happen.

He cleared his throat, and the squad came even more rigidly to attention. "As you will know," he said, "during the last few days the armies guarding our frontiers have suffered massive defeats. This is partly due to the surprise of the German assault, the treachery with which they pretended to be our friends up to the last moment. But undoubtedly it is also in part due to the activities of deviationists, anti-Bolsheviks, traitors, both in our armies and behind our lines in general. Either way the result is the same. At the moment the Germans are advancing, and it may be some time before we can concentrate sufficient forces to halt them. This will be done. Never doubt that. The enemy will be defeated. But the sooner they are defeated the better, and we cannot accomplish this until every man and every woman in Soviet Russia is engaged in the fight, is killing Germans, is dying, if need be, for the Motherland."

He paused to search their faces again. Now they were nearly all glowing with anticipation and patriotic fervor. They thought they were being sent to the front. Well, yes, in a way they were.

"It is our task," he went on, "to lead that fight in its purest form. Our armies have been defeated, their units scattered. Many good Russian soldiers have been killed, and many more have been taken prisoner. But many, many more have simply been overrun by the rapidity of the German advance. They are there, comrades, no doubt bewildered and certainly leaderless, hiding in forests and on hilltops, where the Germans have not been able to find them. They are situated behind the German lines, as those lines, like rubber bands, stretch longer and longer, and therefore thinner and thinner, in their drive into our country. Those men must be found and remobilized. They must be led—not back to us here; we have enough—but against the Germans, behind the lines, where they already are. Once we can cut the German lines of communication, their armies will wither away. J. V. Stalin, to our great honor and glory, has decided to allot the fulfillment of this supremely important task to us. To you."

Once again he paused, and discovered that now they were all watching him instead of looking straight ahead. The initial fervor had died, and they were fascinated, unsure of what was coming next.

Ivan went to the wall and unrolled the huge map of western Russia. From his desk he took a blue pencil and roughly drew in the German line as it had been at the last news from the front. He listened to the sharp intake of breath behind him. Since rigid censorship had been imposed from the very beginning of the invasion, not one of them knew that the Germans had advanced so rapidly or on so broad a scale.

"That is not a line of fortifications, of course," Ivan said, "or even of trenches. It represents the area beyond which there are no longer any regular Red army units operating, and up to which the Germans have occupied such towns and positions as they require. But there are many places where the enemy strongpoints can be penetrated by bold and determined men and women, or by groups of such people. I am dividing you into six such groups. Six groups of three. A commander, and two assistant commanders. You will have full authority to lead, to requisition, to destroy, to execute. You will have powers of life and death over those soldiers, and those civilians, you decide are necessary to the fulfillment of your missions. Each group will be responsible for one area, and within limits you will be able to volunteer for your preferred areas." He turned sharply, to face them.

"Before I call for volunteers, I wish you all to be very sure of one thing. You have been selected for these missions because you are the best we have. You have been taught how to kill, how to wage maximum personal warfare, how to be absolutely ruthless. I now wish you to use those qualities to the utmost. You have also been taught, I hope, how to die. Make no mistake, yours is a desperate prospect. In order to give you the authority you require, it is necessary to give you orders signed by me. If you are taken by the Germans with those orders on you, they will see that you die, slowly and unpleasantly. You must be prepared to do so, without betraying your comrades, without betraying those of our people you may already have been able to contact. Do you understand me?"

They gazed at him. Now the last trace of exhilaration had left their faces. And yet they continued to look determined enough. More determined than before. They were conscious of the patriotic greatness being thrust upon them.

"Good," Ivan said. "Now then, the first area is the most dangerous. It is the Pripet Marshes. In the first forty-eight hours of their attack the Germans managed to cross the entire area of Poland occupied by our forces in 1939, and they are now engaged in two great drives, one to the south, aimed at Kiev and the Crimea, and the other to the north, aimed, my comrades, at Moscow itself, and at Leningrad. They do not consider that the Pripet area is suitable for large bodies of troops, and so they have bypassed it. And there large bodies of Russian troops have accumulated, cut off by the destruction of their commands. These are men with weapons in their hands, capable of once more being led. But the Pripet is also the area furthest behind the German lines. It will take you a long while to get there, always with the risk of betrayal or capture. It will also be the last area to be relieved by our armies when we commence our counterattack. And it will not be possible to fly in any equipment so far behind the German lines, what with their present air superiority. Whoever commands the Pripet will have to manage on his own. Or her own." He looked along their faces. "It is also the area where my wife and daughter, and the others of the Nej Academy of Dancing, may be hiding since their dramatic escape from German custody, so it is an area of great personal interest to me. Now, who will volunteer?"

Gregory Nej stepped forward. "I will volunteer, comrade commissar."

Ivan gave a brief shake of his head. "I have already decided on your duties, Comrade Nej," he said.

"But—" Gregory's face flared scarlet.

"I understand your anxiety for your mother and sister, Comrade Nej," Ivan said. "I feel those emotions myself. But for that very reason you are not suitable for such a task. Whoever goes to the Pripet must not be swayed by any emotion whatever except the necessity of destroying Germans. Step back into rank."

Gregory hesitated, glanced briefly to his right, his cheeks still pink, and then stepped back into line. Of all the futile excuses, Anna Ragosina thought. He will not send his son to almost certain death. But he will send the rest of us. He will send me. This is the reward he promised me. Certain death.

Fighting with Tatiana Nej and her foolish daughter. With Natasha Brusilova, whom she had once arrested. If they still lived. And with John Hayman. The realization came as quite a shock. She had forgotten that he had also been at Slutsk with the Nej women. John Hayman, after all of these years. He would be under her command, forced to obey her, to do whatever she wished of him.

In any event, Ivan Nej was looking at her. She was the best he possessed. She stepped forward. "I will volunteer for the Pripet area, comrade commissar," she said.

The train chugged slowly across the Polish plain—or what had once been the Polish plain, and was now the German plain, Paul von Hassell supposed. It was all a part of the dreadful business in which he, with all Germany, was engaged, in the name of the Führer and of the life of the German people.

He believed this utterly. His childhood memories were of his father weeping in despair as his carefully accumulated savings had suddenly dwindled to less than nothing in the disasters of the early 1920s, of being removed from his expensive kindergarten and forced to attend the free school for the sons of destitute parents. His father had recovered. He had been a hardworking man, and he had carefully rebuilt his lawyer's practice and his own shattered finances. But he had not been prepared to forget. "Germany needs a monarchy," he had said. "A strong hand at the helm. If we are no longer allowed to have an emperor, then our president must be more than a figurehead. He must rule."

Herr von Hassell had been one of the earliest supporters of the Nazis, had encouraged his son to follow the star that would restore Germany to her old greatness, restore the German people to prosperity and safety. He had also encouraged him to aim at the top. If he wanted to be a soldier, where other boys his own age might dream of the Wehrmacht or the Luftwaffe, he should go for the Praetorian Guard, the elite, the Waffen SS, the most exclusive fighting force in Germany, perhaps in

the world. And he had been accepted, as much, he suspected,
for his looks—he had been singled out on the first parade as
a perfect example of blond Aryan beauty—as for his talents.
No matter. He enjoyed being handsome, and he enjoyed being
talented. He knew he was that too. He could shoot straighter
and faster, he could comprehend orders and carry them out
more quickly and efficiently than any of his contemporaries.
His name had been mentioned to the Führer himself, and at
the graduation parade, only four years ago, he had been singled
out for conversation by the great man himself, and patted on
the shoulder, and clearly pointed in the direction of advancement.

That such advancement could come only as the result of a
war, and that such a war would have to be fought against Soviet
Russia, had never been in doubt. He, like all his fellow officers,
had been prepared for it, mentally and physically, had accepted
the Nazi line that the Russians were subhuman monsters, incapable of intelligent or critical thought, that the great Russian
artists of the past—Tchaikovsky and Tolstoy, Rimsky-Kor-
sakov and Chekhov—were a phenomenon no longer possible
since the collapse of tsarism, with all talent submerged beneath
the dull and brutish weight of Bolshevik dogma. The conversion
of such an inferior race into a colony of the Reich had seemed
no more than reasonable.

The arrival of the Nej mission in Berlin in the summer of
1938 had changed all that. Without warning, he and everyone
else like him, which meant all of Germany not actually in
Hitler's confidence, had been told that the Russians were not
so bad after all, that in fact the twin totalitarian systems of
Germany and the Soviet Union were the best hope of a prosperous future for Europe, that the real enemies of the Reich
were the democracies, England and France, who were obsti-
nately standing in the way of the expansion of Germany to its
proper ethnic and cultural frontiers. And however confusing
this abrupt about-face might have been, it had been welcome
enough to swallow. Paul supposed he was as brave as the next
man, and certainly as patriotic, but the thought of going to war
with the faceless Russian hordes had filled him with dread.
The democracies, on the other hand, had not really seemed
prepared to fight. And then there had been the Russians themselves. The first he had ever met were the members of that

mission, and he had never known such delightful people. Madam Nej herself had been the epitome of everything that a great and famous artist should be, her dancers had been the equal of any women he had ever seen, both intelligent and charming. And in Svetlana Nej he had found the perfect woman. To have discovered her was the best thing that had ever happened to him, had seemed to make his life complete. And if their happiness had to be marred by the necessity of winning a war against Britain first, even that could be taken in stride, for with that war behind him, and the rapid promotion that success in war entails, his professional life would then be set on the proper path to equal his domestic happiness.

Well, the war had been a disappointment. It was not that he lacked courage, or talent, but he had found it quite impossible to discover within himself the necessary antagonism, the necessary hatred, to command with the relentless objectivity that modern war demanded. He told himself that it would have been far different had it been a real war, with bloody, vicious battles. Then his innate determination to win, to be the best, would have shown itself. But all the armies opposed to the Wehrmacht—the Poles and the Danes, the Norwegians and the Dutch, the Belgians and the French, and even the hated English themselves—had simply melted away whenever the Panzers had been launched into action. Units like the Waffen SS had never had anything more to do than mop up the demoralized remnants of disorganized regiments. He could only pity those enemies. So, where many of his contemporaries had become majors and colonels, he had remained a captain. It had not seemed important, anymore, when compared with the future, and Svetlana.

Then the Wehrmacht had turned east. These police actions, as they were called, against Yugoslavia and then Greece, were not in themselves disturbing, and again hardly to be considered wars, since the enemy, as usual briefly bolstered by the British, ran away whenever a German force approached. But these actions were accompanied by a persistent, swelling rumor, that this was only a tidying up of the Balkan flank, before the real business began, the business for which they had been preparing all their lives. Most of his fellow officers had found the suggestion incredible, with England, however ineffectively, still in the war, and with the nonaggression pact still having eight years to run. To Paul von Hassell it had suddenly made sense. It had fitted into everything the Führer had said or done from his earliest speech; Paul knew nearly all of them by heart. The struggle, the *Kampf*, was not to be won by words and promises. Those were only weapons, to be used as skillfully as possible. At the end of the day, victory went to the side with the most determination to *win*, the most ruthless approach. Liking the Russians had been a politically desirable phase, necessary for one or two years.

So where did that leave Paul von Hassell, and his Russian fiancée? In an agony of indecision he had visited his colonel, and had been reassured. Svetlana Nej was in reality a Borodin, a direct descendant of Russia's oldest princely family. There could be no question of her being either a Bolshevik, even if her mother was a commissar, or of her being a subhuman. As for her being in Byelorussia, directly in the path of any German advance, well, the obvious thing was to try to get her out of there without giving away any secrets, or failing that, to put one's trust in the certainty that no German soldier was going to harm the daughter of Tatiana Nej.

He had been reassured, even if his application for a transfer to one of the spearhead units had been refused. And he was overjoyed when the news came in that the academy had been taken prisoner *en bloc*, and that orders had been given for Fräulein Nej to be sent to Berlin. It seemed that the entire Wehrmacht was uniting to ensure his happiness.

But that was before the catastrophic breakout. He blamed John Hayman. He could not imagine any woman leading such a concerted act of violence. But Hayman, an American with Russian ancestry, son of a commissar himself... this was a man he had liked but never really trusted, because of his apparently bored indifference to the real purpose of life, to any concept of struggle.

And to have taken Svetlana along with him... Of course she would have resisted, and no doubt had been ordered by her mother, who would have been on the side of her nephew. Of all the crazy, blockheaded things to do. Naturally they had been proclaimed outlaws; they had killed German soldiers. He had nearly had to go down on his knees and beg for this position, for this opportunity to attempt to save her. If she could be saved. If she was not already dead, starved to death or drowned in that pitiless swamp into which they had "escaped."

And if she had not already been coerced into committing some unforgivable crime against the Reich.

The train was slowing. He jerked into full wakefulness, and stared at Prince Peter Borodin, sitting opposite him. They had shared this carriage from Berlin for very nearly twenty-four hours, had eaten together and slept together and shaved together, and had hardly exchanged a word. The prince had remained equally preoccupied.

But he had changed, in the two weeks since they had last met, in George Hayman's company, at the Hotel Albert in Berlin. Then he had been as Paul had always known him, alert and aggressive, almost defiant in his response to criticism, as if he had always known that he was pursuing a wrong-headed path, but was determined to do so to the end because it was *his* path. On this trip his shoulders were more hunched, his whole face sagging. Even his clothes, which were as elegant as ever, hardly seemed to fit anymore. In two weeks he had apparently doubled his age.

It was not difficult to decide why, Paul thought. However much he might pretend to have written off his youngest sister and her family for their Bolshevik connections, he could not help but be concerned as to Tatiana's fate. And in addition, after all his rhetoric, his bombast, his fanatical anti-Communism, he was at last embarking upon the task he had always claimed was his ambition, that of raising a new White army to defeat the Reds. And this time there could be little doubt that he would succeed, with the entire armed might of the Reich behind him. And yet, clearly, he was for the first time recognizing what a tremendous responsibility he was taking upon his own shoulders, that of creating another civil war, when the first had been one of the most terrible encounters in human history.

Still, Paul supposed, the prince would have to pull himself together and do a good job. Otherwise he could not imagine Himmler putting up with him for very much longer, even if he was Goebbels's pet; the propaganda minister regarded him as a perfect publicity tool.

Paul smiled across the compartment. "We'll soon be there," he said. "Isn't it remarkable? You would hardly suppose a war

had been fought over this countryside, I suppose because it is
so vast. But also, I think, it's a tribute to the power of the
blitzkrieg. I suppose it is very true that the more terribly, the
more ruthlessly, war is waged, the more economical it becomes, in terms of human life as well as money."

Peter Borodin stared at him.

"And when it is a necessary war," Paul continued, aware
that he was getting himself into a conversational tangle from
which it might be difficult to extricate himself, "—well, this
*is* a necessary war, Prince Peter. You have always said so
yourself."

Peter Borodin sighed, and looked out of the window. "They
shaved her head," he said, half to himself.

Paul's turn to stare. And then he remembered the Jewish
woman they had discussed with George Hayman. An old friend
of the family's, apparently. But nonetheless, a Jew, and mistress to a Communist official, with a record of Communist
agitation herself.

"I know it is . . . well . . . undignified," he said. "But prison
is an undignified business. And when you herd a lot of people
together, there is the risk of lice. We make our soldiers shave
their heads as well," he said, attempting a smile.

Peter Borodin stared at him once again, his face seeming
to close in on itself.

"As soon as the war is over," Paul said reassuringly, "it will
no longer be necessary to keep subversives locked up. It will
not be long now, especially with your assistance."

"Subversives?" Peter asked, again apparently speaking to
himself. "How can she be a subversive? She hates the Bolsheviks as much as I do. I brought her up to that. She cannot
be a subversive."

Paul frowned. "I'm afraid there is no arguing against
Fräulein Stein's record, Prince Peter. She may hate the Bolsheviks, but she is most definitely a Communist. And a Jew."

Prince Peter appeared to have stopped listening. He was
once again looking out the window, as houses began to appear
and the train slowed still more. "They shaved her head," he
repeated. "Heydrich said they would treat her well. And so
they shaved her head, and took away her clothes, and her
makeup, and made her work in the hospital. A girl like that.
My God." His voice almost broke. "To have spent two years

in a Russian prison, and now this." He turned to look at the young man. "The Russians didn't shave her head. The Bolsheviks didn't shave her head. They didn't ill-treat her at all. They just locked her up, gave her books to read."

Paul could only stare at him; he had no idea what the man was talking about. It occurred to him that the prince might be going mad. After all, it was a tremendous strain, he supposed, attempting to found an army out of people who had been subjected to Communist domination for so many years.

And suddenly he was smiling. Paul began to feel definitely uneasy.

"They wanted me," Peter said. "That is what she thinks. They wanted me, and they took her because I was not there. And having taken her, they didn't know what to do with her, so they kept her. For *two* years, they kept her. Can you believe it?"

Paul shook his head. He did not suppose there was anything more tactful than agreement.

"And do you know," Peter said, "despite all, she is happy? She is happy to be among people again. Despite having her head shaved. She is happy to be able to see the sun from time to time. Can you believe it?"

Paul looked out the window in sheer relief as the train pulled into the station.

Peter Borodin suddenly seemed to return to normal. He sat up straight, and buttoned his jacket. "You'll forget what I just said, Captain von Hassell," he commanded. "I am not supposed to discuss the matter with anyone."

"Of course, Prince Peter," Paul agreed, standing up to put on his cap. "I quite understand."

"Do you?" Peter asked skeptically.

They stepped down onto the platform, where Colonel von Bledow waited. Paul was immediately reassured. Bledow was short and stout, and smiled. His entire face seemed to be composed especially for smiling, or better yet, laughing, and seemed constantly on the point of dissolving into isolated chunks of chubby flesh. Now he greeted the prince with a Nazi salute followed by a handshake.

"Prince Borodin," he said. "How good to have you here, sir. I have placed a building at your disposal, with offices and secretaries and everything you may need. But if you require anything more, why, you have but to ask for it." He chuckled, his uniform jiggling on his body. "A Russian army, fighting alongside Germans! I do not believe it, Prince Borodin. I just do not believe it. But I am prepared to try anything once, eh?"

He left Prince Peter staring, and shook hands with Paul.

"And you will be Captain von Hassell, eh? Ah, love, love." He gave a peal of laughter, and then pointed. "Look there."

Paul gazed at the trees that clung to the southern horizon like an enormous low cloud. But he had seen the Pripet often before. He nodded.

"Have you made any contact with them, colonel?"

"Of course not. They are in there, and we are out here. We have neither seen nor heard them since the night they broke out. But I suspect they are being fed by the villagers on the edge of the marsh. I propose to put a stop to that, but military operations against a bunch of dancers...Bah. It would take several regiments to comb through that swamp. No, no, they can stay there and starve, if they choose. On the other hand, captain, if you can entice them out—" He gave a bellow of laughter. "Oh, yes, if you can entice them out, that would be good, eh? You entice them out, captain. You entice them out."

"Mr. Hayman." Stalin came round his desk, both arms extended. "It seems we only meet in times of crisis. But it is good to see you again. Comrade Molotov tells me you are here officially."

"I happen to be on the spot, your excellency," George said.

"Of course." Stalin ushered him to the leather-upholstered couch in the corner, and sat beside him, while Molotov took the chair opposite. "You were on your way to your stepson's wedding. A terrible affair. When I think of poor Tatiana Dimitrievna, a heroine of the Soviet Union, and one of our most important cultural figures, lost in that hell—".

"There is no news at all?" George asked.

"Nothing," Stalin said. "I have asked my deputy commissar for internal security to come in and tell you what steps he is taking." He looked at Molotov.

"He is waiting outside." Molotov got up to open the door for Ivan Nej. "You know Comrade Nej, of course, Mr. Hayman."

"Yes," George said. "I know Comrade Nej." He did not

offer to shake hands with the man he despised more than anyone in the world.

"Sit down," Stalin invited. "Sit down, Ivan Nikolaievich, and tell Mr. Hayman what steps you are taking to discover the whereabouts of Tatiana Dimitrievna."

"I'm doing all I can," Ivan said. "I have dispatched my best agent, a woman called Anna Ragosina—" He paused, looking at George. He was aware that George knew of Anna Ragosina. It was Anna who helped deliver Ilona Hayman into his hands, at Lubianka. "—into the Pripet area. It is a most hazardous mission, you understand, Mr. Hayman. If she were to be captured by the Germans, I shudder to think of her fate. But she has gone with two aides, to make contact with my wife, if possible."

"And bring her out?"

"If that is possible," Ivan said. But his eyes had suddenly hooded in a way George immediately noticed.

"We are fighting a desperate war, Mr. Hayman," Stalin pointed out. "Every day brings news of some fresh catastrophe. Nothing we do seems enough to stop the Germans. Do you realize they are now only a few hundred miles from Moscow?"

"And only a hundred from Leningrad," Molotov put in.

"We are already evacuating the government to Kuibyshev in the Urals," Stalin went on. "I promise you that your sister-in-law, as well as your stepson and his fiancée, will be found if it is humanly possible, but in these conditions it is not possible to foretell what may happen even tomorrow."

George nodded. "The effort you are making here is stupendous. I read your speech, and if I may say so, your excellency, it was brilliant."

"Ah, thank you, Mr. Hayman. Thank you. We shall fight to the last drop of our blood, you may be sure of that." He smiled genially, as ever. "And certainly to the last shell, the last bullet, the last tank, and the last drop of gasoline that you are able to give us."

"There'll be no shortage of any of those," George said. "Although the administration won't be happy to hear that you intend to evacuate Moscow."

Stalin's smile faded into a frown. "I have no intention of evacuating Moscow, Mr. Hayman."

"But if the government—"

"I am sending the various government departments to Kuibyshev, because they are not necessary here. In fact, they would only get in the way. It is even possible that the climactic battle of the entire war will be fought here in Moscow, so I am evacuating all nonessential men and women. The children have already gone. But *I* am not leaving. I will command the defense here myself. And I promise you, Mr. Hayman, that if the Germans take the Kremlin it will be over my dead body."

He spoke so quietly, in such a matter-of-fact tone, that George entirely believed him, and suddenly believed as well that the Germans would *not* take Moscow.

"And Leningrad?"

Stalin's smile was back. "That too will be held, Mr. Hayman. It is in the care of my oldest associate, and yours—Michael Nej."

George nodded. "I'd like to visit there, when I have finished my work here."

"That would be quite impossible," Molotov said. "The Germans are too close. They are already fighting on the outskirts."

"I have been under fire before, Comrade Stalin," George pointed out.

"Why are you so anxious to visit Leningrad, Mr. Hayman?" Stalin asked. "Is it that you wish to see Michael Nikolaievich again?"

"I would certainly like to do that, your excellency. He and I are very old friends. We shared a battle together against the Japanese."

"A very long time ago," Stalin mused.

"But I would also like to see the city again. I spent a good deal of time there before and during the World War."

Stalin nodded.

"And besides," George said. "Before I go home I'd like to see, if I can, some actual fighting between the Soviet forces and the Germans."

"To report to your government on whether or not their Lend Lease is being wasted?" Molotov inquired.

"That certainly," George admitted. "But I'm also a newspaperman, you know, comrade. I have been one all of my life."

"Of course." Stalin smiled. "A first-hand report, by the publisher of the paper himself. Ah, Mr. Hayman, you have the scent of battle in your nostrils. I can tell it. There is another reason for you to go to Leningrad, you know? Boris Petrov is there."

"Boris? Well then . . ."

"His parents live there," Stalin said. "Poor Petrov, his has been an unhappy life. Well, by all means go to Leningrad." He held up a finger. *"After* you have talked with my defense staff and have sent off your lists."

"Of course," George agreed.

"And if you will promise not to get yourself killed," Stalin said.

"I'll do my best."

"Good. Good." He stood up, and the other men stood with him. "Well, then, perhaps you will do me the honor of joining me for supper. It will be a small party."

"It'll be a pleasure," George said.

"Good. I will see you later."

The three of them left Stalin alone in his office.

"It is time for lunch." Molotov looked at George. "And I know you are tired after your long journey. Shall we make a start tomorrow morning?"

"Okay," George said.

"Then you must excuse me. Comrade Nej will see that you are taken to your hotel."

George glanced at the little man.

"That will be my pleasure, Mr. Hayman," Ivan said. "But first, I thought you might like to have lunch with me. We have a great deal to discuss."

George hesitated only briefly. "I'm sure we do," he agreed.

Ivan Nej ushered George Hayman up the stairs to the restaurant. Despite the daily bombing raids by the all-conquering Luftwaffe, and the streets filled with anxious people staring at the corner news placards, Moscow, like Berlin, seemed to continue a normal daily life. Presumably, George thought, looking around him as he was relieved of his hat and coat, this place was reserved only for high-ranking party officials and equally important army officers—there was a great deal of brass to be seen—but it was full and looked as comfortable as any comparable place in New York.

"You and I have been enemies in the past, Mr. Hayman,"

Ivan said. He had not spoken at all in the official car on the ride from the Kremlin, had obviously been making up his mind what he was going to say. George waited. "It is good to think that we are now on the same side, eh?"

"If you mean that we are both opposed to Nazism, or fascism in any form, then I agree with you."

They were already being led to a table; obviously Ivan was a regular customer here. His was, George supposed, a genuine Horatio Alger story of the little boy rising from the pit to rub shoulders with the highest in the land. Only, in the case of Ivan Nej, the story held ghastly connotations.

"But you still regard me as a monster," he remarked, and smiled. "I read the American press, Mr. Hayman, your newspapers most frequently of all."

"How exactly would you have me regard you?" George inquired.

Ivan did not immediately reply. They had reached their table, set discreetly at the rear of the huge room, one laid for three people. The third was already there, a tall young man in uniform, standing to greet the commissar and his guest—standing to greet his father, George realized with a start of surprise. That Borodin height and those intense features could only belong to Ivan and Tattie's son.

"My son," Ivan said. "Gregory Ivanovich. This is Mr. Hayman, Gregory, from the United States. You have heard me speak of him. You will also have heard your mother speak of him, I imagine."

Gregory shook hands. His face was sad, the mouth too turned-down for so young a man. "You have news of my mother, Mr. Hayman?"

George glanced at Ivan, who sighed as he sat down. "Mr. Hayman *seeks* news of your mother, Gregory. Much as we all do. And alas, there is none."

"I should be there," Gregory Nej said. "I—"

"You are of far more value here," Ivan said quietly, watching George. "Gregory works with me, at Lubianka," he explained. "He is a member of my special branch, and now is helping me train a new special branch. But he wishes to be in the field."

"It is where I should be," the boy said.

"Let us order," Ivan said. "The caviar is good this year, Mr.

Hayman, as is the carp. Meat is scarce." Another brief smile. "The Germans have appropriated most of our cattle, in the Ukraine."

"I'll settle for carp," George said, and studied his host. As a bootblack Ivan Nej had commanded little attention from anyone. Now, despite his uniform and his gleaming leather and brass, the assured way in which he summoned the waiter, gave the orders, and selected the wine, he still had the look of a hungry animal. When the inevitable flask of vodka was placed on the table, he tossed his off as the best Russian soldier might have done, while his son and his guest both sipped theirs. But there was in this older and more experienced Ivan a certainty, an assuredness, which had been painfully lacking in the poor creature who had virtually begged for mercy in 1932 when his plans to destroy the Haymans had been revealed—not, George hastened to remind himself, because the man had matured, had become more of a human being with age and success, but because in the intervening nine years he had made himself more than ever Stalin's creature, the man who had masterminded the arrests and the trials and the executions that had made such a hideous mockery of the Soviet state in the middle and late thirties.

George had an uneasy feeling that this bootblack become Lord High Executioner would no longer cringe.

Ivan smiled. He had certainly been aware of the gaze, and perhaps even of the thoughts that inspired it.

"How would I have you regard me?" he mused aloud. "As a man who is doing his duty by his country, Mr. Hayman. As you are by yours, I have no doubt. I shall not quarrel with you. The issues at stake are too great for quarreling." He leaned forward. "But I wish you to know that I am as concerned for Tatiana Dimitrievna as are you, and that I greatly admire your stepson's brilliant action in getting the academy out of German hands. In that we must be as one."

"You don't think he may have made a mistake?" George asked. "The Germans claim they would never have harmed Tattie."

"You believe them? We have heard reports that several of the girls were taken out and shot, merely for being Russian Jews."

"My God," George said. "I had heard nothing of that. Have the reports been confirmed?"

Ivan shrugged. "It is difficult to obtain confirmation of anything. Perhaps Anna Ragosina may be able to learn something. She has a short-wave radio, and may be able to make contact with our forces."

"If she is not killed first," Gregory said.

"It is a risk she must take. It is a risk we all take, even sitting here enjoying our meal," Ivan pointed out. "And if anyone can survive, Anna Petrovna is that one. But I have no doubt of the truth of the report. It ties in with too many other reports we have received. No, no, Mr. Hayman. Young Ivan Mikhailovich did the right thing, the only thing. Better to die with a gun in your hand than against a wall with your hands tied behind your back."

*As you should know,* George thought. But he did not say it.

"So I would like us to be friends—or at least, shall I say, comrades—for the duration of this struggle, Mr. Hayman. If not longer. We have a common objective, do we not?" He held out his hand.

George hesitated, and then took the offered fingers. "For the duration, at least, Ivan Nikolaievich," he said.

Ivan smiled, and raised his glass. "Then I shall drink to our victory. For we shall gain the victory, I promise you. Now, you must excuse me for a moment."

Gregory Nej watched his father walk towards the toilets. "He means what he says, Mr. Hayman," he said. "I know something of the antagonism between you. My mother has told me."

"Yet you work for him," George said.

Gregory's expression stiffened. "I work for Russia, Mr. Hayman. Is that so very wrong?"

George studied his face. The boy possessed all the Borodin nobility, even with Nej features. He was Tattie's son far more than he was Ivan Nej's. Yet he was a member of the secret police.

But perhaps, George thought, even the NKVD can be civilized, when the bloodstained old revolutionaries like Ivan Nej die off, and their authority is taken over by these young men who have never known anything but a Soviet state.

Perhaps.

It was probably the only hope for their country, and even for Europe. And perhaps even for the world.

"No, Gregory Ivanovich," he said. "There is nothing wrong in that at all."

The crowd was silent, watchful, suspicious, and fearful. It had reason to be. The town square in Slutsk was completely surrounded by armed German soldiers, and there were machine-gun nests on the roofs of the buildings, while the rostrum on which the Prince of Starogan stood was also sealed off by a wall of armed men, their steel helmets gleaming in the morning sunlight.

Peter Borodin wondered how many of his listeners had come here voluntarily. There had been a pronouncement by the mayor, but undoubtedly the Germans had gone around to all the houses, routing out the able-bodied men to come and hear what the Prince of Starogan had to say. But he was beginning to wonder how many of these men even remembered who or what the Prince of Starogan was.

His palms were sweaty, and his throat was dry. Where this should have been one of the greatest days in his life, he could think only of Ruth's bald head. Supposing he succeeded in raising this army, it would be commanded by men who would shave a girl's head and lock her up for no other reason than a flaw in her ancestry. How his mother had railed against him, thirty years ago, when he had even considered Judith Stein as a mistress. "The girl is a *Jew,*" she had shouted, in a mixture of anger and despair. And he had stared at her in equal anger, and asked what difference that could possibly make where there was also beauty and poise and dignity and intelligence and culture?

He had believed that then, and he still believed it now. But his mother had been right, after all. In Russia, as now in Germany and, through German influence, in all of Europe, to be a Jew was to be unnacceptable as a member of the human race. Rachel had at least been spared the suffering inflicted on her daughter and her sister. When he had visited Ravensbrück the commandant had invited him to see the prisoner Stein as well, and he had refused. Seeing Ruth had been enough.

And now he must work for the men who had formulated

this inhuman policy, and were prepared to implement it.

He sighed, and cleared his throat; the German officer standing beside him was beginning to fidget, as was the crowd.

"Fellow Russians," Peter shouted. "You will all have heard of me. I am the Prince of Starogan. For twenty years I have fought against the evil blight of Bolshevism that lies over this fair land of ours, as you would have wished to fight against it, as your fathers and grandfathers *did* fight against it. They lost that earlier struggle, as did I. And so we were forced to bide our time, to wait for our opportunity. My friends, that opportunity has finally arrived! With the aid of the mighty German Wehrmacht, it is now at last possible to sweep Bolshevism away, to destroy the Soviet state, to restore the Russia of the tsars, the Russia of greatness. But we cannot let the Wehrmacht do all the work of cleansing our house for us, nor would they have it so. This is our land, and it is fitting that we should play our parts in its liberation. I intend to do that, and I know that you will gladly follow me toward the happy day when the monster Stalin has been toppled from that Kremlin he so falsely occupies, when all his henchmen have been destroyed, when Russia can again be free, and prosperous and great.

"Now, my friends, I shall tell you how this will be done . . ."

Colonel von Bledow turned away from his office window, which overlooked the square, and gave a contented chuckle. "The prince speaks without conviction," he said. "Mind you, it is impossible to work up any enthusiasm for such a bunch of peasants. You know, Captain von Hassell, the standard of intelligence in Russia must be lower than anywhere else in Europe." He paused by his secretary's desk to give her shoulder a loving squeeze. With some reason Paul supposed. Though she was slightly taller than her employer, and had horn-rimmed glasses and mousy pale hair in a tight bun, her white shirt front contained the largest bust he had ever seen in his life. The rest of her was obviously just as plump, but this clearly suited the colonel.

But he had more important things to consider. "Will they follow him, do you suppose, colonel?"

Bledow shrugged. "It does not matter much either way,

judging by the manner in which they fought against us. Anyway, I doubt they can be trusted. They will run from hand to hand, whoever feeds them best. And they are in a constant state of terror. Come. I will show you an example."

"I really would like to commence my mission, sir," Paul said.

"Soon enough. There is no point trying to negotiate with people unless you understand something of what they are like." Bledow smiled at him. "I understand you are anxious to make contact with your fiancée. But if she is there, she will still be there tomorrow."

"Yes, sir," Paul said. "And it is with her, and her mother, that I shall be negotiating. Not with any *peasants.*"

"You do not know that, Hassell." Colonel von Bledow opened the door and led the way along the corridor and down the stairs. Like a faithful hound, the girl, Ilsa, got up and walked behind him, carrying her notebook and pencil, her black-clad hips swaying as she walked. "For your own benefit, I would have you consider this: Is it not possible that Madam Nej and her daughter and her dancers, having been forced to escape our custody by the madman Hayman, would realize their error and come back to the safety of our protection the moment they understood the enormity of what they had done? But alas, they must have been prevented, and not merely by Hayman. We happen to know that there are also quite a few Russian deserters sheltering in the forest. Think of the joy of those men, hungry, frightened, desperate, at suddenly being joined by thirty beautiful young women. You take my point, Captain von Hassell? Were such a possibility to be the truth, then no blame, no guilt whatsoever could possibly be attached to any of them for what happened here on the night of the twenty-fourth of June."

He had led them down another flight of stairs to the ground floor of the building. Before them, the door to the cellars was clearly locked, for the colonel rapped on it with his knuckles.

"Of course you are right," Paul said, understanding his superior's drift. It was the obvious solution. Unfortunately it left John Hayman out on a limb, but that was a problem that could be solved when the girls were safe. And he had Heydrich's word.

Besides, John Hayman, however sound his motives, *had* murdered twelve German soldiers.

"So you see that you may well have to negotiate with these *peasants* playing soldier after all," Bledow said, as the door was opened by a heavy-set man in his shirtsleeves. At the bottom of another flight of steps, there waited another man in shirtsleeves, while beyond, suspended from the ceiling by a peculiar arrangement of four ropes, one secured to each ankle and one to each wrist, there hung a third man, parallel to the floor and about four feet above it. Paul caught his breath in disgust. A wave of revulsion swept over him, caused partly by the medieval gloom of the cellar itself, the musty walls and the flaking patches of plaster, and its scent, which was a mixture of damp and drains, and human sweat and even human excrement. But mainly he was disgusted by the sight of the suspended man, for he had been stripped, and his naked body gleamed white as he hung there like a carcass about to be slaughtered. Yet, he had not, apparently, been harmed except from a few bruises on his ribs; he was certainly alert and conscious, for at the sound of the door opening he raised his head, which had been hanging backwards, to look at the newcomers.

Paul gave a hasty glance at the girl Ilsa, also standing on the landing. "You should not be here," he said.

She stared at him, her eyes wide.

"Of course Ilsa should be here," Colonel von Bledow said, chuckling as he went down the steps. "She must note down everything he says. Besides, she enjoys it."

The girl followed her master, and then went across the room to sit at the desk in the far corner, notebook in front of her, pencil poised, eyes blinking behind their glasses at the hanging man.

"This device is my own invention," Bledow explained, walking round the Russian, who followed him with his eyes and his twisting head, unable to understand what was being said. "It is very simple, just four ropes and four pulleys in the ceiling. This means that the prisoner to be interrogated can be placed at any angle that is required. For example, should I wish to have him flogged . . ." He snapped his fingers, and one of the shirtsleeved men turned a handle so that the two ropes secured to the Russian's wrists were pulled to the ceiling, and his body went with it, up and up, the sinews in his arms straining, his mouth falling open with discomfort, until he was almost upright, hanging from his wrists.

*"Violà,"* said Colonel von Bledow, with a happy smile, and hit the man across the back with his cane. The body jerked, and the mouth snapped shut.

"And then," he went on, "should we wish to use the water treatment, he can be reversed." Another snap of the fingers, and the wrists came down until they almost touched the floor, while the ankles went up until the man was hanging upside down. The other shirtsleeved man had meanwhile been filling a bucket from a dripping tap in the corner, and this he now placed under the prisoner's head, which he pushed into the bucket. The body above twisted and writhed and jerked, but the SS sergeant held the man's head firmly into the water and refused to let it out.

"You'll drown him," Paul shouted.

Von Bledow snapped his fingers, and the bucket was removed. The man retched, and gasped, and vomited, while water dripped from his ears and eyes and nostrils. "We do not generally let them drown, my dear Captain von Hassell." The colonel smiled. "Interrogation is an art, never mere brutality. But these are all old-fashioned and primitive methods. My system is devised mainly to meet the needs of our latest procedure, which demands that the subject should not have to be in contact with his interrogator in any way. I will show you."

"No," Paul snapped. "No, sir. Interrogation is not my business. I do not wish to observe it. I have a job to do. If you will excuse me, colonel, I will prepare my mission."

Yellow dust plumed into the still summer air and shrouded the column. It was not a large column: two motorcycle outriders, then four trucks, then an armored car, and finally two more motorcycles, this time with sidecars in which sat soldiers with machine guns. The drivers as well as the guards inspected the looming trees around them with interest, but without fear. They knew that elements of the shattered Russian armies were hiding in this enormous patchwork of forest and swamp, so impenetrable that it had been left as a wedge between the army group commanded by General von Rundstedt, instructed to destroy all Russian forces south of the Pripet Marshes, and that commanded by General von Bock, with a similar mission north of the swamp. But no German soldier was going to be afraid to use one of the very few roads through the Pripet; they knew just how shattered was Russian morale.

And certainly they were right, John Hayman thought, nestling on his stomach behind a thick tree to watch them go by. Over the past few weeks more and more deserters had accumulated in the forest. They did not consider themselves deserters, of course. They were survivors, the only survivors of the Russian armies that had attempted to halt the Wehrmacht's onward rush. And having survived the trauma of the blitzkrieg, they were not anxious to fight again. Of course they *would* fight, they said, when the Russian counteroffensive was launched, when they could play a useful part in the defeat of the German armies. Until them, they had nothing to offer, and by lying low, they were not encouraging the Germans to come looking for them in the forest.

John was sure they were right. He was acutely conscious of his own standing in this business, of the fact that he had killed perhaps a dozen men who, if not innocent, were still human beings. And to what end? So that they could fall into the hands of Russians as voracious as the Nazis? Was it better to be raped by a man of one's own nationality than by an alien? The end result was the same. Could any of these girls, having shared so much intimacy with itinerant soldiers, ever pick up their lives again?

There were three exceptions. He rolled on his back to watch the two women coming towards him on their hands and knees; he insisted they move that way when they were within sight of the road. Natasha led the way, wearing a ragged dress she had obtained from the women in the village, her auburn hair now grown longer than when she had dominated the stages of Moscow and Berlin, swaying to either side of her shoulders; she was his woman now, in a manner she could never have been, he knew, had they merely married and honeymooned in the conventional manner. He wondered how necessary it was for a man and a woman to have shared the experience of killing, of fighting side by side, really to learn to understand each other. In Natasha's arms he had discovered an ecstasy he would not have believed possible, and she seemed happy to share the hardest or dampest of beds, so long as she could lie within the reach of his touch. So this devastating war, which had made him into a killer, had also made him the happiest of men, concerned only about their dwindling supplies of food, for with the best will in the world, the muzhiks from the surrounding villages would not supply enough for the growing band of refugees in the woods. And the onset of winter would soon have to be considered.

But what did Svetlana, crawling along beside Natasha, think of it all? She had not been allowed to share in the general camaraderie of the fugitives, even assuming she might have wanted to. Aunt Tattie had been quite definite about that, just as she had kept herself aloof. No doubt, had he not been there, she would have kept her principal dancer aloof as well. Aunt Tattie might be the most egalitarian of all the Borodins, but she certainly believed that some people were more equal than others.

But Svetlana would have been a problem in any event, because of them all, she alone could feel, deep in her heart, that this gypsy existence need never have been. Yet, like a true daughter of Tatiana Dimitrievna, she at least pretended to accept the situation.

"What news?" he asked.

Natasha shook her head. "It is not good. Father Gabon himself came. Apparently the Germans have been requisitioning everything they see. He does not think the village can supply us with food very much longer. There isn't enough, and besides, the Germans have found out about it, too. They captured Efim Vaganian, the postman, while he was on his way to us."

"And done what with him?"

Natasha shrugged. "No one knows. He was taken to the headquarters in Slutsk. But Father Gabon feels it is very bad."

"The father also says that there is not going to be a Russian counterattack," Svetlana said. "He says the Germans have told him this. Their armies are already practically at Moscow and Leningrad, and are about to take Kiev. They say the war is lost. Father Gabon suggests it might be better for us to surrender."

"Now you know that is nonsense," Natasha said angrily. "They would hang John and me, for a start. And your mother."

"Anyway," John said, "that is almost certainly German propaganda. There is no way their armies can be at Leningrad and Moscow already. Why, they could hardly get there this quickly even if there was no resistance at all to their advance—" He stopped suddenly as he realized the enormity of what he was saying.

Natasha had been looking past his shoulder. "We must get away," she said. "Look there."

John rolled back onto his stomach and peered through the leaf screen. The small German column had stopped, and men were climbing out of the trucks.

"They're coming into the wood," Svetlana said, her voice urgent. "The postman must have told them where to find us."

"Keep down," John snapped, holding her wrists, and watching the enormous white flag being unfurled. Now an officer had also left the trucks; he was carrying a megaphone. John wished he had a pair of binoculars, to see his face properly.

"You in there!" The rather hesitant Russian burst through the trees and over their heads. "Madam Nej. John Hayman. Svetlana Nej. Can you hear me? It is I, Paul von Hassell."

Svetlana tried to pull her wrists free, but John would not let her go.

"I am here to help you," Paul shouted. "I have been sent here especially to help you. Come out and give yourselves up, together with all the others. Come out and surrender. I guarantee your lives. You must come out, Svetlana. Otherwise you will die in that swamp. There is nothing to stay there for. Your armies have been defeated, and your government will surrender within a month. Then you will be treated as outlaws. Surrender now, my darling Svetlana, and I can save you all."

The words continued to echo through the trees for a few moments longer, while the white flag was rolled up, and the Germans reembarked. Then the motorcade moved along the road.

"Paul," Svetlana said, at last managing to reach her knees. "That was Paul. I must—"

John shook his head. "You can't."

"It was most certainly Paul von Hassell's voice," Natasha said.

"And I have no doubt at all that it was Paul in person."

"Then—"

"But it has to be a trick. Can't you see that? Do you really think the Germans are going to grant amnesty to me or Natasha, after what we did last month?"

Svetlana chewed her lip.

"Perhaps—" Natasha said.

"Yes," Svetlana said. "I could go to them. By myself. Let me go. They won't harm me. Not with Paul there. And he wouldn't try to trick *me*."

John was silent.

"It may be worth a try," Natasha suggested. "Even if the Germans don't come in after us, and don't win the war very quickly, we will all die when the winter comes, stuck in here without food or proper clothing or shelter."

"They wouldn't let you come back to us," John pointed out.

"Oh, they would. I know they would," Svetlana said. "Please let me go, John. Please."

"Listen," Natasha said. In the distance they could just hear the loudspeaker again. Paul was apparently stopping every mile or so to broadcast his message.

John pushed himself up. "Come along. We'll discuss it with Aunt Tattie."

"Yes," Natasha said. "Tatiana Dimitrievna will know what is best to be done."

The girl hesitated, then also got up—to freeze, as did they all, at the sudden cracking of a twig. None of them was armed; John found the automatic rifle too heavy to carry, especially since he had no intention of killing anyone else with it. Besides, he had only a few rounds of ammunition left. So they turned to face the sound, and the three people who stood there, wearing green uniforms and very heavily armed, with tommy guns, grenades, and pistols at their belts. It took some seconds for John to realize that two of the three were women.

"What in the name of God . . ."

"John Hayman," said the older of the women, walking toward him. His memory surged as he gazed at her pale Madonna face, the black hair that drooped from her forage cap to her cheeks, the bottomless dark eyes that had once watched him as he stood before her, naked and bound.

"Anna Ragosina?" He still could not believe his eyes.

Anna smiled, and looked at the two women. "Natasha Brusilova? Do you not remember me? Svetlana Nej? I am your
father's aide."

Natasha was also staring, because this woman had also
arrested her, once.

"Papa's aide?" Svetlana cried. "But what are you doing
here?"

"I am fighting the Germans. Like you." Anna's lip curled.
"There was a small column down this road, not ten minutes
ago. It could easily have been liquidated. Yet not a shot was
fired. Can you explain that to me, Mr. Hayman?"

"Well, for God's sake," John said. "For one thing, those
Germans were traveling under a flag of truce, and for another,
they hadn't come to fight us. They were trying to negotiate
with us."

"Anyway," Natasha said. "If we ever were to shoot a German, then they *would* come in here looking for us. Right now
they seem prepared to leave us alone."

"To negotiate with you," Anna Ragosina said contemptuously. "To leave you alone. Has it escaped your notice,
Comrade Brusilova, that there is a war on? We do not negotiate
with the enemy, we destroy him. And we do not destroy him
by asking him to leave us alone. We invite him to attack us,
and then we kill him. Take me to your encampment. I wish
to see all your people. We have come here to teach you how
to kill Germans."

# Chapter 9

THE TRUCK GROUND TO A HALT IN A FLURRY OF DUST AND squealing brakes; and was at once surrounded by women. Their heads were tied up in bandannas, they wore a variety of garments, from trousers to skirts, from the very old to the reasonably new, and they were of every age from early teens to late fifties. Although they each carried a spade or a shovel or a pickaxe, and all looked dreadfully tired, they seemed cheerful enough, and waved at the soldiers in the truck and even at the civilian sitting beside the driver.

"You've come to fight the Fritzes," they shouted. "Let's hope you do a better job than the bunch we have now."

On they went, giggling and chattering among themselves. The colonel winked at George Hayman. "Morale is good, eh, Mr. Hayman?"

"Morale seems excellent," George agreed. He had found, throughout the long and painfully slow journey from Moscow, that this was the one constant, and constantly surprising, factor. These people were being literally smashed into the ground—and in a war not for the satisfaction of some monarch's ego or a small commercial advantage, but for their very existence as a nation if Nazi dogma was to be given any credence at all—and yet they could smile, and they could work, too. The evidence of what these women had already accomplished was all around him. For the past hour he had driven through a maze of hastily dug trenches, of hastily constructed antitank obstacles, of pillboxes on which the concrete was still setting. For miles around Leningrad the country seethed like a disturbed antheap, spurred on by the still-distant but ever-growing cannonade to the south and west. Even the sunlit waters of Lake Ladoga to his right were ploughed with ships' wakes as vessels hurried to and fro.

The city itself was the biggest surprise of all, for despite the evidence of an occasional air raid, it remained, virtually untouched. He had not been here since 1922, when he and Ilona had paid a fleeting visit on their way home from Moscow. Then it had not yet recovered from the ravages of the revolution, when it had been a battleground for weeks on end. He had spent some time here during that tumultuous period, and could remember the slow disintegration of what was still the capital of all Russia into a derelict ghost town, with no power being generated anywhere in the city, with great potholes in the roads, with no refuse or sewage being disposed of, so that a poisonous miasma seemed to hang in the streets. But this Leningrad was once again a beautiful and prosperous city, suspended, as it had always been, between the twin waterways of the lake and the Baltic, fed by the unceasing flow of the Neva, basking in the late summer heat. And inside the city the bustle was as great as outside, as it prepared to defend itself against the Nazi hordes.

They were driving along the Nevsky Prospekt, and he could see the spot he had stood on that November day in 1917 when poor Viktor Borodin, in his own way as radical and misguided as his princely cousin, had seized his arm and invited him to come and watch the assault on the Winter Palace. He had run the other way instead, in a desperate hunt for a telegraph office in order to save Ilona and the children from the catastrophe he had then known was certain to overtake Russia. And a few minutes later he had been talking to Michael Nej, about to lead the Bolsheviks into action.

Now Michael was again leading his people into action. The truck had stopped outside the selfsame Winter Palace, and

George was being taken indoors and up a flight of stairs, then into a spacious office nearly filled with an enormous trestle table covered by several maps of the city. Around the table stood half a dozen men, looking up as the orderly opened the door.

"George?" Michael asked. "George Hayman?" He hurried round the table, his arms outstretched. "Is it really you?" He embraced his old rival. "I had heard you were in Russia, of course, but here? It is not safe to use the Baltic, you know. Not now. They have sealed up the passage, even to American and Swedish ships."

"I'm not going anywhere right this minute, Michael," George told him. "I'm here to observe, if you'll let me. Stalin thinks it's a good idea too, for us to let the American people know exactly what this war is like for the ordinary man and woman in the street."

Michael's smile was grim. "There are no ordinary men and women in the streets, here in Leningrad, George. I'm afraid it has to be said that the Germans caught us with our pants down, and of course having the Balts and the Finns coming in against us hasn't helped. Come over here and we'll show you the situation. Have you met Marshal Voroshilov?"

"Mr. Hayman." The soldier saluted before shaking hands. "I have heard of you, sir. Well, the situation is like this. The Finns are here to the north, occupying the whole isthmus between the sea and the lake."

George peered at the map. "But that is only twenty-five miles away."

Voroshilov nodded. "We are within range of their heavy artillery. But the Finns are not fighting with too much enthusiasm, Mr. Hayman. They shell us for a few minutes every day, but take care that their shells fall mainly into the sea. The south and west concern us more. The Germans came on very rapidly in the beginning. We have slowed them now, but you'll see that they hold this line here, and here, and here."

George studied the map again. "If they cross the Luga you'll be cut off, at least by land."

Again Voroshilov nodded. "That is the decisive spot, to be sure. But we are defending it with all we have, and we will hold it, Mr. Hayman. I am sure of that." He glanced at Michael.

"The fact is, George," Michael confessed, "that we are short of front-line troops up here. Most of ours were sucked up in the battles further south. So what we are having to use is the *opolcheniye*—what you might call our national guard, eh?—the factory regiments. But these are only part-time soldiers, and we do not really know how they will stand up to the Wehrmacht." He smiled. "They are eager, though. There is hardly a man of fighting age left in the city."

George scratched his head. "Then who is actually operating the factories? Cleaning the streets? Keeping the city alive?"

"Why, the women, of course. And the children. I am trying to arrange for the evacuation of as many mothers and children as possible, but it is a slow business."

"You must have a hell of a lot of them," George said, "judging by the number I saw on the road these last two days."

"Those are the same women, George. They dig antitank defenses all day and they work in the factories all night. We are at war."

George felt suitably contrite. But he had never encountered a people so prepared to throw every man, woman, and child into the breach if need be. "And you judge that things are going to get worse before they get better," he remarked.

"A whole lot worse," Michael agreed, and then smiled. "But we will hold them. Comrade Stalin has decreed that the Germans will not take Leningrad, and they will not take Moscow, and they will not take the Crimea. It seems that here in Leningrad we shall be the first to defend those limits. We shall hold them. But you must be tired after your journey. You must come home and see Catherine. And Nona, when she gets in." This time his smile was twisted. "She is building pillboxes. Her summer vacation, eh?"

"Yes," George said thoughtfully, thinking of Beth in her studio, happily painting away, and Felicity galloping her horse across the Long Island beaches. They might have been on a different planet. "I'm told Boris Petrov is here."

"That's right." Michael led him down the stairs to the courtyard, where an official car waited. "He is an unhappy man. Have you any news, George?"

"Nothing good. You heard about Tattie?"

Michael nodded. "And John. I am proud. Very proud."

"Even if they're all taken and shot?"

"He will have died like a man, as I would wish to die, if we were to lose this struggle. But I was thinking of Judith."

"She's in Ravensbrück Concentration Camp." He settled back as the car drove away from the palace.

"Judith? But... was there nothing to be done?"

"I appealed to Peter, and he didn't seem interested. I appealed to Goebbels, and he was even less interested."

Michael stared out of the car window; his fingers were rolled into fists. "We must beat these people, George. We *must.*"

"Aren't you going to?"

Michael gave him a quick glance. "I don't know. I can tell you, now we are alone, that I simply don't know. And sometimes I doubt that we can. No one is able to stand against them, it seems. No one at all." He sighed. "When I look around the country, read the reports from the various fronts, realize the chaos my country has been thrown into in just a few weeks... I sometimes despair, George. I simply have no idea where to start, now, beating the Germans."

"My name is Anna Ragosina." She stood with her hands on her hips and looked round the circle of faces. "This is Alexandra Gorchakova."

The girl, a solidly built young woman with black hair, smiled at them.

"And this is Tigran Paldinsky."

The young man, slight and dark, gave a brief nod.

The soldiers stared at them. They had come out of their various hideaways in the forest because of the news of two more young women. Clearly they had not expected two soldiers. Well, Anna thought, I had not expected *them.* Never had she seen such a collection of derelicts, their uniforms nothing better than patchwork quilts, their beards scraggly, their helmets and badges discarded; many were barefoot. And not one carried any sort of weapon.

The women who were with them, the members of the famous Nej Dancing Academy, were hardly better, scarcely bothering to conceal their sun-browned bodies beneath the few scanty garments they wore, hair obviously unbrushed for weeks and nails untended. Even Tatiana Nej herself, almost the last to arrive—she had apparently been sleeping—looked more like some aging wood nymph than the idol of Moscow and Leningrad. And although she must have recognized her, Anna thought, she gave no sign.

Anna glanced at John Hayman, whose shoulders gave a faint twitch. But then he hardly looked much different from the others. In fact the only one of the entire crew who had apparently made any effort to care for herself was Svetlana Nej. Certainly she had never seen the famous Brusilova looking quite so decrepit. Anna did not suppose she was going to prove much of a rival, although Hayman was visibly protective in his affection. But she reminded herself she must not be in a hurry. She wanted to *win* this man, not to command him. And that could only be done by example, by forcing him to admire her.

And anyway, she obviously had a lot of work to do in training these outcasts into a fighting force, before she could even consider her own desires.

The amazing thing was that, apart from Svetlana, they seemed perfectly happy and remarkably healthy, lazily contented with the way they had spent their summer. And there were a great number of them; she estimated not less than two hundred. It would be her greatest exercise in power.

"What unit are you from?" asked the obviously most senior soldier; he was not an officer, but Anna put him down as a sergeant.

"I belong to the NKVD," she said, "as do my comrades."

The men and women seemed to draw closer together.

"From Moscow?" asked the sergeant. "You have come all the way to the Pripet Marshes, from Moscow?"

"Through the German lines, comrade," Alexandra Gorchakova told him.

"But why?" He seemed genuinely astonished.

"We have come to teach you to fight," said Tigran Paldinsky.

The sergeant stared at him, his bewilderment growing even more apparent. Then he threw back his head and gave a bellow of laughter. *"You* are going to teach us to fight?" He looked from the young man to the two women. "You?" Another shout of laughter.

"It is clearly a profession you have forgotten, comrade," Anna said quietly.

The sergeant placed his hands on his hips, to match hers,

and peered into her face. "And who are we going to fight, little girl?" he inquired.

"The enemies of the motherland," she said. "The Germans."

"Ah," he said, and glanced at John Hayman. "You believe this woman?"

"She means what she says," John said.

"Oh, really? So we are going to take on the Germans. With what, little girl? Tell us with what."

"Have you no weapons of your own?"

"We have rifles and some ammunition," Natasha Brusilova said.

"Who asked you to butt in?" the sergeant demanded. "Rifles and some ammunition. We hardly have a dozen rounds each. And our rifles are rusting. And there are only a few of them."

"Then we will get you more rifles," Anna said. "And better weapons."

"You will get them? From where?"

"From the Germans, comrade," Anna said, coming to a decision, although she never altered her expression.

The sergeant thrust out his hand, and stabbed his forefinger into her chest. "Now you listen to me, little girl. We have fought the Germans. We have fought the Germans while you and your playmates have been skulking in the safety of Moscow. We fought them with machine guns and artillery and tanks, when there were hundreds of thousands of us, and we were beaten."

Anna nodded. "You were taken by surprise, and you were badly led. Now things are different. You will take the Germans by surprise, and you will be well led."

The sergeant looked from left to right. "Who is to be our general?"

"I am your general," Anna said. "As of now."

The sergeant seemed to lose the power of speech. Another of the soldiers stepped forward. "You do not understand, Comrade Ragosina," he explained very reasonably. "The Germans have left us alone, all these weeks. They have not been prepared to waste the time to send men into this forest to find us. But if we leave the forest and make nuisances of ourselves, then they will certainly come after us."

"And make themselves easier to kill," Anna said. "Once they come into this swamp, you will have them at your mercy."

They stared at her.

"It makes no sense." It was the first time Tattie had spoken. "I wish to beat the Germans as much as anyone does, Comrade Ragosina, but I do not see that it is possible for us to help. Now, when the Russian armies counterattack, and the Germans are defeated, why then—"

"There is going to be no counterattack," Anna said, speaking slowly and evenly. "Not before next year at the earliest."

She paused to let her words sink in.

"And when it does come, it is not going to reach here for a very long time. The Germans are only a hundred miles from Leningrad and are close to Moscow too. They are attacking the Crimea. They are swarming all over Russia. And when you say that we cannot harm them, you are wrong. We can cut their lines of communication. It is like a pygmy fighting a giant, I know. But if the pygmy can cut one or two blood vessels, even veins, and keep them cut, then the giant will bleed to death, eventually. And you have no other choice. You plan to stay here in the winter, without any more supplies than you have now? You?" She pointed at the nearest girl, Nina Alexandrovna, who shifted her bare feet in embarrassment. "You are going to starve and you are going to freeze. Perhaps you are going to do that anyhow, although I will teach you how to survive even in winter. But if you are going to die, you may as well take a few Germans with you."

The men looked at each other, and the sergeant, having got his breath back, realized that she was beginning to sway them.

"Anyone who listens to this woman is mad," he shouted. "We are mad even to accept her here, appearing out of the blue like some female bandit, claiming to lead us. By what authority do you claim to lead us, *Comrade* Ragosina?"

"By the authority of J.V. Stalin himself," Anna said, and felt in her pocket for the order. The sergeant peered at it.

"Let me see that." Tattie came forward and took the letter. "It is true. She has the authority." She raised her head. "You have been placed in command of *me?* That is Ivan Niko-laievich's idea of a joke."

"This war is not a joke, Tatiana Dimitrievna," Anna said.

"We can negotiate," Svetlana said. "I know we can. Mama, Paul is here. He is with the Germans in Slutsk. I saw him this morning. He made an appeal with a loudspeaker. He said that if we all surrendered we would be treated leniently."

"I heard him," said one of the men.

"And I," said another.

"We can trust Paul, Mama," Svetlana said urgently. "You know we can."

Tattie said nothing.

"Now that makes sense," the sergeant said. "Surrender. Yes, that's the best thing for us to do. If the Germans *are* besieging Leningrad and Moscow, if they *are* about to take the Crimea, then the war is lost. We shall surrender."

"Anyone," Anna said, "who attempts to negotiate with the Germans is a traitor. You have the letter, Tatiana Dimitrievna. Have I not been granted powers of life and death?"

Tattie finished perusing the letter. "That is what it says."

The sergeant gave another guffaw. *"You* have powers of life and death?" he sneered. *"You* have authority to command us? Some chit of a girl. Let me tell you, Anna Ragosina, that I command here, with Comrade Nej. We will decide what is to be done. Stalin is a thousand miles away, running for his life. We are *here,* and what we do will be dictated by that fact. And I say—"

Anna Ragosina implemented her decision. In one movement she slipped her tommy gun from her shoulder, leveled it, and shot him through the chest.

The sound of the shot seemed to bounce from tree to tree for several moments, only slowly dying in the distance. And for all that time no one moved, except for the sergeant, who arched backwards with the force of the impact, for Anna had fired from a distance of not more than four feet. When he hit the ground he rolled several times, but by then he was already dead, a thin stream of blood tracing its way across the grass behind him.

A movement rippled through the gathered soldiers, and Alexandra Gorchakova and Tigran Paldinsky both unslung their tommy guns in turn.

"My God," Tattie said, and ran forward. John was already kneeling beside the dead man, before raising his head to stare at Anna.

"He wished to negotiate," she said. "I have said I will execute anyone who wishes to negotiate."

"You murdered him," Tattie said. "You murdered him in cold blood."

"I executed him, Tatiana Dimitrievna," Anna said patiently. "It was my duty, and I did it. Now I require you to do yours. All of you," she said, raising her voice. "I wish all your weapons brought here so that I may see what we have." She knew that it was essential to capitalize on the ascendancy she had gained, to turn the sergeant's death into an instant victory. "Make haste now. We have work to do."

John stood up. "Are we allowed to bury him, *comrade?*" he asked.

"Let the women do it," Anna said. "You, Tatiana Dimitrievna, have your girls dig a grave for him. It should not be difficult to find some soft earth."

Tattie stared at her.

"I wish it done by the time I return," Anna said. "You, Comrade Hayman. We have heard that you fought like a soldier to escape the Germans. Now it is time for you to do so again. You have a weapon?"

John hesitated, and then nodded.

"Fetch it," Anna said. "Quickly. All of you, quickly. We have to hurry."

John went into the forest.

"Are you going to attack Slutsk?" Natasha asked.

"The Germans are overconfident," Anna pointed out. "There is a small column in the forest at this moment, the one inviting you to be traitors. We will begin with them."

"You cannot," Svetlana shouted, seizing her arm. "That is commanded by Paul."

"Paul?"

"A German officer named von Hassel," Natasha explained. "He is Svetlana Ivanovna's fiancée."

Anna turned to face the girl. "You are betrothed to a German?"

"It happened before the war started," Svetlana explained, flushing. "But he is not a Nazi, he is only a soldier."

"Only a man who is killing Russians," Anna pointed out. "I am sure you will be able to find some nice Russian boy to

become engaged to. Our business is to kill Germans, and this
man is a German. And an officer."

"Mama," Svetlana wailed.

"I am sure it would be possible to have Captain von Hassell
taken prisoner," Tattie suggested.

"Prisoner?" Anna inquired. "We do not take prisoners. Listen to me, all of you," she said, once again raising her voice
to make herself heard by the soldiers, who were starting to
reappear in the clearing, carrying their rifles and their bando-
liers. "Our business is not only to kill Germans, it is to frighten
them, to destroy their morale, their will to fight under the
conditions we dictate. Understand that. We will operate by
terror and by horror. That is what we are here to do. We are
not just going to kill Germans. We are going to make them rue
the day they entered Russia. You, Tatiana Dimitrievna, take
this child away."

Tattie hesitated, then took Svetlana's hand and led her toward the trees.

"Now," Anna said. "How many of you have rifles?" She
counted rapidly. "Forty-nine," she said in contempt. "Forty-
nine soldiers, out of two hundred men. Well, comrades, you
will all have rifles soon. And then you will have to use them.
But for the time being, forty-nine will do. And you, Mr. Hayman—follow me." She turned to Natasha. "Comrade Brusilova, I put you in charge of the burial party."

"I wish to come with you," Natasha said.

"You? You have no weapon. And you do not know how
to kill."

"Then give me one of yours," Natasha said. "I know how
to use it. I have killed before."

Anna Ragosina smiled. She had gained her first convert.

The men lay or sprawled about the grass, panting, chewing
bits of wood to allay some of the hunger biting at their bellies;
Anna Ragosina had not allowed them time to eat anything. Yet
such was her immediate ascendancy over them, the sense of
urgency she had brought to their lives, that they had followed
her at a relentless half-trot for over an hour, splashing through
mudholes and across streams, brushing aside leaves and thorns,
gasping and panting, as they were still doing now, but follow-

ing, until she had at last given them a chance to rest, while she had gone off with her two companions to reconnoiter.

John, as exhausted as any of them—and he had not even had a soldier's fitness before June 22—supposed it had to do with her sex and her personality even more than with the ruthless way she had destroyed their erstwhile leader. She was young, and pretty—indeed beautiful, with that pale face, those almost soulful features, those deep black eyes, and above all the swaying mass of black hair which she had not cut even for the perilous adventure of penetrating the German lines. Her figure was good, her muscles obviously hard. As was her mind. He remembered the gentle, almost casual manner in which she had once threatened to destroy him as he had stood before her in the Lubianka cell. He had not been sure then whether to take her seriously, had attempted to poke fun at her—and had got away with it, thanks to the efforts of his father and George. But she had executed the sergeant in the same quiet, casual manner. It occurred to him, nine years after the event, that it might have been wiser to be as afraid of her as she had meant him to be.

But that was in the past. What was he to decide about the future, if she was right in her estimation that the war would last for at least another year? Even Aunt Tattie was apparently numbed by her powers of authority and decision. But hadn't Aunt Tattie, like all of them, already been numbed, by the life they had been leading these last weeks? Undoubtedly they had been suffering a sense of shock when they had escaped from the Germans. None of their lives, except Tattie's—and that had been a long time ago—had previously been touched by first-hand violence in quite such a crude and abrupt manner. Thus it had been easy for them to wish only to hide, to convince themselves that there was nothing they could do except wait for their rescue by the returning Russian armies. Undoubtedly those watching from afar would not have seen things quite in that light.

But what would the next year bring, under the command of Anna Ragosina? Besides a great deal of sudden death?

Natasha dropped to her knees beside him. "Do you think she will be able to lead us against the Germans?" she asked.

He raised his head. Natasha had also seemed to sink into

the general sloth, after her initial burst of energy fueled by hatred. But now she too seemed suddenly regenerated.

"She terrifies me," Natasha confessed, when he did not answer her at once. But he wondered whether she was merely intending to reassure him. He looked at the three NKVD people returning through the trees.

"The Germans are eating lunch." Anna stood in their midst, her hands on her hips. "Could anything be nicer? They do not regard you as being here at all. Now, Comrade Paldinsky will take fifteen of you. Select your men, comrade."

The young man beckoned to those he wanted, carefully ignoring John and Natasha. When he had finished, Anna nodded, and he set off through the trees again, moving more slowly than before, his men trailing behind him.

"Now," Anna said. "Of the rest of you, I will take half and Comrade Gorchakova will take half. You will come with me, Comrade Hayman—you as well, Comrade Brusilova. Haste, now."

She led the way through the trees, carefully placing her feet so as to avoid making any sound. John ran at her heels, Natasha beside him. But after a few hundred yards Anna slowed to a walk, and then held her hand out and patted the air to make them go down. They crawled through the grass and bushes, and a few minutes later came in sight of the road, and the German party. They were indeed taking it very easy, John thought; they had finished their meal, and someone was actually packing up a folding table at which Paul had been eating. The crazy fool, he thought. But then, was Anna not right? The Russians had been entirely discounted as a fighting force.

He could not see a sentry, but apparently there was one, for suddenly there came a challenge, and someone out of sight to his left fired a single shot. Immediately the rest of the Germans were on their feet, seizing their weapons, but all looking towards the source of the first shot, now followed by a volley. Only one of the Germans was hit, and from the way he threw himself beneath the shelter of the rear truck, he did not appear badly hurt. The rest also went for shelter, automatic rifles thrust in front of them as they returned fire; Paul knelt at the far end of the trucks and drew his pistol, while giving orders in a remarkably cool and collected voice.

"Choose your target," he said, his voice surprisingly clear. "Fire at will. Man those guns." .

Two of his men attempted to board the armored car to reach the heavy machine gun mounted there, and were immediately hit. Then more shots began from the forest to John's right, on the Germans' right as well. Someone gave a shout and fell. Paul immediately commanded half of his men to wheel and fire in that direction, increasing his rate now, smothering the trees with bullets.

"Now," Anna said. "Now it is our turn."

She certainly did not lack courage, he thought, watching her leap to her feet, and run down the slope, her tommy gun thrust in front of her, bucking in her hands as she fired. One of the Germans turned and looked at her, and then collapsed, his tunic a welter of bursting red. Beside him John watched Natasha emptying her pistol, and realized that he himself was firing, that they were all firing, that the afternoon had kaleidoscoped into shrieking noise and flying death, and that the Germans, outnumbered and attacked from three sides, were utterly defeated.

They reached the road itself, and continued their advance, on the run, still firing, until John's rifle clicked on an empty chamber and he knew he had come to the end of his bullets. By now most of the other firing had stopped as well. The Germans had realized that they must make a break for it, and one of the trucks had been started and was roaring up the road, bumping and grinding on two flattened rear tires, but driving straight through the Russians who ran towards it in an effort to stop it. Another of the trucks was on fire, as was one of the motor bikes; the rest were on their sides. And there were at least a dozen dead Germans, sprawled in ungainly attitudes. He had never really looked at dead men before; on the night he had led the escape from the farm, it had been too dark to examine the effects of his handiwork.

Now the Russian soldiers were whooping and cheering as they dragged out the wounded—another half-a-dozen men—and also pushed three apparently unharmed men towards Anna. John looked from left to right. Alexandra Gorchakova was approaching them, completely unmoved by the brief battle, as was the boy Paldinsky, who was busily hunting through the undamaged trucks, having summoned some men to help him, was pulling out discarded rifles and ammunition and various bits of electrical equipment, dismantling the two machine guns, which had hardly fired a shot during the brief engagement. Of Paul von Hassell there was no sign, to John's intense relief.

Natasha knelt beside him, her head bowed. For a moment he thought she had been hit, and stooped to help her, his heart seeming to rise into his throat. But she was merely exhausted and shocked by what she had just been doing. And it was not over yet, he realized with a sinking feeling in his stomach as he watched Anna walking forward. Three of the wounded were badly hurt. "Tie these up," she commanded.

The Russians gaped at her.

"They will die," she said reassuringly, "soon enough. They will bleed to death long before any help can come to them. Tie them up."

The Russians gave another whoop of pleasure, almost as in cowboy-and-Indian films he had seen, John thought disgustedly, and dragged the groaning, blood-smothered men into a row to be trussed with their own belts. He pushed himself to his feet and ran forward. "You cannot mean it."

She glanced at him, then looked straight again. "Tie these others up as well."

"*They* will not bleed to death, Comrade Ragosina," said one of the soldiers.

"Oh, yes they will," Anna promised. "Tie their hands behind their backs and their ankles together, and then take down their trousers. They will bleed to death."

John held her arm. "You cannot. That is not war, that is barbarism. I will not allow you."

She looked down at his fingers, and he slowly released her. "War *is* barbarism, Comrade Hayman," she said. "If you do not want to watch, take Brusilova and go."

John stared at her for a moment, but he was helpless. These men would follow her down the road to hell, at this moment, if she wished it. He turned away and helped Natasha to her feet. "We'll go back to the encampment," he said.

"No," Natasha said. "We are part of this. If we are to remain part of it, we must stay."

He looked back in desperation. The six German soldiers were already lying on the ground, where they had been pushed by their captors, and had submitted willingly enough to being bound hand and foot, counting themselves lucky to have survived. But when the Russians knelt beside them to tear open their uniforms, one at the least suddenly realized what was going to happen to them.

"No," he cried. "No. I beg of you. You . . ." He looked at Anna Ragosina. "You cannot mean this."

Anna knew German, John realized. He watched her smile as she too knelt beside the boy; he was hardly more than eighteen. "Perhaps," she said in her quiet voice, "if you are unlucky, you will still be alive when your comrades come. Then you can tell them that it was Anna Ragosina who did this to you." From its sheath on her belt she drew a long, slim-bladed, razor-sharp knife.

"These," said Colonel von Bledow, "are the people with whom you would negotiate, Captain von Hassell. By Christ, to look at them makes me want to vomit." He stood with his hands on his hips and stared at the dead soldiers, lying in a neat row, already covered by the flies that filled the roadway with a buzz louder even than the idling engines of the hastily mobilized column.

"I should have stayed," Paul muttered. "Oh, God, I should have stayed to die with my men."

"You have a desire, then, to be forced to eat your own balls?" Bledow inquired. "Oh, cover them," he shouted. "I cannot bear to look at them any longer. Cover them." He turned away, swatted the flies that had landed on his sleeve, felt in his pocket, and lit a cigar to combat the smell.

"It was my duty," Paul said. "I gave the order to break out, and thought they would all follow. But I should have been the last to leave."

"Undoubtedly," Bledow agreed.

"It was those trees," Paul explained. "We could see nothing, at first. We could only hear the shots, and feel the bullets. And then they attacked from behind us, while we were still pinned down by fire from in front."

"And you lost your head," the colonel said, not unkindly. "How many of them were there, in your estimation?"

Paul shrugged. "Maybe twenty in the assault. But there must have been quite a few more in the woods." He sighed. "I have behaved very badly, colonel. I should be dismissed."

Colonel von Bledow clapped him on the shoulder. "Everyone loses his head occasionally, Hassell, especially when opposed to guerrillas, who obey no rules. But they are only guerrillas. Men. Perhaps a few women. Not devils or superhumans. We will extinguish them, I promise you that. And instead of running away in disgrace, you will cover yourself with glory." He chuckled. "But let us hear no more talk of negotiating, eh?"

"I am positive, sir, that neither Madam Nej nor her daughter, nor indeed any of the dancing academy, nor even John Hayman, could have had any part in this," Paul said. "They were ladies. Hayman was a gentleman. There is no possibility that they could have allowed such bestiality."

"Yes," Bledow said thoughtfully, staring at the trees. "I am inclined to agree with you, up to a point. For six weeks now our columns have been using this road—some quite as small as yours—without any interference. Now, all of a sudden, we have not only been interfered with, but we have been massacred. Yes. Some new element has entered the conflict, to be sure. Well, we will have to do something about it."

"What *can* we do?" Paul asked, staring into the trees. The evening was drawing in now, and the shadows were growing longer. Behind them the last of the bodies had been wrapped in blankets and placed in the trucks, and around them the soldiers grasped their rifles more tightly as they stared into the gathering gloom, peered down the barrels of their machine guns with anxious eyes. "That forest is too thick, the ground too soft, for vehicles."

"And it is too large to burn," the colonel said regretfully. "They would merely retreat before the flames. But we shall still smoke them out, Hassell. There is no food in that forest. They have survived this long only because of the support of the local population. We shall smoke them out."

"I have never heard of such an absurdity," Prince Peter Borodin declared. He stood in the center of Colonel von Bledow's office on the third floor of what had been the Slutsk town hall, and glared at the SS commander. "Such an obscene absurdity. You would be lowering yourself to the level of the men you are seeking to destroy."

"*You* talk to *me* of obscenity?" Bledow demanded. "You

were not with me yesterday afternoon. You did not see those young men of mine—butchered, cut to pieces while they still breathed. My surgeons tell me that at least two of them *choked* to death. Can you imagine anything more ghastly? Those are not men we are fighting in that forest. They are wolves. And they must be exterminated, however severe our methods have to be."

"And you really imagine that if you start shooting helpless civilians, their families will rush to join my army?" Peter inquired. "I am having enough difficulty in obtaining volunteers as it is."

"Exactly. And why do you suppose that is? Because most of the peasants around here are in sympathy with the men in the woods. They supply them with food. I know they do. There is no other way those wolves could have survived." He wagged his finger. "And do not suppose your own motives are above question. I know your sister is in there. Well, I am willing to go along with young Captain von Hassell's theory that neither she nor her daughter had anything to do with the attack on my men, and certainly not with their castration. But if they wish to survive they had better come out of there and surrender, because I mean to liquidate those wolves, and as soon as possible."

"And I agree with you that they must be exterminated," Peter said. "And of course Tatiana Dimitrievna must be regained, as well as her daughter. But I cannot accept that bringing such extreme pressure to bear on the civilian population will produce the desired result. It can only make my—your—task here more difficult."

"Bah," von Bledow said. "Let me tell you, Prince Borodin, that taking hostages has worked very well in other occupied countries."

"Indeed?" Peter inquired sarcastically. "Has all resistance ceased, then, in France and Czechoslovakia and Norway?"

"It is under control, I can tell you that."

"Nonsense," Peter said. "The shooting of hostages is nothing more than an expression of revenge on your part. It accomplishes nothing."

"Revenge," Bledow said. "Why, yes. It is certainly that. You tell him, Captain von Hassell. Tell him what you saw."

"It was indescribable, Prince Peter," Paul said. "It was the most horrible thing imaginable."

"I am not arguing with that," Peter repeated. "I am just saying that I cannot permit you to answer with an eye for an eye."

"You cannot permit it?" the colonel inquired.

"If you persist in this mad course," Peter said, "I shall resign my position. And what is more, I shall explain the reasons for my resignation to Himmler."

Colonel von Bledow stared at him for a moment, then turned his head at the knock on the door. "Come," he bellowed.

Two soldiers entered. Between them walked a man dressed in a priest's cassock and hat, an elderly man with a deeply lined face and hunched shoulders. Von Bledow surveyed him for several seconds.

"You are Father Gabon?" he asked at last.

"I am, your excellency." Gabon's voice was deep and resonant, used to making speeches in the open air.

"You are the priest of the village of Shelniky, in the Pripet?"

"I am, your excellency."

Bledow wagged his finger once again. "You have been supplying food to the Russian deserters in the woods. Don't attempt to deny it."

"We have been supplying food to the German army, your excellency," Gabon said. "What we have left will barely feed ourselves."

"You are lying," Bledow said. "That postman of yours— he told me what was happening, before I hanged him. I know the score around here, Gabon. Well, perhaps I was lax about it before, but now those partisans have murdered several of my soldiers. *Murdered* them, in cold blood. All because of your support."

"Your excellency—"

"Twenty-one of my men are dead, because of the actions of these guerrillas. Well, Father, I want you to go back to your village and select twenty-one of your people. I do not care whether they are men, or women, or children. I wish twenty-one of your people delivered here to me by tomorrow morning."

The priest stared at him. "What will you do with them?"

"I am going to summon those people in the wood to surrender," Bledow said. "I am going to give them twenty-four hours to do so. If they have not surrendered within twenty-four hours, then I am going to start shooting the hostages. I am going to shoot one hostage every day for the next twenty-one days. Then I am going to take another twenty-one hostages and start all over again. So you had better think about continuing to supply those wolves with food, Father. And if you can make contact with them, you had better tell them what I mean to do, tell them that my leaflets are no idle threat. You tell them, Father."

"You cannot do this, your excellency," the priest protested. "My people have welcomed your soldiers as friends. We have supplied you with all the food we can spare. We have—"

"You have consorted with enemies of the Reich, and are therefore enemies of the Reich yourselves. It is up to you, Father Gabon. When I have obtained the surrender of the people in the forest, I will stop shooting your villagers. It is up to you. Now get out."

One of the soldiers tapped the priest on the arm and led him from the room; he moved like a man in a dream.

"Now you, Hassell," Colonel von Bledow said. "Get to that airplane and drop those leaflets." He chuckled. "And do not get shot down, eh? Or you won't be of any use to that fiancée of yours, even if you do get her out." He glanced at Peter Borodin. "I am sure you have work to do, your excellency."

Peter Borodin stared at him for a moment, then turned and left the room.

The noise of the airplane engine circling overhead roused John Hayman from his reverie. Well, he supposed, he should not have been daydreaming in the first place. He wondered what Anna Ragosina would say should she discover that instead of peering down the slope allotted to him he had instead been thinking of other things, of Central Park on a summer's afternoon like this one, of lazy days playing chess. They were the only safe things to think about. To consider his surroundings would involve too much horror, too much confusion, which he was determined to avoid.

He had an uneasy suspicion, however, that what had happened two days ago was the true reality, and everything else just a pleasant dream. Man was a predatory animal. His entire

history, whether of his conflicts with his fellows or his determined extermination of apparently inferior species, proved that.
Therefore, however thick the veneer of civilization in which
he managed from time to time to cover himself, he remained
always at the mercy of his bloodlust. Presumably soldiers were
trained to develop more of a bloodlust than others, but he had
lived with the other men in this forest for some six weeks now,
and had found them basically simple peasants, the muzhiks that
composed so great a part of the Russian population, men who
had chosen the army—because they had all been front-line
troops, not conscripts—as a way of getting away from their
kolkhozes or from a dull career in a factory. Their dreams and
memories centered on the bucolic pleasures of their boyhoods,
the rivers they had fished in, the girls they had romanced, the
vodka they had drunk, and the scrapes they had got into. Undoubtedly they had been shocked by the tragic ease with which
their units had been destroyed and scattered by the Germans,
and in that debilitated condition had found it too easy to sink
back *into* the pleasures of their youth, especially when they
had so strangely found themselves in possession of nearly thirty
extremely attractive young women. And he was prepared to
accept that, since they were professional soldiers, the habits
of accepting command were so strong that Anna Ragosina's
appearance, and her terrifying execution of their sergeant, had
done nothing more than remind them that they were, after all,
soldiers. There was nothing truly uncivilized or inhuman about
that.

But two days ago Anna had invited them to discard such
unnecessary handicaps and become the animals she had apparently known they were. And they had responded with excited pleasure. The whoops with which they had gone into
battle, the savage ribaldry with which they had gathered round
to watch Anna and her friend Alexandra at their ghastly work,
the utter absence of pity with which they had surveyed the
reeking bodies of the dying Germans . . . one might have supposed oneself consorting with hyenas rather than men.

But he stood and watched as well, and managed not to be
sick. And so had Natasha. They had *felt* sick, as they had been
horrified when they had realized what Anna intended. But this
became merely another aspect of the continual horror that surrounded them. What memories would they have to share, for

the rest of their lives—assuming they had much longer to live; he could not believe the Germans would fail to respond to the butchery of twenty-one of their comrades. But at least, he told himself fiercely, it would be a shared memory, which, if anything, should bind them even closer together.

The snapping of a twig made his head turn, but he knew it would be she, bringing him a scanty lunch of water and some German bread rescued from the destroyed column. He rolled onto his back to watch her, as she slid to her knees beside him. She still moved as gracefully as ever, but over the past few days he had discovered a disturbing heaviness about her, where always before she had seemed to float. And she sweated more than he had noticed in the past; beads clung to her lips now, as she leaned forward to kiss him on the cheek. It had nothing to do with the events of two days ago, since he had made his observation before Anna Ragosina's arrival; she had lived too long on poor and insufficient food. But she smiled as she sat beside him. "My head hurts," she said. "And the forest will not keep still. Is that not silly?"

"If Comrade Ragosina cannot provide us with some decent food, all her plans will be useless," he said.

"Comrade Ragosina," she said. "Did she . . . did you . . . I mean, in 1932—"

"There wasn't really time, thank God," he said. "Ooops. Better look sharp."

Up the slope below them toiled an old woman. At least, she might have appeared, from a distance, to be an old woman, her head wrapped in a shawl, her feet concealed in shapeless boots. But the vigor of her movements, the certainty of her steps, gave her away. Certainly her courage was incredible; John could not imagine what the Germans might do to her were they able to take her, and discover that it was she who had mutilated their soldiers. But it was more likely, he supposed, that in her peculiar mentality she would accept even that as a quirk of fate, would withstand everything that was done to her without a single groan, much less a scream, perhaps would even smile, and die as quietly as she had always lived.

He wondered if he secretly admired her.

Now she threw the shawl back from her head; the black hair beneath hardly looked very different. John rose to his knees. "Is there news?"

"A great deal." She looked up at the plane, which had disappeared over another part of the forest, but had now returned, almost immediately above their heads. "Are they still looking for us?"

"I imagine so," John agreed.

"Well, let them look. We shall show them where we are, soon enough. I have learned that there is a supply train coming through this way in three days. That is our next target."

"A supply train?" John cried. "It'll be well armed. And all we have is two machine guns and some hand weapons."

"They will do, once the train is wrecked," Anna said. "We also have gelignite. I have a considerable supply of it, in my pack. Enough to blow up the bridge just south of Slutsk."

"That's madness," Natasha protested. "That bridge is only a few miles from the town. The entire garrison will be alerted."

"Of course it will take careful planning," Anna agreed, "but wars are not won without risks being taken. We have two days to work it out. Speed will be essential, of course, but I will work it out. Perhaps you would like to help me. I will send someone to relieve you." She looked down at Natasha. "What is the matter with you?"

"Nothing is the matter with me," Natasha said, getting up slowly.

"She does not feel well," John said. "She is not getting the proper food to eat."

"There will be food on the supply train," Anna said reassuringly, and caught Natasha as the dancer nearly fell over. "But you are ill."

"There is nothing the matter with me," Natasha said firmly. "I am just a little giddy."

"Giddy?" Anna peered at her, and then gave a snort which could just have been amusement. "You are pregnant."

"Pregnant?" Natasha glanced at John. "That is impossible."

"Pregnant," Anna said firmly. "I suppose it had to happen. And what use are you going to be to me, with a swollen belly? And even more, with some squalling animal hanging from your tits? You should be shot."

"If you touch a hair of her head . . ." John said. It was impossible to know when Anna Ragosina was serious or merely speaking metaphorically.

"Oh, I wouldn't harm Natasha Brusilova," Anna said contemptuously. "But she will work like everyone else, baby or no baby. Understand that." She looked up at the plane, at the cloud of white leaflets dropping from its opened door. "More negotiations," she said.

John ran through the bushes to catch one as it drifted from branch to branch. Hastily he scanned the writing, in not very good Russian.

"My God," he said. "Bledow is threatening to shoot one villager a day, unless we surrender."

"Oh, yes," Anna said. "That is something else I learned in the village."

"But what are you going to do about it?"

"What do you suppose I should do about it?" she inquired. "Do *you* intend to surrender, Comrade Hayman?"

"My God," he said. "What a decision to have to make." He looked at Natasha.

"It is just a bluff," she said. "They need the villagers for their food. It is just a bluff. A trick to make us keep quiet."

"Maybe," John said. "Well, I guess they're holding the trumps. And I have to agree that I thought that supply-train idea was a crazy one anyway."

"It is not crazy," Anna said. "It has a good chance of working. And that is what we are here for—to kill Germans, and to cut their lines of communication."

"You're not serious?" John demanded. "You attack that train and Bledow will certainly carry out his threat."

"I should think he means to carry out his threat anyway," Anna said. "The people in the village don't think that he is bluffing. I imagine they would like to tear me limb from limb. But if every one of them is shot, then they will have died for the Motherland, even if passively. They will have played their part. As we must play ours. We will attack that train."

# Chapter 10

GEORGE HAYMAN, JR., BROUGHT THE ROLLS-ROYCE SCRAPING TO a halt outside the front steps of his parents' house in Cold Spring Harbor, sending gravel flying in every direction. He drove, reflected Pender, the head gardener, rather like his father, and could never resist experimenting with the family cars. Wearily Pender picked up his rake.

"I'm not sure her acceleration is up to par," George told Rowntree, the chauffeur.

"I will take a look at it, Mr. George," Rowntree agreed.

George slapped him on the shoulder. "And don't look so gloomy. It's not the end of the world, even if we may have to have a new car. I think it's about time, anyway."

He took the steps three at a time, leaving Rowntree scratching his head in time with Pender. Although George junior possessed his father's height and build, strongly set off by his mother's blond hair, it was difficult for any of the Hayman retainers, however long they had been in the service of the family, to imagine Mr. Hayman senior ever possessing such an ebullient nature. That he had once possessed a great deal of energy was impossible to doubt; his record as a war correspondent, his incredible romance with the mistress—still the talk of the servants' hall—and the way, as now, he would go rushing off to see things for himself, whatever the dangers or discomforts involved, proved that. But he did it, and undoubtedly had always done it, with a serious, composed, thoughtful approach which made the difficulties he might encounter no more to be feared than were the pleasures to be overenjoyed. Young Mr. George charged life. And since Mrs. Hayman senior was no less serious a character than her husband, her son had to be a throwback to some ancestor, either quaffing vodka at the side of Peter the Great, or beer in a London tavern—the same ancestor, on the Russian side, at least, who might have fathered his famous aunt. Certainly in the three months that his father had been away, and he had been in control of the *American People* newspaper, an unexpected lightness had been permitted in some of the columns, and had gained more readers than it had lost.

The servants, too, appreciated his boisterous good humor, however much extra work it caused them. Harrison, the butler, was holding the door for him. "Mrs. Hayman is expecting you, Mr. George. And the young ladies are already here."

"Then I must be late. Martinis, Harrison, old boy, to break the ice." He stood in the drawing-room doorway, arms outstretched. "Behold the prodigal. How's my Diana?"

Now she, Harrison reflected, was a true Hayman, even at eight, and despite her dark coloring. She approached her father seriously, and gave him a perfunctory hug. "There's a letter from Grandpapa," she said.

"From Dad?" A shrewd observer, Harrison noticed that although the young man continued to smile as he went toward his mother, a certain watchfulness had crept into his eyes. He was not so lighthearted as not to understand that his father was living very dangerously indeed.

"That's great." He squeezed Beth's hand in passing, blew a kiss at his sister, Felicity, and sat on the sofa beside his mother, his arm around her shoulders to hug her against him as he kissed her on the cheek. "All well?"

"I don't know," Ilona said. "It was when he wrote this letter. But that was over a month ago. August 30. He says, 'Just a hasty note, to catch the last train out. The Germans have forced the Luga position, which was essential to maintain our contact with the rest of the country, and since then the situation has deteriorated. They are now shelling the city continuously, from only twenty miles away. Oops, there goes another one. There is plaster lying all over the place.

"'The fact is, my darling, that I wouldn't give a tinker's damn for the Russians' chances of holding this city. They are now completely surrounded on land, and of course the lake is under bombardment all the time too. Their mainly amateur soldiers have no chance against the Germans, although they all, women as well as men, are fighting with quite incredible bravery. And since there are still a couple of million of them, there'll be a lot more fighting. But that is also the principal problem Michael has here—just too many people, and not enough food. When next you see me I have a feeling that you won't be able to knock my paunch anymore.'"

Ilona raised her head to gaze at her son.

"If he could get a letter out," George asked, "why didn't he come himself?"

"You know your father. He goes on to say, 'But it's more exciting than a health camp. So if you don't mind I'm going to hang on here for a while. Shades of Port Arthur, although I think Michael is going to prove tougher than old General Stoessel. His energy is amazing. But I guess you know something about that. And he seems to have the complete confidence of the people here. They are truly prepared to fight to the last man. I think I may be in the middle of quite an epic, so tell young George he can keep the hot seat for another couple of weeks. It won't be longer than that, I promise you. If the Russians can't open up a corridor before winter, then it's a case of all fall down, and I will be sent home by the Nazis like a naughty schoolboy. No news of Tattie and John yet, I'm afraid, but keep your fingers crossed. I'm sure that if the Germans had captured them they'd have announced it. Oops, here comes another big one...'" Ilona sighed. "I wish to God he'd grow up. He doesn't seem to realize that war correspondents, even neutral war correspondents, can get killed by bombs just like anyone else."

"He'll survive, Mama. I know he'll survive." Beth Hayman sat beside her to hold her hand, and George felt a glow of satisfaction. After the terrible beginning, when Ilona had virtually ordered her future daughter-in-law out of the house, their relationship had steadily improved. Of course little Diana had an enormous amount to do with it. She was the only Hayman grandchild, and the more precious for that. But Beth was also such a warm-hearted person it was impossible to dislike her, even though he was well aware that Ilona still did not approve of her taste for painting nudes.

"Of course he will," he said. "No German bomb is going to bring down Dad. And I have some news."

"What? Johnnie?" Ilona squeezed his hand.

"Well . . . could be. It's come from our Swedish office, via a messenger from Conway, our Berlin correspondent. Seems the Germans aren't allowing news of this nature out of the country, but during the last month there have been some serious attacks on army units in the vicinity of the Pripet Marshes. More particularly Slutsk."

"Attacks?"

"Guerrilla attacks. One at least on a very large scale. They blew up a train, and looted it, killing over a hundred Germans."

"Johnnie?" Felicity cried. "Can that be Johnnie?"

"I don't know. But I'm sure as hell going to publicize the raid as his."

"But—" Ilona still squeezed his hand. "Then the Germans—"

"After what he did back in June, Mama, the Germans would shoot him anyway, if they caught him. Conway's message also says that they're shooting hostages right and left in an attempt to stop these guerrillas, or partisans, as he calls them. He says an entire village has been decimated. It's causing quite a fuss. And you want to know something else? Conway says that Prince Peter Borodin, who was in the Minsk area recruiting men to fight in an anti-Soviet army on the German side, has resigned and gone back to Berlin."

"Oh, good for Peter," Ilona said. "I knew he was never really a Nazi at heart." She sighed. "But Johnnie. And those poor girls. And Tattie. Bound up in something so horrible, killing . . ." She clutched his arm again. "And what about the winter? As your father said, it's only a month or so away now. How can they possibly survive the winter?"

\* \* \*

The crunching, splintering sound awoke Svetlana Nej. For a moment she could not imagine what it was, and incautiously pushed her head from the sleeping bag she shared with her mother, causing Tattie to awake as well.

"In the name of God . . . ugh!" Tattie hastily buried her head again, and in doing so burst into a fit of coughing. She had started to cough soon after the rains had begun, a month before. The hot summer of 1941 had ended with a tremendous cloudburst, which had maintained itself almost without ceasing for nearly a week, and after that it had rained for several hours every day. Then for the first time they had truly discovered why the Pripet Marshes were regarded as such a formidable natural obstacle; in the relative dryness of the past summer they had imagined the place to be an ordinary forest. Now, overnight, the stream beside their camp had risen high enough to flood them while they slept. Two men and one of the girls had actually been cut off and drowned before even Anna Ragosina, who had been momentarily overwhelmed by the sudden natural catastrophe, had been able to organize an evacuation.

But what were the deaths of three people, even if one was an old dancing friend, when they lived in such an atmosphere of death?

The rains had in fact brought a temporary respite from the business of killing or being killed. By the time Anna had led them to higher ground they had virtually been living on an island, completely surrounded by either tumbling water, in many cases several feet deep, or by huge areas of glutinous mud through which progress was next to impossible, even when one managed, as poor Igor Abramov had not, to avoid the spots that had no bottom. Igor had been out scouting and had found himself trapped in the mud. He had sunk so rapidly that although his companions had made a rope of their belts and thrown it to him, they had been unable to pull him free, and had had to watch him slowly disappear, hopelessly reaching for breath to the last sinister gurgle.

Yet Anna remained undismayed. She was not normal, Svetlana had early concluded. Where her mother had been shocked, as had John and Natasha, by the disaster of the attack on the train, when twenty-seven lives had been lost, Anna counted it a triumph: more than a hundred Germans had died, and the partisans had secured enormous quantities of food, weapons, ammunition, and even more important supplies, such as the sleeping bag in which she was now cowering from the cold, and the shirt in which she was sleeping.

The cold! Cautiously, listening to her mother cough, Svetlana again pushed her nose out of the bag. Mother was ill, and she was not going to get better, lying here beneath the frozen trees, in the damp and the cold. Suddenly Svetlana knew what that crunching noise was. Somebody was walking on ice.

It had happened overnight. Yesterday the rain had stopped, the skies had cleared, and everyone had been more cheerful than for a long while. Even Anna had smiled. Anna had been as disgusted as anyone else with the rain, not because the sea of mud in which they found themselves would have stopped her from attacking the Germans, but because the sea of mud in which the Germans found *them*selves had left them confined to the towns where they could not be reached, unable to repair the shattered railway line. "Oh, for another train," Anna had said, over and over again. And when they had stared at her, everyone remembering a comrade who had died, she had shouted at them, "How do you think we will survive the winter, without that train?"

No one doubted that she was right. No one doubted anything about Anna, from the certainty that she would shoot any of *them* who let her down, to the certainty that she would lead them to victory, whenever she decided on an objective. Svetlana could not imagine any group of people being so completely taken over by a single mind, a single determination, a single personality. When Anna smiled, they smiled. When Anna frowned, they all trembled. Even Mama trembled. Or was Mama's trembling just a result of her sagging health?

And Anna's kingdom was constantly growing. She now commanded more than three hundred people, despite all the casualties they had suffered. Men, women, and children had fled to the safety of the marshes as the Germans had commenced their campaign of reprisals. Four of the villages around the town of Slutsk were now empty, burned-out shells, with not even a dog to moan through the streets. And all for what?

There was the terrifying thought. The Germans, with their leaflets and their loudspeakers, hammered the same point over and over again. The war was lost, for Russia. Leningrad was completely surrounded, and about to surrender. Nazi patrols were fighting in the streets of Moscow itself, and their Panzers were sweeping toward the Crimea. At Kiev, when they encircled the city, they had destroyed an entire Russian army group, with millions of men killed or taken prisoner. There was no hope of Russia surviving the winter, much less launching a counterattack. So the Germans said, and for all Anna's sneer that it was nothing more than propaganda, Svetlana believed them. There was no sign of any Russian army approaching from the east, no sound of gunfire, no agitation amongst the German garrison of Slutsk, just as there was never any Russian plane in the sky. Even Anna, with her short-wave radio transmitter, could raise no Russian reply, although she tried regularly, cranking the generator taken from the German train.

Therefore, what were they hoping to achieve? They had become bandits, living by terror and extortion. *She* had become a bandit, although neither she nor Mama had ever taken part in any of the raids, knew only at second hand about Anna's barbarities and her courage. They kept the camp, chopped the wood, did the laundry, such as it was, tended the wounded as best they could, and cared for Natasha and all the girls, such as Nina Alexandrovna and even poor terrified Lena Vassilievna, who had discovered themselves to be pregnant. They were allowed to stay out of the raids because her mother was considered too old, and she was considered unreliable. That was because of Paul's presence in Slutsk. What hell he must be going through, night after night after night!—as she went through a similar hell here. They should have been married by now, and sleeping in the same warm bed together, and being happy together. Instead they were separated by hatred and rain and now by cold, and every day the gulf was growing wider.

Feet appeared in her line of vision, next to the sleeping bag. Svetlana looked out at Anna, rising above her to be silhouetted against the dawn sky. It had been Anna's feet crunching in the ice. It could have been none other.

"I heard your mother coughing," Anna said. "She is always coughing."

"She is ill," Svetlana said. "Very ill. And now that it is getting cold . . . Comrade Ragosina, she must have medicine, or at least warmth."

"There is no medicine," Anna said, "and no warmth. But she may stay in her sleeping bag until she is better. You will do her work for her." She nudged the next bag, and John's head emerged. "There has been a freeze during the night, Comrade Hayman," she said. "Is that not good news?"

"What's good about it?" John asked wearily. He too would have slept poorly, because Svetlana had heard Natasha cry out during the night.

"It means the roads will be passable again, and the Germans will be moving again. It means we can move, too," Anna said. "Get up and dress. I wish to reconnoiter. You can come with me."

John hesitated, and Natasha muttered, "Go with her. I will be all right."

"What is the matter with *her?*" Anna inquired contemptuously. "Is there not room for her belly in that bag?"

"She is hungry," John said, easing himself out of the bag, and shuddering as the icy air struck at him.

"We are all hungry," Anna pointed out.

"But she needs more food than most," John said. "She is feeding two people."

"She should have thought of that before she let you push your prick into her," Anna said. "There are now seven pregnant women in this camp. My God, what a crew! If I start allowing all of them extra food, we shall starve even quicker than we are likely to do now. We need more food, Mr. Hayman. So you had better come with me and reconnoiter."

Svetlana watched them walk down the slope toward the trees, then she pushed herself from the bag and pulled on her ragged clothes.

"Where are you going?" Tattie asked, pausing to cough. "Christ, how my chest hurts. Svetlana, is there nothing warm to drink?"

Svetlana felt the tears burning as they left her eyes and immediately freezing on her cheeks. She realized that in a single night the temperature must have dropped at least thirty degrees. "No, Mama," she said. "There is nothing warm. But there will be. I promise you, Mama. There will be. For you and for Natasha. And for us all. I promise you that."

Paul von Hassell sat at his desk and looked through the window at the snowflakes clouding down. Winter had come early, although the telltale signs had been in the sky for some time. This winter was to have been the happiest of his entire life, and instead, barring a miracle, it was going to be the most miserable.

But for how many German soldiers was that equally true, he wondered? He at least was in southern Byelorussia. What of the men around Leningrad, around Moscow? They had been promised both cities by the onset of the cold, had been promised that the Russian government would collapse, or run away, or surrender by the end of the summer. With that certainty they had embarked upon the campaign with no consideration of a Russian winter, no warm underwear, no fur-lined boots, no proper overcoats.

At least, he supposed, they would still achieve their objectives, even if they froze while doing so. Leningrad was completely surrounded, and by all accounts had very little food. Victory there could only be a matter of days, once the cold really set in. And they were fighting in the suburbs of Moscow, so that would certainly fall before the end of the year, no matter how hard the Russians fought—apparently their resistance had stiffened to a considerable degree—or how many fresh troops were thrown into the struggle from their seemingly limitless reserves of men.

So the other German soldiers did have victory to look forward to, and an end of the war, and a return to their warm firesides and their loved ones. To happiness.

He had none of that. He had been here three months now, and by now he should have been married for more than a month. Instead of which he sat in here, staring out at the snow, and his Svetlana was out there, trapped in a vast morass which would soon turn into a frozen waste. Certainly she must know he was here, desperate to help her. Certainly she must want to come to him. But obviously she was being restrained. By John? Judging by the reports in the American newspaper they had been sent, he was in command. It was quite incredible—

never had Paul so misjudged a man. Far from being the quiet, reserved, introspective fellow he had always considered him to be—a typical chess player, in fact—the American had suddenly turned into a maniac, delighting only in killing and mutilating German soldiers. Paul now knew that he had had some reason for having led the breakout. He had gathered evidence about how Tatiana Nej had been immediately sentenced to death, about how Natasha Brusilova had been publicly flogged. With that evidence he had been quite sure that he could secure John's acquittal, even before a military tribunal, on grounds of extreme provocation. But not now. John Hayman was condemned by his later deeds. There could be no excusing *them*.

Yet his Lana could have had no part in it. Of this he was quite sure. He was not that sure of her mother. Tatiana Dimitrievna certainly had a streak of primitive savagery, which revealed itself in her dancing, and which must have descended to her from her Circassian ancestors of a thousand years ago. But none of that had filtered through to her daughter. He *was* sure about that. Therefore she must be going through sheer hell out there in that forest, desperate to come to him, desperate not to betray her mother . . . as if he would ever let anything happen to Tatiana Dimitrievna now.

If only . . .

There was a rap on the door, and his secretary got up to open it. Unlike his superior, Paul preferred a male secretary, and this was an earnest young man named Engels, who wore horn-rimmed glasses.

The sergeant outside saluted. "Captain, there is someone to see you, sir."

Paul stopped looking at the snow. "Me?"

"A woman, sir. A Russian woman. Peasant stock, I would say. We have searched her, captain, and she does not have any weapons. But if you wish her thrown out . . ."

Paul frowned at him. "A peasant woman? But where has she come from? Here in Slutsk?"

"I do not know, captain. My Russian is not that good. All she keeps saying is, Captain von Hassell. Message. Message." The sergeant smiled. "She is a young woman, sir. Would be quite pretty if she was cleaned up a bit."

"Then you'd better show her in."

"You're sure she has been properly searched, sergeant?" Engels asked. "No knives or grenades?"

The sergeant's smile widened. "She's been properly searched, Herr Engels. Like I said, she's a good looker, under the dirt. And interesting, captain. She's wearing a shirt made in Germany. Army issue. Now how do you suppose she got that?"

"Oh, show her in," Paul said, leaning back in his chair. Some girl pleading for a brother or a father caught out after curfew. As if it was in his power to change the rules for any Russian. The man would be shot, and that was the end of the matter. It was a hateful job. He was a fighting soldier, not a policeman. He loathed having to arrest people, having to shoot them when Bledow's interrogations were finished. He had never reentered the cellar beneath him since that first day, had no wish to know what went on down there—the shattered remnants of human beings he watched being destroyed at the end of it were enough to turn his stomach. Yet the Russians had to be made to understand . . . He shook his head to clear the thought, realizing that he was reasoning just like Colonel von Bledow. He watched the woman come through the doorway.

His first impression was that he had never seen such a rag doll. She seemed to be wearing about three dresses over the shirt, and not one of the dresses lacked numerous great tears and holes. Her legs were bare, her feet clad in shapeless masses that he presumed were home-made boots. A shawl concealed her hair, and flopped half across her face, but her bare arms and calves were almost blue with the cold, and she shivered constantly.

"Well?" he demanded, speaking Russian. "I am told you are wearing a German-made shirt. You will have to tell me how you came by that, before we go any further."

The woman stared at him. "Paul?" she whispered. "Oh, my God, Paul." Her knees gave way, and she knelt before his desk.

Paul von Hassell slowly straightened in his chair, while Engels stared at him in consternation. "Lana?" He vaulted over his desk to land beside her, pull the shawl from her face and hair, and release the golden mass of hair, stiff with dirt and cold, to tumble onto her shoulders.

"Lana. My God, Lana." He scooped her into his arms and carried her before the fire. "Oh, Lana." He kissed her eyes, her nose, her mouth, her chin, held her against him while great shudders tore through her body as the warmth began to reach her. "My darling, darling, Lana. And they searched you. *You?*"

She shook her head against his chest. "It was nothing, really, Paul, nothing. Not now that I'm here with you."

"With me," he said. "Now and forevermore. With me. Oh, my darling, darling."

"Paul . . ." She raised her head.

"I know, my love," he said. "There is so much to talk about, so much to do. But first, we must get you warm, and decently dressed. A bath. A hot bath. That is what we shall get you first."

"A bath? Oh, do you think I could really have a bath, Paul?"

"This very instant. Call Hans, Engels. Tell him to draw a hot bath in my tub, and take Fräulein Nej to it. And Engels— behave yourself or I will have your ears, eh?"

The young man stood to attention. "Of course, captain. But . . . Fräulein *Nej?*"

"That's what I said. You go with Engels, Lana, my own sweet love. He and Hans will look after you. Just tell them what you want. And when she is comfortable, Engels, you will find her some clothes. Good clothes, you understand?"

"Of course, captain." Engels held the door for her.

"But . . . why can't you come too?" Svetlana asked.

Paul kissed her on the forehead. "I will be along in a little while. But first I must go and see Colonel von Bledow, my commander. I must tell him that you are here. Oh, Lana, my love. This is the happiest day of my life."

"It is the cold, you see, comrade commissar," explained Comrade Vaninka. She was a short, gray-haired woman, probably not the least stout, George estimated, but looking like a roly-poly pudding in her three sweaters and heaven knew what extra beneath her skirt. And still she could not keep still, but slapped her hands together as she talked, and shifted her feet.

Well, he thought, he and Boris were doing the same thing.

"It numbs the hands," Comrade Vaninka went on, "and the minds. My girls would rather be out there fighting than in here trying to work their machines. You men are always the lucky ones."

Boris Petrov sighed. He was as warmly wrapped up as anyone, with a scarf round his neck. And like everyone else he shivered all the time. "Nevertheless, Comrade Vaninka, production must be kept up. A five percent fall-off is bad enough, but ten percent is quite unacceptable. We shall not be able to fight at all if our men do not have bullets. You tell your girls that." He paused, and cocked his head, to listen to the sudden, growing whine. There had been one a few minutes before, as there had been similar whines all morning, but this one seemed louder than the others.

There was nothing to be done but stand still and wait, to see if one was still alive after two seconds. George stood at the rail of the dais on which the director's desk was situated, and looked down at the factory floor. There was no longer any electricity to be had, and the lathes and machines were powered by a generator that had to be cranked by hand; half a dozen girls stood at the end of the floor taking turns at the backbreaking task. But they were the lucky ones; they were at least sweating. The others, of all ages from sixteen to sixty, were working the machines themselves, sitting before their tasks, shuddering and making mistakes; they had not even stopped working at the approach of the shell. And when they were finished with their shifts, they would trail towards the suburb of the city where their menfolk were holding off the Germans at bayonets' length, and dig trenches and erect pillboxes as they had been doing for the past six weeks. It would be midnight before any of them got home, and what would they go home for? No heat, no light, and barely enough food to keep their bones together.

There was a dull explosion, and the factory shook. The women went on working, and George followed Boris down the steps toward the door.

"It is the hardest thing I have ever done," Boris remarked, "driving women like these until they drop. But there is no other way. Although . . ." He switched to English. "I cannot help but wonder if they would be any worse off under the Germans."

"Some would," George said. "You have to believe that." You of all people, Boris Petrov, he thought.

They stepped out into the open air, and realized that however cold it might have been inside the unheated factory, the sheer body warmth which had pervaded the place had at least kept the temperature close to zero. Out here it was minus twenty, even though it was noon, and the sun hung in a cloudless sky. But was that the sun, a pale yellow blob that radiated no heat and seemed entirely dominated by the deep, almost royal blue with which it was surrounded?

The glare was tremendous. The city was shrouded in last night's heavy fall of snow, which had now frozen hard; it was not credible, but the day always seemed to grow colder as it advanced. Yet snow was a tremendous blessing. The hard-packed white obliterated so much that was terrible, so much that was unimaginable. Thus the recent crater, the house just destroyed two hundred yards away, were the only visible examples of the destruction wrought yet again in the queen of cities. That they could see the shattered building, drooping crazily sideways toward the street, that they could see the black earth of the street itself, thrown up by the plunging shell, was irrelevant. The houses that once had stood between the crater and the factory, and which had all been destroyed a few days earlier, had now utterly disappeared; their twisted girders and shredded furniture, their mangled bodies, were all neatly concealed by the mantle of white that crunched beneath their feet.

"What next?" George asked, pulling on his fur-lined gloves and working his fingers.

"That is the last one for this morning," Boris said. "I think we will return to the Winter Palace and report. And have lunch, eh?" He gave a brief laugh, because he had retained some of his old humor.

They walked along the street and came to the crater. Two small boys stood on the far side, peering from it to the house, which had caught fire and was now burning. There was nobody else to watch. No one in Leningrad had any time to concern himself with a building hit by a shell, even if it was burning. Or with a hole in the road, even if it was an enormous hole, through which one could see the opened sewers.

But Boris was a commissar, required to interest himself in every aspect of the situation. "Were there people inside?" he asked the boys.

Their breaths clouded before their blue noses. "I do not think so, comrade," said the eldest.

"Maybe Grannie Burtseva," said the younger boy. "She lived on the top."

"But we haven't seen her fall out," explained the first boy.

George looked up at the building. The top floor had been entirely removed by the shell before it had smashed into the road. And even if Grannie Burtseva had miraculously managed to survive that, she would already have suffocated in the clouds of smoke spiraling into the still air to join the other spirals of smoke above the doomed city. Port Arthur had been nothing like this. Or maybe he had been younger, George thought. But what sort of men would these boys grow up to be, forced to spend their childhood with death always at their elbow?

He followed Boris around the crater, plodding behind him as they approached the Nevsky Prospekt, now a deserted thoroughfare, except for one man walking away from them, toward the river front. He must be an old man, for he was obviously not a commissar and therefore had no business to be walking through the city at all if he was fit enough to hold a gun or a spade. He moved slowly, seeming to have difficulty placing his feet in front of each other. No doubt, George supposed, he was looking for anything which could be used as firewood, or, far worse thought, anything that could be used as food. He quickened his stride, to tell the man that there was a whole building back there, which would be available as soon as the flames had burned themselves out, but as he came up to the man the stranger suddenly fell forward, without warning or unusual movement—he just seemed to overbalance and landed on his face in the snow.

George knelt beside him and turned him over. Desperately he rubbed the man's stubbled cheeks, slapped them, attempted to drag him up.

"My God," he said to Boris, standing above him. "He's dead."

"I would say so."

"Just like that," George said. "Walking along, and then . . ."

"He is not a soldier. Not even a factory worker," Boris said. "And not a commissar or an American newspaper correspondent," he added with grim humor. "His ration would have been nine ounces of bread a day, George. Just nine ounces. And three pounds of sugar a month, and eleven ounces of fat a month. Nobody can live on that, when they are also freezing."

George slowly lowered the man's head to rest on the snow, "We'd better find a burial party."

"Where do you suppose we are going to do that?"

"We can't just leave him there," George shouted.

Boris shrugged. "It will snow again before long. By tomorrow he will be buried. At least until the spring." He hunched his shoulders and walked on. "There will have to be a great clean-up in the spring."

George hurried behind him to catch up. "You are saying there will be no one alive in the spring."

"It is a possibility."

"But you're not going to surrender."

Boris glanced at him. "No, George, we are not going to surrender."

George sighed. "Well . . . what about this motor road they're talking about building across the lake? Another few days of this weather and the ice will be thick enough to support it. What about that?"

"We must try," Boris said. "Of course we must try. A motor road across the ice. I do not know." He paused, and looked over his shoulder at the man lying in the snow. "We must try."

George stared at him in consternation, at the tears which welled out of his eyes and dribbled onto his cheeks, immediately to freeze. "We must try," Boris said again. "It is unthinkable to surrender to the Nazis."

"People must eat," George insisted, leaning across the table, late that evening. "What is the point in resisting the Germans, if your people starve to death?"

"Because that is preferable to surrender," Michael pointed out, with infinite patience. "Besides, only a few will die. The old, like the man you saw, and some of the young. The rest will survive, even on what we have, and as soon as the road is built—"

"The road," George said contemptuously. "That is a dream, Michael, and you know it. What you must have is a more equal distribution of food. No one can live on what you are feeding the elderly and the young. While the others—"

"George, I was put here to hold this city, and to tie up as many Nazi divisions as I could, not to save individual lives. The soldiers in the trenches receive twice as much food as the girls who work in the factories. That is as it should be. The girls who work in the factories receive twice as much food as those who merely exist, because they too need their strength. Otherwise they would not be able to work."

George looked down at his own well-filled plate, glanced at Catherine's. "And the commissars receive twice as much as the soldiers."

"That too is as it should be," Michael said, without rancor, "because it is the commissars who have to do the thinking, the planning, who must make the difficult decisions. Without the commissars, and without me at their head, there would be no defense at all. Our judgments cannot be clouded by an empty belly."

"I find that a very fortunate philosophy," George said, "for a commissar. It surely can't apply to a foreign war correspondent."

Michael smiled. "It does, when he is the commissar's friend. Now eat your meal, my friend. There certainly is not enough for any to be wasted. I must lie down and get some rest."

He went to the bedroom and stretched out on the bed. After a moment Catherine followed, to sit beside him.

"Will there really be a road across the lake?" she asked. "Can there?"

"Yes," he said. "There can and there will. As soon as it freezes hard enough. And that will be very soon."

She held his hand. "Pray God that it will be soon enough." She flushed. She had been a devout Christian as a girl, and like so many Russians, whatever the state might decree, she turned to divine aid in her need.

He would not reproach her, even though he could not share her faith. They shared enough else. Finally. He recognized that it was an odd situation, to begin falling in love with one's wife after sixteen years of marriage. Always in the past there had been too many barriers between them. She was the girl he had rescued from Ivan's dungeons because she had shared her imprisonment with Ilona, was there in Lubianka because of the Haymans. She had always known that, had known too that should his protection ever be withdrawn, she might again find herself in the hands of the secret police, with as little cause. Thus she had come to his bed with a desperate gratitude. She had always respected him, or at least given a fair impression of doing so, and they were both healthy, passionate people who had always found sufficient pleasure in each other's embrace, while as one of the most powerful men in Russia he had been able to grant her luxuries denied to the herd.

But there had been no love, none of the instinctive sharing, of desire and intention, that can raise the relationship of two people from the animal to the sublime—until these last few months in Leningrad. Here for the first time they had truly lived, and worked, and fought, shoulder to shoulder. She had been able to recognize the immense strength of the man she had married, a mental toughness that sparked his determination, and indeed his ruthlessness. He had been given a task to perform, and he would perform it as long as even one person remained alive in Leningrad, even as he recognized that that last person would have to be himself. This had appealed to her own Tartar spirit, had roused her own inflexible support and silent courage. But of course there was more. Leningrad was doomed. Even he could see that. There was no room for laughter here, only for silent passion, silent misery. In this bedroom, and on this bed, was all the happiness, all the pleasure, all the comfort either of them could hope to find in the entire city, and it was the more precious because time was so short. In Leningrad they were man and wife, in the fullest sense of the word, where before they had merely been married.

She lay with her head on his shoulder, breathing softly. Perhaps she slept, the most precious of all blessings, in Leningrad.

But only fitfully. She was not sure how much later it was that she heard the sound of feet on the stairs, the outer door banging, but she was instantly awake, and hurrying toward the door. Michael also got up, and opened the door to face Marshal Voroshilov. The soldier's face was red with exertion and excitement.

"Comrade," he said. "My engineers have sounded the ice. It is thirteen centimeters thick. Another twenty-four hours, and it will have reached fifteen. Fifteen centimeters will support a laden truck. My people are sure of this."

"Thank God," Michael said. "You have given orders to begin the road?"

"Immediately." He slapped his gloved hands together. "We will have bullets, comrade. And shells. And fresh troops."

"And food," Michael said. "We will have food."

"And we can send the children out of the city? Say that we can, Michael Nikolaievich," Catherine begged. "Say that we can send the old and the children out."

She was thinking of Nona, and hoped the disturbance had not wakened her daughter.

"That too," Michael said. "Now *there* is a story for George to tell. How the fate of Leningrad, and perhaps of all Russia, all the civilized world, hung upon fifteen centimeters of freezing water."

Colonel von Bledow put down his pen and leaned back in his chair. "You are gabbling, Captain von Hassell. Slow down. Slow down. Ilsa, pour the captain a glass of schnapps. Are you saying that Fräulein Nej is here, in this building?"

Paul realized that he did need the drink. He had been shouting in his excitement, his tremendous relief. He drained the glass, took a long breath. "That is correct, colonel," he said, speaking more slowly and quietly. "She is in my quarters now, having a bath."

"A bath?"

"Well, sir, she was nearly frozen, and...well—" He glanced at Ilsa. "She needed a bath."

Von Bledow nodded. "You mean, she just walked in and surrendered?" He scratched his head. "That is unbelievable. You are to be congratulated, Captain von Hassell. I never believed for a moment that your leaflets and your loudspeakers would work. And of course, it is the cold that has finally driven her in."

"Well, sir, I would say that she had been trying to escape Hayman for the past month, but has been prevented from doing so by the floods. But now that everything is frozen over, why, she has come in to us."

"Indeed she has," Bledow said, getting up and reaching for his cap and stick. "One might almost call it an early Christmas present. I will see this young woman, Hassell."

"Of course, sir. As soon as she is dressed."

"I will see her now. Come along, Ilsa, bring your book." He strode through the door toward the stairs. "She is going to cooperate with us?"

"Well ... why else would she have come?"

"Why else, indeed?" Bledow said. "Captain von Hassell, I shall recommend you for promotion. Oh, indeed I shall. It has been too long delayed. But you are a genius. I shall put that in my report. A genius. Yes." He almost ran up the stairs in his haste. "Mind you, I always knew we would get a break eventually. Patience. That is the secret. Patience." He threw open the door to Paul's apartment, which was next to his on the top floor of the building, and peered at Paul's secretary, Engels, and at Hans, the orderly. "Where is Fräulein Nej?"

Engels came to attention. "She is in the bathroom, colonel."

Bledow glanced at Paul. "Bring her out here."

Paul frowned at him. "I couldn't go in there, sir."

Bledow raised his eyebrows, and turned to Ilsa. "Bring her out here."

"Tell her she can use my dressing gown," Paul said.

Ilsa opened the bathroom door. "You," she said. "Outside."

"She is not a prisoner," Paul protested. "She must not be treated like a prisoner. She came in of her own free will."

"How the Fräulein is treated depends on her," the colonel said, and stared at Svetlana, as did everyone else in the room. For she had soaked, and washed her hair, which lay against the collar of Paul's blood-red dressing gown. The gown itself was far too large for her, and she carried it bunched before her belly, leaving her feet exposed, while its drooping fold also exposed her throat. She was quite the loveliest sight Colonel von Bledow had ever seen. "That is Fräulein Nej?" he asked.

"Svetlana Nej, colonel. This is our commanding officer, Svetlana, Colonel von Bledow. I apologize for disturbing you, but the colonel was as delighted as I am that you should have come to us."

"She is quite beautiful," Colonel von Bledow said, continuing his distressing habit of referring to her as if she were not really there. "Quite beautiful. Do you not agree, Ilsa?"

"Quite beautiful, colonel," Ilsa said grimly.

"I begin to understand your frantic efforts to get her back alive," the colonel said. "Well, well, sit down, Fräulein Nej.

Send these men away, captain. And you yourself may leave.
I will call you when I have finished interrogating Fräulein Nej."

"With permission, sir, I would rather stay," Paul said.
"Fräulein Nej *is* my fiancée."

"Yes," von Bledow said. "Well, dismiss your people." He
waited for the door to close behind Hans and Engels, then sat
down on the sofa and patted the space beside him. "Sit down,
Fräulein Nej." He smiled at her. "Sit down."

Svetlana glanced at Paul, received a quick nod, and sat
beside the colonel. Ilsa sat at the little dining table, her notebook
in front of her. Paul remained standing by the door.

"You have caused us a great deal of trouble," the colonel
said, with increasing joviality. "Hiding in that forest. Murdering my men." He shook his finger. "That was very naughty
of you, Fräulein."

"I . . ." Once again she looked at Paul.

"I am sure Svetlana had no part in any attacks upon German
soldiers," Paul said.

"Would it not be better for her to answer for herself?"
Bledow inquired, smiling at her.

"I . . . it was Anna Ragosina," Svetlana explained.

"Anna Ragosina?"

"She is a colonel in the NKVD, sent to command us. She
made us fight. She made us . . . do everything."

"Anna Ragosina," von Bledow said softly. "Make a note
of that, Ilsa."

"Yes, sir," Ilsa said.

"And it was she who kept you prisoner," Paul said.

"Well . . . yes, I suppose it was. I wanted to come to see
you, Paul, that first day. But she wouldn't let me. She made
us attack you instead."

"You were there?" Bledow asked. "That first day?"

Svetlana shook her head. "I refused."

"Good girl." The colonel patted her on the knees. "Oh,
good girl. You are going to be a boon to us, Svetlana. Do you
mind if I call you Svetlana?"

"Of course not," Svetlana said. "I should like it. Colonel
von Bledow, my mother is very ill. She has pleuresy, I think,
and cannot stop coughing. She'll die, out there in the open,
with winter upon us. I thought perhaps . . . some medicine . . ."

"Of course," von Bledow said. "Of course. As soon as she

comes to us. Yes." He leaned back, still watching the girl. "But you understand that I must destroy these vermin, this Anna Ragosina and this Hayman. They are enemies of the Reich."

Svetlana stared at him with huge eyes. "They will never surrender. Not now."

"I did not expect them to. So I must destroy them. They have a camp, have they not? A hideaway?"

Svetlana nodded slowly, her face seeming to close.

"Of course. A camp that is quite inaccessible to assault by any large body of troops, at least in secret. But I could bomb it, Svetlana. Downstairs I have a large-scale map of the entire Pripet Marshes. If you will show me on that map where this Anna Ragosina has her camp, then I will blast it out of existence. Do not fear, I shall call for their surrender first. For your mother's surrender, at least. But those who refuse to come to us—why, they must be destroyed."

"I couldn't tell you that," Svetlana said.

Von Bledow frowned at her. "Why not? You agreed that they had to be destroyed."

"But John is there," she explained. "And Natasha." She looked at Paul. "Natasha is pregnant."

"Ah," said Bledow. "So they do not spend *all* their time murdering my soldiers, eh?" He chuckled. "But this John, this Hayman, is guilty. You have just agreed with that."

"I . . . he's only done what Anna has made him do. If they could all come out . . ."

"Yes," the colonel said, "if you could persuade them all to come out . . ."

"But John *is* guilty, Lana," Paul said. "I'm afraid there can be no excusing what he has done these last three months."

Colonel von Bledow sighed, and shook his head, to himself.

"I . . . I couldn't betray Johnnie," Svetlana said.

"You are a naughty girl," Colonel von Bledow said playfully. "You are going to make me very angry with you." He leaned forward and chucked her under the chin. "Do you know what I do with girls who make me angry?" He smiled at her. "I *burn* them. You would not like that, Svetlana."

Svetlana gazed at Paul with enormous blue eyes.

"I must protest, colonel," Paul said. "Fräulein Nej is not a prisoner. We agreed on that."

*"You* agreed," Bledow said. "To me she is a gift from the gods. If she will cooperate with us, then no harm will come to her. You have my word as an officer and a gentleman. But if she will not—well, I have my orders to exterminate these vermin in the Pripet by whatever means I can discover, and she is certainly a means, is she not? Now I tell you what we will do, captain. We will attempt to end this business as soon as possible. You will get into your airplane and fly over the forest, with your leaflets. You will tell these people that we now hold Fräulein Nej, and that if they do not surrender within forty-eight hours, she will be executed, in the slowest and most painful manner I can devise, and her body exposed for them to see."

"Colonel von—"

"And at the same time, I shall endeavor to persuade the lovely Fräulein to give me the location of the guerrilla camp. Shut up and listen to me, Hassell. I am being very generous. I will settle for *either* alternative. If the guerrillas surrender, the Fräulein will be set free. If she gives me their camp site, she will be set free. I cannot offer more than that."

Paul stared at him, then at Svetlana. "Lana..."

"I couldn't betray them, Paul. Not Johnnie and Natasha. They saved Mama's life. Don't let him hurt me, Paul." She was breathless, and shocked, and disturbed, but being Tattie's daughter she could not believe anything terrible was really going to happen to her.

Paul came to attention. "I cannot permit this, colonel. She is my fiancée, and the daughter of one of the most famous dancers in the world. I cannot permit it."

Colonel von Bledow gazed at him for a moment, then he got up and opened the door. "Sergeant Brinckmann," he bellowed. "Sergeant Brinckmann!"

"Coming, sir." The sergeant panted up the stairs.

"You will place Captain von Hassell under arrest," Colonel von Bledow said, "for insubordination. If he resists you, shoot him." He turned back to Svetlana, smiling at her. "Now you, Fräulein Nej, my dear Svetlana. You will come with me."

Svetlana found herself on her feet, without knowing how she had got there. She stared at Paul, who was returning her gaze, his face a distortion of uncertainty, anger, and fear min-

gled with the rigidity of the career soldier who has just been
told he is under arrest. But it could not be happening. Not to
Paul, and not to herself.

She watched the sergeant tap him on the shoulder. "Your
pistol, captain."

Paul seemed to jerk into wakefulness, as he unfastened the
cover of his revolver holster. Draw it, she wanted to shout.
Draw it and shoot them all. Because she, who had never wanted
a single soul on earth to die, suddenly wanted everyone in this
room destroyed, except Paul and herself. She now knew she
had made a mistake. She now knew that Anna Ragosina had
been right from the very beginning, that these people *could*
only be destroyed. Therefore their only hope of salvation lay
in her taking Paul back to the forest, to survive the winter as
best they could, at least in the company of friends.

But it was not going to happen. She watched Paul draw his
revolver, but carefully, holding the butt between thumb and
forefinger only, and reverse it to hand to the sergeant.

"Paul . . ."

He turned his head, and then looked away again. He seemed
to be in a state of utter shock. Now he sucked air into his lungs,
noisily. "Tell them where the camp is, Lana. Please tell them
that."

Then he was gone. She could hear his boots on the stairs.

"Good advice," Colonel von Bledow confided. "Although
I will tell you something, Svetlana. I should be disappointed
if you did. Can you believe it? But I am looking forward to
getting to know you better. Ah, well. Come along."

Svetlana's brain seemed to slow. She was only aware that
she must concentrate, on little things, on stopping time from
moving on. "My clothes . . ."

Colonel von Bledow chuckled happily. "You will not need
clothes, Svetlana. Clothes will only be a hindrance. But," he
said generously, "you may keep the dressing gown. At least
for the time being. I am sure that Hassell will not miss it. Come
along."

Her feet were moving before she was ready, and she was
at the top of the stairs, the colonel and the woman he called
Ilsa immediately behind her. The stairs themselves were narrow
and steep, at the top of the house. If she were to throw herself

off, here, she would probably break something. Perhaps even her neck. An impulse to do it surged rapidly through her mind, and as rapidly evaporated. They were not really going to hurt her. She was sure of that. And if they *were* going to hurt her, having a broken leg was not going to deter them.

Besides, she was already too late. The landing beneath her was clustered with men, watching her approach. Word had spread through the building that Captain von Hassell had been arrested, and that his fiancée was also under arrest. They wanted to see.

Perhaps even to touch. She went toward them, found herself in their midst, holding her breath as she clutched the dressing gown closer, aware only of their grins and their breaths. But they did not touch. She was the property of the man walking behind her, the man who was going to hurt her; suddenly that realization, once admitted to her brain, obliterated every other consideration. He was going to hurt her, and he was going to enjoy hurting her, and he would smile while he was doing it. Her mind became a raging tumult of fear and disgust, reaching down to her stomach so that she felt sick. And yet she was moving, because to stop would be to bring the moment closer. As long as she could move . . . but she had gone down another flight of stairs, and then another, and along a corridor, and was now in an office, and the colonel was standing beside her, and indicating the straight chair before his desk.

"Sit down, Svetlana," he invited. "I think you need to sit down, eh? Your knees keep knocking against each other. Ha ha."

Svetlana sank into the chair and discovered she was panting; she could hear herself breathe.

Colonel von Bledow turned his back on her and busily unfolded an enormous map on his desk. Suppose she were to leap up and grab the pistol butt protruding so invitingly from his holster? She was sure she could do it, and then—But the girl Ilsa was standing immediately behind her chair. She could smell her perfume. She herself hadn't worn perfume in three months.

The awful thought crossed her mind that she would never wear perfume again.

The colonel spread the map on the desk. "Here we are," he

said. "The Pripet Marshes. Study it carefully, Svetlana." He
held out a blue pencil. "All you have to do is circle the area
of your encampment. And then, do you know what I will do
for you? I will rescind my order of arrest on Paul von Hassell,
and pack you both off to Germany together. Won't that be
nice?"

Svetlana stared at the map. Won't that be nice? Oh, won't
that be nice! All she had to do was betray Johnnie and Natasha—and Mama as well, no doubt. But wasn't Mama going
to die anyway, if she didn't cooperate? They would all die, if
she didn't cooperate. This way she was at least saving her own
life. All she had to do . . . A sudden great light seemed to burst
in her brain. All she had to do was circle an area of forest.
Even after he had sent in his bombers, there was no way Colonel
von Bledow could ever know whether he had hit the camp or
not, whether the continuing attacks upon his people merely
meant that he had been unlucky, and Anna Ragosina had been
away when the bombs fell.

In a fever of excitement at her own stupidity, her own lack
of guile to combat these people, she picked up the blue pencil,
surveyed the map quickly, chose an area some ten miles away
from where she judged the actual camp to be, and circled it.
And became aware that the colonel was standing behind her
now, his fingers on the nape of her neck, caressing her flesh,
sliding under her still-wet hair, coming round in front to stroke
her throat.

"Hm," he said. "Somewhat further off than I had supposed.
Still, it is good to know that you are being so cooperative,
Svetlana. Good to know." The fingers on her throat suddenly
tightened, stopping her breath, filling her chest with pain, forcing her mouth open, although she was determined not to
scream.

"You promised," she gasped.

The hands released her, and slid away. She seemed to crum-
ple on the chair, desperate to caress herself, refusing to admit
to the agony.

"Of course I did," he said. "But we must be sure. Come
along with me, Svetlana."

This time he led the way, and the girl Ilsa followed behind
her. She gathered the dressing gown, had again to bear the

gauntlet of the stares and grins. But he had promised. Her brain was in a whirl. He could not *know* that she was misleading him. He could not.

The cellar door opened, and she recoiled at once at the stench and the sight of the two men waiting for them. She did not need to be told what their profession was. But there was no way she could stop now; when she hesitated, Ilsa poked her in the back.

"Here's a pretty little girl for your collection," Bledow said with a chuckle. "Do you not agree, Johannes?"

"She is pretty, colonel," said one of the men, eyeing Svetlana's legs as they emerged from the dressing gown on her descent.

"I will let you look at her," Bledow said. "Take off the dressing gown, Svetlana."

"No," she said, and hugged it tighter.

Bledow laughed at her. "Oh, take it off. You have been in the woods for three months with hundreds of men. You can have no modesty."

"I have never undressed before any man," she said.

"Is that a fact? And here we are, dismissing all Russians as immoral peasants. Fräulein, I apologize." He came closer to her, again chucked her under the chin. "But you will have to take it off anyway, you know. You don't really want us to tear it off you, now do you? It is Paul's dressing gown. It is his favorite, I can tell you that."

Svetlana hesitated, looked to Ilsa for feminine support. But Ilsa had seated herself at the desk in the corner, and the eyes behind the spectacles suggested those of a wolverine. Svetlana drew a long breath. "I protest," she said. "I—"

Bledow snapped his fingers, and the two men moved against her with a speed and violence she had not supposed possible. The dressing gown was ripped from her shoulders even as she was thrown to the stone floor with such force that all the breath was knocked from her body. While she was still gasping, she saw ropes being brought down from the pulleys in the ceiling, one to be secured to each ankle and each wrist. Then she felt a tremendous tugging on her wrists and found herself being raised from the floor, to dangle, arms above her head, almost pulled from their sockets. But she could not stand, either, for

her ankles had also been raised so that she was hanging in a
crescent shape, all her weight centered in her belly.

Bledow stood immediately in front of her, smiling at her.
"The area you circled has a name, on the map," he said. "You
must know the name, Svetlana. Tell me the name."

She attempted to think. He was only testing her. If she told
him the name that she had circled, he would believe her. But
she hadn't looked. Oh, of all the stupid things! She hadn't
looked. And she couldn't think, with the ropes sawing into her
wrists. They had moved from the Hollow, which had been
flooded, to the Knoll, where they now were. Those were the
names to tell him. But there were others . . .

"It is called Peter's Island, isn't it?" Bledow asked. "That's
where you moved to. See, I am trying to help you. Isn't it
Peter's Island?"

She nodded before she could stop herself. "Yes," she
gasped. "Yes . . ." She actually heard the stroke and felt the
cane hitting her before the pain came, but she knew it was
coming, and it was unlike anything she had ever heard before.
Her body arched upwards, reversing the crescent for a moment,
while her words trailed away in a noiseless scream of agony
mingled with outrage. But the man standing behind her hit her
again, before she could settle back, and for the next few minutes
she seemed to be flying through the air, arching this way and
that, while the cane slashed into her buttocks and thighs and
shoulders. When it stopped, again without warning, she was
exhausted, knew she was sagging like an empty carcass, while
tears poured down her face, and she could only dimly see
Bledow, smiling, or Ilsa, staring at her.

"That was naughty of you," Colonel von Bledow said. "You
are a *naughty* little girl, Svetlana. And naughty little girls get
punished." He reached forward and stroked golden strands from
across her face, wiping away some of the tears as he did so.
"Now, if you do not tell me the truth, I am going to *hurt* you."

She gasped, and attempted to focus, attempted to get her
racing brain under control, attempted to suppress the raging
agony that was her back.

"So where was it?"

She couldn't think. Her brain had gone dead. She couldn't
even invent. But she dared not invent. He was going to hurt

her. How could he hurt her more than he had already done? How . . . She was being lowered. She gazed at the ceiling, realized that she was now parallel with the floor, her ankles having also been raised so that she was about four feet above the stone. She was spread-eagled on a bed of air, at the mercy of this smiling monster, who had now produced a towel and was gently drying the sweat from her breasts, massaging the soft flesh with a tender expression. She stared at him, anticipating sexual assault. But she had known this was coming, had to come. She began to get her breathing under control, looked past him at the girl Ilsa, who was carrying some kind of box. Despite her pain and her fear and her humiliation, she was curious. She turned her head to see what he was doing, looked down at the alligator clips, opened her mouth in surprise and fresh discomfort as he pulled one nipple as erect as he could, and then enclosed it in the clip. The little steel teeth bit into her flesh and she thought he was mutilating her, in some especially fiendish fashion. She gave a little moan of pain, and felt the same thing happening on her left breast. And then she watched him step back, until he was standing three feet away from her, smiling at her, holding the box in both hands. From the center of the box there emerged a little handle, like the one on a telephone, she realized, while from the bottom of the box there trailed away a thick wire, again like a telephone, she thought. A telephone? He was going to telephone through her breasts?

Bledow smiled at her. "Now," he said. "Now, I am going to hurt you. Do you know, my pretty little Svetlana, my men have a bet that when I turn this handle, and the electric current passes through those lovely tits of yours, you are going to leap so far you will touch the ceiling. Do you think you will do that, Svetlana?"

She gazed at him, her mouth opening to speak, but there was nothing she could say, nothing she could do, nothing . . .

Smiling, Colonel Bledow turned the handle.

"I must go to her. My God, I must go to her! You cannot stop me! She is my daughter. I must go to her."

John had never seen Tattie so distraught, had never supposed that such a fate could overtake his aunt. She knelt in the freezing cold of the morning, coughing and gasping for air, and gazed in supplication at Anna Ragosina and in hope at the other people gathered around. She kept crumpling the leaflet between her fingers.

"You cannot go to her," Anna said. "She has betrayed us, and that is the end of the matter. These leaflets are nothing more than a German trick. We must evacuate this island as rapidly as possible, and move to another. Alexandra Igorovna, you will see to packing up our things. Haste now, there may be bombers here at any moment."

"I cannot believe Svetlana would betray us," John protested.

"Of course she wouldn't," Natasha said. "She went to see if she could negotiate, make a deal."

"And that is not betrayal?" Anna demanded. "I will tell you this, comrades, if she ever returns, I will execute her as a traitor."

"Then execute me now," Tattie wailed, "because I sent her."

"You?" Anna frowned.

"Yes," Tattie said fiercely. "I cannot stand living here any longer, like animals. I cannot stand this cough. I am dying. We are all dying. And so I sent her, to tell Paul I would surrender. I sent her."

Anna's lips parted in the semblance of a smile. "I do not believe you, Tatiana Dimitrievna. But in any event, you are not going to die. Not just from a cough. Put her back in her sleeping bag, and wrap her up warmly," she told Alexandra Gorchakova. "And make a litter for her. You are not going to die, Tatiana Dimitrievna," she said again. "And when this war is over, you can tell everything you have done to your husband." She turned her head as a man came running through the trees, staggering and slipping on the ice. "Yes? What is it? Are there bombers?"

He shook his head. "It's the girl, I think. The girl. Svetlana Ivanovna."

Anna hesitated for just a moment, then began to hurry through the trees. Without a word the rest of the partisans ran behind her. Natasha helped Tattie to her feet and she also ran, gasping and coughing. John ran with them, his heart pounding. But we are going to our deaths, he thought. If it's a trap . . . It was the first sign of human weakness he had ever seen in Anna Ragosina. For she was leading the rush, oblivious of the need for concealment, for reconnaissance, for anything save that of seeing Svetlana, of knowing what had happened to her. And yet it could not possibly be a trap. The Germans had no idea either where the partisans' headquarters were, or what their reaction might be. They had merely dumped Svetlana's body on one of the many roads leading through the marsh, knowing that she would eventually be found, knowing the horror and the fear that her death would create in the hearts of her comrades. And suddenly John realized that he had immediately assumed she was dead.

The same thoughts were obviously crossing Anna's mind, as she came to a halt. "It may be a trap," she gasped, instinctively unslinging her tommy gun.

"It's not a trap," the man protested. "They drove along the road at great speed, and just threw her out. They didn't stop. There's no one else around. I swear it, Anna Petrovna."

Anna gazed at him for a moment, then nodded. "Nevertheless, we will spread out, and cover the road," she said. "And move carefully." She went forward herself, with John just behind her. She liked him there, counted him her best support. They had almost struck up a friendship, over the past few weeks.

For his part, John could do no less than loathe everything she stood for, but he could also do no less than admire her quite remarkable courage, her self-possession, her utter coldbloodedness. They were qualities he might have wished for himself, qualities which she, remarkably, supposed he already possessed.

And today, he realized, he liked her more than ever, because of the unexpected dropping of her guard, the fact that she could be as emotionally bound up in learning what had happened to Svetlana as any of them.

They knelt in the bushes, shoulder to shoulder, and gazed at the naked sliver of flesh lying crumpled beside the road. Anna took out her binoculars and studied the body for several seconds. Then she said, "Cover me."

"Let me look," he said.

She put the binoculars in their case. "Cover me," she said again. "And when Tatiana Dimitrievna arrives, do not let her come down."

She got up, slid down the frozen slope, landed on her feet,

and walked toward the body. As she did so, she slung her tommy gun. John watched her kneel beside the body, turn it on to its back, bend lower. He could not see properly, since her body was between him and Svetlana's, but he was aware of a rising feeling of sick anger in his stomach. Svetlana had been so vital, so lovely . . . and so very much in love.

He heard Tattie's cough, turned on his knees to watch her and Natasha stumbling through the trees. "Take cover," he said.

But they remained standing, looking at the two people on the road.

"Help me down," Tattie said.

John stood up to hold her arm. "No," he said.

"Johnnie . . ."

"No," he repeated, and watched Anna Ragosina straighten and come toward them.

"I must go to her," Tattie shouted.

"You will leave her there," Anna said.

"Leave her? Are you mad? You are obscene. You are disgusting . . ."

"You do not wish to look at her, Comrade Nej," Anna said, and as she climbed the slope John realized that her face had grown older in a matter of seconds. Perhaps she was realizing that what she had just seen was what she too would look like, when the SS finished with her.

Tattie gripped her arm. "What did they do to her?" she begged. "What—"

"They killed her," Anna said. "Can't you understand that? They killed her," she shouted in a sudden fury. "They slaughtered her like a beast. They spared her nothing. Nothing, do you understand? There was semen on her thigh. Nothing. And then they slaughtered her."

Tattie stared at her, her mouth agape. "My Svetlana?" she whispered. "My Svetlana?"

"But I would say," Anna went on, "that she never gave in to them. Both because of what they did to her, and because there are no bombers. She died like a heroine. Like Tatiana Nej's daughter." She put her arm around Tattie's shoulder. "Perhaps," she said, "you will now help me to kill Germans, Tatiana Dimitrievna."

\* \* \*

White snow dust plumed away from the racing wheels, making a pattern against the dawn sky almost as if the ice had broken and was allowing a fountain of water to spout through its brittle surface. In places it had indeed broken, for the Germans were also up and about, their planes wheeling and diving above the huge lake, unloading their bombs to scatter great clouds of ice and snow into the air. The resulting gushes of water added their roar to that of the engines, to the cheers and screams of the watchers on the Leningrad shore, to turn the morning into a kaleidoscope of sound and movement and cascading death.

But nothing, George realized, his eyes now stinging although his binoculars were tinted against the glare, was going to stop the Russians. They had built this road across the ice, in the face of the most resolute German bombardment, and now they were using it. For as far as he could see, the trucks raced along at tremendous speeds, and now the leaders were almost within reach of safety.

The cheering rose to a crescendo as the first truck left the ice, skidding sideways as it encountered the snow-covered earth of the ramp, but soon brought under control by the exultant driver wrestling with the wheels. More than fifty eager assistants ran forward to push the truck straight and get it onto the roadway, to make room for those thundering behind. Catherine Nej gave a squeal of utter joy and threw both arms around George's neck to kiss him on the mouth. He had never before observed such delight in so normally reserved a person. But he had got to know her better during the months he had lived here with her and Michael, shared their increasingly meager food, and understood something of the deep happiness that had grown up between them. He was happy for them both, after all the traumas, all the tragedies that they had endured together.

Over these months he had come to respect them both, as well as all the defenders of Leningrad. He had no idea how many men, women, and children had died during the past three months. No one had any idea. The number of bodies that must be lying under the hard-packed snow—victims of German bombs, of starvation and cold, of German gunfire in the slit trenches and pillboxes—defied computation. And no one had any idea how many more would have to die before the Russian armies could raise the siege. But now, as the trucks roared into safety one after the other, each to be greeted with a tremendous cheer, it could no longer be doubted that the city would hold. It, and its heroic citizens, had withstood everything the Germans had been able to throw at it, and was now about to be helped.

And the greatest admiration of all had to go to their leaders—to such men as Marshal Voroshilov, who had commanded the army, like Commissar Zhdanóv, the head of the Leningrad Soviet, and of course to Stalin's special representative, Michael Nikolaievich Nej.

He heard his name being shouted, and turned, Catherine still in his arms, to see Michael Nej and Boris Petrov hurrying toward them.

"Michael," he shouted. "You've done it! The road's open. You'll hold the city."

Michael's face was alive with delight. George had never seen it so animated. "We'll hold, George," he said, coming up to them. "We'll hold, and we'll win. We have just received a message over the radio."

"A counterattack?"

"A counterattack, yes," Michael said. "But better even than that. The day before yesterday the Japanese attacked the American fleet at Pearl Harbor."

George could only stare at him, for the moment unable to believe what he had heard.

"The Japanese are claiming a great victory," Boris said. "Several battleships were sunk. But that does not matter. It means that you are in the war, George. Yesterday the United States government declared war not only on Japan, but on Nazi Germany as well."

"My God," George murmured.

Catherine squeezed his arm. "What are you going to do, George?"

"Do? Why . . ." He looked at Michael. "I must get home. I must be there."

Michael nodded. "Of course you must. You will return to

the mainland with these trucks, tonight. As soon as we have them unloaded. We will get you home just as quickly as is humanly possible." He laughed again, and embraced George and Catherine together. "But you will be back. You will be back, because how can anyone stand against Russia, and Great Britain, *and* the United States? You will be back, George, to celebrate our victory."

# Chapter 11

GEORGE HAYMAN LOOKED UP FROM THE DECK OF THE LINER AT the towering skyscrapers of Manhattan. It was the most reassuring sight in the world, he thought: a symbol of the wealth and the power that was now entering the war, was going to win the war for freedom and for democracy. He had no doubt about that.

But he could only feel sick, that this power had waited for so long on the sidelines, when it had been so terribly needed, for so long.

The two telegrams lay side by side in his pocket. It was impossible to decide which was the more appalling, the more unbelievable, the more pregnant with horror for the future. David Cassidy's death at Pearl Harbor was a catastrophe for his entire family, but he must have died cleanly and well, George thought. The Nazi claim to have "executed" Svetlana Nej, with all that that ghastly word implied, was even worse, for if Svetlana had been taken, what then had happened to John, and Tattie, and Natasha? He was sure they had not been captured; the Nazis would have certainly crowed about that. But could John, at least, have permitted Svetlana to be taken without dying first?

It was a terrifying thought that had Roosevelt been able to take his advice, more than two years ago now, this huge tragedy might not have occurred at all.

The horns and the cheers grew louder, obliterating the clanging of the telegraph from the bridge. The tugs completed their work with triumphant blasts on their whistles, and the great ship slowly and almost imperceptibly slipped alongside the dock. The gangplanks were immediately lowered, but before any official or sailor could venture onto them they were filled by the solid block of reporters who came charging up, breaking through the barriers between first and second class as they made for the upper deck, and the lonely figure standing by the rail.

"Tell us about Russia, Mr. Hayman."

"What about Leningrad, Mr. Hayman?"

"Is it true your stepson is leading a guerrilla movement behind the German lines?"

"What are your thoughts on Pearl Harbor, Mr. Hayman?"

"Where do you think the Japs will move next?"

"Do you think we can hold Corregidor?"

"Can you describe Marshal Stalin, Mr. Hayman?"

George spotted his son at the back of the throng. He held up his hands. "Now, boys," he said. "You know I've got a lot to do, now that I'm back. I'll tell you what I'll do for you, though. Come on down to the *People* building tomorrow morning, and I'll give you all a story. And—" He raised his finger. "—there won't be a word in my own papers until after that."

"At least tell us how you came back from Russia, Mr. Hayman. It must have been quite a journey."

George sighed. "I guess it was. I traveled via Moscow, Samarkand, New Delhi, and Bombay, and there picked up a ship for Cape Town. Then it was home via Puerto Rico."

"Quite a journey," the reporter repeated. "And what do you figure happens next, Mr. Hayman? You know Singapore has fallen? The Japs are running wild. They're saying even Corregidor can't last too long. You think we're in trouble, Mr. Hayman?"

"Trouble?" George smiled at them. "None we can't get out of. They've taken us by surprise, that's all. Corregidor may well fall. But the Japs can't lick us and the Australians and the British, all together. They just don't have the resources."

"Yeah, but with the Germans knocking down the Russians—"

"Forget it," George said. "The Germans haven't got the resources either. If they didn't win that one by Christmas, they're never going to win it. Leningrad is still there. So is Moscow. They're not going too much further."

"It's good to hear an optimist, for a change," someone said.

"Now about Stalin, Mr. Hayman..."

"That's enough boys," George said. "Tomorrow, at the *People* building." He elbowed aside their protests, pushed through them to grip his son's hand.

"Where's your mother?"

"In the car. She wouldn't come up." George junior pushed people out of the way as well, as, assisted by a hastily marshaled squad of sailors, escorted his father to the gangplank. "But she's awfully glad you're back." He flushed. "So am I."

"You've been doing a good job, I hear," George said, hurrying down the sloping ramp. "I've been thinking that you're ready for a vice-presidency. Even the presidency. I'm getting old."

"You'll be feeling young again after a good night's sleep. Anyway, no vice-presidency. Not for the moment, Dad. I want to see action."

George stopped to look at his son. "You're not serious."

"Of course I'm serious. We're at war."

George found himself at the door of the Rolls, still surrounded by people slapping him on the back, pulling and tugging at his coat, even whipping his hat from his head. He dived inside, found himself against Ilona, and took her in his arms. The crowd cheered.

"Oh, George," she whispered against his ear. "To have you back. To know you're safe." She pushed him away to look into his face. "I've dreamed of submarines every night for the past two months."

"Well, we never saw one." He kissed her on the nose. "We hurried, you might say."

"But George, the news—"

"Is pretty grim. But it'll change. There's no doubt about that."

The other door slammed as George junior got in, and the

car started to move away through the crowds.

"It's good to have you back, Mr. Hayman," Rowntree said.

"It's good to be back," George agreed.

"Must have been pretty rough in Leningrad," George junior said.

"It was pretty rough."

"President Roosevelt wants you to call, just as soon as you can, George," Ilona said. "He wants a long chat."

"Just as soon as I can. Felicity?"

Ilona sighed. "She won't speak. She won't eat. She just sits there, in her room. George . . . it was the *way* it happened. The ship apparently turned upside down, and David was below. Do you know, they could hear men tapping on the hull for hours, even days, afterwards, but they couldn't get through to them. Can you *imagine?*"

George thought of the old man walking along the street in Leningrad, and just falling over. "Yes," he said. "I can imagine." Had the last war been anything like this one? Anything like as terrible? Probably it had, but it hadn't seemed so to him—because he had been younger, and stronger, and tougher?

"And now, this one, wanting to go off," Ilona said.

"Now, Mother," George junior said, "there does happen to be a war . . ."

"And there's a draft," Ilona pointed out. "That's supposed to take care of the men who have to fight. Your name hasn't come up yet, so why anticipate it?"

"What does Beth think about the idea?" George asked.

"Well . . . she's not enthusiastic, but she knows it's something I have to do."

"Why?" Ilona cried. "In the name of God, why? For God's sake, this war has only just started for us, and it's already been on too long. Felicity is a wreck, she thinks her life is ruined; Johnnie is lost, maybe dead, together with Tattie; and Svetlana . . . oh, poor, poor Svetlana . . ." Tears welled out of her eyes and rolled down her cheeks. "And when I think of you, George, in Leningrad . . ."

"And Judith," George said. "Don't forget Judith. Judith was always right about those concentration camps, you know. Remember that evening in 1938, when we sat with her and Boris, and talked? She was right and I was wrong. Maybe if I'd pushed it a bit harder in the paper I could have done something then. But for her sake, and John's sake, and for Svetlana's too, and David's, we have to win this war just as soon as possible, and that doesn't mean waiting to be called up. You've got my blessing, George. Just kill a few for me."

The bell clanged, and Ruth Borodin tapped the man on the shoulder. "It is time for you to go," she said.

He preferred not to move, continued to lie half across her, lips sucking at her neck, groin wedged into hers, left hand ruffling the soft down that carpeted her scalp. He was very young, younger even than she, she suspected, and very afraid. This was his last furlough, before departing for the Russian front, as he had repeated over and over again while undressing. What a contrast to the men who had come here last summer. Then they had been eager to participate in the splendid drive to Moscow, in the dismembering of an ancient country. But over this winter the euphoria was dying. Not officially. That the German armies might be bogged down in snow and ice, in temperatures so low it was impossible to start the engines on tanks or trucks unless fires were kept burning beneath them all night, was, in the words of the Nazi-controlled press, nothing more than an unfortunate aberration of nature. The advance would certainly be resumed with the coming of spring, and then the continuing rout of the Russians would be brought to a satisfactory conclusion.

But the victorious paeans of the newspapers were apparently becoming difficult for the ordinary readers to accept, because the older ones among them could remember the last war, and the difference that the entrance of the United States had made. However well things were going at the moment, however much the Nazi Party might reiterate that the Americans were on the verge of being smashed by the Japanese and that, in any event, it would be years before their full power could be brought to bear, either industrially or on the field here in Europe, there were many who remembered that a very similar story had been propagated the last time.

And then there was the steady trickle, growing now into a stream, of wounded and shattered men returning from the eastern front. These she knew at first hand, because some of them, those who had been considered capable of regeneration into fighting soldiers, had been brought to the "clinic" for a spell before being reassigned. These were men with strange shadows across their vision, with peculiar twitches, and lurking horrors at the backs of their minds, men who muttered about the paralyzing effects of the Russian cold, about comrades found frozen stiff after a few hours on guard duty, and others who had gone blind from looking too long at the snow-clad wastes, and who whispered too about the horrific anger of the people they had conquered, of the vicious brutality with which the partisans went to work.

And men too, who knew the reasons. "It is an endless process," they would say, lying on their backs beside her and staring at the ceiling. "We execute them, they murder us. Endless. But with them it is often the women. To be held down and chopped into pieces before your own eyes by laughing women..." These were soldiers who were being destroyed psychologically, who would never be good for anything again.

This boy had obviously talked with a friend, or even a brother or an uncle or a father, who had returned from the Russian front. Even his sweat smelled of fear. But she must not slip into the trap of becoming sorry for a German. The sooner he went to Russia and got his head shot off, the sooner the war would end.

She thumped him again, harder than before, but not very forcefully. This was her problem, feeling sorry for people. Even these people. Once she had supposed that two years in solitary confinement, with only Anna Ragosina's twisted mentality for company, was the greatest misfortune that could possibly befall any human being. Now she knew that the cell in the depths of Lubianka had been nothing more than the antechamber of hell. But if the concentration camp had to be hell itself, what words could she possibly find to describe the camp brothel? Even the horror of being branded on the forearm, the pain and the nauseating stench of her own flesh on fire, had been less terrible than the mental destruction of having to submit her body, several times a day, to men she feared and hated and abhorred—and felt sorry for.

In fact, she now knew that but for the experience of Anna, she would have been unable to survive this place, would have gone mad, months ago. The imprisonment in Russia, with Anna as her keeper, had toughened her. And the empty pit of hatred that was Anna's mind had been almost a joyous place when compared with the mentalities she had encountered in this camp, whether of the amoral guards, or the greedy, frightened soldiers, or even the fear and hate-crazed inmates. Mercifully, in her mind many of them had merged into meaningless gray misery, but there were pinpoints of terrible depravity that had burned holes into her brain, and which she could never hope to forget. Such as the occasion she and Judith had been used in an experiment, forced to make love to a man who had been immersed in freezing water to the point of death, because one of the doctors in the camp had a theory that Luftwaffe pilots shot down in the North Sea and dying of exposure could be saved by the application of animal warmth, animal stimulation. The theory had not been proved; the man had died. And when they had been returned to their barracks Judith had looked at her with those deep, brooding, but determinedly defiant eyes of hers, and said, "These people are mad. It is existence turned inside out to be the only sane people in a madhouse."

Anna at least had not been mad. She had merely been a woman for whom life and training—she had never tired of talking about either aspect of her existence—had combined to remove too much humanity. But not all. Anna, for instance, had still supposed she could love. Why, she had even supposed she loved Ruth Borodina. She could not understand that love to her was only possession, submission, conquest; she desired with all the bloodcurdling lust of a female praying mantis.

Yet she was almost an admirable figure when compared with these monsters who guarded and used the concentration camp, so brutishly bewildered by the power thrust upon them by their Führer.

Perhaps worst of all was the terrifying thought of what would happen to her when the war finally ended. If the Germans were defeated, it would be necessary for her to start living all over again, and that was an impossible thought, because no matter where she went or what she did or who she traveled with, she would always be Ruth Borodin, the girl who had spent two years in solitary confinement in Russia, and who had afterwards been an army whore. For such a person there could never again be any laughter, any pleasure, any feeling. So perhaps she was better off here, where she didn't have to feel, where being able to feel was unthinkable, for it would mean reacting to every menial task she was forced to perform, every careless kick or slap from the guards, every thrust of every penis, twenty times a day.

Far better to think and dream, and imagine, than ever to feel again.

But the boy would have to go. Not only would she get into trouble if she allowed any of them to overstay their time, but he was the last on her shift. Ahead of her lay food and rest, and it was still daylight. She could look up at the sun; even the winter's sun was worth looking at, and she could dream.

She thumped him for a third time, the hardest yet. His head raised. "You must go," she said.

He sighed, and pushed himself up. "When I come back, I will try to come here again," he said. He stroked her head for the last time, allowed his hand to drift down to her breast. She did not protest. They all wished for some last caress.

"Yes," she said.

"If I come back," he said, and she saw tears welling into his eyes.

"Yes," she said again.

He waited for a moment, hoping for some word of sympathy, some suggestion of understanding. Then he sighed, pulled on his clothes, and left.

And she could dress, and leave. And she suddenly remembered that this was a special day. Judith's time off was coinciding with hers. If there was one person with whom she could be happy, it was Aunt Judith.

Anna Ragosina knelt against the tree trunk and levelled her binoculars down into the abandoned village of Schelniky. John Hayman knelt behind her, waited, and watched. They were alone in the forest. This was Anna's decision, as it had been increasingly Anna's decision since Christmas. Where she went, John Hayman must accompany her. When he might question her choice, she would smile at him. "But I trust you," she would say. "You shoot straight."

Anna Ragosina. Anna had come to dominate their lives more than ever in the horrible weeks since Svetlana's execution—weeks of empty bitterness made far worse by the increasing cold, which had cost the lives of several of the partisans, had left Natasha and himself deeply worried about

Tattie, as much for her mental state as for her physical health, weeks of dwindling supplies that left them all hungry, left the soldiers more anxious to fight each other than the Germans, unavailable and snug inside their winter cantonments. Where even her two companions, Alexandra Gorchakova and Tigran Paldinsky, had from time to time seemed to droop with exhaustion, Anna had remained the essential leader, invigorating them with her demonic energy, making them laugh at each other with her often cruel jokes, quelling the slightest hint of mutiny with her thin lips and her bottomless black eyes, and with the curl of her finger on the trigger of her tommy gun. John sometimes thought that she was the true spirit of the resistance of Russia, assuming that there was any resistance left in Russia, and that they were not, as the German leaflets claimed, fighting a private war in an unending vacuum, a war that must come to an end with their own deaths from starvation and exposure, or failing that, when the Wehrmacht was ready to launch its final, decisive attack.

He found her fascinating to watch. She possessed none of the grace of, for example, Natasha—even at six months pregnant—but she possessed a special grace of her own, the unequaled grace of supreme fitness and supreme confidence. He did not suppose even George Hayman possessed quite such an instinctive confidence in his own powers, such an obvious certainty that there was no one in his particular world who could possibly stand up to his determination or his excellence. The difference was that George Hayman stood for everything that was decent in the world, would be an essential part of the peace-making process when this holocaust came to an end; Anna Ragosina stood only for death and destruction. Mars was her god, and none of the others had even a tiny part of her personality. And when the holocaust ended, then too, he suspected, would Anna Ragosina end, her *raison d'être* no longer able to sustain her.

She handed the binoculars over her shoulder. "The square," she said.

He focused, and picked out the deserted houses, the frozen stream that meandered toward the trees, and then the improvised gallows and the slowly swinging body, still wearing its priest's cassock.

"Father Gabon."

"Obviously," she said. "There was nobody left to hang. But look at the house behind him."

John raised the glasses and watched the men in brown fatigue uniforms worn over a variety of sweaters that probably had been hastily and recently culled from the home front. The men were moving to and from the doors of what had once been the town hall. Those who went in were empty-handed, those who came out carried lengths of wood over their shoulders, and now he could see that they were filling trucks parked down a side street.

"They're stripping the town hall," he said.

"For firewood. That is obvious too," she said. "But they will not finish today. It is going to be dark in half an hour and there are another hundred-odd buildings in the village. The Germans are the most methodical people on earth. Once they have decided to use Shelniky for firewood, they will use all of it. They will take several days, perhaps a week, to get all they wish."

"I guess you're right. But there's nothing for us down there."

"There are Germans down there," she said.

John swung the glasses to and fro. Now that he knew what he was looking for, he could pick out the two machine-gun nests controlling the square, and the two armored cars down another side street. "They're well protected."

"But those machine guns aren't going to spend the night there, John. If we were in position when they arrived tomorrow, I think we could perhaps liquidate that entire force."

"It'd be quite a battle," he agreed. "But what's the point? For a couple more machine guns, a few more rifles, and some ammunition? We'd lose too many people."

She almost snatched the glasses back from him. "The point is that it is necessary," she snapped.

He met her angry gaze. "The point is that you haven't actually murdered anybody for three weeks now, and you're getting hungry."

"Yes," she said. "The point is that *none* of us has killed any Germans for three weeks. We have done nothing but shiver in our sleeping bags, and die with cold, and dwindle, in our minds, and think of Svetlana's body, lying in the road. An army exists to fight. When it does not fight, it gets like its weapons—rusty. And men's minds get even more rusty. Besides, do we not owe the Germans something, for Svetlana? We have not yet avenged her death." She jerked her thumb at the village. "Or that of Father Gabon. Come along and we will make our plans."

She turned on her hands and knees and began to crawl back through the frozen bushes. From behind she seemed a shapeless mass, with the flaps of her fur-lined *shlem* drooping over her ears, the tommy gun draped across her back, the grenades hanging from her belt, her fur-lined jacket and pants, her fur-lined boots. Like her two assistants, she had come prepared for the winter. The others might suffer from frostbite, but not Anna Ragosina. She did not offer to share. Well, he supposed he could understand her reasoning. She was their brains. She could not be distracted from her plans and her disciplines by any personal discomfort.

Yet she never used her rank to take more food than was her share. Often, indeed, she ate *less* than her share. But then, he did not suppose food interested her. She made him think of a vampire, needing only blood to sustain her.

Her gloved hands slipped on an unsuspected piece of ice, and she slid away from him, falling heavily on her stomach with a gasp. He held her shoulders and raised her up again, and realized that she had hit her chin; there was a gash there through which the blood seeped, immediately coagulating as it reached the air. He was quite surprised. He had hardly expected her to bleed, however severe the injury.

Her eyes were shut for a moment, and when they opened, they flickered lazily before closing again. He felt a momentary spurt of panic. Before her coming, he had traversed this forest quite freely and without fear; since her arrival, to go anywhere or do anything without Anna had been unthinkable. And now the silly girl had knocked herself out.

"Anna?" he asked. "Anna," he begged. "Wake up." Desperately he turned her in his arms, held her against him, her icy face against his. Her breath fluttered against his. "Anna?"

He didn't know what to do. Carrying her was out of the question, she was so heavily laden, and abandoning any of her equipment was equally out of the question. It was the one unforgivable sin, in her eyes.

But he didn't want to leave her, either, even to go for help. With her eyes shut, and her mouth relaxed, she looked more like a Madonna than ever. She was quite exceptionally beautiful.

"Anna," he said. "For God's sake, Anna, wake up."

Her eyes opened, and took him by surprise. He could feel his cheeks burn.

"Would you not be happy to see me dead, John Hayman?" she asked. "Then you could all go back to being castaways, in the middle of your forest. As you have said so often, if you do not trouble the Germans they will hardly trouble you."

He gazed at her, uncertain whether or not she had been play-acting the entire time.

Anna smiled, and turned in his arms, and before he could stop her, her arms went round his neck. "No," she said. "I do not think you would like me dead, John Hayman. I think you would regret that."

She kissed him on the mouth.

In the freezing predawn darkness they moved slowly, clumsily and noisily. Ice crunched beneath their feet, rifles slipped from nerveless fingers and clattered on the brittle surface beneath them, breaths clouded the air to turn the morning into a fog. Despite Anna's angry remonstrances they had long since burned flat the batteries in the flashlights they had taken from the train, but this, John thought, was all to the good; he could not believe that there wasn't a German sentry, somewhere, listening and hoping to see what was happening so noisily in the deserted village.

But gradually Anna got them where she wanted, concealed in the houses surrounding the square, in those down the street where the armored cars had been parked the previous day. She placed a great deal of reliance upon her enemies' lack of imagination.

The principal ambush was laid in the town hall itself, for again with great organization the Germans had begun their procedure of stripping the wood and furniture from the top of the house, and so the two lower floors were still untouched. "I will command in here," she said. "You will take the house across the street, John. And remember, I will fire the first shot. No one is to make a sound until he hears that first shot. Any man who disobeys is a traitor and will be dealt with as a traitor."

Her gaze swept her section commanders. "Do not forget that. Now go."

Tigran Paldinsky went to the left, Alexandra Gorchakova to the right. John crossed the square, unable to keep from looking up at the still-hanging body of the priest, nearly a solid block of ice now. He was quickly inside the building alloted to him, once the general store.

The ground floor contained a long counter, with shelves behind it, all empty now. Here he had six riflemen. Upstairs, where bedrooms and a living room overlooked the street, he had placed his machine-gun section, their weapons pulled back into the gloom of the house. "No one will fire until he hears a shot," he reminded them. "Then move to the window and open fire on every German you can see."

They nodded. With their bearded, ice-caked faces and their ragged clothing, they reminded him of wolves. And having seen them in action, he knew that they *were* wolves, in thought and in deed. He could not doubt that today was going to be as terrible as those others.

But what would it bring for him?

He returned downstairs, to be with the six riflemen concealed behind the counter; this was the position of most danger. It was the position Anna herself would have taken; he could do no less.

Had she, then, conquered him so easily? As he had come to know her so well, to understand the way she laid her plans and the slow and methodical way she implemented them, he could no longer doubt that *he* had been among those plans, from the moment she had arrived in their camp. Yet until yesterday, she had done nothing, had waited, with that deadly patience of hers. She could not doubt that he loved Natasha, that he already regarded her as his wife. But she had not doubted, either, that since he was a young and healthy man he would feel desire, in the course of time. And now Natasha was too heavily pregnant for them to continue sharing a sleeping bag.

Yesterday Anna's patience had borne fruit. For a few seconds he had held her in his arms, and it had been almost impossible for him to let her go. And yet, being Anna, she continued to spin her spider's web of a plan, refusing to deviate in the slightest, however opportune the moment. Yesterday afternoon he had wanted only her. Even as their tongues had touched, his hands had been seeking ways through her layers of fur. He had never seen her body. She wandered away into the forest by herself whenever she felt the necessity, and no one dared follow Anna Ragosina and spy on her. He did not even know if she undressed in her sleeping bag; she was invariably the last to go to bed and the first about in the morning. But that her body would match her face could not be doubted.

And she had laughed, gently, and kissed him some more, and given the front of his pants a gentle squeeze. "Tomorrow," she had said. "Tomorrow, after we have won a victory, we will celebrate. You and I will celebrate, John Hayman."

Had Natasha guessed? There was no way of telling. Natasha, like Lena Vassilievna or Nina Alexandrovna or any other of the pregnant girls in the encampment, lived permanently in a state of deep depression, aware of their growing handicaps when so much hard labor was required just to keep alive, and aware too of the enormity they were perpetrating, that of bringing another human being into this living hell. Women in such a position needed loyalty and support and continual comfort. So last night he had sat beside Natasha and held her in his arms, and kissed the tears from her cheeks—and wondered if she could hear the wild beating of his heart as he had looked across the camp to where Anna sat, cleaning her tommy gun and smiling. She was a monster of destruction. To surrender to her desires would be far more than merely betraying Natasha. It would be a betrayal of self, of the last hope he possessed of emerging from this war—if he was ever to emerge from this war as a human being instead of a seething psycopath.

But not to surrender to so much animal magnetism, animal power, and, he never doubted, animal passion as well . . . would any man have that much strength, much less John Hayman?

Dreadful thoughts to be thinking when he was about to command the men under him to kill or be killed. For now, seeping through the sudden daylight, he could hear the clanking of the chains on the German tires. They were up early, to work while the brief daylight lasted.

He looked along the row of men. They wiped frozen spittle and frozen sweat from their faces with the backs of their sleeves, and held their weapons the more tightly. The noise came closer, and now he could discern the pitches of the various engines. He did not dare stand up, but peered instead around the end of the counter and through the half-opened door at the square. He could just see Father Gabon's dangling boots; suddenly he feared that he had not left the door at exactly the angle it had been yesterday. Then a truck appeared, between himself and Father Gabon's feet. The tailgate came down, and out climbed the Germans. If they had brought rifles at all they were not carrying them now; apparently they were secure in the inactivity of the partisans since before Christmas and in the cover provided by the armored cars and their comrades. Beyond the first truck he could just see another, also unloading some twenty men. They seemed cheerful enough, laughed and joked even as they were marshaled and given their orders by their sergeant, and trooped off towards the town hall. Now, he thought. Now. But there was no sound from the town hall. Anna, of course, would wait until they were actually under her gun muzzles before she would open fire.

An officer suddenly appeared in John's line of vision, and stared straight at him. For a moment he could not believe it, had to make himself keep still by an act of will. But the man was approaching, slowly and nonchalantly, his brightly polished boots flicking slivers of ice from the roadway. Slowly, with infinite care, John shrank against the counter, until he could no longer see the approaching German. With childish optimism he assumed that therefore the German could not see him. He glanced at the men beside him, who were watching him, aware that something was happening. But Anna had said she would execute the man who fired before she did, and no one could doubt Anna would carry out her threat. Even if it meant killing John Hayman.

The door creaked, and the man beside John stirred, sucking breath into his lungs. John shook his head violently, listened to the boots hitting the wooden floor of the shop. He almost stopped breathing. Surely it was impossible to stand in a room containing seven men, and not know they were there, even if you could not see them. Surely—

A shot rang out, a sudden lonely, and for a brief second, unsupported spurt of sound, surprising even those who had been waiting for it. But it had been fired. John stood up, and his men stood with him. The officer had turned at the noise, and was framed in the doorway, his back to them, his mouth open, the first notes of a shouted question already booming into the air, to continue on and on and on across the frozen morning as seven bullets crashed into the back of his greatcoat, reducing it, before he ever hit the ground, to shredded gray cloth soaked in blood.

"Get to the windows," John shouted, even as, from above him, the machine gun started to chatter, to be drowned in the general cacophony as every rifle and machine gun in Shelniky opened up. He crouched in the doorway and watched unarmed men spilling from the town hall, many already hit and staggering before they encountered the hail of bullets coming from the general store, from his own rifle as well, as he fired again and again, pausing only to feed fresh clips of ammunition into his magazine. The morning became a tumult of dying men and flying bullets, of crashing noise and shouting voices. One of the trucks in the square caught fire and exploded in a gigantic bang which ignited the other, causing another huge flame to leap for the sky. A driver ran across the square, his jacket blazing, and fell, writhing in pain, with a bullet through the belly. Father Gabon disappeared as his body too caught fire. Bullets crackled into the store, and one of the men at the window spun around and hit the floor with a dreadful crash but without a sound from his shattered throat; his rifle struck John across the back.

But the battle was already over. The square was nothing better than a charnel house, and the final acts were coming from down the side street in the dull explosion of grenades. John stood up, slowly and carefully, still leaning against the doorway, looking down at the German officer sprawled in front of him. His throat was dry and he could smell nothing but gunpowder. It was too cold for even death to smell. He wondered if, when the spring thaw came, all Russia would suddenly become one vast stench, from the millions of unburied bodies lying now beneath the snow.

The partisans began to emerge from their concealment, from the town hall, from the floor above him. Yet again they had fought and won, under Anna Ragosina's leadership. They whooped and cheered, kicked the dead bodies they encountered, and began hunting for the still living. Anna was one of the last to appear. Her cheeks were pink with the pleasures of destruction, but already she was breathing slowly and evenly, in control of the situation.

"Strip these bodies," she commanded. "There are good boots there, good cloth. Collect all unspent bullets, all weapons." She stood with her hands on her hips and surveyed the burned-out trucks. "Now there is a pity. They will have brought their midday meal. But those others in the armored cars will have rations in their haversacks. Collect them. Hurry, now. All this noise must have been heard in Slutsk. You, make me up a list of our casualties, and bring out the wounded. Hurry, hurry."

She walked toward John. "I wish to know who fired that shot."

"Didn't you?"

"No." She turned towards Paldinsky and Gorchakova, who were approaching from the side street. "I wish to find out who fired that first shot, in direct contravention of my orders," she said.

Alexandra Gorchakova snapped to attention. "I did, Anna Petrovna."

"You?" Anna was incredulous.

Alexandra Gorchakova drew a long breath. "My weapon slipped, Anna Petrovna. I tried to catch it to keep it from hitting the floor, and it went off."

"Well," John said, "we were lucky. The timing was perfection."

Alexandra Gorchakova continued to gaze at Anna; she hardly seemed to breathe.

"You are under arrest, Alexandra Igorovna," Anna said quietly. "Take off your weapons."

Alexandra hesitated, then unslung her rifle, and removed the belt holding her revolver holster and her one remaining grenade. Her face had lost all expression. She handed the weapons to Paldinsky, who was also waiting, his face expressionless.

"And now your clothes," Anna said.

"You can't be serious," John said.

"They are good clothes," Anna pointed out sternly. "Spe-

cially made fur-lined jacket and pants and boots. One of the
girls at the camp will be very grateful for such clothes, perhaps
even your Natasha."

Alexandra unfastened her jacket, took it off, and immediately began to shiver.

"But she'll *freeze*," John shouted.

"It is a quick way to die," Anna said.

John gave a despairing glance at the girl, who was sitting
on the snow to remove her boots.

"You can't do that!" he cried, aware that they were suddenly
surrounded by people waiting and watching. "What difference
does it make if she fired out of turn? You still won your victory.
You still killed a whole lot of Germans." He pointed at the
shivering, terrified men being marched towards them, only
twelve out of all the hundred or so who had come to the village
this morning. "You still have your prisoners to butcher."

"You are coming very close to insubordination," Anna said,
still speaking very quietly. "You should remember, Comrade
Hayman, that should I find it necessary to execute you, I will
certainly then execute Comrade Brusilova as well. She remains
alive, in her unproductive condition, only because she is your
woman. Remember that."

. John stared at her, and she returned his gaze for a few
seconds, before turning to Paldinsky. "Take a dozen men and
break the ice on the river."

Paldinsky nodded, and summoned his squad. He did not
even look at Alexandra, who was now standing, quite naked,
flesh already turning blue, desperately trying to contain her
shivering, horribly aware that there was not a man or woman
in the village who was not looking at her.

Anna pointed toward the stream where Paldinsky and his
people were busily smashing the ice with their bayonets and
gun butts. "That way," she said. "If you stop walking, Alexandra Igorovna, I will shoot you. But you are a good soldier
and a good comrade, are you not, Alexandra Igorovna? You
will not make me waste a bullet."

Alexandra hesitated, as if she would have spoken, then she
turned and walked down the street, the cold already turning her
feet and toes white and numb, preventing her from doing more
than stumble.

"Now you," Anna said, addressing the Germans in their

own language. "Follow the example of Comrade Gorchakova, and attempt to die like men. Strip."

They gaped at her, seeming to huddle together. They all knew what had happened to other soldiers captured by the partisans.

"Strip," Anna said, "or I will kill you myself, slowly. But if you behave, you may walk away from here."

They glanced at each other. Better to die of exposure than to be butchered, they were thinking. John suddenly felt sick, as he had known he would feel before this day was done. But each time was even more horrible than the last.

The men tore off their clothing and threw it on the ground.

"And the boots," Anna said. "But," she added, "you may keep your helmets. Now rope them," she commanded in Russian.

The partisans gave a whoop, and a rope was passed around the twelve men, pulled tight to force them into an obscene huddle, shivering as they too began to turn white and blue.

"Over to the river," Anna commanded. "Follow Comrade Gorchakova."

Paldinsky's men had managed to smash a six-foot hole in the thick ice coating the stream, and now they had formed a double line through which Alexandra Gorchakova had to pass. She hesitated—no doubt, John realized, debating her chances of running either to left or right to avoid the water, but understanding that they would easily recapture her and make things worse than they already were. She drew a long breath, and stepped into the stream. It was only about eighteen inches deep, but rose above her knees. She began to hurry, splashed forward, reached the ice beyond, got her knee up and with a tremendous effort pulled her body behind, slipped and fell on her face but regained her knees again, and attempted to crawl forward. But to his horror John saw that the water on her legs was already turning to ice—something she had discovered as well. She turned, and brushed at it with desperate haste, realized she could make no impression, turned again, on her knees, tried to stand up, slipped again and fell, and this time lay sprawled on her side, incapable of further movement.

"For God's sake shoot her," he said, his voice low, the words distorted with saliva.

Anna glanced at him. "She is already dead. Or at least

unconscious. Hurry those men up," she shouted.

The Germans were driven into the water, unable to do more than shuffle as the Russian soldiers, whooping and cheering, pulled on the ends of the rope. There was a great splash, accompanied by cracking ice, for the exposed stream was already beginning to freeze over. And now the men realized the enormity of their fate. They turned to face the shore, shouting their pleas, attempting to scramble back out and being prevented at once by the rope and by the frantic movements of their companions in hell.

"They too will be dead in seconds," Anna said. "But do you know, there is not room for them to sink to the bottom under the ice. So when the other Germans come here, they will still be there in the river, frozen solid. That will give those others something to think about. Make haste now," she shouted. "Gather up these clothes. We must be on our way." She hurried to and fro, forcing the men to stop watching the dying Germans, driving them to work and then into the forest, until only she and John were left in the village.

"It is a pity about Alexandra Igorovna," she said. "She was a good girl. But always inclined to carelessness. I told her this, even when I was training her. I told her, 'Alexandra Igorovna, that carelessness of yours will be a disaster, one day.'" She sighed. "But she would never learn." She held his hand. "That is the way of life, is it not, John Hayman? Now let us hurry." She smiled at him. "But not back to camp. I know a little hollow where we may go, and be alone. It will be cold, but it is sheltered from the snow, and we will warm it, eh? After all, we have won our victory, our greatest victory yet. And you have been promised your reward."

John Hayman looked down at her, then pulled his hand free. "You'd best waste that precious bullet, Anna Petrovna," he said. "Because one day I am going to have you hanged."

He walked away from her, after the receding partisans.

*"Heil* Hitler!" The adjutant threw out his arm in the Nazi salute. "Prisoner will come to attention."

Paul von Hassell brought his heels together, stared to the front. After six months' confinement to quarters, he was about to hear his fate. And did it matter?

But he was surprised to discover that the officer entering

his room was not Heydrich. The Obergruppenführer had personally conducted his trial, just before Christmas, and found him guilty of unsoldierly conduct.

"Well, Hassell." This man was as tall as Heydrich, but far broader and more heavily built; his close-cropped black hair suggested that in his time he had been a regular army officer. "What have you to say for yourself, eh?"

"I have nothing to say, general," Paul said.

"Indeed? You should have. You have been given time to reflect, to consider where your true obligations lie. Oh, stand at ease. Sit down. You may go, Rennseler."

The adjutant saluted and left the room, closing the door behind him. The general sat down, crossed his knees, took out a gold cigarette case, and held it out. Paul hesitated, and then took a cigarette.

"Time to realize how mistaken you were," the general said.

"Fräulein Nej was my fiancée, sir," Paul said stubbornly. "We were in love with each other. We were going to get married. I could not have acted differently, either in love or in honor. Nor can I ever forgive the act that caused her death, nor the way it was carried out."

"Fräulein Nej was a partisan, Hassell."

"I will never believe that, sir," Paul said. "Never. She was an innocent caught up in circumstances beyond her control."

"That must remain an open question," the general said, puffing contentedly. "She most certainly knew where the partisans were to be found, and it was her business, if she truly intended to become the wife of a German officer, to help us eradicate these pests. Pests? In the Pripet Marshes they have become positively a menace. Their boldness is quite remarkable, and it is this man Hayman who is responsible. During the past few months they have killed nearly five hundred Germans, many in the most brutal fashion. Can you really condone such uncivilized behavior, Hassell? And do you know"—he stabbed the air with his cigarette—"it is catching. You have not asked where Obergruppenführer Heydrich is."

"I assume he will wish to see me, in due course, general."

"See you? Let me tell you, Hassell, Obergruppenführer Heydrich will never see anyone again, ever."

Paul's head swung, involuntarily, to look at his superior.

"Because he is dead, Hassell. Dead. Cut down in his prime.

Murdered by a bunch of Czech anarchists. Oh, they shall pay.
By God, they shall pay. The death of Richard Heydrich will
never be forgotten by any Czech or any German. But as long
as the world contains such madmen, careless of their own lives
and the lives of their families, it will not be a decent place to
live in. And the fact is, Captain von Hassell, that you are guilty
of conniving to keep these people alive and strong. It is possible
to reason that but for a mistaken supposition that you would
be able to rescue her from her predicament, Fräulein Nej might
well have told Colonel von Bledow everything he wished to
know, and we would have been rid of these Pripet vermin."

Paul could think of nothing to say. He found it difficult to
believe that Heydrich was actually dead. He had known him
since his first parade as a member of the Waffen SS, had
admired his singlemindedness, his elegance, his confidence,
had consciously attempted to model himself after so splendid
a figure—and over these past six months, had come to hate
him and everything he stood for, because it was Heydrich who
had confirmed Bledow's actions in Slutsk. And now he was
dead, struck down by the surest of all equalizers, a flying piece
of lead.

"Something to think about, eh?" the general asked.

Paul kept his head straight. "Yes, sir."

"Quite. I knew that you would have used these months well,
would have reflected deeply upon your position. The Reich
needs young men like you, Hassell. Make no mistake about
it, we are engaged upon the greatest, the most titanic struggle
in our history. It is a struggle we shall win, of course. There
can be no reversal now. But the Russians and the British seem
determined to fight to the last drop of their blood, and when
we have drawn that last drop of blood, we may have to help
our Japanese allies teach the Americans some facts of life, so
this war is likely to last a few years yet. Therefore we need
every talented young man we have. And you are certainly a
talented young man. So you will be pleased to know that the
Führer has signed an order restoring you to your rank and your
regiment. A position will be given to you in due course, but
for the time being, you have two weeks' vacation. You can
visit your mother, *Captain* von Hassell. And you can wear that
uniform with pride again. Is that not splendid?"

Paul gazed at him.

"I knew you would feel that way," the general agreed. He stood up. "Well, I must be off. Remember, wear that uniform with pride." He gave the Nazi salute and left the room.

Paul followed him more slowly, grateful that in the middle of the morning the huge building was empty of his fellow officers; the orderlies and clerks had had to salute him anyway, even during his confinement.

The sun shone with all the energy of a good spring day. It was the first time in six months that he had been allowed to leave the building except under guard, and he had not been allowed away from the barracks at all. He walked through the gate, returning the salute of the guard with almost self-conscious pleasure, and caught a tram into the heart of the city. A meal at the Albert. He had dreamed of that for six months.

And then a train down to Wiesbaden, and his mother. She had been shattered at the news of his disgrace; she would be overjoyed to see him again, to know that he was restored to rank and favor.

In order to return to Russia. He had hardly allowed himself to think about Svetlana, these last months. She had been everything to him, but at the end she had chosen country and family over a lifetime of happiness with him. Had he not accepted that, he would have gone mad.

And yet, she was the heroine, and he was the villain. There was no escaping that fact, either. A return to Russia would mean obeying commands that would involve torturing other young girls to death, hanging priests and mayors who sought to do nothing more than protect their people, slaughtering helpless hostages who had no wish to participate in the war. And to take the risk of being captured by the partisans himself, and butchered like a pig for the market.

The sun went in as if someone had drawn a blind, although it still shone brightly enough on the street. He left the tram and walked slowly up the Unter den Linden. The general had said this war might last for years—years of slaughter, of outrage and terror, of catastrophe. Of which he would be a part. A prime cause. He and all Germans. Because it was they who had gone to war with the English and the French, the Poles and the Czechs, the Norwegians and the Belgians and the Dutch. And the Russians. In every case it was the German army that had taken the irrevocable step of crossing another country's frontier, of attempting to dominate by force, always spurred on by the demonic ambitions of their Führer.

He wondered if there were any other Germans who felt as he did, who dared admit such thoughts to another. And if there were, what could they do about it? How could they seek to influence the warlord on his insane course?

Never had he felt so helpless, so despairing, and so angry at having survived Svetlana, when all the world seemed destined for disaster. And never had he suddenly felt less like a meal at Albert's.

He stopped, and turned away from the hotel, and heard his name called.

"Paul von Hassell? My God, but it is you. Come and sit down. I am sure we have a lot to talk about."

It was the Prince of Starogan.

# Chapter 12

AT THE TOP OF THE FLIGHT OF STAIRS, PETER BORODIN STOPPED and looked back at the young man. "You understand," he said, "that this is your last chance to turn back?"

Paul could just see his outline, looming above him, for the hallway was dark; the skylight had been blown out by a bomb blast, and had been patched with slats of wood. But he suspected that this hallway had always been dark. It was in a dark part of Berlin. To this, then, had the great Prince of Starogan been reduced. But he supposed even this tenement was better than a concentration camp; the prince was lucky. No doubt Himmler considered him a harmless madman, who might still have his uses. Once the eastern war was won, they would need a figurehead to set up as a puppet to reconcile the Russian people to their new masters. The renegade Vlasov, who had taken over the prince's role as the organizer and leader of the Russian army prepared to fight for the Nazis, had none of Peter Borodin's international stature.

But Himmler would certainly change his attitude were the prince to be discovered guilty of plotting against the regime. As for those who had attempted to aid him . . . and if they actually came from the ranks of the SS . . . Besides, the whole idea was utterly absurd. Better than anyone else, Paul knew the vast, all-embracing grasp that the Nazi machine had on the life of Germany. For a handful of civilian amateurs, even if aided by a soldier or two, to challenge that power would be utter madness.

And yet he was here, at least partly because of his fascination with the character of the prince himself. He had watched the man leave Slutsk, apparently crushed by the realization of just how unimportant he was. Yet here he was, bouncing back as ebulliently as ever, and with as much determination as ever, having selected a new course to be followed with all the fervor of the old.

Perhaps his motives were once again partly personal. Perhaps, for all his disclaimers of interest, he was determined to avenge his niece's death, and equally, perhaps, he was more than ever anxious to obtain the release of his Jewish friend from Ravensbrück. Were Paul von Hassell's motives any less personal?

He had realized he was going to stay. The only alternative was to turn his back upon everything that had happened, forget about Svetlana and about his dreams, forget about all his notions of honor and the future greatness of Germany, and become a true Nazi, utterly and without restraint, as he was already supposed to be.

That would not be survival as a human being.

He smiled into the gloom. "Having brought me this far, Prince Peter, would you not then immediately have to kill me?"

"If I did not suppose you could be trusted, Hassell, I would not have invited you back here at all," Peter pointed out seriously. "What I do not know for sure is your steadfastness, in the face of what may seem insuperable odds. And dangers."

Paul gave a brief laugh. "I'll not let you down, your excellency. I gave you my word."

Peter nodded, and opened the door. There were already seven people in the candlelit room, five men and two women, and as one they rose, less at the sight of the prince than of the uniform of his companion. One of the men instantly drew a pistol, while one of the women stifled a scream.

"Put that thing away," Peter Borodin said, and closed the door. "Captain Paul von Hassell is one of us."

They stared at him, refusing to believe such a thing was possible.

"The niece of mine who was executed in Byelorussia by the SS," Peter went on quietly, "was Captain von Hassell's fiancée. When he refused to accept the sentence, he was in turn arrested, and has spent the last six months confined to his quarters. He has now been released and restored to his rank. You'll agree, therefore, that he is a most valuable recruit to our cause."

"Released?" inquired one of the men. "And restored to rank? I find that difficult to accept. If he *did* oppose the sentence."

Peter smiled at them. "Captain von Hassell is somewhat of a protégé of the Führer."

Once again they stared at him.

"But the Führer is no longer his god, I am happy to say. Sit down, please. There is really no need for such alarm. I trust this young man, and he trusts us, or he could not have come."

"Unless ordered to do so, by Himmler," someone growled.

"In which case we are already dead," Peter pointed out. He watched them slowly settle back into their seats. "But how did you suppose we would progress toward our aim? By sitting here in this room and talking about it? We are engaged upon a great and dangerous enterprise. That is implicit in our intentions. Therefore risks have to be taken, in order to give us a chance of success. Paul is a calculated risk, and there will have to be others. For nothing we can say, or even do, has any chance of success without support from the army. The army is the crux of the entire matter. And here we have our first recruit from the army. I think this is a great day. Now Paul, I would have you meet the other members of the group."

The names rattled around in his head. Some of them he already knew, or knew of. Carl Goerdeler; Fabian von Schlabrendorff and his wife, Bismarck's granddaughter, no less. The others were just names. Intellectuals, men who had the time to think and who were trained to think, not blindly to obey orders. But there would have to be orders, eventually, when it came time to act, rather than discuss. And those orders would have to be carried out blindly, whatever reservations the intellect might have.

"So now," Peter said. "Perhaps you would like to say something, Paul."

"I am here to learn," Paul said, "to understand." He looked

around the circle of faces. "Prince Peter has given me to understand that you—that we—seek a change of government, a change of direction for Germany, an ending to the senseless war that has now ranged the entire civilized world against us—and an ending to the uncivilized behavior here at home. I am for all of these things. I will support you to the hilt. But as the prince has said, it is a great and dangerous enterprise. It will not be accomplished by words."

"There speaks your soldier," Peter agreed. "But you must not forget, Paul, that I too was once a soldier, and am ready to be one again. I think you will agree that this regime has betrayed us all. It has betrayed your hopes of a better, a greater Germany, by launching itself upon this self-destructive course of conquest. It has betrayed me also. I came here because Nazi Germany appeared to me to be the last, the only bulwark against international communism, the pernicious system that has seized my own country by the throat. And what do I find? That the Nazis are even worse than the Soviets. That their idea of liberating a nation is to reduce it to a desert. How can I possibly reign over a restored Russia if I have first been a party to the execution of thousands of my own future citizens, for no other crime than that of wishing to defend themselves? Therefore, I repeat, there can be no difference between us as to the aims we mean to achieve.

"Nor, as I have said, can there be any difference as to the methods. It will have to be by means of a coup d'etat. The arrest of all the Nazi leaders at the same time, and then the implementation of a carefully laid plan by which loyal army units, which will have already been positioned in key areas, such as here in Berlin, will take over. That there are such units, and certainly a large group of senior officers who agree with our thinking, is not in question. But at present all such groups are isolated, uncertain of the others, disorganized. The organization must come from us. By the time we strike we will have a new head of state chosen, and ready. He will immediately broadcast, informing the German people of the changed situation, and inviting the democracies and their Soviet allies to discuss an armistice. You will note that I am not advocating anarchy, or surrender. The Wehrmacht will remain in being, and will be prepared to continue its victories, should our enemies be reluctant to come to terms. But the offer will be there.

And the regime will have been changed to one with which they will be able to negotiate in honor." He smiled at them grimly. "You will also note that I am sacrificing more than any of you, in that I am prepared to accept the continuance of the Soviet regime in Russia, at least for a while longer, in order to end this senseless slaughter. But that is by the by. The important point is that we can proceed no further until certain vital army elements and commanders are secured to our cause. That will take time; they will have to be approached with utmost caution. But at least we have made a beginning. Have you any thoughts on how we may continue, Paul?"

"Well, sir," Paul said, "it is going to be immensely difficult. You may well be right that there are many people in Germany, and even many in the Wehrmacht, who are appalled by what is happening, by the slaughter in Russia and the terror here at home. But sir, being appalled and breaking one's oath are two totally different things. Every man in the German armed forces has taken an oath of personal allegiance to the Führer. The mere fact that Hitler is in custody, and justifiably so, will not cause them to break that oath."

"As you have broken yours," someone said.

"As I am prepared to break mine," Paul said. "Perhaps there are not many of my comrades with as much reason."

"I said that there would be no differences between us," Peter insisted, "and Paul is quite right. To ask a soldier to break his oath of allegiance is a terrible thing. What we must do, as part of the coup d'etat, is remove the object of the oath. And here, Hitler has assisted us. As Paul has said, the German soldier has not taken an oath to uphold the Nazi government, or any other government. He has taken an oath of personal allegiance to the Führer. Therefore, my friends, the Führer cannot merely be arrested. He must be executed. Hitler's death is the lynchpin upon which the success of our entire project depends."

Natasha Brusilova lay on the warm grass, her body twisting to and fro. Tatiana Dimitrievna had taken away the sleeping bag, exposed her to the wind and the sun—and even worse, to the gazes of the partisans—because there was nothing else to do. Now, as she moaned and whimpered, she looked up at Nina Alexandrovna, who was holding her wrists, and pressing them into the ground. Nina was also pregnant, but not due for another few weeks. Natasha Brusilova was the first of the girls from the academy to give birth here in the forest.

The heat was intense. Part of it was caused by her agony, but it was also a warm May day, the best day they had had so far. The spring rains had ended over a week ago, the high streams had started to subside, the bogs that abounded inside the forest had started to form a crust on the top. It was the true beginning of the year, the start of something new. Spring flowers burst forth among the roots of the giant trees, and the birds sang in the leaves. Butterflies flitted to and fro, and above everything, the sky was blue. Of all the times of the year, there could be no better time to give birth. .

As if there could ever be a good time to give birth, here in the forest, living like a hunted animal, and surrounded by so many more hunted animals. The thought made her twist again with pain, and cry out. Tatiana Dimitrievna stroked her stomach and thighs, and begged her to relax, and promised all would be well.

Fingers closed on hers. Strong, brown fingers. Her husband's fingers. Her husband before God, if not yet before man. But more than just a husband. A man among men. Of all the partisans, only John Hayman's name was equal to that of Anna Ragosina. Together they had made themselves immortal in the annals of this strange and brutal conflict, here in the Pripet Marshes. That John spent so much time trying to civilize his commander, trying to civilize them all, mattered nothing now. He did not often succeed. But his courage, his ability, his determination had earned even Anna's respect.

So, what had she earned from him? Natasha's eyes opened, and she smiled wanly at him, and saw Anna Ragosina standing behind him. Even she was interested in this supreme act of nature, in which she had never allowed herself to take her part. But her interest was purely academic. Her face remained expressionless—as it had, from all accounts, last January when she had ordered her companion in arms, Alexandra Gorchakova, to her death. That had been too much for John. He had returned to the camp and thrown himself on the ground, and waited for her to come and shoot him too. But she had not. She valued him too highly. And gradually, once again the barriers of hate and disgust had been broken down, because she was Anna Ragosina, because she was supreme in this way of life into which they had been thrown. And she was a woman, young and lovely, and for all her skills, helpless if enough of the men here remembered those essential facts. So she dominated by her courage and her brutality, her apparent insensitivity and her utter lack of fear.

And so, despite all, she continued to rule even John Hayman.

Natasha wondered if she was jealous of Anna. She had been so helpless these last few months, so much a burden to everyone, while Anna had gone from strength to strength, laying her plans, raiding isolated German posts, blowing up bridges and tearing up railway tracks, always with John at her side. Sometimes they had been gone for days on end. How and where and when did they sleep? It was not a question she really wanted answered. To be jealous of Anna Ragosina was hardly practical, and to force John to make a choice between them was to take too great a risk. She knew he loved her, and despite the circumstances, bearing this child of theirs was the most important thing she had ever done.

And surely that vital moment was here, at last.

"There," Tattie said. "Now, Natasha, now." John's fingers tightened on hers as the cramps welled up through her entire body. Her eyes flopped open and she watched the men coming closer, standing around, some muttering at each other, one or two even grinning—but with embarrassment, she decided. Most looked utterly absorbed by what they were watching. A free anatomical lesson, she thought, and closed her eyes again as her mouth flew open with pain.

She listened to noise, huge, burgeoning, unending sound, the roar of a hundred angry hornets, buzzing through her brain. Then there were other noises as well, shouts and screams. The hands holding her wrists suddenly relaxed and disappeared, and were immediately replaced by others, and these again she recognized: Johnnie's hands. Then the ground was heaving and something even fell across her face, but in the same instant the pain ceased and she heard Tattie's exclamation of pleasure, followed by a crisp smack and a thin wail of anger at being so rudely welcomed to the world.

Natasha was swept from the ground, and opened her eyes to look up, first, at the sky being darkened by the low-flying bombers, sideways, left and right; then in desperate terror, at the crater a hundred feet away, at the sprawled bodies half in and half out of it, at Nina Alexandrovna, who had fallen not fifty feet away, blood seeping from her back, and then up again, at Johnnie, as he ran with her further into the recesses of the forest.

"My baby," she screamed. "My baby."

"Aunt Tattie has it," he gasped, and fell to his knees in the shadow of a huge bush. "It will be all right. Aunt Tattie has it." He gave her a smile. "Has him."

"My son." She nestled her head against his chest, unable to grasp for a moment the fact that it was over, raising her head again at another huge explosion near at hand. "Johnnie . . ."

"We knew it had to happen," he said. "They wouldn't leave us alone forever, my love."

"But Johnnie . . ."

She watched him raise his head, to look past her.

"She will be all right now, Comrade Hayman," Anna Ragosina said. "She is the mother of your child. Now leave her and come with me. Where there are bombers there will also be soldiers. They mean to destroy us this time."

She crawled through the undergrowth in front of him. How many times had he watched her do this? But in the summer it was less easy to remember who and what she was. The *shlem* was discarded, and so were the fur-lined jacket and boots. Her shirt was unbuttoned and dragged out of her pants by her exertions; her shorts allowed him to see the ridges of white flesh above her thighs as she moved, the flopping tommy gun slung across her back.

Now she stopped crawling, and propped herself against a tree trunk, her glasses leveled at the distance. Her sleeves were rolled up, and he could watch the muscles in her forearm and at her bicep. Her collar was open, and there were her throat and neck to be observed as well, the little trickles of sweat descending the pale flesh to disappear into the fragrant wonderland that lay between her top button and her belt. She was a monster. He had had to remind himself of this, time after time after time, all through the winter and the spring. That she had not used her powers to destroy him was the result of chance. He was not at all sure what lay behind it, whether it was animal attraction to him or, more likely, orders from Ivan Nej. But that her own feelings came into it he could not doubt. Now, as she waved him alongside her, he watched her fingers playing with the top button of her blouse.

"Look there." She handed him her binoculars. He focused on the regiment of tanks slowly maneuvering into formation on what had once been a bog, the infantry forming themselves behind the tracked vehicles, the motorbikes with the machine guns mounted on the sidecars.

"They mean business," he said.

"It had to happen," she said. "They have only been waiting for some decent weather."

He looked down at her. She had rolled onto her back, her forage cap discarded, her face lazily relaxed. "And you are happy that it's come," he said.

"Once they enter this forest, however many of us they kill," she said, "we should take five for one. This is the moment we have all been waiting for, the moment they come after us. All my plans have been laid for this."

"What plans?" he demanded. "We have about four hundred people. So we take two thousand Germans with us. *That* is going to make a difference?"

"Everything we do makes a difference," she said fiercely. "We may only kill two thousand of those men, but a whole division is tied up there, just to destroy four hundred of us. That alone is a victory."

"And you do not care whether you live or die."

"Oh, yes," she said. "I care, John Hayman. I care. Not so much as you, perhaps. I have no little boy squalling his anxiety to live in this world. I have no loved one waiting to feel me in her arms. But I care. Do you doubt that?"

"No," he agreed. "I cannot doubt that, Anna Petrovna. Everyone must care. But if we are going to destroy the Germans in the right proportion to ourselves, then we'd best get moving."

She shook her head, to and fro on the grass. "There is no hurry." She pointed, her fingers languid, at the bombers still wheeling overhead. "They will not advance until their aircraft are finished. And you know what you have to do."

"I know how to die," he agreed.

"Then you may as well live, while there is yet time," she said. "Make love to me, John Hayman."

Never in his life had he had such a direct invitation. She

had unbuttoned her blouse from neck to waist; her breasts were larger than he had supposed, her nipples pointed and anxious, her entire body suffused with desire.

"Why do you hate me?" she asked. And when he did not immediately reply, she went on. "Because of what I am? Because I am a member of the NKVD? Because I have tortured and killed and maimed? It is a part of the job, John Hayman. I am what I am. I am what I was made to be. But you, you could make me something different. All I lack is love, John Hayman."

What an absurd conversation to be having, with the world about to fall apart, he thought.

"All you lack is love, Anna," he said. "But you have to be able to love first."

She took his hand, placed it over her nipple. "Do you not suppose I could give that love, John Hayman?"

She was the devil incarnate. A vicious monster who had condemned her only female friend to death, and made her die in the most inhumane and miserable fashion. She was a woman to be shunned, and feared, and hated.

And she was a woman to be respected and admired, and followed into the very gates of hell.

And he was the lover—the husband, in all but law—of the most beautiful, the most marvelous woman in the world and the father of her child.

Her smile was lazy. The intensity he would always associate with that gaze was, for the moment, lacking. "It is three years," she said, "since I have had a man." Her shoulders twitched. "I have not wanted one, except for you."

"And you always get what you want, Anna," he agreed, his mind raging with guilt and desire.

"Is it not always possible?" she asked seriously. "With patience. And determination."

"And certainty," he said, "that you know what you want."

"Of course," she agreed. "Without that, success is impossible."

"Then you know what *I* want," he said.

"Of course," she agreed again. "You want Natasha Feodorovna, and your son, and a house with a garden and beautiful furniture and a car. You want all the good things in life, because your name is Hayman, and you consider that you are entitled to them."

He sighed. "Well, then..."

"Oh, do not weep for me," she said. "Because, you see, you are much more certain than I can ever be. I am just a creature, John Hayman. You are out to make what you can of life. I can only be what life has made me. I do not look for happiness, because I know I can never have it. I can look for ecstasy. I can look for pleasure, as I feel when I am causing pain. Am I not a monster? But even monsters feel, John Hayman. And even monsters weep, in the secrecy of their sleeping bags, where they cannot be seen or heard. And even monsters yearn, even if they know that the yearning can only be for moments, rather than eternities."

He could only stare at her, and watch her smile.

"Did you not suspect that monsters can also share their feelings, John Hayman?" she asked, and then frowned. "Listen."

The earth had stopped shaking; the drone of the bombers was suddenly dwindling.

John pushed himself up. "Now the assault will begin."

"They are still over a mile away," she said. "There is time."

"You'd like us to die, here in each other's arms," he said.

She shook her head. "I had that in mind a few minutes ago. I thought then: now is the time to die, Anna Petrovna. I thought that you and I would charge those Nazi scum, killing down to our last breath, so that our souls would go winging through all eternity together, gun in hand, shoulder to shoulder."

"And now you've changed your mind."

"I have taken many lives," she said. "Now I would like to give a life back. Your life, and Natasha's life, and your son's life." Her face twisted. "It will be the first time I have ever failed in my duty. Which is not to say," she added, "that we should forget that Germans are there to be killed." Once again she knelt by her tree, and watched the approaching columns through her binoculars. "Give me your rifle."

He did as she asked, knelt at her shoulder, wanted to touch her again. But the time for that was past, just as her softness and her femininity were also in the past now. He watched her raise the rifle, check the mechanism, wedge the butt into her shoulder, and peer along the barrel. The binoculars had been laid on the ground, and he picked them up to look through them himself.

The tanks came first, a squadron of them, now crossing the roadway beneath them before beginning their push into the trees. Their hatches were open, and their commanders were inspecting the forest before them, also using field glasses. The scene reminded him a great deal of the German advance on Tattie's farm, the previous year. But this time there would be a difference. Would there have been a difference then, if Anna Ragosina had been in command of the defense?

Behind the tanks the infantry also advanced, in extended order. They moved slowly, utterly confident. But utterly determined, too, from the expressions on their faces. They were here to liquidate vermin who had been allowed to flourish for too long.

The movement of Anna beside him was almost simultaneous with the crack of her rifle. Instantly the leading tank commander threw up his arms and fell backwards, held still in his turret by the weight of his legs, body sprawled backwards. His cap disappeared to reveal blond hair, his tunic was a sodden red mass, and his face was utterly expressionless.

"Down," Anna shouted, throwing her shoulder against his to send him to earth. Bullets tore and slashed through the branches above their heads, punctuated by the deeper booms of the cannon. John realized that Anna's mouth was against his ear, but it was some seconds before he could hear what she was saying.

"Get out of here," she bawled. "Find Natasha, and Tatiana, and the child. Get into the forest."

He frowned at her. "I have my people to command."

"And I am relieving you of that command, today. Paldinsky can handle it. Now go."

He hesitated, and she kissed his forehead. "Do not disobey me, comrade. I will not have my orders disobeyed. Even by you."

He crawled into the bushes as fast as he could, looked over his shoulder, and saw her going the other way. Relief spread through his system; for a moment he had feared she had, after all, been overwhelmed by her urge to glorious suicide. A moment later she was lost to sight, and he had descended a dip

and could get up and run, forcing his way through the under-
brush, while the roaring cacophony behind him raged over his
head, and steadily advanced.

"Johnnie!" Tattie stood, hands on hips, gazing at him.
"What in the name of God—?"

He panted up to her. "Where's Natasha?"

"Over there, with the boy. Johnnie—"

"Into the forest," he said. "Deep into the forest." He grabbed
her hand and dragged her through the trees. "Natasha," he
bawled.

Her head came up, from a hollow in which she had been
lying, and she rose to her knees, the baby in her arms. He
reached her, and threw his arms around her shoulders to raise
her to her feet.

"Oh, Johnnie," she said. "Thank God you're back. But
Johnnie—"

"We're not going to fight," he said. "Anna's orders. We
melt into the forest."

"Thank God for that," Tattie said. "Give me the baby."

"But Tatiana Dimitrievna—"

"I know more about babies than you do," Tattie said. "You
take care of yourself."

"But he's hungry," Natasha said, as the child started to cry.

"And you have no milk yet. He will just have to do the best
he can. Come along." In the excitement of the birth, and now
of the battle, she had at last thrown off the inertia that had
clung to her throughout the winter, caused partly by her illness,
more by the horror of her daughter's death. But now suddenly
she was the old Tattie again, energetic and commanding. It
was as if, with Natasha's delivery, she had discovered a new
daughter, as well as acquired a grand-nephew.

She led the way, John and Natasha following. To left and
right, others of the girls were also hurrying, calling out to one
another, while from behind them there came the barking of
rifles and automatic weapons, to suggest that either Anna or
Paldinsky had made contact with the advancing Germans.

"Follow me," John shouted at the women. It was last year
all over again, except that there were now nearly a hundred of
them, and most of them were armed—but still running, away
from the black-clad menace, as he sometimes thought they
would run for the rest of their lives.

A sudden volley took him by surprise, left him too bemused by the horror of what had happened to understand for the moment. He could only stare; Lena Vassilievna, as pregnant as Natasha had been only a few hours ago, lay on her back, her entire head shot away, and several other girls were scattered on the ground, arms and legs flung to and fro in the ghastly ballet of death.

"Down," he shrieked, unslinging his rifle and returning fire, not sure where the ambushing Germans actually were. Natasha lay beside him, panting, looking left and right. Tattie was nowhere to be seen.

"My baby," Natasha shouted. "My baby," she shrieked.

Machine-gun fire scattered through the trees, whipping the bark away to leave white nicks on the tree trunks. From away to their left someone was screaming, and then there was another volley, and the screams seemed to redouble in their intensity. He watched the bushes in front of him move, watched, too, the gray-clad figures rising up, bayonets gleaming.

"My baby," Natasha moaned. "My baby."

John lay absolutely still. To fire was to die. But would *not* firing make any difference? He watched the Germans running forward, watched another girl start up out of a bush fifty feet away, gaze at the Germans, throw her empty pistol at them before turning to run, and trip, to fall to her knees; watched the bayonet thrust forward, watched her head tilt back in a wailing scream of agony and despair, watched the German place his foot on her buttocks to pull the bayonet out, watched her lie there, watched the blood-red steel drive forward again, and watched, too, the German spin round and hit the earth with an audible thud. John gazed in horror along the barrel of the rifle he had just fired with instinctive anger.

As if his shot had triggered some universal mechanism, the forest around him exploded into flame. Several of the Germans fell, others started to retreat, and still others sought shelter as they returned fire. But now they were being attacked from the left as well, the trees seeming to tremble with the deadly bees that buzzed to and fro. John became aware that he was loading and firing, loading and firing, while Natasha clung to his legs and wept. Until feet appeared beside his, and he looked up at Anna, panting, face blackened and her midnight hair in wild tangles.

"Retreat," she said. "Come on. There may be other flanking parties. Into the swamp, comrades. Into the swamp."

"My baby," Natasha moaned. "My baby."

Anna gazed questioningly at John.

"He was with Tattie. Aunt Tattie!" he bawled, his throat dry and his voice hoarse. "Aunt Tattie!" She could not be far away. The thought of one of those bayonets driving into that white flesh, and finding the child as well, made him want to vomit. "Aunt Tattie?"

Bushes heaved, and Tatiana Dimitrievna stood up. She had opened her blouse to allow the child to chew, and still held him close.

"Alexei," Natasha screamed, and ran forward.

Anna Ragosina smiled at John. "There, he has a name. And he was born in battle, your son. He will go far. Now let us hurry." She held his hand to pull him forward.

"But—the Germans—"

"Oh, they are still coming. But they will stop eventually. They count this a victory. They will write it up in their newspapers. They have killed several of us. But we have killed more of them. And when they go away to celebrate, we will still be here, John Hayman. We will always be here, until they go away for good."

## Chapter 13

"YOU MAY GO IN NOW, CAPTAIN HAYMAN," THE ADJUTANT SAID.

George Hayman, Jr., stood up and tucked his cap under his arm. He stepped through the opened door and immediately came to attention. There were four other men in the room, two of whom he recognized: the balding figure of General Eisenhower, seated at the huge desk, and the dapper, sharp-featured British Field Marshal Montgomery, standing at his shoulder. They had been studying a report lying on the desk in front of Eisenhower, but looked up together as George came in.

"Captain Hayman, Army Intelligence, general," the adjutant said.

"You compiled this report?" Eisenhower asked.

"Yes, sir."

"Based on these named contacts with enemy agents?" Montgomery asked.

"Yes, sir."

"You're young for such a position."

"I had the contacts, sir," George explained. "My father's newspapers had many correspondents in Europe before the war. Several are still there, and none are Nazis. So I was given the

335

task of contacting them through field agents, and correlating their reports."

"And you believe what is down here?"

George stared straight in front of himself. "There definitely is a plot against the Hitler regime, general. Against Hitler himself."

"But the conspirators want assurances that we will then deal with Germany as an honorable enemy, and even join with them in fighting the Soviets," Eisenhower said. "You know that I can give no such assurances, even if I wished to. These men may now know that deposing Hitler is their only hope. That makes them no less guilty of supporting him for the past eleven years."

"Yes, sir."

"So this report is meaningless. I cannot, and I will not, make any deals with any officers of the Wehrmacht, except to accept their unconditional surrender."

"Yes, sir. I think they know this, sir."

Eisenhower frowned. "Explain."

"They obviously would like such a deal, sir, but they know they're unlikely to achieve it. I think the plot will go ahead. But it requires something positive on the part of the Allies to spark it. The conspirators have to present the German people with a situation that is quite desperate, where the war can be seen to be irretrievably lost, and where only a non-Nazi government has even a hope of making an honorable peace. That situation has not yet arisen."

"You wouldn't call Stalingrad desperate, for Germany?" Montgomery asked. "Or the situation in Italy?"

"Apparently they wouldn't, sir. Italy is beyond the Alps, Russia is beyond the Ukraine. The Nazi fortress Europe—bounded by the Pripet Marshes, the Carpathians, the Alps, the Pyrenees, and the Atlantic—is still inviolate, and the German people believe that it is too strong ever to be invaded. When the Second Front is launched, sir..." He paused.

"You think a successful landing in France may trigger this conspiracy, captain," Eisenhower offered.

"Yes, sir. I do."

Eisenhower nodded, and glanced at the calendar on his desk; the date was May 3, 1944.

"Well, captain," he said. "Let us hope that you are right. When the time comes. Good day to you. And thank you."

The telephone jangled, and Paul von Hassell picked up the receiver.

"Prince Borodin for you, Colonel von Hassell, from Brandenburg," said the girl.

The Prince had left Berlin over a year ago; he claimed it was safer, and easier, to control the conspiracy from thirty miles outside the city. No one had apparently minded. The Nazis seemed determined to ignore their difficult protégé's existence—unless, Paul had often thought, they were merely giving him enough rope to hang himself. And his accomplices.

"Yes," he said, attempting to remember all the many code words and phrases he had been supposed to learn by heart. Schoolboy stuff. And about as real as games played by schoolboys, as well.

"Good morning, Paul," Peter Borodin said. "And a very good morning it is too, considering yesterday."

Paul sat up straight. Peter had just told him to stand by. It was not the first time this had happened, however.

"Yes," he said.

"Because," Peter went on. "I have finally settled accounts with that rat in the bathroom. I knew you would be pleased to hear this, seeing how often he troubled you."

Paul held the receiver away from his ear, stared into it, and discovered that his secretary was watching him. But it was not credible. After all this time?

"How can you be sure?" he asked, forcing his voice to remain quiet, and calm.

"I had Stauffenberg help me," Peter said. "Well, you know he was anxious to try. I am too old to go crawling around hunting for rodents. But Stauffenberg did everything, and he assures me the brute is dead."

"When?" Paul asked.

"Ah. About four hours ago. You see—"

"Four *hours?*" Paul shouted.

"Yes. I had some problem in getting through, and of course I had to wait until Stauffenberg could tell me himself that he was sure. Well, I won't detain you. I know that you have a great deal to do, and the sooner the better. Don't you agree? Call me here, in three hours, and tell me how you are. Goodbye, Paul."

The receiver went dead, and Paul slowly replaced it on its hook. For a moment his brain seemed to have gone blank. He had not expected it ever to happen. Not after two years. Two years of slowly building up the group that would control the coup, whenever it happened. This had taken much longer than any of them had supposed possible, and even when it had been completed it had hardly seemed more than a game. They had finally obtained the support of Field Marshal Beck, who, before his dismissal by Hitler at the start of the war, had been commander-in-chief of the Wehrmacht, and was the one man, apart from the Führer, whom they thought the German soldiers would obey without question. Through Beck they had managed to approach several other high-ranking officers, and met with a remarkable amount of success. But the prerequisite had always been the same. No soldier was going to take action while Hitler lived, and the assassination of Hitler became daily a more difficult matter, since he had responded to the worsening military situation by spending most of his time in the East Prussian headquarters of Rastenburg, where he was entirely surrounded by the most faithful of his people.

For that had been another concomitant of their long crawl toward a viable plot—the disasters that had overtaken the Wehrmacht since the heady days of the summer of 1942. Since then there had been the Battle of Alamein, the American landings in North Africa, the catastrophic invasion of Italy and the collapse of that country, and, overshadowing them all, the tragedy of Paulus and the sixth army at Stalingrad, from which had started the steady but apparently irresistible counterattack of the Red army, mowing down all who attempted to oppose it.

And then, the final blow, only two weeks earlier, as the Americans and the British had landed in Normandy. They were still being contained. There was still the possibility that this invasion might be thrown back into the sea. But the fact that they had been able to land so many men with so much equipment at all meant that the military defeat of Germany must be in sight. Thrown back here, would they not soon land somewhere else? And how could the Wehrmacht fight on three fronts at the same time, as well as hold down the subject peoples of an entire continent?

Certainly not while regiments such as his own, a thousand of the finest fighting men in Europe, were kept on garrison duty in places like Prague. Perhaps it was necessary. The Czechs were proving almost as recalcitrant as the Russians, and even though he refused to have anything to do with interrogation or executions, he still had to sign all the necessary orders. He was not so very far removed from Colonel von Bledow, after all.

Undoubtedly, though, having a regiment such as his in Prague had been an essential part of the operation. With the aid of loyal staff officers, Peter Borodin and Beck and Stauffenberg and the other leading conspirators had worked hard to have every important city or marshaling point controlled by troops whose commanders were in the plot with them. But Paul had not even had to apply for this posting. It had been given to him, perhaps because he was still not yet considered trustworthy. It would be necessary to prove that he could control a captive population before he could be sent back to Russia. But the regiment would have been of more use in Normandy.

These past months had also been months of doubt. Even now he doubted. That Nazism had been a ghastly mistake, on his part and the entire nation's, he could not doubt. That the men who had executed Svetlana Nej, and so many others like her, and sent so many others to concentration camps, deserved at best to be hanged, this again he could not doubt. And that Hitler, as the font of so much misery, also deserved to be executed, he could not doubt. But as every attempt had failed, because of either defective explosive mechanisms or failure of nerve, and as Germany's situation had deteriorated, the doubts had grown. Peter Borodin had claimed that they were not going to surrender, that the Wehrmacht would be kept ready to resume the German victories if the Allies refused to negotiate. But that was hollow talk now. Trying to hasten things, Paul had even volunteered to be the assassin himself, but had been refused. He was not senior enough, could not be sure of gaining access to the Führer. A staff officer had to be found, however long it took. "One does not succeed in ventures of this nature," Peter had said often enough, "by impatience."

Paul had even suspected them all of being no more than

theoretical conspirators, men and women who liked to meet and mutter over ersatz coffee but were not prepared to take the risk. Meanwhile he could feel himself, with his being sustained solely by the existence of the plot, dwindling into nothing. Until Stauffenberg. "Stauffenberg," Peter had said, "is the man for it. He is utterly fearless, and he is a man of decision. And he is a senior staff officer."

It was difficult indeed not to have the utmost confidence in Stauffenberg. His courage and decisiveness were legendary. But could a man who had been blown up by a mine in North Africa, losing one eye, one arm, and two fingers on the remaining hand, be capable of carrying out an assassination?

Apparently he had. And Paul von Hassell was still sitting at his desk, brooding on it, when there was so much to be done. The Wehrmacht was still a formidable force, a force with which the Allies would be glad to make peace could it rid itself of its demonic leader.

He leapt to his feet. "I have just received information," he said, "that the Czech partisans are about to attempt a coup, a seizure of Prague, in league with traitors in our own command. Get me Captain Roedeler, and issure orders for the battalion to be ready to move out in fifteen minutes. We must seize the radio station and command headquarters, place the city under martial law, and await further orders. Hurry, Fräulein. The entire fate of Germany is in our hands."

General Schmitt looked down the barrel of Paul's Luger, then slowly removed his own pistol from its holder and laid it on the desk in front of him.

"You," he said without heat, "are going to hang, Hassell. I am of the opinion that you are quite mad."

"And I am still hoping that you will show some sense, general," Paul said, "and join us. This city is entirely in the hands of my men."

"And do you suppose they will remain your men, when they learn what you are about?" The general leaned back in his swivel chair, half-turned it to look out of the window, and allowed his hand to droop down the side of his desk.

"If you attempt to press one of those buttons, general," Paul said, "I shall be forced to kill you, and whoever enters this room in answer to your summons. My men are also in control of this building. But please, sir, why do you not telephone Berlin? Ask to speak with Field Marshal Beck."

Schmitt frowned. "Field Marshal Beck? He is retired."

"He has returned from retirement to head the government and the Wehrmacht, now that the Führer is dead."

Schmitt gazed at him for a moment, then slowly picked up the telephone.

"And please remember, Herr General," Paul said, sitting on the edge of the desk. "No tricks."

Schmitt merely continued to gaze at him, gave the necessary instructions, and waited, fingers drumming on the desk. "If the Führer *is* dead," he said, half to himself, "then possibly the entire situation will have to be reviewed. Possibly."

Paul began to breathe more easily. If he could win Schmitt to his side, with all the German divisions in Czechoslovskia under his immediate command . . .

"Yes," Schmitt said into the phone. "Herr Field Marshal?" He listened for a moment, began to frown again. Then he said, "I do not understand. Under *arrest?*"

Paul stool up again, his stomach churning.

Schmitt was looking at him, but still speaking into the receiver. "I was given to understand, Herr General," he said, very carefully, "that an attempt has been made on the life of the Führer, and that Field Marshal Beck had been recalled. That is not true?" Again he listened. "The Führer is alive? You have spoken with him on the telephone?" He gazed at Paul. "Herr Goebbels is in control? I see. And the Field Marshal is under arrest. To be shot? Yes. I understand. The others . . . Stauffenberg . . . to be shot? Yes. Yes, I understand. Oh, there is no trouble here, I assure you, general. I shall take the necessary steps. It may be necessary to shoot one or two here as well, of course . . . carte blanche? Thank you, general. You may rely on me."

He replaced the telephone, as slowly as he had picked it up.

"You are bluffing," Paul said. But he knew it had been the truth. There was no way Schmitt could have chosen the name of Stauffenberg as one of the conspirators; it had to have been told him over the phone.

Schmitt shrugged. "I suggest you telephone for yourself.

But I would more earnestly recommend that you holster that gun. Of course, you can shoot me now, Hassell, but you will be taken. And handed over to the Gestapo. I do not think they will be in any hurry to shoot you, colonel. But I tell you what I will do. Because I have known you for a great many years, and because I have even liked you, once upon a time, I will get up and leave this room. You will still have your revolver. I will not return for fifteen minutes. You have my word as an officer and a gentleman." He pushed back the chair, and stood up. "Believe me, it is much the best course to follow."

Paul gazed at him for a moment, and then leaned forward and with a sweep of his arm caught his superior a blow across the side of his head with the pistol barrel. Taken utterly by surprise, Schmitt fell without a sound; Paul had time to catch him and lower him into his seat before he struck the floor. Then in quick movements he removed the general's boots and tie and socks, used them to bind and gag him, and secured him to the chair. This was action, and suddenly his whole mind was crying out for action, even as his stomach seemed to be filling with great lumps of lead. Peter Borodin had been so sure, so definite—it had to be a bluff. But not from Berlin. For some reason things had gone wrong in Berlin, and Beck and Stauffenberg were both under arrest, both about to be shot. But if things had gone wrong in Berlin, even if Hitler was dead, then the game was up. With Goebbels in command, things might even be worse than if Hitler were alive.

He realized he was panting. He had no idea what to do. He wanted to get away, but where? He was about as securely buried in the very center of German-occupied Europe as possible. Besides, they would immediately be closing all frontiers to Switzerland, even if he could get that far.

He chewed his lip. Peter Borodin! Peter Borodin was the center of the conspiracy. He would know what had gone wrong. He would know how to put it right.

He picked up the phone, gave the number. But the operator came back immediately. "Brandenburg has just been bombed, colonel. The lines have been cut. But there is a call from Berlin, for General Schmitt."

"No." Paul said. "General Schmitt will take no calls. General Schmitt is not to be disturbed until further notice." He replaced the receiver. Of all the bad luck! But Peter Borodin was still the only hope the conspirators now had of saving something from this catastrophe. Certainly he could not stay here, and wait to be arrested.

It was only two hundred and fifty miles from Prague to Brandenburg.

He roared up the autoban at seventy miles an hour, hand flat on the horn whenever he encountered other traffic. Since he was in uniform and driving an official car, most of the traffic—it was all military—got quickly out of his way.

But what was he doing? Running away. The realization came as quite a shock. He had never doubted his personal courage. But he was running away. Again. As he had run away from the partisans, as he had run—or allowed himself to be led—away from Svetlana.

For a soldier to understand that he may be a coward is a horrifying shock. For a moment the car slowed. But there was no point in changing his mind now and attempting to die like a hero. By now Major Helsingen, whom he had left in command in Prague, would have entered the general's office, if only out of curiosity. So Prague was lost, because Helsingen was not in the plot, had only been obeying orders. And undoubtedly the same thing was happening all over Germany. All over Europe. Only in Berlin could the situation be rectified. And only Peter Borodin would know how to go about accomplishing that, because only Peter Borodin had the full list of conspirators, knew exactly who could be called upon. There had been talk that Rommel and even Model might be involved. Or Rundstedt himself. If one of those, or better yet all three, would come out against Hitler now, the day could still be saved.

But time. It ticked by on the clock on the dashboard of the Mercedes, every tock the death knell of one more hope, and no doubt also the moment of death for one of his confederates. At least he retained the option of suicide; his pistol was still on his belt. But he would postpone that to the last possible moment, until he had spoken with Peter Borodin, until they actually appeared before him, gun in hand. He was suddenly filled with a wild sense of desperate exhilaration, partly caused by the tumultuous drive, partly by a lurking suspicion that he could yet escape, if he acted the coward boldly enough, and with enough determination. And if he made himself remember, constantly, that the only alternative was death.

The car felt its way through the streets of Brandenburg, a seething antheap in the hot June afternoon. Fire engines wailed to the accompaniment of police sirens. Houses burned and civilians aided wardens and firemen in pulling at collapsed rubble. Others stood around in shocked groups, nerves temporarily collapsed under the pervading destruction showered on them by the American flying fortresses. They all gave way instinctively to the SS colonel.

He hardly noticed them, was vaguely aware of being hungry, since he had not had any lunch, but he also knew that there was no hope of eating anything, with his stomach so turbulent. He brought the car to a halt on the side street, expecting Gestapo men to appear from behind every bush. But this street was deserted, and undamaged. He took the stairs four at a time, reached the top, and banged on the door.

"Who is it?"

Thank God for that, he thought. "Paul von Hassell."

"Paul? Are you alone?"

"Yes. For God's sake hurry, Prince Peter."

The door opened, and Peter stared at him. That he knew what had happened was obvious; his eyes said that. But he did not look particularly frightened. "Why are you not in Prague?"

"Don't you understand?" Paul snapped. "Goebbels is in charge in Berlin. What in the name of God went wrong?"

"Would you believe it? Those fools failed to take over the radio station. And they argued. And Hitler wasn't dead at all."

"But how on earth? If Stauffenberg planted the bomb in the conference chamber . . ."

"I have no idea," Peter confessed. "Sometimes I think that man must be protected by some evil genius, some devil." He went back into the room and poked the roaring fire, a sufficiently strange sight on a warm June day.

"What are you going to do?" Paul demanded, closing the door behind him.

"Do?" Peter continued to poke. "There is nothing to be done. I am sorry for Stauffenberg and Beck, and those others in Berlin. We must hope that they know how to keep their mouths shut."

"Are you going to do *nothing?*"

Peter turned his head. "What *can* I do, except start again? If I am allowed to."

"You will just sit here and wait to be arrested? And then tortured by the Gestapo?"

"I shall take poison before arrest," Peter said. "But there is still hope. If no one breaks down—"

"For God's sake," Paul shouted, "of course they will break down! The Gestapo will reduce them to such a state that they won't know what they're saying. And what of people like me? General Schmitt will have a warrant out for my arrest by now."

"Then you'd better see if you can get away," Peter said.

"And you won't come with me?"

"You mean run away?"

"Oh, come now," Paul said. "You ran away from the Bolsheviks, in 1918, because there was nothing else for you to do. And by doing that you lived to fight another day. Listen to me. I have a car downstairs, and we still have a few hours. I have my uniform, and several passes. I have been thinking about it. If we can get to Warnemünde, near Rostock, before the fishing fleet puts out tonight—I have an old friend there, a skipper named Jürgen. When I was a boy, I used to go crewing with him. He will help us. He has a Swedish wife. They will take us across to Sweden. I'm sure of it."

"Cross the Baltic? That is absurd!"

"It is a chance," Paul insisted. "The only chance we have. If we're sunk, then we'll drown. It's better than having electrodes shoved up your ass." He turned to the door. "I'm going to try it, anyway."

Peter hesitated, chewing his lip. Then he said, "A car. Rostock. You will drive by Ravensbrück."

Paul frowned at him. "That is madness. Every moment is vital. And besides—"

"You have several military passes. And you are still Paul von Hassell, as I am the Prince of Starogan. The very last place they will think of looking for either of us is a concentration camp." He came across the room and took Paul's arm. "We are going to die, Paul. You know that. There is no way we can survive this."

"And you wish to take that Jewish woman with you. To hell."

"Judith? Why, yes. I will take Judith. But it is my daughter I want. Ruth is also in Ravensbrück."

Paul stared at him. "Your *daughter?* But—"

"She disappeared five years ago. Oh, yes. A long story. But the Nazis have had her in Ravensbrück for the past three years. They shaved her head. Can you imagine? Paul, we must try to get her out. If we die there, it is just as good as drowning in the Baltic. But we must *try.*"

It was Paul's turn to hesitate.

"And Judith," Peter said. "I treated her very badly, Paul. I treated her worse than any woman should ever have been treated."

Paul sighed. "And you assume they'd rather be dead."

"Than pretending to live, in a place like Ravensbrück? Why, yes. I think they would rather be dead. With me. You drive me to Ravensbrück, Paul, and then I'll help you to get to Warnemünde."

The car scraped to a halt. The guard saluted, then inspected the pass. It seemed to take forever, and Paul could only lean back and gaze at the barrackslike buildings, the sign over the gate. He had never actually been inside a concentration camp before. That it was a prison was obvious; the barbed wire and the guard towers with thier machine-gun barrels protruding so disturbingly indicated that. And the smell of disinfectant, which hung on the still afternoon air. But apart from that, nothing.

The guard returned his pass, saluted. "The commandant's house is on the right, sir."

Paul smiled at him. "Have you no inmates?"

"They are working, sir," the guard said seriously.

"Of course." Paul took his foot off the brake, allowed the car to ease forward. It was necessary to drive with the utmost confidence, smile with the utmost confidence, refuse to admit to himself that he expected to be arrested at any moment, that he could not keep his mind from what Prince Peter might be doing back in the village. They had decided that, since Peter had visited Ruth before, and might just be remembered, it was best for Paul to attempt the escape on his own. Prince Peter did not know that he had placed his life, and that of his daughter, in the hands of a coward.

Or was Borodin playing a trick, he thought? His brain was

clouded with suspicion of everything. But it could not be a trick. Prince Peter would not desert his own daughter. And besides, without this car he was as lost as anyone.

The car stopped in front of the building with the flagstaff from which the swastika lazily drooped. Now he could hear a sound like the cooing of a thousand doves. It reminded him of visiting a girl's school, many years ago. This was also a female world. Two uniformed young women hurried down the steps, opened the door for him, stood at attention.

"The commandant?"

"Is in her office, sir. Is she expecting you?"

"No. But it is very urgent."

The girl nodded, hurried in front of him, and knocked on the inner door. The other secretaries and typists stared at him.

"Well?" The commandant was a large blonde, who must have been quite pretty once, he thought. Now her face was twisted with impatient arrogance.

"Paul von Hassell," he said.

She appreciated his rank and saluted. "I am told it is urgent."

"It *is* urgent," he said. "You have two women in this camp. Judith Stein and Ruth Borodin."

The commandant frowned at him. "I have those women, yes."

"They are to accompany me to Berlin."

The frown deepened. "You wish me to release two members of this camp, without authority?"

"It is a very urgent matter. You may as well know the truth of it. There has been an attempt on the Führer's life, accompanied by a coup d'etat in Berlin. Oh, do not worry. The attempt has failed, and everything is under control. But it is certain that Prince Borodin of Starogan is deeply implicated. The prince has escaped, for the time being. Herr Goebbels wishes the two women, the prince's daughter and his sister-in-law, to be taken immediately to Berlin for questioning."

"Questioning?" The commandant gazed at him, her mind obviously in a turmoil.

"Immediately," Paul said. "But I am afraid I shall have to impose on you, Fräulein. I cannot possibly take two women on my own. I am instructed to requisition from you—" He hesitated in turn, but it was necessary to convince her, by overwhelming reassurance. "—two of your people as guards."

"Well...I suppose that could be arranged," the commandant said uncertainly. "But the whole thing is very irregular."

"I shall require them to be armed," Paul said. "And trained to use their weapons. These women might well prove desperate."

"Yes," the commandant agreed. "Fetch the two women," she snapped to a subordinate. "And you, Helga, and you, Inge. You may have a trip to Berlin. That will be good, eh? Go and pack some things, and arm yourselves."

"And make haste," Paul said. "That is vital."

The absurd ease of it astonished him, left him feeling at once flattered and apprehensive. Of course the real difficulties lay ahead. But he did not suppose either Helga or Inge were going to be difficult, as long as he could steel his mind to what he had to do. And this was simple. He had but to remember that these two pretty girls were concentration-camp guards, that they spent their time torturing other innocent women, that they were of the same breed as Colonel von Bledow's secretary, Ilsa, who had undoubtedly sat and smiled as Svetlana had screamed and died. He was more worried about the two women they were rescuing.

The Stein woman sat in the back seat, between the two guards. He had estimated that she, being so much older and presumably more experienced, would be less likely to have hysterics when he killed the guards. But it had been a difficult decision to make, because her eyes had no more life than did those of the young one, the prince's daughter. Of course, she supposed she was being taken to a Gestapo torture chamber. And she had obviously not suffered as much as he had expected, in the camp; both of them looked surprisingly well fed, and even well groomed, except for the very short hair, and the ever-present smell of disinfectant. But they had come from the camp brothel. They had spent nearly three years in the camp brothel. Any woman would have dead eyes after that.

He gathered, from the guards, and the remarks of the commandant, that they had been two of the women most sought after by their soldier clients. This he could understand. Judith Stein was still remarkably handsome, with bold features and a voluptuous body, while Peter Borodin's daughter was a delight to look at, even with her cropped head. Should have been a delight to look at. Except that he did not wish to look at her at all, because when he looked at her she looked back, and he had to gaze into those eyes.

Well, they were Prince Peter's problem. But he hoped they would behave when it came to the moment, because that had to happen before the village, when they would meet Prince Peter. It had to be now; they were out of sight and out of earshot of the camp. He turned off the road on to the grass shoulder, and applied the brake.

"What is the matter?" asked Helga.

Paul twisted on the seat, rising to his knees as he did so, his pistol already drawn. It was simply a matter of thinking of Svetlana. But it was not as easy as he had hoped. As he gazed into Helga's shocked, alarmed eyes, he hesitated—for less than a second, he supposed, but it was a second too long. For as he squeezed the trigger, watched Helga's tunic dissolve into red, watched her head jerk forward and her entire body slump into the bottom of the car, he felt a tremendous jolt in his own body, which threw him sideways, and realized that that fatal hesitation had given the woman Inge time to draw her weapon.

Her second bullet went wide, because he had fallen against the door so hard that it opened and he found himself in the road. He was paralyzed, unable to use his weapon. But there was no other shot, only a cry and a series of grunts and gasps. He looked up and saw Judith Stein holding the other Luger.

"Is she—?" he panted.

"Unconscious." Judith knelt beside him. "You are badly hurt."

"You must kill her," he said. "And . . ." He sighed. How difficult it was to concentrate. "Her uniform . . ."

Judith gazed at him for several seconds, then she nodded, and turned. "Bind up his wound," she said. "Use the woman's clothes."

Paul could raise his head no longer. It flopped back and his eyes shut. Fingers touched his shoulder, opened his jacket, tore away his shirt. His eyes opened again, and he gazed at the girl. Ruth Borodin's face was expressionless, but she worked busily, tying up the wound with pieces of already bloodstained khaki cloth. Dimly he heard another shot, and gazed at Judith, coming around the car.

"Did you . . . ?"

"Through the head," she said. "There is blood, but none on the uniform. You wish me to drive?"

She seemed able to read his mind, needed to ask no questions, stooped only to inspect her niece's handiwork.

"Is the bullet still in there?"

Ruth Borodin shook her head. It occurred to Paul that he had not yet heard her speak. Perhaps she was dumb.

Judith Stein disappeared again, for how long he had no idea; time seemed to have slowed. When she reappeared she was wearing Inge's uniform, except for the cap. But he watched her lean into the car and take the cap from Helga's head, before dragging the body out and rolling it into the ditch.

Paul drew a long breath. "You must drive into the village. Prince Peter is there. Hurry."

"Peter?" Judith's face changed for a moment; he could not be sure of the expression. Then she nodded. "And you?"

"I hope you'll take me with you."

"If only to explain," she said, without smiling. Between them they lifted him up and put him in the front. "Ruth, you will have to change clothes." Judith looked at her niece. "You can do that in the back seat as I drive. There must be something that will do, in one of those suitcases."

Ruth merely nodded and fetched the suitcase.

Judith hesitated again, but Ruth Borodin got into the back without a word. Paul sat in the front seat, tried to keep his breathing under control, to stop the great shivers from tearing his body apart, the pain from driving his mind into a coma. Judith got behind the wheel, and put the car into gear.

"You are badly hurt," she said.

"Drive, Fräulein Stein," he muttered between clenched teeth. "For God's sake drive."

As she pulled on to the road, he looked in the rear-view mirror, saw two bodies, one white in the sunlight, the other a crumpled mass of bloodstained khaki. At least, he thought, Svetlana has been avenged.

"My God," Peter Borodin said. "Is he dead?"

"I don't think so," Judith said. "I'll drive, if you tell me where."

"There is a little port called Warnemünde. It is at the mouth of Rostock Bay, due north fifty-odd miles." He got into the back seat. "But to see you . . . Judith . . . Ruth . . ."

Judith watched him in the rear-view mirror, as he put his arm round his daughter's shoulder, hugged her against him. Judith refused to believe it. She refused to believe that she was sitting behind the wheel of this car, driving slowly through the streets of the town, being regarded deferentially by the civilian passersby on their way home from work, and then faster as she reached the open road. She refused to believe that she had just shot Inge through the head. For how long had she dreamed of being able to do that? From the first moment, three years ago, when she had entered Ravensbrück and been commanded to strip, by that same Inge.

So there it was, a dream. And undoubtedly she was over-sleeping, and was therefore about to receive an almighty kick in the ribs.

"She won't say anything," Peter complained. "What has happened to her, Judith? What has happened to her?"

"I think she is too surprised," Judith said. "We are both too surprised. This man . . ."

"A friend of mine."

"An SS officer?"

"He and I have been working with others to overthrow the government," Peter said.

"The government? But . . ."

"The plot has failed. We are wanted men, now. But we have a chance, if we can get to Warnemünde. Hassell knows it well. We will have to wake him up."

Judith sucked air through her nostrils. It was not, then, a dream. But it might as well be. Because they were going to be caught, soon enough. Men on the run. And now women on the run too. But at least she had a pistol at her belt. She would die decently, before anything more could be done to her.

"Ruth, my darling Ruth," Peter was saying. "You never doubted I would get you out, eventually? You never doubted that, did you?"

At last Ruth spoke. "No, Papa," she said. "I never doubted that."

"And it was not so bad, eh?" Peter begged. "You do not look too bad. Your hair will grow, and . . . It was not too bad, eh?"

"No, Papa," Ruth said again. "It was not too bad."

"Working in the hospital, eh? In the clinic? Why, they'll have taught you a profession. To be a nurse. Your mother was a nurse, in the last war. So was Aunt Judith."

"The clinic was the name for the brothel attached to the camp, Papa," Ruth said.

Judith drew a long breath.

"The . . . the *brothel?*" Peter asked.

"Yes, Papa. I have spent the last three years as a whore."

"As a . . ." Peter Borodin's voice faded. Judith could not see him any longer in the mirror.

"But we were the fortunate ones, Papa," Ruth explained, as she might have explained something to a child. "We were well fed, and we were beaten only now and then. We had to stay plump and pretty, you see, for the soldiers. We were the lucky ones, Papa."

Oh, yes, Judith thought, staring down the ribbon of road in front of them, heart leaping into her mouth as they passed a squadron of tanks slowly rumbling south toward Berlin. But the commanders merely saluted the apparently sleeping SS officer in the front seat. *We were the lucky ones.*

She suddenly realized that that was exactly true. They *had* been well fed, compared with the others, and they had not been beaten very often. Only when Inge had a hangover. Inge undoubtedly had hangovers far too often, but at least not every day. And what had they been forced to do? Lie beneath men. Men who could only take possession of their bodies, who had never been allowed the time to grasp at their minds. So the men were not the slightest bit important, to her.

But Ruth. Ruth had been a virgin, had cried out in fear and pain and humiliation that first day, had brought Inge and Helga and even the commandant rushing up to see the fun. She had recovered. She had revealed a quality of courage Judith would not have expected to find in any woman, much less in an innocent girl. She would smile, and laugh, and pretend to be happy. "There are other people," she would say. "In Russia there were no people."

Only Judith had been able to judge the utter black misery which must lie beneath the smiling, brittle falsehood of the face. How could it be otherwise? Ruth's first memories would be of the early twenties, when her father and mother had begun that decline from being the darlings of New York society into the netherland of poverty that had eventually driven Rachel to suicide. Then she had been dragged around Europe while her father had sought support for his anti-Bolshevik plans, and finally she had been made to settle in this state of prehistoric savagery. Only to be taken from there to solitary confinement in a Lubianka cell, for two years. And then three years in a brothel. There could not have been a single moment of true happiness in all that time. Merely a waiting for the next disaster to occur, the next blow to fall. So how could she possibly even react to what was happening now? She must know that this madcap drive would end in disaster.

But Judith wanted her to survive. No life could possibly be so hopeless, so empty of hope or love or pleasure, and then end so abruptly. Judith found herself wrapping her fingers around the steering wheel, and peering into the gathering gloom. Therefore *she* had to survive too, if only to teach her niece how to be happy. It was a determination she had not known in years.

"Oh, Ruth." Peter once more held his daughter in his arms. "Oh, my darling Ruth. But we will get away, you'll see. And I will make you happy, I swear it. Oh Ruth..."

Von Hassell stirred and raised his head. "Where are we?" His voice was thick.

"We've passed Rostock, colonel," she said. "Warnemünde is straight ahead, four kilometers."

"Drive straight to the docks," he said, and looked at his watch. "My God. Pray we are not too late."

The car raced through the empty streets, had to slow as it entered the town, but this too was uncrowded. Except on the waterfront, where the fishing fleet was getting ready for sea; engines were roaring, mooring lines were being cast off, jokes were being exchanged. Judith slowed, and twisted in and out of wives and girlfriends waving good-bye. Her heart was pounding now; this was the real crisis of the day, of their lives.

"There," Paul said, pointing with his good arm. "Number one seven two. And it is still alongside. Pull in there."

It was only just alongside. The boy in the stern was already casting off, and his mate stood in the bow, ready to drop the line the moment the skipper gave the command. Black smoke belched from her little funnel, and two other men sat amidships, inspecting the drift net.

The car stopped, and Paul leapt out, arms folded against the agony that had to be tearing through his body. "Hans," he bellowed. "Hans Jürgen."

A glowing pipe appeared in the wheelhouse window. "Herr von Hassell? Why, it's been four years!"

"Four years too long, Hans," Paul said. "I would like to come on board. With my friends."

"Hold that bow line," Hans Jürgen shouted. "Of course, Herr von Hassell. But only for five minutes. There are fish, eh?"

Paul steadied the rail, and Judith helped Ruth across. Passersby stopped to stare. In the ill-fitting clothes of the much heavier Inge, and with her close-cropped hair, she was a peculiar sight. The door to the cabin was opened, and they stumbled inside; Paul had already gone up the steps to the wheelhouse. Two of the sailors stood in the doorway to stare at them.

"Cast off forward," came a shout from the wheelhouse. "Mind those fenders."

The two sailors went outside again.

"Ruth," Peter begged. "At least smile at me. We're on board. We're safe. We're going to escape."

Ruth looked at Judith, her eyes fathomless pits of black despair. She dared not allow herself to believe. But then, she did not *want* to believe. To be free, to have escaped, was too great a hazard to be faced.

Judith got up, went to the wheelhouse step, and saw Paul come down. His face was deathly white, and he staggered and shivered. She realized that he would have lost a lot more blood during the past five minutes' exertion.

But he smiled. "He and his men will do it."

Judith sighed. "They'll find the car, colonel. They'll send planes out, and ships. We cannot possibly be in Sweden before tomorrow morning."

"But we *will* be there," he said. "The forecast is for fog tonight. They won't find us. We will be there." His knees gave way, and he sat. He attempted to smile at her again, and suddenly fell forward, his head striking the table.

Beneath them the engine noise increased as they gained speed. They were out of the harbor. They were, after all, free.

And their savior was dying.

"There are bunks down here." A woman had entered the

cabin, from aft, and introduced herself as Frau Jürgen. Over
her shoulder Judith could see the winking lights of the village,
beginning to fade.

"Help me," she said. Between them they got Paul down the
companion ladder and laid him on the bunk. Frau Jürgen took
off his boots while Judith removed the bandages and looked
at the wound. It was quite terrible, for there was blood everywhere and it was almost impossible to discover where the bullet
had even entered. Certainly at least two ribs had been shattered.
But as Ruth had said, the bullet had exited again, and they
must hope it had touched neither lung or kidney. The colossal
loss of blood was the most dangerous thing, as far as she could
tell. Frau Jürgen brought warm water and a cloth, and then
more bandages. Judith bound Paul up again, and put him under
the blanket. But he shivered, and his teeth chattered.

"His temperature is too low," Frau Jürgen said. "It is the
shock of the wound and the loss of blood. It does not look
good, Fräulein. He is an old friend. It would be terrible if he
died."

"Terrible for us all," Judith said. "He has just saved our
lives. Is there no way we can make him warm?"

"There are other blankets, and I will get a hot drink. Yes,"
Frau Jürgen said. "If we can wake him up enough to take a hot
drink, and then wrap him in blankets..." She looked up as
Ruth Borodin came down the steps.

"I will warm him up," she said. "I know how it is to be
done. Leave us here alone, and I will warm him up."

# Chapter 14

THE NOISE WAS UNENDING, A TREMENDOUS GROWL THAT encompassed the entire eastern sky, and was steadily growing closer. Often at night the partisans could even see the glow of the barrage, lighting up the treetops. The skies, too, had changed character. Now hardly a German plane was to be seen, and in their place Russian transports swooped low over the forest, parachuting arms and ammunition, food and medical supplies. And orders. Now they were given precise instructions as to where they should attack, and when, what bridges were to be destroyed to coincide with an assault in the east, what railway installations to be damaged. Sometimes the order was merely to create a great deal of activity, again to distract the Nazis in coordination with some movement of the Red army.

The orders came addressed to General Ivan Nej. Strangely, Anna did not apparently mind. Having lived so long in the shadows, she seemed content to remain there. And besides, this "Ivan Nej," this so-publicized guerrilla commander, was clearly an act of policy. Here was an émigré, returned to fight for the Motherland, to fight for Soviet Communism, to link the peoples of the United States with the peoples of the Union of Soviet Socialist Republics.

357

John suspected the hand of the real Ivan Nej behind that one; from the news items that were also dropped by the planes, he gathered that his own father was far too busy in Leningrad. But it was good to know that both father and son were working, with growing success, toward the same goals.

Even Uncle Peter had come in for his share of publicity. Here the newspapers were less kind. No deed could truly excuse the arch-traitor, Peter Borodin of Starogan, a man who, in addition to his lifelong opposition to Bolshevism, had worked for the Germans, had attempted to raise a White Ukrainian army to fight against his own people. But even in the case of so dyed-in-the-wool a villain, his true Russian blood had come shining through at the end, according to *Pravda*. For Uncle Peter, apparently, and incredibly, had been one of the arch-conspirators in an amazing plot against Hitler's life, details of which had just been unearthed, since it had only happened a week ago. He was now being sought by the Gestapo, and would undoubtedly be hanged by the Germans. But at least he was going to die as a Russian should.

What a tangled world it had become! John lay on his back and watched the last of the planes returning over the Russian lines. His men were roaming through the woods to find the precious parachutes, and his women were busily cooking, no longer even considering concealment. Since their failure to liquidate the partisans two summers ago, the Germans had only sought to contain them, had built a series of blockhouses around the forest—as if mere blockhouses could contain Anna Ragosina.

And now, after three years, this war was on the point of ending, for him, for Anna, and for them all. And the most incredible thing of all was that John Hayman no longer wanted it to end.

He raised himself on his elbow, watched little Alex playing in the dirt. After her first frantic scream of his name, Natasha had insisted upon using the American equivalent. He was a lonely, solitary child, despite the presence of other babies around the encampment. Not one of the then-pregnant girls had survived the German attack, so the children who had since been born were all at least several months younger than Alex. Yet he was happy, because he was the idol of the entire group, men as well as women. Even Anna from time to time swept him from the ground, to hug him and dance with him, when she was celebrating some special coup by drinking too much vodka.

But what was he going to do with a boy who had been born in the middle of a bombardment, whose first sounds had been those of men and women dying, who had never seen the interior of a house much less slept in a warm bed? Wouldn't such a childhood have to lurk at the back of his subconscious for the rest of his life?

And what of his mother, who now walked across the grass to kneel beside her husband, and offer him a mug of steaming tea? Here was beauty, and self-possession, and radiant happiness. Like them all, Natasha Brusilova had become a creature of the woods. She even danced, from time to time, to the great joy of the partisans. Would Natasha ever be able to acclimatize herself, now, to the restrictions of kitchen and drawing room, traffic jam and cocktail party?

And Aunt Tattie? Tattie was magnificent, as much the general of the camp as he or Anna were the generals of the offensive. Her word was law within the forest, and there was not a soul—not even Anna, he suspected—who would have had it otherwise. Perhaps even more than dancing, Tattie was the essential spirit of the woods, moving through the trees, wearing, in summer, hardly more than a tattered shirt, golden hair still unstreaked with gray as it trailed to her thighs, powerful limbs gleaming in sun and wind-tanned splendor. Only sometimes, as they sat in the evening and sang, did he see the dark tragedy lurking in the depths of her eyes. It was more than just the death of Svetlana. It was the utter destruction of the academy, of the girls she had trained and nutured. Of all the thirty excited, chattering dancers who had gathered round her on that fateful twenty-second of June, three years ago, only five remained. So she had managed to replace them, temporarily, with the even greater responsibility of coping with the domestic needs of several hundred people. But the ending of the war would mean, too, the ending of that. Tattie would have to let go of all her threads, and see which others she could gather in their place.

And what of John Hayman? Could he ever go back to being a sports editor, to recording the deeds of others rather than playing the hero himself?

He watched Anna Ragosina coming through the trees, moving quickly as always, face flushed. She carried her radio, for over the past week she had made contact with the advancing armies, from her excited face, it was clear she possessed news of some fresh Russian triumph. Perhaps she was the greatest problem of all. Because, in delving into the blackened turmoil that was her mind, he had uncovered more than he had expected. He did not know why he should have been surprised. Anna Ragosina was a twisted, violent, vicious personality. But she was also a human being, who felt and wanted and even feared, like any other human being. And who also loved, or wished to love, like any other human being. Only her own fear of rejection had always kept that love on a selfish, almost angry plane. But she no longer feared rejection from him. That he still attracted her sexually could not be doubted, any more than she could doubt her own attraction for him. But she had accepted his greater loyalty. He thought perhaps she valued his friendship the more for that—because they *were* friends, at last. For all her savagery in battle, he thought that Anna was more of a human being than she had ever been before, and that was mostly because of him. What then would the end of the war mean for her, a colonel in the NKVD, with Ivan Nej as the ultimate arbiter of her destiny?

She knelt beside him in turn, alongside Natasha. Incredibly, the two women were even friends.

"It's here," she said, voice quivering with excitement. "The end is here."

John sat up. "What do you mean?"

"It just came through on the short wave," she said. "Our armies are about to drive for Minsk. They want the partisans to launch an offensive at the same time, from behind the German lines. Our target is Slutsk."

They were in position by dawn, having spent the night in transporting themselves and their equipment out of the marsh, past the German blockhouse and across the river on their inflatable rafts. They were accustomed to the operation by now, but they had a great deal of equipment to move. Gone were the days when it had been only men and women, with a few rifles and tommy guns and some gelignite. Now they were several hundred strong, a battalion of irregular infantry with all the supporting firepower, machine guns, and even several of the terrifying katyusha mortars, which had probably done more than anything else to destroy the German morale in this war.

"We're just in time," Anna whispered, pointing. "They're preparing to move out."

They crouched in the shelter of the last clump of trees, only a hundred yards from the derelict houses that marked the out-skirts of the town—long since looted for firewood—and watched the beehive in front of them. The main road out of Slutsk seethed with long rows of trucks being loaded with gear, with groups of civilians standing around, unable to believe their eyes, with women clamoring to be given a place, well aware of the fate that waited them if they remained to be denounced as whores for the Germans.

"There are noncombatants there," John pointed out.

"And Germans," Anna said. "I will give the order to open fire."

He sighed, but she was right. There was no other way to surprise the Germans, to have any real chance of victory. He nodded, and she twisted on her elbow, flashlight in hand. Behind her, sprawled on the uneven ground outside of the town, waited the assault force; behind even them, concealed in the hollow by the riverbank, were the mortars. The heavy machine guns were also placed here, to cover their retreat, if that should be necessary. He realized he had never thought like that before; always, in the past, retreat had been accepted as inevitable. But then, never before had he led an assault upon a town, and a full German command. The wheel had finally turned full circle.

Anna's torch flashed, and the katyushas exploded. The dull sound was probably hardly audible within the town itself. But the first shell burst among the transports with deadly accuracy, throwing pieces of truck, spark plugs, and tires into the air together with pieces of men, setting the fuel tanks on fire, and immediately igniting those to either side, even as the rest of the mortar shells exploded close by. In an instant the road had been turned into an inferno of raging death.

John scrambled to his feet and raised his arm. Now was the moment. Now. He ran forward, tommy gun thrust in front of him, knowing that Anna was just behind him, that the rest of the partisans were following. For several seconds, as he raced toward the flames which were now reaching the houses behind the trucks, he saw nothing, heard nothing but the crashing of the mortars, which had now extended their range into the town itself, and the roaring of the flames. Then as he got closer, panting, and slowing, he could hear the screams, punctuated by shots. He fired a burst into the inferno, crouched as he ran along the ditch beside the road, saw an opening by an unexploded truck, and darted through, to face three Germans, knocked over by the initial blast and only just getting up, reaching for their weapons. Another burst from his tommy gun sent them scattering backwards, a jangle of disconnected arms and legs. He leapt over them and faced a group of Russian women, fallen to their knees in supplication. "Into the cellars," he shouted. "Take cover."

From either side of him now he heard the sound of the other tommy guns, quite obliterating the isolated, heavier thumps of the German rifles. The defenders of Slutsk had certainly not expected an attack, much less such a furious one. Nibbling at trains and outposts and isolated columns was one thing; a full-scale assault had been beyond their anticipation.

John ran along the street, faced the square, and dropped to one knee, both to regain his breath and to reconnoiter. He looked over his shoulder and saw some fifty of his men behind him, following his example. Of Anna there was no sign.

He looked into the square. Outside the town hall, several command cars stood silent, ready for loading, the dawn breeze whisking an occasional sheet of paper from the boxes waiting beside them. But the swastika still waved above the building, and he could not doubt that it was defended, while from further into the town he could now hear a more general exchange of fire, as the mortars ceased their bombardment and the Germans started to recover. Taking the town hall was an urgent necessity.

"Small arms fire," he shouted. "Pin them down." He chewed his lip. A mortar or a heavy machine gun would soon settle the matter, but did he have the time to wait while one was brought up.

"You," he snapped. "And you and you. Grenades. Follow me."

He drew a long breath, stood up, and ran round the corner. From around him a tremendous fire was opened by his men, but now the town hall replied. And the Germans certainly had at least one machine gun. Bullets tore up the pavements, cut ruts into the road. John threw himself forward, rolling over and over to come to rest against a stone horse-trough; water spurted across his face as the bullets crashed into there as well. From behind him there came a dreadful growling explosion and he realized one of his men had been hit in a grenade blast. But the other three now crouched behind him.

"The cars first." He drew the first pin, counted, and hurled the grenade. It fell short, but rolled across the road and came to rest against the front tire of the second car. Three more grenades bounced amid the cars, all exploding together. One car went immediately; the front of the town hall was covered in a vast sheet of flame and flying stones and earth. John was on his feet and racing forward, feeling the heat surging at him to take his fading breath away. Then another car exploded, and the blast knocked him over, sent him rolling against the curb, his hat gone and his shirt torn.

He reached his feet again, waved his arm, and ran for the outside steps. Behind him his men gave a cheer and charged. A German soldier appeared at the head of the steps, but only to come tumbling down as he was hit several times. Yet there were enough others to hold the place; a hail of bullets swept from the windows, and John found himself on the ground again, gazing in utter consternation at the blood dribbling down his right leg, soaking the heavy material, making his feet sticky inside the boot. And there was no one around him. His entire force had either been destroyed by the machine-gun fire or had gone to ground. Absurdly, he felt no pain.

He looked up. For the moment he was out of sight of the windows, having fallen behind the stone balustrade of the steps. This alone had saved his life. But he would have to die, if he wanted to get the attack going again. It seemed so senseless, suddenly, and yet that was not a judgment that had any bearing on the situation. The John Hayman who wished to live, who dreamed of taking Natasha and little Alex back to America, was a formless creature, hovering over his head, intruding upon his thoughts. The wounded man on the ground here was a soldier, who understood only that his task was to get up those steps, and encourage his men to follow him.

The firing had slackened as the Germans awaited the in-

evitable assault. Slowly John pushed himself to his knees, and
listened to a sudden increase in noise. It came from the near
distance—the grinding of tanks, the deep sounds of their artillery. German tanks, or Russian? That it came from the east
was meaningless. But if he was going to die, it hardly mattered.
And there was new noise from closer at hand, the quick chatter
of tommy guns from the rear of the building. He gave a roar
and hurled himself at the steps. He heard bullets but was not
hit as he went up behind the bucking, heat-angry gun, threw
his shoulder against the already shattered door, kicked open
the one on the left of that, fired a long burst at the already dead
Germans inside, ran back into the hall, and saw his own people
crowding through behind him. He turned to face Anna Ragosina, followed by a dozen men.

"They are running," she shouted. "They have heard our
tanks."

"Our tanks? Are you sure?"

She laughed, and tapped the radio strapped to her back.
"Our tanks. But there are still people in here. I have seen no
sign of Bledow. We must have him. You—" She pointed at
two of her men. "—check the cellars. I will look upstairs."

John ran at her elbow, up to the second floor, heart pounding, breath coming in great gasps; three men followed. The
victory was theirs. Russian tanks! But since the victory *was*
theirs, it was a time to call a halt to the savagery, to begin the
return to normality. Whatever his crimes, Colonel von Bledow
was now a prisoner of war. Even Anna must understand that.
Whatever her hidden lusts and angers, she was a woman, as
she had proved often enough these past two years.

A woman he could almost love, at this moment.

"There," she said, pointing at the door. One of the men
nodded, and ran at it. The others stood to either side, tommy
guns thrust forward.

"Remember," Anna said. "We want him alive."

The door was hurled open, and the men sprang inside, guns
weaving to and fro. Anna shouldered them aside as she followed. She halted to gaze at the desk and the slumped body
behind it. A pistol lay on the floor, and a thin gray-and-red
thread of blood and brains trailed across the blotter.

"I guess he was sensible, at that," John said.

"Sensible," she spat, and turned to look at a girl who stood against the wall, panting, glasses misty with fear. She also held a pistol, but it was at the end of her fingers, drooping beside her.

"But you were not sensible," Anna said in German.

Ilsa opened her mouth, closed it again. Her enormous bosom heaved against her shirt.

Anna smiled. "You are his secretary," she said.

Ilsa nodded.

"I have heard of you," she said. "You were present at all interrogations."

Ilsa gasped for breath.

"Drop the pistol," Anna commanded.

The weapon fell to the floor with a thump.

"You should have used it," Anna said, going closer, her voice caressing. "You will pray that you had used it." She reached out and took the glasses from the girl's nose, and threw them on the floor.

"Take her downstairs," John said. "She is a prisoner of war. Remember that, comrades."

The men moved forward.

"No," Anna said. "We will deal with her, here and now."

"She is a prisoner of war," John repeated. "We can take prisoners now, Anna. The war is over, for us."

"She is a Nazi swine," Anna said. "She will hang, anyway. But we will save her from that."

Ilsa, with only a smattering of Russian, looked from one to the other, anxiously. Her panting was dreadful to hear.

"I said—"

"You said nothing," Anna spat. "I command here. I have always commanded here. You are nothing but a figurehead. Without my flanking movement we would not even have captured this building, and you would be dead, Comrade Hayman. Go and have your wounds seen to, and leave us to our work." She snapped her fingers. "Strip her."

Ilsa gave a thin wail of despair. John caught Anna's shoulder. "For God's sake, Anna," he shouted, "that is over and done with now. Even for you. Finished. Can't you understand that? Now is a time to stop hating. We have to live with these people. You won't do that by mutilating young girls."

The blow took him by surprise, was delivered with such force and such anger that he found himself stretched on the floor before he had even absorbed the pain. Anna Ragosina stood above him, eyes a seething mass of battle-inspired bloodlust. "Hate?" she shrieked at him. "What do you know of hate, John Hayman? Hate is all I have. I will never stop hating. I hate all of you, every single one of you, everything that breathes. I hate you, hate you, hate you," she screamed.

Her fingers were white on her trigger, and for a moment he thought he was about to die. Then she turned away from him with as much violence as she had hit him, slung her tommy gun, and drew her knife.

"Help me," Ilsa screamed, throwing her body this way and that, but held against the wall by two of the partisans. "Oh, God, help me."

Anna reached for the heaving shirt front, and John managed to get to his knees. He had already unslung his gun, and now he fired, a single shot, smashing through white shirt and flesh and bone, to end all the fear and the agony and the hatred in a single eternal thump.

But he had not shot Anna Ragosina. He had shot the girl Ilsa.

The signal was given, and the band burst into martial music. The six heroes, four men and two women, marched forward together; the partisans from the Pripet Marshes had no monopoly on courage.

But how odd to be alongside five Russians, and wearing this strange uniform, so hastily concocted for him. He had spent his last week in learning this march—each leg thrown out in front of him in a straight line, raised as high as he could manage. Not half as high as any of the others; even Anna Ragosina was far more military than he. But then, his leg still hurt if he stretched it too far.

Anna Ragosina. Throughout the train journey to Moscow she had not spoken to him once; nor had she spoken to him at all during the past week. If he regarded her as having reverted to type, then she undoubtedly thought the same of him. But he had quickly recognized that her bloodlust was entirely the result of the mania that seemed to overtake her in battle, and which was undoubtedly responsible for her remarkable courage, and thus he had been prepared to forget and forgive. But in her eyes, he had committed the unforgivable sin of questioning her commands, her wishes, her desires, in front of other members of the group. Only his technical superiority in rank had saved his life; the memory of her blazing eyes, of the bloodstained knuckles hardening on the trigger of her tommy gun as she had swung away from the dead girl, had convinced him of that.

Perhaps she counted that failure to kill him as her greatest.

But they were all heroes of the Soviet Union now, as they approached the group of officials standing at the other end of Red Square, which seemed to glow as the sun began to sparkle from the huge onion domes on the Cathedral of St. Basil. The crowd burst into tumultuous applause, drowning out even the strains of the band. He could recognize faces, Stalin's certainly, for although he had never met the Party secretary he had seen enough photographs of him, and then his father, standing beside Stalin, and Ivan Nej beyond that, and Aunt Tattie, smiling at him and once again dressed with the flamboyance of the immortal Tatiana Nej, and beside her Clive Bullen, wearing the uniform of an English Colonel, and then Natasha, with little Alex in her arms. Only his mother and George were missing from the gathering. But they would be at the pier, waiting for him, and for Natasha and Alex, when they got home to New York.

New York! It seemed light years away, another planet, where Moscow, the bomb damage and the graves, the uniforms and the utter dedication of this entire people winning the war, were merely the logical extension of the blood and the cold and the anger and the bestiality of the war in the marsh. But he was remembering New York in the spring of 1941. Perhaps that too had changed.

They stood at attention, and Marshal Stalin passed slowly down the line. He had started at the other end, and John had been warned not to turn his head. But now the mustache was parting into a smile as he reached Anna.

"Comrade Ragosina," Stalin said. "I have heard of you. We need women like you, to lead our people."

"I thank you, comrade," Anna said.

Stalin pinned the medal on to the left breast of her tunic.

"And there is much to be done," he said. "Much."

"I am ready, comrade," Anna said.

He nodded, held her shoulders, kissed her on each cheek, and stepped back to accept her salute. Then he faced John.

"Comrade Hayman," he said. "Or should I say Mr. Hayman? I am told you have expressed a wish to return to the United States."

He had known this was coming. "It is my home, comrade," he said, "and my mother's home."

Stalin frowned at him. "Soviet Russia is your home, Mr. Hayman. As it could be your mother's home, would she but choose it." Then he smiled. "But perhaps you *will* choose it, in the course of time. For now, if you wish to go back to the United States, then that is where you will go. Yours has been a long war, but a successful one, Ivan Mikhailovich. Remember us, when you are across the ocean."

He pinned the medal, kissed John upon each cheek, and stepped back for the salute. Then the band, which had sunk to a whisper during the actual presentations, boomed forth once more, and it was necessary to about-face, and march back, boots thumping on to the cobbles, chests inflating with the sheer immensity of the occasion, with the knowledge that, for them, the killing and the dying were over, and that they had been acclaimed as heroes even among a people whose collective will to win had been no less heroic.

The band stopped, and they were dismissed, to be immediately surrounded by their families, their friends, and their well-wishers. All except for the pair from the Pripet Marshes. Occasional strangers wished to shake their hands, but there was no affection. John Hayman's family and well-wishers were at the other end of the square, with the official party. He had only to turn round and walk back toward the gleaming onion domes.

But Anna Ragosina had not a single well-wisher in all Moscow, he realized. In all Russia. In all the world.

He touched her shoulder, and she turned. For a moment they looked at each other. Then he held out his hand. "We fought well together," he said, "after you had taught me how to fight. And there were moments when we were happy together, too. Anna Petrovna, I salute you. I shall not forget you."

"As I shall not forget you, John Hayman," she said, and

turned away, without touching his hand. A moment later she was lost in the crowd.

A ringing doorbell, when one is a fugitive and sought by the most powerful organization on earth, must send shivers down the spine. But it was the *once* most powerful organization on earth, Judith reminded herself, as she dried her hands on her apron and faced the door. Yet still capable of seeking to avenge itself. But even after ten months?

"Who is it, Judith?" Peter called from the tiny living room overlooking the harbor. Spring had only just reached Stockholm; the ice was still a recent memory. But Stockholm, the most beautiful city in Europe in the winter, only redoubled its beauty with the coming of spring. Surely it was also the safest city in Europe, perhaps in the world.

"I am about to see," she said, and slipped the bolt. She blinked at the heavy-set man in the topcoat and the slouch hat, for a moment quite unable to understand who it was.

"Judith," Boris said. "My God, Judith."

She realized her mouth was open, and hastily closed it.

"Won't you let me in?" he asked. "I have tremendous news."

Slowly Judith released the chain, allowed the door to swing back. "How did you find me?"

"By looking." He held her shoulders, brought her against him. She did not resist him, but would not open her mouth for his kiss. "It took quite a while. But your prince has been writing articles for Swedish newspapers. That made it easier."

"We had to live," she said.

"Of course. Judith . . ."

"Judith?" Peter called again. "Who is that?"

"It is no one. A delivery boy." She pushed Boris through the door and out to the landing, and closed the door behind herself. "He still hates anything, or anyone, Communist."

"And you have lived with him for ten months."

She met his gaze. "I have kept his house for ten months, and I have looked after his daughter, and that poor boy who helped us escape from Ravensbrück. Prince Peter was responsible for that, you see. But I do not think even he would wish to make love to me, Boris. Not after three years in Ravensbrück."

His hands closed on her shoulders again. "If you knew—"

"I do."

He sighed. "Oh, my dearest, dearest Judith. But it is over now, all the sadness, all the tragedy is over, my love. I have found you, and there is nothing more to fear."

She gazed at him.

He kissed her on the nose. "I heard it this morning, as I drove into Stockholm. Hitler is dead. It *is* all over, Judith."

Her gaze slowly turned into a frown. "I must tell Peter," she said.

"And then? You do not look very pleased."

She shrugged. "I will have to understand. It is difficult to understand." She turned back to the door, and he caught her hand.

"You will have time to understand, Judith. *We* will have time."

She hesitated, and then shrugged herself free, pushed up her left sleeve, allowed him to look at her arm. She did not watch his face.

"I know," he said. "Judith—"

"I spent my time there in the camp brothel," she said.

"Do you suppose that would matter to me?" he asked. "Or to you, Judith? You are Judith Stein. You do not get crushed by things like that. And I love you."

At last she turned. "No," she said fiercely. "I do not get crushed by things like that. But neither can I forget them, or forgive them. I have spent too much time in turning away from my responsibilities, from what I should be doing with my life. I am a Jew, and during these past six years my people have undergone the greatest persecution in history. They are *my* people, Boris, and I must be one of them, and be *seen* to be one of them. You tell me Hitler is dead. I believe you. I believe that the last vestiges of Nazism are about to be swept away. But that cannot be an end for the Jewish people. That can only be a beginning. Out of the thousands, perhaps millions, of us who were beaten and tortured and killed we must create something, otherwise it will all have been an even greater tragedy." Her eyes softened, and her tone, and she rested her hand on his cheek.

"I love you, Boris. I know that now. If I survived Ravensbrück, it is because I had the dream of you to sustain me. But what do you want me to do? Come with you to Russia, marry you, become a pillar of Soviet society? Can you really expect me to do that? Oh, I no longer loathe the Bolsheviks as I did. I have learned that there are many worse things in the world than Bolshevism." She smiled. "I think I have even forgiven them for murdering Momma and Poppa. But it is a *sterile* society, Boris. It is as much based on physical control as the Nazi society was. You deride the Americans for thinking only of money, but what do *you* think of, Boris? At least, to make more money, you have to work harder and think harder and try harder. You have a goal. What is your goal?"

He sighed. "Perhaps to see Russia grow into an ideal society."

"What nonsense. Do you believe that can ever happen? It is a Socialist dictatorship."

"It will never happen, Judith, unless someone tries to make it happen. Turning your back on it will not accomplish that. And Judith, never before has Russia been so ripe for change. Perhaps it will not come with Stalin, or any of the old guard. But there is a new guard coming along, men who fought and saw their brothers and sisters die, for Russia. It is where you belong, Judith. After all these years, it is where you belong. Because you are Russian, just as much as you are a Jew. And Judith," he said, gently pulling her into his arms, "there are still millions of Jews in Russia, waiting to be helped, waiting to be led, just waiting."

The door behind them opened, and Peter Borodin looked out. "Judith? What on earth—?"

"Peter." She kissed him on the cheek. "There is wonderful news. Hitler is dead. The Germans are surrendering all over the place. The war is over."

Peter was staring past her at Boris. "You? Coming here? You?"

Boris nodded. "But if I can find you, your excellency, so can others. It might be a good idea for you to move."

"Move?" Judith cried. "But you said—"

"Oh, you have nothing to fear from the SS, any longer. But Prince Peter is on the list of war criminals."

"Of war— That's impossible!"

"He began the recruitment of the White Russian army in

Byelorussia. He was in Slutsk when many of the atrocities there took place."

"He resigned because of those atrocities!" Judith shouted. "And then he took part in the plot against Hitler. That's why we're here, Boris."

"These things will have to be proved." Boris's tone softened. "I do not think you will ever be convicted, your excellency, in view of all that has happened. I just felt that you should be warned."

Peter stared at him. "Warned?" he demanded. "By you? A war criminal? As you have just admitted, that is rubbish, Petrov. Your Bolshevik thugs cannot harm me, here in Sweden. But I will tell you something. *I* can harm *you*. And I intend to. This conflict with the Nazis was just an interlude. A bubbling up of something filthy from beneath our feet. It will have no effect on the mainstream of history. That stream is, and has been for twenty years, the determination of every man of honor, sense, and understanding, to bring down the Bolshevik system. Well, sir, I intend to return to the forefront of that fight. And you can tell your masters in the Kremlin what I have said."

He turned and went back into the apartment. Judith ran behind him. "Peter, you can't mean all of that. For God's sake, the war is *over*. Let's call a halt to all wars. To everything like that. Boris wants me to go back to Russia with him, to help him to rebuild it, to make it a better place, to submerge old Bolshevism in something good, something better than tsardom ever was, or could ever be."

"You have more sense than to believe that, Judith," he said.

"I have enough sense to hope," she shouted.

"But you'll never go back to Russia. Not you, Judith."

She drew a long breath. "I will stay with you, Peter, if you'll give up this crazy private war."

"I am the Prince of Starogan. Others may have been deflected from their duty, but I have not, and never will be. I swore an oath to oppose Bolshevism in any and every way I could until it has vanished from the face of the earth. I shall not tarnish my honor."

She stared at him, and took a step backwards.

"As you will be neglecting your duty if you abandon me now," he said.

She shook her head. "I have never abandoned you, Prince Peter. But you have abandoned me, time and again. I think you are mad."

He smiled at her. "The last refuge of those who do not understand. Well, then..." He walked to the window. "Look down there. Do you not have a duty to them?"

Judith looked down at the square outside the apartment building, at the seat, at the two people who sat there, holding hands. Paul had still not regained his full strength, still wore bandages over the terrible wound in his side. But he was on the way to health, and he would complete the journey. With Ruth at his side? After all her fears that the girl would never smile again, Judith saw that she had found something utterly precious in the man whose life she had saved. Would she love? Could she, after her experiences? And such a man? But in the way he had risked his life to save theirs, and had all but died because of it, Paul had surely expiated the last vestiges of Nazism in his soul. Ruth thought so, anyway. As to whether their love could ever be physical, well, only time would prove that. But was not what they now possessed even more valuable?

I have never possessed anything like that, Judith thought.

"They will never desert me," Peter said. "Ruth will never desert me, and neither will Paul von Hassell."

Judith sighed. But she knew it was true. Ruth would never desert her father, and Paul would never desert Ruth. And no doubt, under the influence of his personality, they would wind up working with him against Bolshevism, following his hate-filled course to its inevitable end.

"No," she said. "They will never desert you, Peter. I pray to God that you never desert them, either." She turned and walked out of the apartment, Boris at her side.

# Chapter 15

"AND SO YOU WISH TO SAY GOOD-BYE," JOSEPH VISSARIONOVICH Stalin held both of Tattie's hands, and brought her forward for a kiss. "This is a huge decision you have made."

"My work here is done," Tattie said. "My girls are dead. My academy is destroyed. I could not possibly start all over again. Besides, Joseph Vissarionovich, am I not entitled to a little happiness in my old age?"

"Have you never been happy in Russia?"

"Of course I have been happy, Joseph Vissarionovich. But my heart is elsewhere."

"In England." Stalin shook hands with Clive Bullen. "You are a lucky man, Colonel Bullen. You are leaving Russia with our brightest star. But perhaps you will let her return to visit us, from time to time, when the shooting has finally stopped."

"It will be my pleasure, your excellency," Clive said. "I will even accompany her, if you will let me."

"That will be *my* pleasure," Stalin beamed.

Tattie had passed on down the room, past the huge dining table where her farewell banquet had just been celebrated, past the row of smiling guests, aglitter with medals and jewelry, to where Michael and Catherine and Nona waited for her. Michael also wore the Order of Lenin. His defense of Leningrad had made him, even more than before, one of the immortals of Soviet history. And whatever he thought of her decision, he would not criticize. Michael Nej would never criticize Tatiana Borodina. So there was no necessity for words, no use for them. They had been friends all their lives. They would remain friends in their mutual twilights.

Gregory stood by the door, wearing the uniform of a captain in the NKVD. Tattie forced a smile. "Can you forgive me?"

"A man must be able to forgive his mother anything," he said. "Besides, what you are doing has the approval of Marshal Stalin himself."

"It is your approval I desire."

His face remained stiff. "This is our land, Mother. Svetlana died for it. Our blood has watered its soil. I cannot understand your wishing to leave it."

Tattie sighed, and glanced over her shoulder at Clive, still saying good-bye to Michael and Catherine. "And you refuse to recognize the power of love. Or perhaps you have never known it."

"I have never known it, Mother."

Tattie hesitated, then took his face between her hands, and kissed him on the lips. "Then one day when you learn that power, you will understand, and you will forgive. And then perhaps you will come to see me, my own dear boy." A last squeeze of his hand, then Clive was at her side, and it was time to leave the room.

Stalin left the banqueting hall by the other exit, walked along to his office, opened the door, switched on the light, and gazed at the little figure hunched in the chair before his desk. "Perhaps," he said, "you should have come to the banquet."

"A man does not attend a banquet," Ivan said, "thrown by his recently divorced wife, in order to celebrate that divorce."

"I gave the banquet, Ivan Nikolaievich."

Ivan raised his head.

"And betrayed you?" Stalin asked, sitting down. "I do not betray my faithful friends, Ivan Nikolaievich. But sometimes a head of state must dissemble—more than he might wish to, more than his friends can understand."

"Yet she is gone," Ivan said. "Tomorrow she will be gone."

"Yes," Stalin said. "Tomorrow she will be gone. I wish her to leave in style, Ivan. I wish you to supply a car for her and her paramour to travel to the airport together. I wish you to do that."

Ivan slowly raised his head.

"You and I discussed this long ago, Ivan Nikolaievich," Stalin said. "We realized, long ago, that Tatiana Dimitrievna, however useful to Soviet Russia, however brilliant an advertisement for our culture, would one day outgrow and outlive her usefulness. Now she wishes to leave us, to go and live in the West. And who can possibly doubt that a woman like Tattie, once she has forgotten all the benefits she has received here, with a few lavish speeches will undo in an hour all the good she has accomplished over twenty years? Besides, is it not a sad thought?—all that beauty, all that grace, all that excitement, slowly dwindling into old age."

"Yes," Ivan said. "Yes." His face suddenly came alive with excitement. "How I have waited for this moment, Joseph Vissarionovich. I have dreamed of it, night after night. I shall arrest her immediately. I shall arrest them both. I shall—"

"Ivan, Ivan," Stalin said sadly. "Have I not made myself clear? One cannot just arrest Tatiana Dimitrievna, any more than one can arrest an officer in the British army. The British, after all, are our allies, and I have publicly given Tatiana permission to emigrate. No, no. Whatever happens must be an accident."

"An accident?" Ivan asked, his enthusiasm fading.

"An accident," Stalin said firmly. "You will see to it. There must be no mistake. To the world, it must be an accident. Indeed, I wish you to make sure that there are adequate witnesses."

"An accident," Ivan muttered.

"It will give you something else to dream about, tonight," Stalin beamed. "But make sure it is done, and done properly."

"Yes," Ivan said, some of his enthusiasm returning. "She, at least, at the final moment, will know that it had to be I who was responsible."

"Perhaps she will," Stalin said. "Off you go. Let me repeat, there must be no mistake."

Ivan got up. "There will be no mistake, Joseph Vissarionovich. And I thank you." He saluted, and left the room.

Stalin remained for several seconds, gazing at the closed door, then he pressed the intercom on his desk. "I wish you to find me Colonel Ragosina," he said. "She may be traveling down to the Crimea. Find her and have her brought back to me here, privately. Use an airplane if necessary. I wish her to be here by dawn tomorrow."

"What does it feel like to be leaving Russia, Madam Nej?"

"Tell us what you expect to find in England, Madam Nej."

"What are your marriage plans, Madam Nej?"

The reporters crowded round, as Tattie and Clive Bullen emerged into the hotel foyer. Tattie smiled at them.

"I am told you are flying on the same plane," she said.

"Well, most of us," said the correspondent from the *American People*. "We were only told last night."

"Well, then, interview me on the plane. I will hold a conference, on the plane. How can I tell you what it feels like to leave Russia, until I have left it?"

This raised a laugh, and Tattie swept past them, into the doorway, to stop in surprise at the sight of her former husband.

"Well, Ivan Nikolaievich," she said. "Don't tell me Joseph has changed his mind, and I am to remain in Russia."

"Joseph never changes his mind," Ivan said. "I have come to wish you good-bye."

*"You* have come to wish *me* good-bye?" Tattie demanded, incredulously.

"I hope," Ivan said, "that you are very happy where you are going." He glanced at Clive. "With Colonel Bullen."

"I intend to be," Tattie said.

"I have no doubt of it. Will you not kiss your husband farewell, since it is forever?"

Tattie hesitated, then leaned forward and kissed him on the cheek. "You saved my life, once, little man," she said. "I have always been grateful for that. It is a pity you are such a louse, or we might have been happy. No doubt you are content with your Ragosina."

"I have sent her away," Ivan said. "I shall never see her again."

Tattie raised her eyebrows. "Well, then, no doubt you will find someone else. Come along, Clive. We have a plane to catch."

She waved to the crowd that had assembled to say farewell to their favorite dancer, even this early in the morning, and sank back on to the cushions of the official car. Clive squeezed her hand. "No regrets?"

They pulled away from the curb. "Of course I must have regrets, my darling," she said. "I am leaving my home. As Gregory said, my daughter's blood is in this soil. I am leaving my people. I am leaving my fame. All for you." She kissed him on the cheek, smiled through her tears. "It is only the last I do not regret."

Clive looked through the heavy glass rear window at the carful of reporters following them out of town. "You'll never lose your fame."

"Bah," she said. "Once I have had my press conference on the plane, they will forget all about me, and I shall fade into nothing. You wait. But I will not be nothing. I will be Mrs. Clive Bullen." She sighed, and rested her head on his shoulder, as they left the houses behind for the drive to the airport. It was still not yet seven o'clock and there was no other traffic; the car was slowly gathering speed. They shot around a bend, and Clive looked over his shoulder, and saw that the reporters' car had disappeared.

"Hello," he said. "Our friends seem to have lost us." He leaned forward to tap on the window that separated the passengers from the driver. The chauffeur slid it open and half-turned his head. "The car behind," Clive explained. "It seems to have stopped. Perhaps they have had an accident."

The driver shrugged.

"Don't you think we should go back, to see?" Clive asked.

"My orders are not to stop for anything," the driver said, and closed the window.

"Those would be Ivan's orders," Tattie said. "He is afraid I may be kidnapped. He cannot stop being a policeman for a moment."

"Well, I wish his driver could stop pretending he's chasing a crook," Clive said, as they took another corner on two wheels, and then, surprisingly, slid to a screeching stop, in the middle of the road, on a short straight stretch before the next bend. "What the devil—" He stared in amazement as their chauffeur opened his door and got out, not standing, but throwing himself on to the road and rolling across it, to come to rest in the parapet at the side, bruised and cut, his clothes torn and smeared with dust and mud. "He's gone mad."

"Clive." Tattie sat up, her fingers tight on his. She was looking forward, at the enormous truck which was coming round the bend, driving very fast. "Clive," she screamed. "Clive!"

He reached for the door, discovered it was locked by some external device. As was the other one. And the windows. And there was a solid sheet of plate glass between them and the front seat.

"Ivan," he gasped.

"Ivan," she whispered, and squeezed herself against him, just before the impact.

The man was breathless; his cap was askew. "It was terrible, comrade commissar," he gasped. "Terrible."

Ivan gazed at him. "What is it you are trying to tell me?" His voice rose. "Are you trying to tell me that Tatiana Dimitrievna is dead?"

"It was a head-on collision," the man stammered. "Right in the middle of the road. The driver saw the truck coming, and jumped clear. He has been taken to the hospital, suffering from shock."

"Indeed," Ivan said. "And Tatiana Dimitrievna, and the man Bullen, they did not jump clear?"

"It is supposed the doors were locked, comrade commissar. Anyway, there was no time. The truck could not stop. It drove right over the car."

"My God," Ivan said, and got up to walk to the window, hands clasped behind his back in an unconscious imitation of his master. "There were witnesses to this?"

"Oh, yes, comrade commissar. The driver of the truck . . . he was alone, you see. He has also been taken to the hospital, suffering from shock. And then there was a carload of journalists, following behind Madam Nej. They were delayed by a flat tire, but they arrived only minutes after the accident."

And are also no doubt suffering from shock, Ivan thought. "I am horrified," he said, turning back to face the room. "How can these things happen? Tatiana Dimitrievna . . . You will have the two drivers transferred to one of our hospitals, Igor Simonovich. There are sure to be a few who will imagine the drivers are guilty of some crime, just because they survived. You will see that that is done immediately."

"Of course, comrade commissar. Immediately." The man hesitated. "And Madam Nej?"

"I must go to the morgue," Ivan said. "I must..." He took off his glasses to polish them, and the man gave a murmur of sympathy, and stepped outside, closing the door behind him.

Ivan replaced his glasses on his nose. Oddly enough, he did feel like weeping. He had hated her, but he had also loved her. When he remembered the voluptuous, laughing girl he had married, or even more, those faraway days on Starogan, when the bootblack had watched the young mistress going about her careless life, or that tumultuous day in 1918, when he had led the mob against the house, and taken her for himself... to think of all that energy, all that beauty, lying in a bloody heap on the back seat of a car... But then, as Stalin had said, it would have been equally tragic to think of her growing old, of that powerhouse dwindling.

The door opened again, and he turned, frowning. There had been no knock. Then his frown turned into an incredulous stare. "You? I sent you to the Crimea."

"And I have been recalled, Comrade Nej." Anna Ragosina took off her cap and hung it on the hook by the door.

"You..."

"I have a warrant here," Anna said, "for your arrest."

"A warrant? For my arrest?" He seemed unable to think.

Anna sat down in his chair, behind his desk. "I also have a confession, which I have typed out for you. If you sign it, Comrade Nej, you will be sent to a labor camp for life. If you do not sign it freely, I will have you taken downstairs to the cells, and there interrogated until you are willing to sign. Then you will be shot. The choice is yours." She tossed the paper on to the desk and leaned back.

Ivan stared at her, at that immaculate beauty, that flawless complexion. Even three years in the Pripet Marshes had not affected her in the least, except, apparently, to cause her to lose her mind.

"You are mad," he said. "Quite mad." He turned to the open door, where four armed guards waited. "Take this woman downstairs and beat some sense into her," he said.

The guards looked past him, at Anna Ragosina.

"Why do you not be sensible, and sign the confession?" Anna said kindly. "A labor camp is not so bad. I spent five years in one, remember? It was you who sent me there. They will cut off your hair and shave your body, and they will beat you from time to time, and they will give you cold baths in the middle of winter, and they will starve you. But that's not so bad. What is bad is the people you meet there, Ivan Nikolaievich. The people you sent there in the first place. That is bad. But I survived it. I am sure you will survive it too. Sign the paper." She smiled at him. "It is better than being tortured, and then shot, comrade. Because I will attend to that, personally."

"Mad," Ivan said. "Quite mad. Do not just stand there," he shouted at the guards. "Arrest her."

Anna put another piece of paper on the desk. "Perhaps you would like to look at the warrant," she said. "It is signed by Stalin himself."

Beth Hayman opened the bedroom door to the knock, tried to close it again, and was gently but firmly pushed to one side.

"Johnnie!" Ilona cried, when she saw her son. "You can't come in here. It's bad luck."

"We've used up all our bad luck," John said, and closed the door behind him as he gazed at Natasha. She was dressed all in white, and had just fixed her veil; beside her, Ilona and Beth, the one in royal blue and the other in pale blue, glowed, but not as radiantly as the bride.

"Well . . ." Ilona glanced from one to the other, and took Beth's hand. "The guests are probably arriving. But you only have five minutes, Johnnie."

The door closed behind them. Natasha remained, staring at her husband-to-be. She had wanted to postpone the wedding, had had to be persuaded by Ilona that it was what Tattie would have wanted—what, indeed, Tattie had planned for her.

"Think you can make it?" he asked.

She nodded. Her eyes glistened.

"I mean the whole thing," he said. "Being here. Living here. Not just marrying me."

She turned away, stood at the window, and looked down on Central Park. "Yes," she said.

"Convince me."

Her shoulders rose and fell. "It is different. So very different. Different even from what I expected. You know Russia. You can understand that."

"Of course I do. But is it *better,* or *worse?*"

She turned, and smiled despite her tears. "You think I have to say, nothing could be worse than Soviet Russia. Of course you're right."

"There's a but, though."

She sighed, and sat down, her hands on her lap. "I do not know America," she said. "I have only seen New York, and a little piece of Long Island. I only know what you have told me, what Tatiana Dimitrievna..." She hesitated, and he squeezed her hand. "What she told me as well, to add to those first impressions. But I can see that it is a great country, and that you are a great people. And yet, with all your resources you have had greatness thrust at you. You are like a man born and living all his life in an orchard, with nothing to do but pick the fruit, or even wait for it to fall into his hands." She smiled. "There are not many orchards in Russia. Am I being absurd, or am I right to fear for a people too blessed by fortune?"

As usual, he was quite astonished by the depth of her thought, the intensity of her feelings. He sat beside her. "Don't think we're soft," he said. "I would have thought we'd proved differently, these past four years."

"Your soldiers are the best in the world, John. But America has never been invaded, never been torn apart like the Ukraine and Byelorussia."

"Good point," he agreed thoughtfully.

She squeezed his hands. "But I will tell you this, Johnnie. I am glad, so glad, that I am going to be one of you. And even more, that Alex will grow up as one of you."

He kissed her on the nose. "And being Mrs. John Hayman doesn't come into it at all?"

She kissed him back. "I have been Mrs. John Hayman, at least in my mind, for several years. Today can make no difference to that."

"And so, ladies and gentlemen," George Hayman said. "To the bride and groom!"

The crowded room, hushed for so long while he was speaking, burst into excited sound, cheering, laughing, as the throng swept forward to shake John's hand, to kiss his beautiful auburn-haired bride. George stepped away, around the table where the cake still waited, leaving them to the plaudits of their friends. He found himself next to his wife.

"Oh, George," she said, "I don't know what to say. If only Tattie . . ." There were tears in her eyes. He could not remember Ilona ever weeping before.

He kissed her forehead, but could restrain himself no longer. "Something came in on the wire yesterday," he said. "I didn't want to tell you, while all this is going on—"

"What, George? That it wasn't an accident, after all?"

"Well . . . we'll never know about that. But Ivan Nej has been convicted by a special court of anti-Soviet activity, and has been sent to a labor camp."

"Ivan? But he was Stalin's absolute right hand."

"Not anymore, apparently."

"And you think it may be something to do with Tattie's death?"

"As you say, he was Stalin's right arm, up to that moment."

"Ivan!" she said, her nostrils flaring. "I felt all along that he had something to do with it. It would be just like him. Oh, Stalin should have had him hanged. He should have—"

"Just hold on a moment," George said, squeezing her hand. "I have an idea, for a start, that Ivan will find a labor camp a lot less pleasant than a noose. But think about this, my love: has Ivan ever done *anything* in his life, at least since Lenin's death, which was not commanded by old Joe himself?"

She stared at him, her eyes wide. "My God!"

"Quite," George said. "It makes you think." He looked across the room to where little Alex was being held by his nanny; hers was a difficult task because the child spoke no English, and she spoke no Russian. "Thank God they got out."

"Thank God," Ilona agreed, watching George junior, and Beth, and young Diana, in her bridesmaid's dress, pushing into the crowd around the table. "If only . . ." She had caught sight of Felicity, in her bridesmaid's dress, but standing alone against the far wall, her face in its familiar mask of depression.

"It'll turn out all right," George said. "It must."

"Did it turn out all right for Tattie?"

"Tattie lived her life more fully than any other human being

I have known," George said. "And she always knew the dangers she was playing with. So did Clive. They died together, while they were happy. I don't suppose anyone could ask for more than that, Ilona. Yes, it was right for her. And it'll come right for Felicity too. It must."

They were separated by the crowd, overflowing from the happy couple to congratulate the parents in turn. To these people the death of the famous dancer Tatiana Nej, who also happened to be the groom's aunt, did nothing more than add to the glamour of the occasion—again, George thought, with grim humor, as Tattie undoubtedly would have wished.

He allowed himself to be pushed toward the balcony, and the fresh air, where he could light a cigar, and look out over Central Park and the pulsing city.

He heard movement behind him, did not have to turn his head. "She's changing?"

"Yes," John Hayman said.

"We'll talk when you get back."

"I'd rather talk now," John said. "George, about the sports desk—"

"I know," George said.

"It's just that—well, I'm not really the man for it." He smiled. "I guess I'll have to get myself a job."

"Don't rush at it," George said. "As of this moment I'm commissioning your memoirs, the Memoirs of General John Hayman, Partisan leader. Will ten thousand be enough?"

"Now, George—"

"It's not charity," George said. "I'll make ten times that much out of the story, serialized in the *People.*"

"If you really think I can do it . . ."

"If I didn't, I wouldn't have suggested it. You have a story to tell, John. A story I'm looking forward to hearing."

"If I dare."

"I'll want every last drop of blood, John. Because once you've written something down, you can set about forgetting it."

"Forgetting? George, if you knew . . ."

"I was in the last one," George reminded him. "In Russia. Civil war can be even worse than the Nazis. Write it down."

"And then?"

"Then? Then forget all about Russia, and start to live."

"Do you think I'll ever go back, George? Will Natasha and I ever go back?"

George flicked ash over the balcony, watched the glow fade as it slowly sank towards Fifth Avenue. "Just because we all seem to love each other like brothers at this moment, don't count on it. I don't think the Soviets are about to change their ideology, and I sure as hell know we aren't. So whether we meet them again as friends or as enemies..." He smiled, and threw his arm round his stepson's shoulders. "That depends on Comrade Stalin."

THE BORODINS
BOOK V

# RAGE
# AND
# DESIRE

Will Be Published in
November 1982

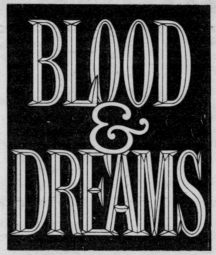

# Bestselling Books
# for Today's Reader –
# From Jove!

__**CHASING RAINBOWS**                     05849-1/$2.95
Esther Sager
__**FIFTH JADE OF HEAVEN**                 04628-0/$2.95
Marilyn Granbeck
__**PHOTO FINISH**                         05995-1/$2.50
Ngaio Marsh
__**NIGHTWING**                            06241-7/$2.95
Martin Cruz Smith
__**THE MASK**                             05695-2/$2.95
Owen West
__**SHIKE: TIME OF THE DRAGONS**          06586-2/$3.25
**(Book 1)**
Robert Shea
__**SHIKE: LAST OF THE ZINJA**            06587-0/$3.25
**(Book 2)**
Robert Shea
__**THE WOMEN'S ROOM**                     05933-1/$3.50
Marilyn French